UNDER THE MAYHAW TREE

Charlotte Boyett-Compo

SWEET VICTORY

Small-town football star Drew Dunne sacrificed everything for friendship and guilt. He's spent most of his life unloved and unwanted. A kind touch, a gentle smile, an encouraging word are all wisps of memory from before the accident. For him there is only family, duty, loyalty. And longing. Until he meets Allison.

When Allison Bennett looks in the mirror, she sees a woman whose life has gone from bad to worse. At the mercy of an abusive husband, sweet tenderness is something she can only dream about...until she finds it in the arms of Drew Dunne.

Not every sacrifice is worthwhile, not every promise is worth keeping, and events in a small Georgia town will test this pair to the very depths of their souls, but at the end of the journey is the truth that—if you're willing to pay the price—true love can conquer all. Drew Dunne will finally be with the woman he loves. Or die trying.

PRAISE FOR THE WORK OF CHARLOTTE BOYETT-COMPO!

30 DAYS TO SIN

"Whether it is the smooth writing style or the way the author chose to spin the storyline, this is one of those unforgettable stories that will have a lasting place on my keeper shelf. 5 stars!"

—Romancing the Book

"A true but unconventional love story. Highly recommended! 5 stars and a Top Pick Award!"

—Night Owl Reviews

HARDWIND

"Charlotte Boyett-Compo has once again made me cry before the end of the first chapter. She has such a mastery of the written word that she can, and will, rip your heart out. To have your emotions rollercoaster the way that they do while reading her books makes each one a bittersweet experience."

—Fallen Angels Reviews

"Looking for a story wrought with danger, insanity and a love worth dying for? Then you need look no further…. Sit down, buckle up and be prepared to be taken."

—Love Romances Reviews

IN THE ARMS OF THE WIND

"This book is terrific if you love mystery and romance combined…. Another hit on [Charlotte Boyett-Compo's] long list of wonderful reads."

—Romance Junkies Reviews

DANCING ON THE WIND

"A wonderful offering…. There is just something so compelling about Charlotte Boyett-Compo's writing that catches me up and keeps me reading, regardless of the material."

—ParaNormal Romance Reviews

"One hell of a book. If you have never read anything written by this author then I suggest you do, and if you're already a fan make sure you don't miss this one." An A+ Rating and an Outstanding Read Award

—Simply Romance Reviews

UNDER THE MAYHAW TREE

Charlotte Boyett-Compo

www.BOROUGHSPUBLISHINGGROUP.com

UNDER THE MAYHAW TREE
Copyright © 2015 Charlotte Boyett-Compo

ISBN 978-1942886-22-8

To all the kids I grew up with in Colquitt who said I'd never get published. Guess what, guys? 100 published books later...

ACKNOWLEDGMENTS

Joyce Rix McNease, Marti Conley Holloway, Gloria Mock Jenkins and Kay Rooks (may she rest in peace), and Mildred Weaver. You kept me sane while I was growing up. Thank you, ladies. David Cox...the inspiration for Early.

UNDER THE MAYHAW TREE

10

CONTENTS

Part One

Chapter One

Life was bad, Drew thought.

Very, very bad.

He had the radio up as loud as his ears could take it. That was the best way he'd found to drown out his thoughts. The Christian country rock station was blasting him with hard rhythm—skirling electric guitars, tinkling banjos and a bass beat that had him tapping his palms on the steering wheel. The words pouring out of the lead singer's mouth were uplifting and the gals singing backup were in perfect harmony with the guy's rich tenor voice. It was a song meant to invade your senses and it did. To soothe you and it was doing just that. To stay in your mind and he knew it would. It was the best kind of mind worm.

Behind him the four-lane blacktop of U.S. Highway 27 was scorching hot for it was late August in southwest Georgia, and the temp was somewhere north of ninety with the weatherman prophesying the mercury would hit the century mark that afternoon. With no clouds in sight or expected to make a show, the fields by which he passed were wilting and heat devils were dancing across them. Even the sign stating he had just passed into Early County seemed to be glowing neon white from the heat. Despite having the driver side window down, the wind pressing against the side of his face did little to cool him. It ruffled his hair and brought with it the faint smell of the honeysuckle growing across a gray weathered fence.

Taking his hand from the wheel of his rebuilt 1966 Chevy C10 pickup, he reached down for the beer that rested between his legs. Lifting the can, he took a long, satisfying sip of the cold brew, then rested the base of the can on his thigh as he spied a car approaching. From the distance that separated them he couldn't tell if the silver gray car was a state trooper or not but he didn't want to take a chance of being caught with an open container in a dry county. There would be hell to pay if he got a ticket.

Keeping his eye on the vehicle he was relieved that it wasn't a cop car, unless it was unmarked, for it didn't have a push bumper. Besides, there were two people in the front seat, and as the car got closer he swept his gaze down the front grill where a tag bore the unmistakable University of Georgia big red G. He smiled sadly for UGA had been his alma mater once upon a time. As the car sped past him, the guy gave him the good ole boy pistol shot greeting and he nodded back.

"Huh," he said and glanced up to the rearview mirror to watch the silver sedan. "Gotta be the new coach."

For the life of him he couldn't remember if he'd ever heard the man's name. Lord knew, he thought, he'd heard everything else about him over the last two months while the last minute scramble for a coach was going on. He recalled hearing the man had been an assistant coach in Milton, Florida, before accepting the job as head coach at Miller County High—home of the Pirates—but didn't care enough to be interested. Unlike every other red-blooded male in the county he hadn't absorbed all the particulars of the who, what, where and how of the man's sports credentials. He simply didn't give a damn about football and hadn't for a long time.

Not since an injury ended his own career at the University of Georgia, thanks to a vicious, brutal UF linebacker who'd had it in for him.

"Chip Brantley," he said aloud, remembering the player. He hadn't thought about that son of a bitch in a few years and wished he hadn't thought about him now. The game that had effectively put an end to his dreams of becoming a professional football player had put him in the hospital with a right femur broken in two places. A metal rod inserted into the marrow canal, then secured with three titanium intramedullary nails had sent his life spiraling in a direction he had never wanted it to go.

And given him a painful reminder of that day every time the weather changed.

As it always did when his memories took him back to those long, painful months it took for his leg to heal, anger washed over him like acid. He clenched his teeth, and then absently ran the beer can up and down the long scar on his thigh. While it throbbed from time to time—especially in cold or wet weather—the leg had healed well enough that he had only a slight limp and then only when he'd been standing for too long at a time.

"Stop thinking about it," he snapped and forced the memory aside. It was just one of many that had changed his life in ways over which he'd had no control.

He took another sip of the beer and took his foot off the gas. With no other cars in sight, he didn't bother with the turn signal as he turned onto a two-lane blacktop heading west. Four miles down the road—singing along with the Royal Disciples band—he backed off the accelerator. His destination was a few hundred feet down the road so he reached for the handle to roll up his window. The two-mile-long red clay road down which he turned would be boiling with pale peach dust as soon as his tires bit into the dirt. It wouldn't take much to come billowing through the window to choke him. Despite the sweltering heat that would build up rapidly inside the truck cab, that was preferable to suffocating, getting a mouth full of Georgia red clay. Besides, he had every intention of putting the hammer down and taking the dead-end road like he owned it.

Which in essence he partially did.

Hickup Road led to the family farm where he'd been born and raised, and where his cousin, Early, lived with his wife, Bea, and four of their five towheaded brats. The farm had been in their family for over one hundred and sixty years. His great-great-grandparents, Jonas Hazel Rawls, and wife, Matilly, built the original farmhouse—which burned to the ground during the Civil War when it was struck by lightning. The second dwelling was destroyed when heavy rains washed away the foundation and the homestead collapsed—killing all but one of the nine inhabitants. The lone survivor, Ellis Ray Rawls, whose twenty-first birthday had been celebrated only two day before the disaster, built the third structure, which is still standing. The clapboard structure had been added onto several times, indoor plumbing and electricity added and a double-wide carport erected right off the kitchen door. Though it was badly in need of paint and the roof sagged in a couple of places, the old farmhouse held a special place in his heart. His beloved mother, Mary Nell, had died there when he was ten years old—ovarian cancer snuffing out her life as easily as a strong breeze against a candle.

His mother's only brother, Carlton, had inherited the farm and promptly kicked his sister's drunkard husband out the back door.

Literally.

There had never been any love lost between Carlton Rawls and Wade Dunne. Those who professed to know the truth of the matter said Carlton went to his grave cursing Dunne.

He turned onto the dirt road and braked to a stop. Ahead of him the red clay road was a straight shot between two fenced peanut fields. Lifting the beer can to his lips, he tossed his head back and guzzled the last of the now-tepid brew. Crushing the can in his hand, he pitched it onto the passenger side floorboard, and then flexed his fingers around the steering wheel. As the music from one of his favorite Christian rock bands blared from the radio, he nodded in time to the heavy beat, started rolling, shifted through first into second, popped the clutch, then stomped his booted foot on the accelerator, sliding the four-speed synchromesh tranny into what Early called the rocket gear. The tires of the half-ton C10 dug in and the truck shot forward with all the power housed within the 327 V8 engine roaring like a banshee. Picking up speed, red dust rolling in on itself in a long plume behind the tailgate, the seat belt dug into his lower abdomen. He glanced at the speedometer and grinned. Zero to sixty mph and the heavy-duty front and rear shocks sent the truck skipping along the pitted road like a rock over a frozen pond. At seventy the truck was still solid but when he hit eighty, there was a bit of vibration. At ninety, he didn't like the way the engine was straining so he shifted down—disappointed once again he hadn't finally made it to the mystical one hundred peg.

"Time for another tune-up," he mumbled as he neared the termination of the road and the sawed-off telephone poles that marked the end of the line.

Sometimes—and today was one of those times—he was of half a mind not to stop, not to downshift, but to plow the truck into the poles going ninety. There was a steep gully past those poles and a half-ass creek that was deep enough to accommodate the front end of the truck. Slamming through the poles would certainly put an end to him, he thought, and the misery that had been his life since that fateful night on the football field in Gainesville.

Coming to a stop about fifty feet from the wooden barrier, he shifted the truck into neutral, gunned the engine. Gunned it again—his eyes locked on the poles. His heart beat heavily in his chest. His palms grew slick with sweat. All sound vanished as though it had been sucked into a vacuum. He pushed his foot down on the accelerator but he couldn't hear the revving of the motor. He didn't hear anything save the steady whooshing of the blood in his ears.

He thought about turning the truck around and going back to the highway, turning and making the drive back along the dusty road. About racing toward the poles at top speed, keeping his foot on the accelerator until he rammed through the barricade as the needle pegged out at the magical, mystical century mark on the speedometer. To crash through the barrier, slam into the gully with enough speed and force to cave in the front end. Fingers flexing around the wheel, he looked down at the seat belt that anchored his hips. He took his right hand from the wheel, reached down to the lift the lever and release the clip. The belt came undone. There was nothing holding him to the seat.

The past rose up like a dust devil to swirl in front of his eyes. He watched it moving in slow motion across the hood of the pickup like slides in a projector. Each slide stayed in his vision long enough for him to recognize just what it was. The images were as clear as glass.

A cold, moonlit night on a lonely stretch of Georgia asphalt.

Ogrelike oaks crouched over the highway with their branches drawn into gnarled claws.

A dark yellow diamond emblazoned with a reverse curve symbol flashing by in the swath of the headlights.

Silver hood pointed directly at a telephone pole.

He put the heels of his palms over his eyes to blot out the pictures. They had haunted him for sixteen years. They went to bed with him each night, slept beside him and he woke to them each morning. Not for a second of any day did they leave him. The pictures were etched into his very soul and with them the guilt born of that ill-fated night.

If only he could rewind the clock, turn back time. Things had been much simpler, more manageable back then. The happiness and peace that had eluded him all his life was within his reach. Like the proverbial carrot on a stick, a rosy future dangled before him. He had graduated salutatorian of the class to his best friend's valedictorian. They'd both gotten full-ride scholarships to the University of Georgia—where they had been accepted on the Bulldog football team. Going along for the ride had been his best friend's fiancée who had been the head cheerleader at their high school. They'd had it all planned.

He would get his bachelor's degree in athletic science, then hopefully get drafted to play pro ball. Playing for the Georgia

Bulldogs had been his dream since he was a little boy. Going on to play for the Dallas Cowboys was more than a dream. It was a religion to him. No one in his family had ever graduated from college, and to be the first was a goal he had set for himself early on. To get a job doing what he loved most, to travel, to *be* somebody was all he could think about.

From the first day they met in first grade and all the way through school, his best friend had encouraged him every step of the way. They had been inseparable. Closer than brothers. He wanted to play ball and his friend wanted to coach. Together they were going to be invincible.

But the best laid plans of mice and men…

They'd left Colquitt with stars in their eyes. The brand new 2002 Oldsmobile Cutlass that had been his friend's graduation present was loaded down with all the things they would need in the dorm room they would be sharing. His truck—a graduation present from his uncle—had furniture crammed into it.

Furniture that would be going into the dorm room of his friend's fiancée.

That girl wasn't fond of him. He suspected she was envious of his relationship with her fiancé. She was always hanging around, trying to push him out of his friend's circle, but her efforts never worked. Over the years, theirs had become a begrudged association made compulsory by their mutual love for his friend. She had tolerated him at the best of times and ignored him the rest, but she had not out and out hated him.

"Not back then," he said aloud.

Back then, she had accepted that he was a necessary evil in her life. She treated him like a lackey for she was a spoiled rotten little socialite whose father's was the wealthiest man in the county. An only daughter, she was treated like the princess she likened herself to be. Snooty, arrogant, she fit in well with the sorority she joined.

Because he loved his friend, he put up with the girl's uppity manner although he was no fonder of her than she was of him. Since childhood she'd treated him like gum stuck to the sole of her sandal and nothing changed the older they got, even when they went off to college. If anything, she dismissed him entirely.

Until she needed help with a class or a paper or a strong back when his friend's wasn't available. Then butter wouldn't have melted in her mouth she was so nice to him—bestowing smiles and giggles and the occasional pat on the shoulder.

When his football career ended after that god-awful afternoon at the University of Florida's Ben Hill Griffin Stadium, she'd even helped take care of him—though it was fairly clear to him that she resented having to do so. He suspected the only reason she got roped into it was because his friend had insisted.

He revved the engine again, reached down to mold his hand around the gearshift. The wooden poles seemed to be dancing in the heat of the afternoon sun. They were calling to him, motioning him to come on down! He rocked his foot on the accelerator as other memories flitted across his mind.

The girl—furious at his friend—coming to him for a shoulder to cry on. Awkward pats on her back to calm her. Her makeup ruining his one good white shirt. Her arms slipping around his waist, her lips parting as she gazed up at him in what he realized now was mock helplessness, pretend need.

He should have known better, he thought. Hindsight being what it was. But he'd been lonely. He hadn't dated in high school and though he wasn't a virgin, sex wasn't something he'd had very often. Her attention—even if it had been extended in order to spite his friend—should have been a red-flag warning.

Yet it hadn't.

Back then he didn't drink. Alcohol and drugs and smoking were not a serious athlete's friend. He'd refrained from all three, although his friend had imbibed far too much for his own good. The girl partook of marijuana, Southern Comfort, and whatever illegal drug she could find with fervor.

"Come on, Drew, loosen up. You're being a prude." she'd told him that evening. *"For once in your life pull that stick out of your ass and live a little!"*

One shot of the booze had become two, then three, then four. He rather liked the taste of it but had liked the looseness it gave him even more. Never having smoked before that night, he'd thought he was going to cough up his lungs as she made him hold the smoke in until stars danced in the periphery of his vision. And whatever drug she'd had him swallow had sent him on a wild journey to a place he'd never have gone on his own.

Ecstasy, he thought as he sat there gunning the motor.

She'd given him something that completely wiped away all his inhibitions. Took away each of the Big Three: reserve, restraint and respectability. He'd found himself slithering along the underbelly of deviant behavior he'd only heard about.

He shuddered as he went back to the night he had lost his friend. All the terrible, wicked things that had happened that night in the dorm room he'd shared with his friend had been thrown at him like the contents of a slop bucket.

"He fucked me in the mouth and the cunt and the ass!"

If he lived to be a hundred he would never be able to forget the look of surprise, then shock, then revulsion that had passed over his friend's face as the three of them sat in the seedy little bar.

"He shoved his cock so far up my twat I could taste the cum when he came."

Eyes filled with revulsion swung to his guilty ones and held.

"He told me he loved me, has always loved me and begged me not to marry you. He said you were cheating on me anyway."

Though he had shaken his head and sworn none of that was true, the revulsion in his friend's gaze turned to anger. It had turned to fury at her next words:

"And now I'm knocked up with his brat! What the hell are you going to do about it?" she'd hissed. *"Am I supposed to have his white-trash baby and you give it your daddy's name?"*

He'd been as stunned by her words as his friend was. The news had rocked his world and he knew—beyond a shadow of a doubt—it had effectively ended a friendship that had lasted for thirteen years. There would be no forgiveness for the disloyalty.

His friend and the girl were three sheets to the wind but he'd only had a couple of beers. He'd sat there as his friend pushed clumsily to his feet, then stared down at him.

"How could you?" his friend asked. *"How could you betray me like that?"* His friend turned to stumble away with the girl clinging to his arm like kudzu.

He shot to his feet, demanded his friend give him the keys, but his friend turned and shoved him. He staggered back, slammed into a table and rolled off the top and onto the sticky floor. By the time he got up, his friend and the girl were in the parking lot. He ran after them—pleading to be given the keys—but his friend ignored him.

He and the girl got in the car but before either of them could lock the back door, he had it open and dove into the seat.

"Get the fuck out of my car," his friend ordered.

"Let me drive. You're drunk and—"

"Get out of my car!"

He refused and his friend had turned the car on and sprayed gravel as he gunned out onto the highway.

It had been a wild ride with the girl berating his friend for allowing him to stay in the car. His friend bellowing at him, accusing him, condemning him for his betrayal.

Then he'd spied came the reverse curve sign.

"Slow down," he'd ordered. *"For the love of God, will you slow down?"*

His friend had snapped his head around to pin him with a nasty glare.

"Watch out!"

He'd screamed those words a second before the car began to skid.

Drew let his chin sag to his chest, took his foot off the accelerator, realized he was trembling—as he always did when the memories of that night came back to haunt him. All of it, everything bad thing that went down that night had been because of a lie.

She'd lied to him. He knew it now, but back then he'd been so starved for affection he'd bought into her lies. He'd *wanted* to believe her. He wanted to be loved.

So desperately wanted to be loved.

When he'd awakened the next morning, she had been lying in his bed staring at him. He was stunned to find her there and could remember little of what had happened the night before.

"What did we do?" he asked for he realized he was naked beneath the sheets.

"You fucked me," she stated. *"What the hell do you* think *you did?"*

"No," he denied, shaking his head that felt twice its normal size.

"You weren't half-bad," she told him. *"Clumsy as hell but not half-bad. I* almost *enjoyed it."*

He'd watched her leave his bed, averted his eyes to her nakedness.

"You can't tell him," he said.

"I have no intention of telling him," she'd lied. *"He'd beat the shit out of you if I did."*

Drew raised his head to stare at the thick wooden poles at the end of the road. No, he thought, Jackson died because of what I did.

The guilt had kicked in long before the night of the accident. Guilt at having betrayed his best friend. Guilt at hiding what he'd done. Guilt at lying to him.

After the accident had come even stronger guilt.

Guilt at having impregnated his friend's girl. Guilt at not wrestling the keys away from him. Guilt at having to go through her, to pull her out of the wrecked car in an attempt to reach his friend. Guilt at fearing for his own life, his own pain. Guilt at backing away. Guilt at failing to rescue a man he loved so dearly. Guilt at standing there as that man died before his very eyes.

Guilt.

All that horrible, horrible guilt because he had failed to be the man he should have been.

So many layers of guilt pressing down on his shoulders, impacting his life in ways he could not have imagined as he sat in the hospital that night. That guilt brought with it a responsibility, a culpability he could not deny. He—and he alone—had ruined his life and two others, so it was up to him, it was his obligation to make things right.

So he had done what had been demanded of him and not hesitated. He took his medicine, shut his mouth and swallowed it—along with any pride he had. He voluntarily gave up his dreams, his future, his life, sacrificing it all on the altar of the immense guilt that was riding him with wicked spurs. He'd put himself in a prison of his own making. He'd allowed the girl to become his warden. He'd willingly put his entire existence into the hands of people who hated him because of what happened that night on a lonely stretch of Georgia asphalt.

To atone for his sins he'd slipped on the hair shirt, girded his very soul with a barbed cilice and drawn it so tight it could never be removed. It was the least he could do for his betrayal. In his mind he deserved every evil, crippling thing that was done to him, and he had freely sacrificed his life on the altar of guilt.

Obviously God also thought he needed to make amends for his treachery else He would not have allowed the retribution to go on for so long.

He eased his foot back onto the accelerator. There was, however, a solution to the problem. Yeah, slamming through the poles would certainly put an end to his situation, but it would also put an end to the C10 and that would be sheer sacrilege. If there was anything—other than Early, Bea and their towheaded, booger-eating brats with the picket fence smiles—that he loved, it was his truck. It had been a graduation present from his Uncle Carlton and he took better care of it than he did himself.

Well, him and Early, who was the head mechanic at Five County Motors where they both worked.

He turned his head to look at the short gravel driveway that led up to the house where he'd been born. The house where he had been permitted to keep living when Carlton Rawls sent his father packing. The house where he'd known the only happiness and love and respect and genuine caring he'd ever experienced. His uncle had had his back.

"Some father you are! You ain't got no business raising that boy!" his uncle had shouted before planting his size fourteen work boot against Wade's ass. *"I'll be responsible for him from here on out. You get and stay gone!"*

* * * * *

From that day until he had gone off to college, his uncle had treated him no differently than he did his own son, Early—the joy of Carlton's life. The two boys had grown up as close as brothers, and he had been the best man at Early's wedding to Bea. Unfortunately he hadn't been allowed to have Early as his best man when he'd been forced to marry…

"Don't think about *that*, either," he berated himself and yanked on the wheel to turn the truck down the gravel drive. Rocks struck the undercarriage, the engine bucked and stalled. For a second or two he growled, then slammed his palms hard against the wheel, leaned forward with his arms over the top of it, closed his eyes and laid his forehead on his crossed wrists.

He hated his damned life, he thought. Hated it bad enough that he often daydreamed of killing himself. Not that he ever would—wasn't that committing a sin of the worse kind?—but he thought about it far more often than he knew he should. Wouldn't it be a relief to put a gun in his mouth and be blown into the darkness? Toss a noose over some branch and swing his way to oblivion? Swallow a bottle full of his wife's sleeping pills and drift into the hereafter?

"My luck I'd wind up in hell with her at my side for eternity," he mumbled. "Stuck to me like stink to a dead polecat."

Lifting his head, he stared through the dust-coated windshield and sighed. Bea was standing on the front porch with a hand shielding her eyes as she watched him. Beside her was Melody, the most precocious of her brood. The four-year-old was clinging to her mama's skirt, sucking on her thumb. Both girls were barefoot as yard dogs and that made him smile. It warmed his heart in ways that put a tingling behind his eyes. He reached over to turn the radio dial to off, though the loud music was no longer playing thanks to him stalling out the pickup. Turning the switch, he started the truck and rolled slowly up the driveway.

Bea waved at him and he waved back as he parked the C10 behind her ten-year-old car.

"I heard you coming two miles away," she said when he exited the cab.

"No, heck you couldn't," he replied. He climbed the three steps up to the porch, leaned in and gave her a peck on the cheek before hunkering down in front of Melody.

The little girl moved behind her mother's leg while keeping a firm grip on Bea's dress. Her thumb never left her mouth as she peeked at him around her mother.

"And who's this pretty girl?" he asked.

Melody giggled around her thumb. "You know," she muttered.

"I sure don't," he said. He reached a hand into the pocket of his shirt and pulled out one of the suckers he'd brought with him. He looked at it, twirled it between his thumb and index finger. "I can't read the name on this sucker."

"It's Melody!" the little girl cried.

"Nah," he said, shaking his head. "Melody's my girlfriend and if this was her sucker, she'd be hugging me to get it."

"I'll hug you!" she said with a giggle. She released her mother's skirt and rushed forward to throw her pudgy little arms around his neck.

Bea shook her head. "You're spoiling her, Drew," she told him.

"Ain't got none of my own so I'll spoil yours," he replied. He kissed the child on the top of her head, then handed the lime sucker into her keeping, telling her she was welcome when she thanked him for the treat.

Melody gave him a sloppy kiss on the side of his face, and then ran into the house, shouting for her twin brothers that she had a sucker and they didn't.

"Early's out to the barn hooking up the boat," Bea said. "You boys better bring us home some big catfish."

"You make up the hush puppies and the coleslaw, slice up some Vidalia onions, open up the ketchup bottle, and we'll supply the catfish, woman," he promised as he kept squatting in front of her.

She folded her arms over her more than ample chest. "You got beer out there in the cab of your truck, Drew Dunne?"

"Got a crushed beer *can* out in the truck," he said.

"Well, I can smell that one on your breath." She narrowed her eyes. "You got a six-pack or two in the truck bed?"

He slapped a hand to his chest. "I got an eight-pack right here, baby. Wanna see it?"

She rolled her eyes. "No, you don't. You wish you did. Get on out to the barn with you." She pursed her lips. "And don't you men be coming back here drunk as John Kirk."

"We're leaving here boys and coming back men," he said with a wink and a cluck of his tongue. "Beer will do that to you, Beatrice."

"Only thing beer does is give you a pot belly, Drew Dunne," she shot back.

The screen door slammed open and the twins came running up to him. The three-year-olds were grimy from head to toe, and something was sticking out of the older boy's hair that looked like it had come from the backside of some animal.

And smelled like it, too, when Drew opened his arms for them to hug him. Their appearance was the reason he'd stayed hunkered down.

"Whatcha brung us? Huh? Huh?" Kelvin, the stinky one asked. "Whatcha brung us?"

Fishing his hand between them and his pocket, he took out one grape sucker and one cherry. Kelvin grabbed the grape and Delvin the cherry. Both boys peeled the candy in record time, and then shoved the confections into their mouths.

"Bye!" they both cried and ran for the door.

"What do you say?" Bea called after them.

"Thank you!" the boys shouted in unison as the screen door slammed shut and their running footsteps echoed from the living room.

"You're welcome!" he replied as he got to his feet. "They're growing like weeds."

"You seen Travis lately?" she asked of her six year-old. "I swear that boy outgrows his tennis shoes every other month. He's gonna have as big a foot as his granddaddy had."

He chuckled, then asked after her child, Nell.

Bea's smile slipped away. "She's doing okay. We're gonna go see her on Sunday after church."

"Tell her I love her," he said. Not that it would matter to the five-year-old child for she was mentally challenged and blind and had been that way since birth. He ducked his head—not knowing what else to say—and started to step off the porch.

"Drew?"

He looked around but kept walking. "Yeah?"

"Did he tell you?" Bea asked.

"Tell me what?"

She smiled, then put a hand to her belly and rubbed.

That brought him up cold. "Are you *kidding* me?" he asked, eyes wide. "When?"

"March," she said. "We're hoping for another girl."

"Don't you two know how to do anything except—"

"Don't you say it," she warned with a shake of her finger at him. "Now go on. Early's waiting on your lazy butt. Them fish ain't gonna catch themselves."

"I'm happy for you, Bea," he said. He gave her wide grin, then dug his hands into the pockets of his jeans and turned toward the barn. As soon as she couldn't see his face, he let the grin fade. What he wouldn't give to have a child of his own, he thought.

But that wasn't going to happen.

Ever.

He had resigned himself to the fact long ago and although it still hurt each time someone he knew brought a new life into the world, he understood that it wasn't in the cards for him and never would be.

"Just one more kick in the ass, Dunne," he mumbled.

He heard Early's Dodge Ram start up and stepped to the side as his cousin pulled his johnboat out of the old barn. He couldn't help smiling for the boat was as precious to Early as Drew's truck was to him. Both had been graduation presents from Early's dad. The truck stopped and Drew came over to open the door.

"Damned boat motor was giving me fits," Early said as his cousin slid into the seat. "I hope to the good Lord we don't have no trouble with it whilst we are out on the lake."

"We better not," Drew told him. "I'm in no hurry to spend the night out there floating among the cypress trees being eaten alive by skeeters."

"Well, I ain't got the money to buy me a new one," Early said as he honked his horn—his way of saying good-bye to the missus. "You know how much a new trolling motor would set me back?"

"Depends on the motor but the way you get us lost I'd say get one with a GPS and that would be about six hundred dollars."

"Six hundred dollars, my ass," Early said with a snort. "Try more like a grand, son, but if you were to give me a raise…" He cranked his head around to look at Drew but his cousin didn't take the bait.

"You remember to put the beer in the cooler?" he asked Early.

"Does the pope wear a funny hat?" Early scoffed.

"Bea thought I brought it."

"What she don't know ain't gonna hurt me," his cousin replied. He reached over to crank up the air conditioner, turned onto the dirt road that led to the highway.

"I got news for you, Early. She didn't see me go back to my truck to get anything so she's gonna know you already had it. We come back here snockered and she's gonna box our ears."

"So long's we got her a mess of catfish, she ain't gonna get too hot under the collar 'bout it," Early pronounced.

"You go to church with a hangover tomorrow and it won't be her collar you should be worried about," Drew replied.

Early grunted. "She tell you our news?"

"That she's got another bun in her oven?" Drew asked. "Yeah, she told me. I should congratulate you but I'm not going to 'cause you think you did it all on your own."

"Then don't."

"I wasn't planning to."

They were silent for a moment, then Drew looked over at Early. "I think I saw the new coach today."

"That Bennett guy?"

"Is that his name?"

"Yeah," Early answered. "Clay Bennett."

Drew frowned. "Clay Bennett? You sure that's his name?"

"Think so. Graduated Georgia back in ninety-eight if I remember right, then went on to be assistant coach somewhere down in Florida."

"You know where he's from?"

Early hooked his wrist over the top of the steering wheel. "Let me think." He nibbled on the end of his ragged, unkempt mustache, then shrugged. "Somewhere up in north Georgia. Marietta, I believe but don't quote me on that. Why?" When Drew didn't say anything else, Early glanced over at him. "Why?"

"I think I might know the bastard," Drew said. He thought back to the man who had passed him on the highway but he hadn't been paying that much attention. Couldn't recall his face.

"Well, he was at Georgia the same time as you," Early told him. "He'd be four years older than you, right? Graduated your freshman year."

Drew clenched his jaw. "Yeah and if he's the one I'm thinking about, he's a real piece of bad work."

"You have trouble with him?"

"No but I knew some guys on the team who did. He liked to brawl and there were a couple of times he did some real damage to a couple of the younger guys who pissed him off. He also had a reputation for being a player."

"Liked the ladies, did he?"

"They sure as hell liked him although he treated them like shit," Drew replied. He remembered there had been two people in the car that had passed him. "Is he married?"

"Yeah. I think Cal told me his wife went to Georgia, too." He chuckled. "Hell, you might have known her."

"It's a big school, bubba," Drew reminded him. "Unless I had a class with her or she was on the cheerleading team, I wouldn't have had any reason to know her. If you remember, I wasn't dating back then."

"I remember," Early said, casting him a quick look before turning onto the highway that would take them down to Lake Seminole. "Wish things had been different for you, Drew."

"You and me both," Drew muttered. He laid his head back on the seat, turned his face to the window. For the second time that day, his mind went to his wife of sixteen years and he ground his teeth. Memories of his last three months at UGA came back to him like acid scalding his soul and he closed his eyes.

* * * * *

"You're worthless," she told him. "What good are you to me like that, Andrew Allan? You can't even carry my books."

He hobbled along behind her on crutches that were biting into his underarms with a vengeance. His cast was a living nightmare on his leg—the top of it chafing the crook of his leg as he moved. He was striving to keep pace with her but it was getting harder and harder to do. His arms were giving out and he was breathing heavily. "Terri Anne, wait up. Please?" he asked.

Terri Anne Carver Thompson came to an abrupt stop and turned to face him. "What, Drew? What? What?" She stomped her foot, reached up to fling her long hair over her shoulder. *"What?"*

He stopped—drooping against the crutches—and tried to catch a decent breath. Sweat was running down his face and the palms of his hands were slick with it as he gripped the crutches.

"I'm waiting," she snapped.

"I'll do the paper for you," he told her.

"Damned straight you will," she said. "You owe me, Drew."

"But I can't do it today. I've got physical therapy and—"

"I told Professor Mattingly I'd turn it in *today*," she yelled at him—drawing the attention of passersby. *"Today,* Drew. Not tomorrow. Not Thursday. *Today."*

He sighed and hung his head. "What time today?"

"Sometime before six p.m.," she replied.

He winced. "Okay, I don't know how I'll manage it but I'll get it done."

She took a few steps over to him and reached out to put her palm on his cheek. "Good boy," she said with a bright smile. "I'm counting on you."

That said, she spun around, waved at a few people she knew, then hurried toward her dorm.

"Good boy," he said, staring after her. "Fetch. Heel. Roll over."

"Play dead," a guy from his English 101 class told him as he walked past.

"I wish," he called after him.

"Grow a pair, dude," the guy said.

* * * * *

"Earth to Dunne," Early shouted.

Drew jerked and snapped his head toward his cousin. "What?"

"You fall asleep on me?"

Shaking his head, Drew sat up in the seat, plowed a hand through his hair. "I was just thinking about her."

Early didn't need to ask who the man beside him meant. "I try not to," he said.

"So do I but it's hard to do when I live with her," Drew told him.

"Hell, son, you don't live with her. You're a guest—and an unwanted one at that—in her house. Separate bedrooms does not constitute living with someone."

"Ooh, Rawls learned a big word," Drew said. "Sure you didn't mean constipate?"

"Fuck you, man," Early grumbled. "I have a high school diploma."

"Yeah, you graduated at the bottom of your class but what the heck, huh?" Drew ribbed him.

"Fuck. You," was the reply.

They were silent for a moment, then Early reached over to turn on the radio. It was set to an Alabama country station and the song that came warbling out of the speakers was about a man and his cheating wife and his dog.

"What's the dog got to do with it?" Drew asked.

"Man, don't insult a guy's dog. Dog won't cheat on you," Early answered. "He's your best friend."

"My best friend's a horn dog," Drew said. "Does that count?"

"I say again—"

"Yeah, yeah, yeah," Drew interrupted. "But I'm not the one who can get my wife pregnant just by sneezing in her general direction."

"Insensitive dickwad," Early pronounced with a sniff.

Tooling along, listening to the caterwauling of some female country singer berating her man for God only knew what the poor bastard had done, the men settled into the companionable silence they'd always preferred—each lost in his own thoughts.

Early's thoughts were on his wife and family.

Drew's were on a freedom he knew he would never have.

* * * * *

"Well?" Bea inquired.

"Terrific as always," Drew complimented her. He leaned back in his chair. "I may have to let my belt out."

"Always nice to hear," Bea said with a smile. She left her chair to go to the center island where a pecan spice cake waited. She looked at Drew and lifted a brow.

"If you insist," he said, rubbing his chest. "I'll force it down if need be."

Bea snorted as she cut him a hefty-sized piece, then slid it onto a dessert plate. "You want ice cream, too?"

"What's cake without ice cream, woman?" Early queried. "'Course he does."

"Will one of you crack the back door?" Bea asked. "The place smells like fried fish."

Drew waved Early back down in his seat and got up to do as she asked. He opened the door, then stood looking out at the gathering dusk. He spied the car parked down the driveway and sighed.

"She out there?" Early asked.

"Who, daddy?" Kelvin asked.

"I think your daddy means Miss Terri," his mother replied.

"Is she?" Early pressed.

"What do you think?" Drew replied. He stared at the black Lincoln, then shook his head.

"She's always welcome to join us," Bea said.

"Like she would ever lower herself to eat with us po' folks," Early quipped. "That would be sacrilegious."

"Two big words in the same day," Drew said. "I'm impressed, Rawls."

"What other big word did he use?" Bea asked as she scooped ice cream on Drew's slice of cake.

"Constitute," Drew provided.

"Sure he didn't mean constipate?" Bea asked and the four brats at the table giggled at the word.

"I *know*, right?" Drew commented.

Early shot them both a narrowed look.

"Why is Miss Terri just sitting out there?" Melody inquired. "Why don't she—"

"Why doesn't she," her mother corrected.

"Why *doesn't* she come in?" Melody questioned.

"She's watching Cousin Drew," Delvin pronounced. "Trying to catch him doing somethin' wrong."

Drew looked at Early who cocked a shoulder.

"Out of the mouths of babes," Early said in a soft voice.

"Are you doing somethin' wrong, Cousin Drew?" Melody asked him.

"No, baby girl, I'm not," Drew replied. He took a bite of the cake and ice cream.

"*Have* you done somethin' wrong?" the little girl asked him.

"That's enough," her mother said sternly. "What Cousin Drew does or does not do is none of your business, missy, and it's rude to ask such a question."

"He done something wrong," Travis—the oldest of the kids— stated.

"What do you think I did, Trav?" Drew inquired, then held his hand up when both Bea and Early would have spoken.

Travis shrugged. "Dunno."

Drew looked the boy in the eye. "I haven't done anything, son. Okay?"

"Yes, sir," Travis said.

32

"Why don't you guys take your cake into the living room and watch TV?" Bea said.

"Yes, ma'am," the kids whooped and swiped up their dessert before she could change her mind. Once they were gone, Bea brought her cake to the table and sat down.

"What is it she thinks you're going to do here, Andrew?" she asked.

"How t he hell would I know?" Drew said on a long sigh. "Bring some woman here to screw?"

"Not in my house you won't," Bea said with a snort. "She knows better than that and if she doesn't, I'll set her uppity butt straight."

"She just wants to make sure she knows where he is all the dangblasted time," Early stated. "But if she could catch him with a woman…"

"She'd run to Big Jake and he'd send the Klan after my ass," Drew proposed.

"And they'd tear you a new one," Early said with a grin. "Better keep it in your pants, old son."

"Watch your mouth," Bea warned her husband. "Little pitchers have big ears."

"I think they're a little young to know what I meant, Beatrice," Early groused.

The sound of a car engine starting cut off whatever response his wife was about to make. She pursed her lips, then got up to start gathering plates.

"We'll do that," Drew offered. "You cooked. We clean."

"You," she said. "Better get on home. You'll probably catch holy H E double hockey sticks as it is."

"She's right," Early said. "Much as I'd love to whip your sorry butt in a few rousing games of checkers, you'd best be on your way, my man."

"Yeah, I guess so," Drew said. He stood, leaned into Bea to give her a kiss. "I really enjoyed the meal, sweetie."

"My pleasure," she said.

Early walked with him to the door. "See you at church tomorrow," his cousin said, slapping Drew on the back.

"Yep," Drew agreed. He opened the screened door and took the two steps down to the concrete carport pad. Hunching his shoulders, hands thrust into his pockets, he headed for his truck.

* * * * *

Terri Anne Dunne had always been a reckless driver but when she had a few under her belt—and tonight she'd had more than a few—she was a menace on the road. Driving too fast, she passed slower cars like they were standing still and when she couldn't, blinded the drivers with her high beams.

"Get the fuck out of my way, asshole," she shouted at the car going ten miles an hour under the posted limit. The handicap tag on the back of the car didn't cut any ice with her. She laid on the horn until the driver moved over to the side of the road to let her pass on the curve they had entered. She shot past the car—flipping the bird as she sped away.

All the way home she cursed the man to whom she was married. She hated him—had hated him for a long, long time. No, she amended. She despised him, *loathed* him. He was everything she found repulsive, and to her way of thinking he possessed no redeeming qualities whatsoever. Someone should just shoot the bastard and put him out of his misery.

"Ugly, deformed little piece of shit," she seethed. "Sawed off runt."

A smiling image of Jackson Mackie appeared before her to blot out the long stretch of darkened highway for a moment. Blackjack Mackie, as he'd been known since high school, had been the perfect man. Tall, dark and handsome with eyes the color of rich caramel, he'd had a rock-hard body to go with his devilish good looks. Son of the second richest man in Miller County, captain of the football team, prom and homecoming king to her prom and homecoming queen, he had been absolutely perfect for her. She'd started planning their wedding while they were still in grade school. By the time they entered high school, she was so hopelessly in love with him no other boys existed for her. They had been *the* couple. No one spoke his name without adding hers.

And Blackjack had loved her as much as she did him.

"Until that worthless bastard killed him," she shouted so loudly she knew she'd strained her voice.

Forced to slow down as she neared the city limits, she turned on the radio and cranked the dial up to ear-splitting volume. It was the only way she could keep her mind off wanting to rake her fingernails down Drew's despicable face. If she didn't, she was liable to do just that as soon as he showed his sorry ass at her house.

Her house, she thought. It was *her* house and not his. Never his. His horrid name wasn't even on the deed and the pre-nup her daddy had made him sign ensured it never would be. If anything ever happened to her the house would go back to the man who built it.

"Daddy," she said. It didn't do to think what would happen to it if anything were to happen to both him *and* her. Her worthless brother would inherit it.

Forcing her mind away from her husband, she drove sedately past the Colquitt town square until she was on the southern outskirts of town. With no cars in sight, she pressed her foot down hard on the accelerator. With her CD player spitting out AC/DC it didn't take her long to reach the long, twisting lane that led up to her house.

* * * * *

Taking his time getting home, for he had no reason to want to be there, Drew drove with his arm out the window. He hummed one of his favorite hymns from childhood, a song his mother used to sing to him. The melody never failed to soothe whatever ache he had in his soul. As much as he'd hated going to Sunday school and church when he was a boy, that was the only bright spot in his week other than the one Saturday a month in the summertime when he went fishing with Early. That roughly two hour span between Sunday school and the end of the church services gave him the only solace he would get for the remainder of the week. He sure as hell wasn't going to get any at home.

Home, he thought as he passed the cemetery where his mother, Uncle Carlton and both sets of his grandparents were buried. He glanced at the entrance and smiled.

"Hey, Mama," he whispered. "Take care of her Uncle Carlton."

It made his heart ache that two people he had loved so dearly and who had loved him unconditionally were no longer there for him to confide in. His mother had been dead nearly thirty years and his uncle close to seventeen. The wound their passing had created in his soul would never close.

When he turned into the serpentine drive that ended at the house where he existed—he had never really lived there as Early had pointed out to him so many times—he felt his gut begin to churn. There would be a fight as soon as he entered. There always was. She'd be waiting for him with a drink in one hand and a cigarette in the other. Her eyes would be filled with vengeance and her lips twisted with hate.

Driving the truck up to the garage, he reached onto the dash to activate the door opener. He was half-expecting it not to work and wasn't surprised when it didn't. She had turned the handle so the door would need to be lifted manually. It was just one of the nasty little spites she liked to throw at him from time to time. He let out a long breath, opened the truck door and got out to roll up the door. She surprised him by standing right in the middle of the place where he would have parked the truck. Her fists were clenched and her eyes bored into him.

"It took you goddamn long enough to get back," she snarled. "What the hell were you doing?"

He didn't want to fight—never did—but from the way she was slurring her words he knew what he wanted didn't matter.

"You know where I was, Terri," he said tiredly. "You were out there spying on me."

"I guess you needed to take your whore home is why you took so long to get here," she threw at him.

"Yeah," he said, clenching his jaw. "She lives in Boykin so I…"

He stopped when he saw her eyes flare and knew he'd said the wrong thing. She flew at him with her hands up and fingers curled into claws. Her wickedly long red nails came toward his face but he managed to grab her wrists before she could rake them down his flesh.

"Stop it," he ordered as he twisted his body away from the knee she tried to drive into his groin. He pushed her away from him but she sprang at him again. This time she managed to drag the nails of her left hand down his right forearm. Blood welled up as the sting crawled over his nerve endings. She tried it again and this time he was ready for her. He snagged her arms and pinioned them behind her.

"Coward," she yelled. "Filthy, murderous coward."

She struggled—twisting and turning and trying to head-butt him. He tightened his hold on her and positioned himself where she couldn't use that wicked knee of hers to cripple him as she'd done so many times in the past. When she realized she couldn't get free, she bit him—clamping her teeth into his left bicep. He yelped and shoved her away from him.

"That's enough," he shouted. "So help me God, Terri, if you don't stop I'll beat the shit out of you."

Her mouth dropped open. He had never said anything like that to her but she'd hurt him tonight. His arm burned and the bite on his bicep throbbed.

"What did you say to me?" she all but whispered.

"You heard me," he said. He glanced at the door that led to the mudroom and hoped she wouldn't attack him when he headed for it.

"I'm going to tell Daddy what you said," she told him.

He ground his teeth. There was no doubt in his mind that she would and Big Jake would find a way to punish him for having made the threat.

"I hate you, Drew. I loathe you. I pray every day some drunk driver will hit you on the way home so I can bury you and be done with it," she hissed.

He'd had enough.

"You know what, Terri? So do I," he snapped, then walked past her, reached into his truck and turned off the engine before heading to the mudroom.

"It should have been you," she shouted at him. "You instead of Jackson that died that night."

Yeah, he thought as he strode through the mudroom, past the laundry room and into the kitchen. He wished it had been, too.

Trudging up the back stairs behind the kitchen, he kept listening for the sound of her coming after him. He had a twitch between his shoulder blades, but he made it up the stairs and down the hall to his bedroom without her running after him. He entered his room, locked the door behind him and threw the security latch he'd bought for added protection, then began stripping off his sweaty clothes.

What he needed was a long shower.

And a stiff drink, but the only booze was down in the great room and he really didn't want to risk running the gantlet with her again that night. He made a mental note to buy a couple of bottles of bourbon to stash in his room for those occasions when she was on the warpath. Idly he wondered what he'd done to set her off this time, then remembered he said he'd gone to Boykin.

"Stupid shit," he called himself for having used the name of that place. There *was* a woman in Boykin—one he had known in high school. She'd been his first and his wife knew all about her. Hell, the entirety of five counties—Miller, Early, Baker, Decatur and Seminole—knew about her. She was the reason Terri had attacked him.

Not that she needed a reason to go ape-shit on his ass, he thought as he yanked the T-shirt over his head and winced. He looked down at his bicep and cursed. She'd gotten him good this time. Did a number on his arm, too. There were four long gashes that were still oozing blood. The woman had been close to foaming at the mouth when she'd laid into him. Grimly he wondered if he needed to get a rabies shot.

"Mean little bitch," he said quietly. She meant to hurt him and she had. Just one more set of marks on his body to go with the ones she'd already put there over the years.

He thought about the woman in Boykin and shook his head. It had been years since he'd visited her. Six years his senior, she had taught him all the things a man should know and for that reason he would always think kindly of her. Even now when he saw her on the streets of Colquitt or Bainbridge or Donalsonville she'd smile. He'd smile and remember the big rusted iron bed where she had made him a man.

"Corinne," he whispered, seeing her peroxide blond hair falling around her face as she brought his body to a fevered pitch.

Still thinking of her, he sat down on the edge of the tub, pulled off his boots and laid them aside. Standing, he unbuckled his jeans, ran down the zipper, then shucked off the fishy-smelling denim. He balled them up and put them next to the door instead of adding them to the hamper because he didn't want it to smell.

Opening the glass shower door, he fished inside for the dial and turned the water on full blast, adjusting the temperature before he stepped in and closed the door. The hot warmth cascading over him felt good until it hit the scratch marks on his forearms and the bite on his bicep. He winced at the discomfort, then hung his head to let the water beat down on his shoulders. He stood that way for a moment or two then lowered his hand to his cock.

It had been over a month since his wife had demanded he service her. It had been a perfunctory fucking that had been about as satisfying as a root canal. He'd gotten his release but it had left a bad feeling in his gut. For some reason he'd felt shame that night like he never had before. But despite the disgust he had for himself, the contempt he had for her for demanding her marital rights, he needed the relief of the act itself. He was a man and he had the appetites of a man. The needs of a male in his prime. He craved a woman's soft body cushioning his. He ached to slide between silken thighs and plunge deep. To ride a body that was willing. That wanted his.

Shifting his legs apart, he slid his hand along the length of his shaft, gently twisted the head and pulled the skin toward his groin until it was taut. His body appreciated the handling and his cock came alive. Finding the rhythm that would take him where he wanted to go, he closed his eyes, laid his forehead and the palm of his left hand against the shower wall—the water pounding his back and neck as he worked his shaft. He tried to keep Corinne's face and lush body in his mind's eye but she faded into the background. He opened his eyes. Another face and body appeared in his subconscious but he couldn't make out the features. He had an impression of long, dark, wavy hair flowing past creamy shoulders to a small waist. Green eyes peered at him through the wavering mist of the hot water pummeling him. He couldn't make out the lips but he imagined them slightly open, ready to take him between them.

The speed of his tugs, the force of them increased as he pictured himself atop the mystery woman, straining between long, shapely legs. Pounding his cock into her receptive body. He imagined those legs wrapped around him. Soft arms cradling him against firm breasts as hard little nipples pressed against his chest.

"Love me Drew," she whispered to him and he could almost feel the spiral of her breath in his ear. He shivered as though that breath had entered his ear canal.

His strokes turned frenzied as he jerked his flesh. He panted with his teeth clenched against the pleasure building in his groin. His chest heaved as the hot seed left his balls and spewed in thick jets—

washed away by the cascading water. Breathing heavily, he stood there holding his shrinking cock in his fist and realized he was crying.

Chapter Two

Allison Bennett stood in the center of the tiny kitchen of her new house and wanted to cry. The stainless steel appliances felt all wrong to her. They made the kitchen look cold, unwelcoming and institutional. There was no window above the stainless steel, triple-compartment sink, which made the room all the more uninviting, almost claustrophobic. A door led out to the double-wide carport but it was a solid panel. That corner of the kitchen was dark, heavy with shadows and there was a strange smell she couldn't identify. The only light came from a single casement window by the small table that overlooked a miniscule backyard fenced in with white PVC panels for privacy. Out of the five rooms in the home, only one didn't make her feel like a prisoner, and that was the living room. At least it had a big picture window that let in plenty of sunshine.

She looked at the pale yellow Formica countertops that clashed horribly with the stainless steel appliances, then down at the floor. The vinyl beneath her sandals made her cringe. It bore a white brick pattern that would be hard to keep clean. She hated it.

As she hated everything in the little 900-square-foot house.

From the master bedroom—labeling it such almost made her laugh—with its pea green walls and dark brown shag carpet to the pink tiles on the bathroom wall, the house was an eyesore. She wanted to scream at her husband for the choice he had made in their living quarters. Had he consulted her before buying the god-awful place she would have flatly refused to sign the papers.

But he hadn't. He was content with the house and expected her to be as well.

"So what do you think?"

She looked around at her husband of fifteen years. "It's okay," she said for she knew better than to criticize any choice he made for them.

"I like it," he said. He walked over to the window beside the kitchen table and put his hand on the tabletop and smoothed his hand over the Formica surface. "Got this for twenty dollars at Goodwill." He smiled. "Can you believe that?"

Looking at the fifties style chrome monstrosity with its green cushions, she almost told him Goodwill should have paid him to take it off their hands. She thought longingly of the beautiful old oak table that had belonged to her grandmother—the one he'd sold when they left Milton.

Like all the furniture she had brought to their marriage from her family home, because he didn't want to pay to have it shipped up to Georgia.

"We'll get all new when we get to Colquitt," he'd lied. When she'd seen the rest of the hideous thrift store things he'd purchased for the house, she wanted to sit down and tear out every strand of her hair.

All to save money. To Clay, saving money was as important as sports. She suspected he still had the first dollar he'd ever made. That he came from a very wealthy, influential family who lived in a big-ass mansion in Marietta and stood to inherit millions when his father passed on made his penny pinching all the more bizarre.

"Stop sulking," he snapped. He gave her a hard look. "What are we having for supper?"

She didn't need to look in the pantry. She knew there would be all his favorite canned and boxed food there. The cupboards and drawers were no doubt filled with the same thrift shop purchases. Mismatched plates, flatware, pots and pans—things he had bought with the money he'd gotten from selling her mother's good china, silverware and cookware. She had no doubt he put most of that money in a savings account to which she did not have access.

"Whatever you want, Clay," she said.

He nodded and strode over to the pantry. Opening the door, he stood there for a moment, then pulled a box of mac and cheese from the shelf, a can of butter beans and a can of corn. He walked over to put them on the counter by the stove.

"There are pork chops in the fridge. Let's get supper on the table by six. I've got a meeting with the mayor at eight," he told her, then turned and left the room.

Shoulders drooping, tears threatening to spill with every ragged breath she took, she went over to the sink to wash her hands. A memory she hated flowed through her mind like the water from the spigot…

* * * * *

She thought he was the handsomest boy she'd ever seen. Tall—well over six foot—with black hair and pale blue eyes and a killer smile, he had all the girls sighing over him. Broad shoulders, great physique, he was on the UGA football team and that made him all the more alluring to those girls. His status as a senior only added to the husband potential for many of them.

Not that she was looking for her husband. It was her first year at Georgia and she had her career all planned out. A teaching degree, her Master's in creative writing, then her doctorate that would lead her to a position at a good private school. It was all she'd ever wanted—to teach and to write. Maybe five years into the job and after the release of a book or two she'd consider getting married. At nineteen, the future looked bright and the world was her oyster.

That was until the boy with the black hair, blue eyes and killer smile turned his full attention on her.

"You're Judge Thad Bailey's daughter, aren't you?" he'd asked as he braced his hand on the wall above her head. He was looking down at her with the most sensual gaze she'd ever encountered.

"Yes, I am," she managed to agree. "Do you know my dad?"

"Yeah, I do. He and my dad are frat bros. Delts," he told her.

"Delta Tau Delta fraternity," she replied. "Are you a legacy?"

"Indeed I am," he said. He moved in closer until she felt his body heat, smelled his cologne. "What say me and you go get a cup of coffee and talk about all the pretty babies we're gonna make?"

She felt the blush spreading across her face and lowered her head. His devastating blue eyes were doing strange things to her lower body and when he hooked a finger under her chin to lift her face, the warmth went straight between her legs.

"You are such a pretty little thing," he said, caressing her chin, sweeping the pad of his thumb across it. "I'm gonna love making those babies with you."

Then he had swept in to kiss her. His lips were firm, his tongue warm as he slipped it past her lips. The man knew how to kiss. Her knees felt weak by the time he pulled back and reached for her hand.

"Let's go."

He threaded his fingers through hers and tugged her away from the wall. He'd given her no chance to protest as he led her away.

* * * * *

He'd given her no choice then and he had continued that behavior from that day on. Every decision had been his. From her dropping out of college to marry him to the wedding date. From the church in which they said their vows to the wedding gown she wore. From how she dressed and what she wore to the style of shoes she put on her feet. From where they lived and how, to what went on the walls and where. If she disagreed with his choices, she would regret it. As heavy-handed as he was with the decisions, he was more so with an open palm to her cheek or a bruise-making fist wrapped around her arm.

Sitting silently at the table with him, she watched him devouring the pork chops. Knife in his left hand, fork in the right, he had his arms on the table and was hunched over his plate like a troll as he shoveled the food into his mouth. He would eat four out of the five chops, then inhale most of the corn and beans. She'd already refilled his glass of iced tea twice—all without a word being said by either of them. She had learned early on in their marriage that he did not tolerate idle chitchat when he ate. Just as with his precious sports, he took eating very seriously and had no desire to be distracted while engaged in either endeavor.

Her stomach in knots—as it always was when she was this close to him—she slowly ate the meager portion he allowed her to have in order to maintain her one hundred and ten pound weight and waited for him to look up at her. That would be her cue to fetch the same dessert she'd been making for years—banana pudding with whipped cream.

"You remember that girl I dated before I met you?" he asked, surprising her with the opening gambit.

"You dated a lot of girls," she said and when his head came up sharply, she forced a smile to her lips, put her hands in her lap and clutched them tight. "You were a very popular guy. You had your choice of girls."

"Yeah, I did," he said. "And look who my daddy chose for me."

The words were bitter—as they always were when he mentioned his father or her father and the decision those two men had made regarding his life. It was best to humor him, cajole him or the bitter words would turn to something physical.

"Which one of your girlfriends are you referring to?" she asked in the hopes of staving off the anger she saw building in his eyes.

"The one from Colquitt, of course" he snapped. He picked up his napkin to swipe at his greasy lips. That was her cue to get the dessert.

She pushed her chair back, reached for his plate, put it in the sink, then stepped over to the refrigerator. Since she wasn't allowed the calories in the pudding, she got one dessert cup only and brought it back to the table, placing it before him with care. "I don't recall her name."

"Terri Anne Thompson." He rolled his eyes at her. "You had an economics class with her. Cheerleader? Red hair and tits like a cow's udder?"

That brought the image of the girl to her mind and she nodded. "I remember her now."

"She still lives here," he said. "Married some local yokel. She goes to the First Baptist Church. Thought I'd look her up tomorrow after the service. Catch up on old times with her."

If memory served, he'd only had a couple of dates with the redhead and that was only because the girl had broken up with her steady boyfriend. She couldn't help but wonder if he'd been pining for Terri Anne Thompson all these years, and if the reason he'd taken a job at a small school like Miller County High had been because of her.

Not that it mattered one way or another. She had grown accustomed to the philandering that began right from the start of their marriage. If he was screwing some other woman, he was leaving her alone. His brutal lovemaking was something she tried very hard to avoid.

"Her daddy's the richest man in Miller County and someone I need to have in my pocket," he continued.

That explained it, she thought as she took her seat. Her husband rarely did anything unless it benefited him. In Clay's mind, if he seduced the Thompson girl, had her eating out of his hand, her father would no doubt be pleased. What man wouldn't be to have his daughter garner the notice of the new football coach—a star defensive end at UGA?

She watched him gobble up the pudding. If he wanted another, his body posture would make it evident. When he pushed the cup aside and got to his feet, she felt a moment of relief.

That didn't last long.

"I'm gonna want you tonight when I get back," he said as he headed for the carport door. "Get yourself prettied up as much as you can."

Those were words she didn't want to hear. They made her shudder. Once the door closed behind him she slowly looked around the hideous kitchen, then let fall the tears she'd held at bay all day.

Chapter Three

Dressed in his Sunday best—suit, tie, polished loafers. Sitting quietly in the pew watching friends and family and neighbors filing into the sanctuary. Smiling at those friends and family and neighbors. Nodding at those he didn't particularly like or actively disliked because that was the Christian thing to do on Sunday. Trying not to let his thigh touch Terri's as she perched rigidly on the seat beside him. Reaching for the hymnal just to have something to do with his hands. Idly tuning in to the talk around him.

"Henrietta looks like butter wouldn't melt in her mouth, don't she?" someone asked.

Turning his head toward the choir, he zeroed in on the woman being discussed. She was sitting ramrod straight at the organ and looked so prim and proper. No one liked the prune-faced old bat, considering she was the town's most vicious gossip. Scanning over to the choir members, he mentally shook his head. Ed Carter beat his wife and children on a regular basis. Marvelle Dickson had a drinking problem that rivaled his father's. Jody Hatcher and his wife Leigh Ann were loan sharks and bookies on the side though their day jobs were those of grade school teachers. Brothers Thad and Boyd Dykes cooked and sold the best moonshine in the five counties. Georgette Myers's son, J.T., was now her daughter ,Judy, and Georgette was fresh out of the sanitarium where she'd tried to cope with the change.

And the choirmaster?

Drew locked his gaze on Bobby Daniels. He and Bobby went *way* back. The bastard was the sheriff of Miller County—like his daddy and granddaddy before him—and like them was as corrupt as they came. Rattlesnake mean, brutal and just plain evil. Born and raised in Donalsonville—a town thirteen miles to the south of Colquitt—Bobby D. had been a defensive end for the Seminole County Indians. He took great delight in coming after Drew every chance he got on the field. Bobby despised Drew and sacking the star quarterback for the Pirates every game earned him a place of honor with the D'ville Indians.

No doubt sensing Drew's eyes on him, Bobby turned around and stared right at him. The slow, nasty-spirited smile that pulled at the man's thin lips made Drew want to knock Bobby's teeth down his throat. When those green eyes slide over to Terri and the smile became something more, Drew looked away. His stomach churned—not because he knew the two had slept together and probably still did on occasion, but because the thought of Bobby pounding into any woman made him physically ill.

"Hey, Daddy."

Drew stiffened as Terri bumped into him to send him farther down the pew. Her father had made his appearance—coming in later than most folks so he would be sure to be noticed—and plopped his bulk on the seat he considered his own.

"Hey, baby girl," Big Jake Thompson said. He put a pudgy hand on his daughter's knee and patted it like he would one of his blue-tick coon dogs.

There was no greeting for him, but then Drew hadn't expected one. Big Jake hated him as much, if not more, than his daughter did.

The man sitting on the other side of Drew leaned around him. "Morning, Jake. How you doing?"

Terri's father turned his head toward the speaker. "Fair to middling. How's things in your neck of the woods?"

"The same." The man was a cousin of Big Jake's and—as such—was entitled to sit in the pew reserved for the Thompson family. The wooden bench even had the name Thompson engraved on a little brass plate that was screwed into the side to warn away potential perchers that it was off-limits to anyone other than the Thompson clan.

Big Jake's upper lip curled as his gaze raked over Drew. He didn't do the Christian thing and nod at his son-in-law, he simply ignored him and turned his attention to the front of the church.

That didn't bother Drew. He disliked Jake just as much. The less they said to one another, acknowledged one another, the better. He was about to open the hymnal when a tall man appeared at the end of the pew in front of the one in which Drew was seated. He glanced up expecting someone he knew.

He knew the man, all right. It might have been sixteen years since he'd been in the same room with the bastard, but he recognized him.

"Clay Bennett," the man said, thrusting his hand toward Big Jake.

"Welcome to Colquitt, Coach," Jake said, pumping Bennett's hand. "This is my daughter Terri Anne."

Drew saw Bennett's ice-blue eyes shift to Terri and a look of desire flashed over his sun-tanned face a split second before he shut it down. He stepped back to reveal a diminutive woman who was standing behind him. "My wife, Allie," he introduced.

It felt as if all the sound had been sucked out of the room. Drew saw Bennett's mouth moving but he didn't seem to be able to hear what was coming from the thin lips. In the periphery of his vision people moved about but seemed to be doing so in slow motion. His entire attention was riveted on the woman at Bennett's side as she stood there with a smile frozen on her lips, hands clasped in front of her. When her gaze swung to him, he felt the breath catch in his throat.

Then fell in love for the first time in his life.

* * * * *

He couldn't take his eyes off her the entire service. She was sitting right in front of Terri so all he saw was her profile. Her black hair was plaited and wound into a tight, sleek bun at the nape of her neck. The creamy expanse of her swanlike neck, the delicate shape of her chin, her small nose, her slender shoulders and the thick length of her dark lashes did things to his body that the hymnal helped to hide. Luckily there wasn't that much standing to do, else Terri would have seen what he was trying to keep from view.

And her voice was absolutely beautiful. It carried clear and crisp and with just a hint of vibrato. She seemed to know every hymn by heart for she rarely glanced down at her hymnal. As he listened to her singing—tuning out Terri's nasally rendition of whichever hymn was being sung—he felt an inner peace he hadn't known in a long, long time. He could listen to her voice for hours.

"The coach's wife ought to be in the choir," he heard Jake comment to his daughter.

"I guess," Terri replied with a sniff.

Bennett turned around in the pew and grinned. "She'll be up there next week," he told Jake. His icy eyes flicked to Drew and he frowned. They stared at one another for a few heartbeats, then Bennett turned back around.

When the service was over and the congregation began to file out noisily, Drew sat where he was. Jake was on his feet and once again pumping Bennett's hand. Terri was half-heartedly inviting the coach's wife to join the garden club.

"She'll do that," Bennett said and his scrutiny slid to Drew. "Have we met?"

"My son-in-law," Jake said, making it seem like an afterthought. "He went to Georgia. Didn't graduate though."

"What year were you there?" Bennett inquired.

"He was there in ninety-eight and ninety-nine," Jake answered for Drew.

"You look familiar," Bennett said. "Did you play any sports?"

"He played freshman ball," Jake replied. "Got hurt in that sorry mess what went down at Florida."

Bennett's eyes lit up. "You the one got his leg broke so bad?"

"That was him," Jake stated.

Bennett pointed at Drew and wagged his finger. "I remember." He nodded his head, dismissed Drew, then looked at Terri. "And I do believe we've met before, too, haven't we?"

"We have," Terri said. "We dated for a while there."

"Yes, indeed we did," Bennett affirmed. "The prettiest girl on campus my senior year."

Terri laughed. "And you were the handsomest boy," she returned.

Drew saw Allie Bennett's head go down, her shoulders slump and lowered his gaze to her hands. She was clutching her fingers tightly together. So tightly the knuckles had bled of color. Her body posture told him all he needed to know. Her husband was a cheater and she knew it all too well.

"Did you go to Georgia, Mrs. Bennett?" he asked to bring her into the conversation.

She looked up, surprised. "Yes." Her eyes were filled with gratitude that he had acknowledged her.

"She only went the one year," Bennett said. He slipped an arm around her waist. "Went there to find a husband, didn't you, sweetie?" He grinned crookedly. "Caught my eye right out of the stall. I had to marry her to keep her honest."

Allie Bennett winced and looked down again. Her cheeks flooded with color. Her full bottom lip trembled.

"Any man would be lucky to have as beautiful a woman as Mrs. Bennett for a wife," Drew heard himself say. Despite having three shocked glares settle on him he didn't care. He ignored his wife, father-in-law and the coach. It was the beautiful green eyes that lifted to his that mattered.

"Thank you, Mr...." Her blush deepened. "I don't know your name."

"Andrew Dunne," Jake snapped. "He runs my car dealership for me."

Much to his delight, Allie Bennett held out her hand. "It's a pleasure, Mr. Dunne."

"Drew," he said, taking that small, soft hand into his.

"Okay then," Terri said with a hiss. She all but tore his hand from the other woman's as she grabbed his arm and pulled him back. "We need to get going."

"Guess I'll be seeing you around, Coach," Jake said, casting Drew a nasty look. He put out his hand yet again to shake with Bennett.

"You sure will," Bennett said. He flicked his narrowed gaze over Drew, then put an arm around his wife's shoulders to draw her in close. "We'll have to have you and your daughter over for supper some night, Mr. Thompson."

"Jake," the older man corrected.

"And you as well, Drew," Bennett's wife stated.

"It would be my pleasure, Allie," Drew told her. He pretended not to see the anger than flitted over the faces of the three people standing there with him in the sanctuary.

* * * * *

"Why didn't you just fling her skirt up then and there and fuck her?" Terri snapped as he opened the car door for her.

"You don't fuck a woman like her, Terri," he said. "You make love to her." He held her hard gaze. "Slow and sweet."

Before he could move back, she brought up her hand and slapped him as hard as she could.

"Fuck you, you goddamned piece of shit," she spat at him.

* * * * *

Across the parking lot, Clay Bennett shut the passenger side door of his pickup. He had witnessed the slap as had a man who was about to get into his own truck. They looked at one another and laughed.

"Wonder what's going on there," Clay said to the stranger over the hood of his truck. "Woman embarrass me in such a way, I'd return the favor."

"He's used to getting slapped in public," the man said. "His daddy made it a way of life for him earlier on, and Terri Anne is just carrying on the tradition." He skirted the hood of the truck, put out his hand. "Bobby Daniels. I'm the sheriff here. Welcome to Colquitt, Coach."

"Just call me Clay," Clay told him. He cocked his head toward the Lincoln where Dunne and his wife were arguing. "He needs to get that filly in hand."

"Takes balls to do it and he ain't got none," Bobby replied. "You got plans for the rest of the day?"

"Gonna sit in front of the TV with an ice-cold brewski and my hand down my pants while my woman makes lunch," Clay said with a grin. "How 'bout you?"

"The same except I'll be making my own lunch. The bitch I was married to is long gone."

Recognizing a kindred soul, Clay asked him if he would like to come over to share lunch with him.

"Your missus won't mind?" Bobby inquired.

"What would it matter if she did?" Clay countered. "She's a fucking woman."

"I hear you," Bobby said with a grin.

"Why don't you follow me up to the house?"

"I can do that," Bobby agreed and opened the door to his truck. He took one last look at the Dunnes, shook his head and climbed inside.

Clay went around the front of his own truck and slid behind the wheel. He reached over to take hold of Allie's wrist. Wrapping his fingers tightly around it, he pulled her arm up so the back of his hand rested on her shoulder. He leaned in until his lips were against her ear.

"You ever put your hand into some other man's hand and by God I will break it," he said between clenched teeth. "You hear me, Allison?"

She nodded, her lips pressed tightly together as the pain built on her face.

"'It's a pleasure to meet you, Mr. Dunne,'" he mocked and increased the pressure on her wrist until she whimpered. "Don't think for a minute I didn't see the way you were looking at that sawed-off little pissant. Look at him like that again and I'll beat the shit out of you."

Allie cried out as he ground the bones of her wrists and tried to pull her arm free, but he wouldn't allow it. He flicked out his tongue and licked the side of her face.

"Your cunt belongs to me, bitch, and it's mine whenever I want it," he said then let go of her wrist, laughing as she cradled it to her chest. He fished in his pocket for his keys and pushed them into the ignition. Nodding at the new friend he'd made, he put the truck in reverse and backed out of the parking slot.

* * * * *

All the way home Drew listened to Terri's commentary about everyone she hated who attended the First Baptist Church of Colquitt. She wasn't talking to him. She was on her cell phone talking to her best friend, Janice.

"Did you see that hideous dress she was wearing?" she asked and he ground his teeth. She was talking about the coach's wife and the more she insulted Allie Bennett, the madder he got.

It was bad enough she had slapped him right out in front of people they knew. He'd seen the smirks, the pursed lips, the raised eyebrows of the men who had witnessed his shame. The women simply looked the other way. The old folks shook their heads. The children laughed and pointed. Which was par for the course. He was a laughingstock in Miller County. He was accustomed to the humiliation. It had been his to endure for as long as they'd been married.

"Yes! I do," Terri said breathlessly. "I knew him in college. I *dated* him! I…" She glanced over at him, then lowered her voice. "Well, you know. Yes. Yes. You better believe he was."

He knew she was trying to hurt him but he didn't care. Her attempts at making him jealous had never worked and he wondered why she even bothered. She didn't give a damn about him so why try to make him jealous? It never had made any sense to him, but then again, most of what his wife did didn't make sense. Spoiled little rich girl with an entitled complex and daddy issues. That was Terri Anne.

"Are you kidding me?" she said with a hateful laugh. "Can't hold a candle to Clay Bennett." Once more she looked at him. "The difference between a cocktail wienie and a salami."

The laughter that followed set his teeth on edge but he didn't give her the satisfaction of glancing at her. He kept his eyes on the road and thought about Allie Bennett.

"The difference between an ice storm and a sizzling fire," he mumbled.

"What?" Terri snapped, pulling the cell phone from her ear. "What did you say?"

"Nothing," he replied.

"Yes, you did," she said, then put the cell phone against her ear. "Jan, I'll call you back. *He's* being a fuckhead again." She pressed the disconnect button, then tossed the cell phone into her purse before swiveling around in her seat.

He didn't need to see her face to know her eyes would be narrowed, her lips peeled back from her teeth and her nostrils flaring. "Now, what the fuck did you say?" she demanded.

"Since you were comparing me to Clay Bennett, I was just comparing you to Bennett's wife," he said. He turned to give her a steady look. "Ice to fire."

She hit him—slapping at his head with her open palm—and he nearly lost control of the car. The vehicle fishtailed across the blacktop. The back tires slid into the gravel at the edge of the road, and he had to fight the wheel to get them back on track.

"God*damn* it, Terri, what the hell's the matter with you?" he shouted. "You trying to get us killed?" He got the car under control, then pulled off onto the side of the road, panting as his heart raced.

"You bastard," she shouted back at him and hit him again though he threw his arm up to block her hands. "I wish *you* had died instead of Jack."

"I do, too," he bellowed and got a moment's satisfaction when her mouth dropped open and her eyes widened. Her face drained of color—making it impossible to stop the words that came pouring out of him. "There's not a day that goes by that I don't wish I had been the one they buried instead of him. Not a goddamned day, Terri. Not a goddamned *day!*"

She gawked at him, then moved back to wedge herself against the passenger door as though she feared he'd attack her as she had him. He could almost hear the hard swallow she took. The hand she put up to push a wisp of hair from her cheek was shaking.

"I tell you what," he said, bracing his forearm on the steering wheel as he faced her. "Why don't you take one of your daddy's guns and blow my fucking brains out while I'm sleeping some night? Why don't you do that and put both of us out of our misery?"

"Don't think I haven't thought about it," she said.

"Then fucking do it and get it over with it," he said, turning around and putting the car in gear. "I'm tired of this shit." Gravel spewed as he accelerated onto the highway.

* * * * *

Terri Anne stood in the foyer and watched her husband take the stairs two at a time. As much as she hated to admit it, Andrew Allan Dunne was a handsome man. She liked looking at his body if not his face.

Despite being only average in height, he managed to catch the eyes of women who didn't know him. He had chiseled features and broad shoulders, a narrow waist and flat belly. He carried himself well. With a head full of thick chestnut hair, striking blue eyes and a gravelly voice, he seemed to mesmerize some women.

Not those who had grown up with him, though. Those women knew him for the coward he was. Even though he had been the quarterback on their high school football team, he hadn't been the captain and he hadn't been popular by any stretch of the imagination. The girls stayed away from him because he was Wade Dunne's son, and the boys left him alone for the same reason.

Everyone except Jack Mackie. For some reason she had never been able to fathom, the two men had been tight as thieves growing up. Best friends until the day Jack left her world.

As it always did when Jack's smiling face flashed through her memory, she felt her throat close and her chest grow tight. Her eyes filled with tears.

God, how she had loved that boy, she thought as she sat down on the bottom stair and buried her face in her hands. She missed him with every breath she took. Over the years she had tried to lose herself in first one man and then another to try to dull the pain of not having Jack with her. None of them had come close to doing for her what Jack had and the guilt she felt afterward only made it worse. Though they had never been intimate, she had fantasized herself into believing they had.

It wasn't like you could cheat on a dead man, anyway, but that was what her one-night stands made her feel. When she felt bad about herself, she went after her worthless husband—the man her father had forced her to marry. The man she hated so violently.

She had done—and still did—everything in her power to punish her husband. She held him responsible for Jack's death, but as the years passed, it didn't seem to matter as much anymore. Drew hadn't crumbled beneath her mental torture but he *was* beginning to show a few cracks here and there. He had surprised her by his outburst in the car. For the first time he admitted he wished he'd died in Jack's place.

"I wish you had, too," she said aloud.

As much as she had loved Jack, she hated Drew. Had always been envious of his relationship with Jack. She'd never understood the bond the two had and had tried time and again to break them apart, but it seemed the harder she tried, the tighter that bond got. They were closer than brothers, loved one another, understood one another and that just pissed her off.

Getting to her feet, she turned and headed up the stairs. He was at the top, coming down. She bit her lip for she could not control the wayward part of her that found the worn jeans that hugged his runner's thighs sexy. That part of her wanted to rip the faded blue check shirt from his chest and peel it down his shoulders.

"Stop it," she said and forced her mind to think of Clay Bennett. As she watched her husband descend the stairs, she thought of the tall, darkly handsome football coach and remembered his big hands on her breasts a long time ago.

Broad shoulders, hairless chest. Dark hair accentuated with blue eyes…

She shook herself as Drew passed her for he was the same physical type as Clay—and Jack for that matter—and that annoyed her. She gave him a hard look but he never shifted his gaze to her as he passed her on the stairs.

"You are a fucking limp-dick bastard," she threw at him.

"Right back at you," she heard him reply.

Now that was something new, she thought as she turned to watch him walk into the kitchen. He normally did not respond to her jibes but that was three times in one day that he had done so. Her anger rushed to the forefront of her mind and she almost turned to storm after him, to slap him as hard as she could, but her commonsense got the better of her and she continued on up the stairs. Once more she used the image of Clay Bennett to push aside her husband's.

Tall—maybe three inches or so over six foot—and muscular. That thick wavy dark hair. Those icy blue eyes that she remembered well gazing down at her as he pumped his big cock into her body. His strong hands had gripped her ass almost painfully as he thrust. His hips had swiveled like a piston—the sound of his balls slapping against her music to her ears. He had owned her that night and the night after that. He'd been rough—borderline violent—with her but that had only added to the allure.

That and the fact that she was cheating on Jack, getting back at him for cheating on her with that whorish cheerleader, Danielle Foster—the bitch.

And for that she blamed Drew as well. Had he not introduced the slut to Jack…

Just one more nail in the coffin of her hatred for her husband. One more reason to make his life as miserable as she could.

* * * * *

When Big Jake Thompson built the palatial home for his only daughter, he spared no expense. Second in size only to his own Southern mansion, the plantation-style home he had given Terri Anne as a wedding present was as ostentatious as it was out of place in Miller County. Boasting six bedrooms, seven full baths—one of which was inside the pool house—a den, a living room, dining room, kitchen with two industrial-size ranges and refrigerators, library, solarium and wraparound porches on both the first and second floors, the 8000-square-foot house was simply pretentious. With only two of the bedrooms in use and absolutely no need for industrial-size ranges and refrigerators, for the Dunnes never entertained, the house was nothing more than a waste of money. But then, Big Jake had more money than he, his daughter and son could ever spend in their lifetimes.

Skirting the outdoor pool with its archway that led to the indoor pool that was used in the winter, Drew noticed the door to the sauna was open but he didn't care. Coons and possums and any other critter who wanted to take advantage of the steam could be his guest. It wasn't his sauna any more than was the grandiose house.

He paid no attention to the manicured lawns on either side of the elaborate fieldstone walkway down which he walked. Underfoot, expertly maintained moss grew between the cracks of the pavers. The trees he passed were likewise pruned to perfection and as symmetrical as possible given their variety. Ahead of him was a fully-stocked catfish and perch pond with a long dock that jutted like a sore thumb into the perfectly oval basin around which grew redtop bushes. Evenly spaced around the pond were weeping willows that swayed gently in the summer breeze.

To the right of the dock was a roofed platform that was used as a seating area. Four chaise lounges, two gliders and a table with four chairs sat primly in place upon the intricately laid redwood floor panels. A large stainless steel grill with four burners was set into the middle of a long counter with a three-compartment stainless sink set off to one side. A semicircular bar and four stools fronting it faced the grill. On the far side of the platform was a five-foot long wooden swing.

Walking down a slight incline to the long dock, Drew looked out across the pond and smiled. There were two peafowls—a cock and a hen—strutting about among the willows and with them were two chicks. On the pond were a couple of ducks and they had their little row of ducklings trailing in their wake.

Reaching the end of the dock, he sat down, took off his tennis shoes and socks and put his feet into the water. Which wasn't a particularly smart thing to do. Cottonmouth moccasins were known to make the pond their home although the gardener did his best to keep out the venomous snakes.

Bracing his hands on the weathered wood beneath his legs, he leaned forward to look down into the gently lapping water. He saw a few fish wriggling past his feet so he kept them still. Hopefully he wouldn't attract the attention of anything that might be slithering beneath the surface.

He realized his life was as murky as the waters into which he was staring. Unhappy, depressed, restless, miserable—his entire existence was one long sad adventure into old age. With a woman who hated him at his side to always remind him what a loser he was.

"You wouldn't do that, though, would you, Allie Bennett?" he asked quietly.

No, he thought, she wouldn't. She would be supportive and encouraging. She would stand at his side with her hand in his and face whatever life had to throw at them. How he knew that, he couldn't explain had his life depended on it, but he was as sure of it as he'd ever been of anything.

Beautiful woman, he thought as he pictured her standing there in the sanctuary. He longed to take the pins from that wealth of black hair and fan it out over her shoulders. It would be soft, silky and wavy. He didn't know how he knew that, either, but he did. It would smell of gardenias for he had inhaled that perfume when they shook hands. Her big green eyes had held him in thrall as he gazed into them. There was laughter hiding in those pretty orbs. Kindness and gentleness and respect. There was compassion and consideration for others. There was interest and empathy.

"And need," he whispered.

Like recognized like, and he had seen in her lovely eyes and sweet face a need as great as his own to be loved and wanted and desired for the woman she was and not an object to be used. That her husband did not treat her as she should be treated was evident in the way he spoke of and to her.

"Typical asshole," he said, lifting his head.

A player. A womanizer of the first order. Oh, he knew all about Clay Bennett. What he hadn't known was that he had fucked Terri. It didn't matter but it had been a surprise that they'd had a relationship.

"One you're gonna rekindle, huh, Terri?" he asked.

That didn't matter, either. If she was wallowing under some other man, she wasn't wallowing under him. Just the idea of screwing her made his flesh crawl. She was a beautiful woman, but she was as mean as a polecat, too. She always managed to drag her wickedly sharp nails down his back or gouge them into his ass when she came.

"But you wouldn't do that, either, would you, Allie?" he questioned the sweet face that was hovering in his mind's eye.

He wanted her. God, how he wanted her. Wanted her as he had never wanted any other woman he'd ever known. He longed just to hold her hand, to touch her, to make her smile. He wanted to talk to her, walk with her, sit quietly beside her with his arm around her slender shoulders.

How, he wondered, could a man fall so helplessly in love with a woman he had just met?

Because you are desperate for affection, fool.

He shook his head, then allowed his shoulders to slump. He closed his eyes, hung his head and felt a tremor in his arms as he braced himself on the dock planking.

Across the pond the peacock shrieked and the peahen answered in an equally raucous tone. For some reason that struck a chord in Drew and he dug into the pocket of his jeans and pulled out his cell phone. Punching in Early's number, he pulled his feet from the water and stood, then bent over to retrieve his tennis shoes.

"Hey, it's me," he said when his cousin answered. "You got anything planned for today?"

"Just watching Braves baseball," Early replied. "Why?"

"Where's Bea?"

"At her mama's. Why?" Early drew the repeated question out as though he was talking to a child.

"I need to get away from this place," Drew said.

"Ah, she gonna let you do that, cuz? I thought Sundays were when she made you braid her hair or paint her toenails or the like," Early countered.

"I'll be there in twenty," Drew said and ended the call.

Not bothering to go through the house, he went around its side directly to the garage, then to his truck, grateful he hadn't shut the garage door. He was barely inside the cab, didn't have the door shut, before the mudroom door opened and his wife appeared.

"Where the hell do you think *you're* going?" she yelled at him.

"Away from your crazy ass," he said quietly. Although he knew she couldn't possibly have heard him, she hurled a succession of filthy curses at him. He put his arm on the back of the passenger seat, turned his head to look behind him and gunned the engine. He backed out of the carport as she came running after him.

"Don't you *dare* leave. You better listen to me, Drew," she yelled. "You can't leave."

"Watch me," he replied.

* * * * *

He got halfway to Early's house and realized he was bringing trouble to his cousin. There was no way he was going to make Early have to deal with Terri today. She'd follow him as sure as God made little green apples, so he went through town and took the road east to Albany. He doubted she'd even think about him leaving the county, and she knew nothing about the little house in East Albany that he had purchased a few years back. He went there when things with her got too rough around the edges. Lately, things weren't just getting rough, they were beginning to scour his soul like coarse sandpaper. He needed some time alone to think.

Reaching into his pocket for his cell phone, he thumbed in Early's number to let him know he wasn't coming.

"Hey, cuz," he said. "I—"

"Don't come out here," Early cut him off. "I just got off the phone with her and she's spittin' mad that you left without her permission. I think she's on her way here so go somewhere else unless you want to have her bring hell down around your ears."

"Man, look," he said. "I'm sorry I dragged you into this. I—"

"Don't worry about it. I can handle the wicked witch of the south," Early interrupted. "Just don't come out here. All right?"

"Okay," he agreed.

"And be careful, Drew," Early said. "She sounds rabid."

"She *is* rabid," he told his cousin, then ended the call.

As he drove he tried to force Terri's sneering, bug-eyed face from popping up in front of him. Even from miles away he felt the woman's venom searing him. There would be hell to pay when he got home but it wasn't going to be any time soon. He wished it would be never but that wasn't an option.

Reaching over, he turned on the radio, but the sad, mournful hymn depressed him even more so he twisted the knob—moving past talking and commercials and the hard rock he detested until he landed on a melodic string of notes that caught his attention. As the male singer began putting words to the music, he took his hand from the dial.

"I was lost before I found you, girl. All alone in this cold, hard world."

He settled back in the seat.

"Your tender smile eased the ache in my heart. The touch of your hand kept me from falling apart."

The face of Allie Bennett pushed Terri's completely out of his mind.

"My life has meaning now that you are here. Gone is the loneliness; gone are my tears."

His hands tightened on the wheel.

"Put your arms around me, hold me tight. Lie here with me 'til the morning light."

As the song continued, he got lost in the lyrics. The singer might as well have written the words with him in mind. Humming along with the mesmerizing melody, he joined in on the chorus.

"'Baby, baby, let me lean on you. That's the only way I'll make it through. There's no one else to care if I do. Baby, baby let me lean on you.'"

When the song ended, he pulled onto the shoulder of the road and just sat there with the engine idling. He was about two miles from the Decatur County line but he wasn't worried about Terri coming after him. He'd taken the turnoff to Bainbridge instead of going on toward Albany—where she could conceivably think he'd gone. Sitting there with a hot, stale wind coming in through the window, he stared at the highway without really seeing it. His mind wasn't on the road or the quickly heating truck cab or the too-chipper prattle of the D.J. giving out useless information about the singer coming up next. His mind was on Allie Bennett and the loneliness he'd seen reflected in her pretty green eyes.

A loneliness that mirrored his own.

He knew—beyond any shadow of a doubt—that she would let him lean on her if he needed to. She would wrap him in her arms and hold him close, pull his head to her shoulder and whisper softly to him. She would keep the cold, hard world at bay.

"Are you as lost as I am, Allie?" he asked.

He thought perhaps she was. There had been something so bleak in her gaze, so hopeless. He wanted to put happiness on that lovely face. Hear unrestrained laughter escaping her soft lips. Feel the touch of her hand on his brow. His cheek. Anywhere she wanted to put it on his body.

That thought made him draw in a quick breath and his cock pulse against his jeans.

He squirmed against the hot vinyl beneath him. Just the wayward notion of her putting her hands on him turned his blood as hot as magma flowing through his veins. It made him ache with a need he hadn't felt since he was in his late teens. It brought moisture to his mouth and he swallowed hard, his breath coming harsh and heavy to his lungs.

"I want you, Allie Bennett," he whispered.

A car raced by him—startling him. The unexpected interruption took him out of the moment and brought him back to reality. He stared after the car until it disappeared over a rise in the road. He shook his head, glanced in the rearview mirror, then pulled back onto the road. He didn't have any particular destination in mind but his stomach was rumbling. There was a convenience store that served what were arguably the best hotdogs outside of Jimmy's in Albany and it was there he headed as another man/cheating wife/hound dog song came over the airwaves.

"What *is* it with the dog?" he mumbled.

That made him shake his head again. He'd never had a pet growing up and Terri would not abide an animal in her fancy digs. Early had a mangy old mutt that slept in the barn but the canine preferred his own company to that of the human variety. Corinne— the woman who had eased him joyfully into manhood—had had a little calico cat that she'd loved with a passion, but the cat hadn't cared for Drew and Drew had disliked the cat just as much. He liked animals, wouldn't ever hurt one, but he simply did not see the fascination some people had with keeping them in their homes.

"She took my money. She took my chaw but she went too far when she took my dawg."

The song made him chuckle and he needed the laugh. By the time he pulled up to the convenience store, he was in a better frame of mind.

* * * * *

"You'd better not be lying to me, Early Rawls," Terri said with a hiss. She flicked her eyes down him as though he were a piece of offal, then pivoted on her heel to stomp back to her car.

"You don't own him, Terri Anne," Early called after her.

"Like hell I don't," she snapped. She jerked the door open, then turned to give him another hateful look. "I own that boy's ass and the crack that runs down it."

Early folded his arms and stared at her as she cranked the car, raced the motor, then slammed the vehicle into reverse. He couldn't help but wince at the brutal way the woman treated the Lincoln. As a master mechanic, he had a deep, abiding love for automobiles and had worked on hers several times. The abuse she heaped on the blameless thing shot his hackles up.

"Goddamned hateful bitch," he labeled her as she whipped the car around at the end of the drive and gunned the motor.

He hated Terri. Had hated her since they were children. Not just because she had been a spoiled brat who turned into a world class hellcat. He hated her for the way she treated Drew. The woman had all but emasculated a good man who had never done anything to deserve the treatment she dished out to him. Any other male would have left her mean ass long ago. He knew the only reason Drew stayed with her was because of the guilt he felt over Jack Mackie's death. Hell, the whole town knew that's why he stayed with her, though the spiteful ones said it was because of Big Jake's money.

"He don't give a rat's pecker about that old bastard's money," Early grumbled as he turned to go into the house. "Ain't got a good goddamned thing to do with money he ain't never going to see anyway."

Just as he closed the door behind him, the phone rang. He went over to answer it. The caller ID told him it was Bea and he grinned, picked up the receiver and said, "She ain't home yet. You better hurry on over if you want some of what I got waitin' for you."

"Ha, ha," Bea said and he could picture her rolling her eyes—which she did more than he liked. "Is she gone?"

"Who? My wife? Yeah, I just told she—"

"Will you behave?" Bea asked with exasperation. "You know who I mean."

"How'd you know she was here?" he countered.

"I saw her streaking through town like a hound dog with a swarm of bees after his fanny," his wife replied. "Where else would she be heading?"

"She just left. Madder than a bear with a sore paw."

"Drew wasn't there, then?"

"He called and I told him not to come," Early told her. "I don't know where he went but that poor boy's gonna get pounced on soon as he lights to home. She had that look in her eye and that don't bode well for Drew."

The sound of a long sigh came through the receiver. "I wish he would leave her," Bea said. "I really do. It's just gonna keep getting worse and worse until something bad happens, Early. I can feel it in my bones."

"Yeah, babe," Early agreed. "You may be right."

* * * * *

"I want you to kill him, Daddy," Terri sobbed into her phone. She was speeding down the highway much faster than she should have. She knew it, but she didn't care. She'd been driving since she was ten and could handle anything with four wheels.

"Now, baby girl," her father said calmly. "You know you don't want no such thing."

"Then get Wade to beat him to a bloody pulp," she shouted. "You can do that, can't you?"

Her father chuckled. "I could and would take great pleasure in doing so, but I got to know what the little son of a bitch did first."

"He left the house when I told him not to," she told him.

"Well, now, that ain't grounds for me ordering a beating, sugar. A talkin-to, yes, but not a beating."

"He disrespected me. I want him punished for it," she stated.

"And I will take appropriate measures, but Terri Anne? Darling? Don't you go tearing into him and hitting him like you're apt to do when you're mad. You let me handle him. You hear?"

"I'm gonna scratch his eyes out," she snarled.

"No, you ain't. Just leave him to me. Okay? I'll take care of it."

"Promise?"

"I promise. Now why don't you come on over here and spend the night? Me and you and your brother can have a good meal together and maybe watch a movie or two. Would you like that?"

"I guess."

"Then that's what we'll do. You haven't been over here in a coon's age. Bossy misses fixing you your favorites. How 'bout I have her whip up some of her special garlic fried chicken and mashed potatoes. Bake us some cathead biscuits. How does that sound?"

"All right," she said, mollified by the prospect of the maid's cooking. "What about *him*?"

"Well, now, he ain't invited. Let the little bastard fend for himself. Do you really care whether he eats or not?"

"He can starve to death for all I care and I hope he does," she stated.

"That's my baby girl," her father said with a chuckle. "Now you drive safely."

Terri ended the call and pitched her cell phone into the passenger seat. As much as she wanted to light into her hated husband and pound him senseless, the thought of eating Bossy's delicious meal was a lure she couldn't pass up.

Chapter Four

Allison winced at the loud whoop that came from the living room as she closed the carport door behind her. She fed the two men, cleaned up the kitchen and was dismissed—relegated to some place where Clay wouldn't be bothered by her presence. The backyard and the old wooden swing was her destination. In her right hand was a book and in her left a glass of iced tea. It was her intention to stay outside until Clay's new friend left. She didn't like the way he ogled her or the snide way he whispered whatever it was he'd whispered in Clay's ear that made her husband look at her with narrowed eyes.

"Make yourself scarce, woman," Clay had snapped.

She was all too happy to do just that. The less time she was around him the easier her life was.

Placing the tea on a small metal table beside the swing, she sat down on the slatted bench, drew her legs up and propped her back against the Y-shaped support chain. She opened the book and began to read.

Woman's porn, her husband called the dark fantasy romance novels she preferred and maybe it was. There was plenty of sex in the books—detailed descriptions of it—but it was gentle, all-consuming sex without pain and humiliation and indifference. The heroes adored and cherished their women. The heroines loved and honored their men. There was no physical abuse by either gender and the happy-ever-after endings always made her sigh. What she wouldn't give, she thought, for a man like the hero in the book she held.

She put her finger on the page, closed the book and looked up to stare across the postage stamp yard. Sometimes it didn't do to wish for things you knew you could never have. Such thoughts could be depressing as hell and hurt more than a hard punch to the stomach.

She'd seen Drew Dunne's wife slap him at the church, but in her very soul she knew he never laid a hand to his woman. Violence wasn't in his eyes or in his body language. There was a gentle soul behind that handsome face and she had wanted to caress the cheek Terri Dunne had hit so viciously. To soothe away the shame that she knew the slap brought.

"He's used to getting slapped in public," according to Clay's new friend. *"His daddy made it a way of life for him earlier on and Terri Anne is just carrying on the tradition."*

Had Drew Dunne been abused as a child? she wondered. It certainly sounded like it and there was no doubt in her mind that he was being abused now. There was meanness in his wife's stare—a pitiless ferociousness that turned her pretty face to a mask of evil.

"I know all about being abused," she whispered.

Too much, she thought.

"But you would be a gentle man, wouldn't you, Drew?" she asked. "Kind and tender and incredibly sweet."

She couldn't help but think she'd met him somewhere before although that seemed an impossibility. He looked *so* familiar to her. His face had grabbed her immediate attention and she couldn't shake the notion that she knew him.

Or maybe wanted to because he was so…

"Handsome?" she said aloud.

Dear Lord, yes, he was *gorgeous*. His was a calm, temperate face holding lips that would not tighten and twist with unrepressed fury. Soft blue eyes that would not flash with murderous intent. She could well imagine he had gentle hands that would not punch and slap and pinch savagely.

And when he made love, he would carefully cover his woman's body with his own—not throw himself down on it to rut like a wild stag. He would make love to—not rape—his woman. He would not use vulgar, nasty words as he took her. His lips would be soft yet firm. His body would have just the right amount of weight to press her into the mattress.

She closed her eyes—imagining his body covering hers. She could almost feel his knee gently pushing her legs apart as he settled the hard bulge of his shaft in the V between her thighs. His kiss would be soft, tentative at first but grow more heated as his body strained to possess hers. He would taste sweet as he thrust his tongue inside her mouth. Her nipples would harden as he slid a questing hand to her breast.

"Don't," she said, snapping her eyes open.

Her body was on fire. She felt a pulse beating between her legs. She ached as she never had before. For the first time in her life, she wanted a man and not just any man, she wanted *him*. She wanted Drew Dunne.

"And you can't have him," she whispered.

As much as she wanted him, there wasn't a snowball's chance in hell that she would ever be with him.

But that did not stop her from imagining what it would be like to have him.

* * * * *

"Dunne couldn't keep his eyes off your wife at church today," Bobby said in between sips of beer. "You better watch him, Clay. He's got the worst marriage in the world. Far as I know he's never cheated on Terri Anne but he's got the want in his eyes in the worst way. I recognize that look."

"What look?"

"The kind that says he's on the prowl. That he's got his sights set on a target."

Clay snorted. "Last thing I need to worry about is Allie cheating on me. I'd beat her within an inch of her life if she so much as looked like she wanted to cheat. She knows what side of the bread the butter is on."

"Just telling you about Dunne," Bobby replied.

"What's the story on him, anyway?"

"Son of the town drunk," Bobby told him. "Mother died when he was about ten, I think. She owned the farm where they lived but she left it to her brother Carlton because she knew Drew's daddy would piss it away. Old man Carlton told Drew he was welcome to live on there, but he kicked his daddy out along with the trash. Pissed that nasty old sot off something fierce."

"So he didn't come from money like Terri Anne?" Clay questioned.

"Fuck no. The Dunne's are farmers. Always were, but times got bad and Early Rawls, Carlton's son, went to work as a mechanic to make ends meet. Been with Five County Motors since he graduated high school."

"I assume this Carlton paid for Drew to attend Georgia, then."

"Drew won a full-ride on a football scholarship. He was a helluva quarterback back in the day. Good as they got."

"Until he got hurt down at Florida," Clay said with a smirk.

"Yep. Ruined whatever chances he had to ever play pro ball, which was what he wanted," Bobby replied. "Man, he wanted out of Miller County like nobody's business."

"So how did he wind up with the daughter of one of the richest men in Georgia?" Clay asked.

Bobby reached for another beer out of the cooler sitting beside their recliners. He popped the top, took a sip, then leaned back.

"Terri Anne was Jackson Mackie's girl," he said. "Blackjack Mackie, we called him. One of the best noseguards you'd ever want to play against. Nice guy, too. Graduated valedictorian of his class. Was prom king, homecoming king, class president. You name it and that was Blackjack.

"Everyone liked Blackjack. Everyone. Even those of us who played ball against him. We respected that boy. Hell, I'd even go so far as to say we loved him—in a brotherly way, you know? Thing was, he was Drew's friend. His *only* friend. Those two were like Frick and Frack. Where one went, the other followed and despite him being the son of the second richest man in Miller County and set to get a shit pot full of money when his old man kicked it, Blackjack was Drew's sidekick. He looked up to Drew." Bobby snorted. "Ain't that a kick in the nuts?"

"How do the town folk feel about Dunne now?"

"They fucking despise him," Bobby answered.

"Why?"

Bobby ticked off the reasons on his hand, starting with his thumb. "Poor people hate Drew because of what he has. Rich folk hate him because they don't think he *deserves* what he has. The men he went to school with despise him for getting the girl they crushed on in high school and because he was a jock. Hell, you know what that's like. The older people hate him because of his father." He put up the thumb of his other hand. "And the younger generation hates him because he's a rich man living in a mansion yet driving an old Chevy pickup."

"Trying to be just one of the good ole boys, huh?"

"Exactly," Bobby acknowledges.

"Was Dunne in love with Terri Anne?" Clay inquired.

"Shit, no. He disliked her as fiercely as she disliked him. He knew she was a spoiled brat and stayed the hell away from her, but then Terri and Jack went through a rough patch and I heard she went after Drew to make him jealous. Got the bastard drunk one weekend and fucked him—apparently until he put one in her oven."

"Man, that's a bitch," Clay observed. "Bet that was when I met her."

"Did you fuck her?"

"You better believe I did. Had that bitch every way but Sunday for two nights in a row." He laughed. "She was walking funny when I was done with her."

Bobby grinned. "Brat could have been yours, then," he said with a wink.

"Not a chance," Clay stated. "I had myself clipped when I was in high school. Went down to Mexico to have it done 'cause I didn't want any squalling rug rats nipping at my ankles. Didn't want no bitch telling me I got her in the family way and had to marry her ass." He shook his head. "Not for this boy."

"Me, neither," Bobby agreed.

"So Dunne gets her pregnant and old man Thompson made him do the right thing," Clay said. He belched, then reached for another beer.

"Well, something bad happened before that," Bobby said. "Something that really fucked up Drew's life worse than getting his leg broke."

"Which was?"

Bobby was silent for a moment, then took a deep breath. "Jack Mackie died and Terri told the state troopers Drew was to blame."

"How so?"

"They were coming home for Thanksgiving break and had stopped in Columbus to drop off some friend of Terri's. They found this bar and all three of them got drunk as pissants. The bartender said he heard the girl yelling at the taller of the two boys. Said the boy didn't seem concerned about it but the shorter boy did. He kept trying to shut Terri up but she wasn't having any of that. Terri let it slip that she was pregnant and that it was Jack's. I imagine he knew better. He had to know who the father was. Knew what she'd been up to behind his back.

"You see, his old man and Terri's old man expected them to get married. Their daddies had planned their wedding since the two of them were children. Jack didn't care one way or another. He didn't love her but she was…" He looked away. "A cover, you know?"

Clay frowned. "He was queer?"

"Yeah. As a three-dollar bill," Bobby said. "He'd met this guy and they were meeting secretly. Terri thought it was one of the cheerleaders he was fucking, but it was this boy from North Carolina."

A low whistle came from Clay. "That sucks." He shrugged. "No pun intended."

"Terri still doesn't know about it, but Drew knew. Had probably known a long time what Jack was. Hell, I suspect Jack was in love with Drew but that's neither here nor there. Drew would never have told anyone. Never has. Only reason I know is because my daddy is a lawyer and Jack left that North Carolina boy some money in his will. I saw the paperwork on Daddy's desk and read a letter Jack had left to be given to the kid. Daddy never sent it. He should have, but he didn't want Jack's daddy to find out his son was gay."

"Understandable."

Bobby nodded. "I never understood why Daddy kept that letter until he got nominated for the Georgia Supreme Court. Jack's daddy endorsed him although the two of them hated one another like you wouldn't believe."

"Blackmail," Clay stated.

"That would be my guess."

"So what happened that night?" Clay asked.

"Like I said, they were all drunk. Shouldn't have been allowed to leave the bar. Bartender should have taken the keys. None of them had any business driving."

"Disaster waiting to happen," Clay said softly.

"Blackjack was driving," Bobby said as though he hadn't heard. "Weaving all over the road according to someone who saw them. This was on Highway twenty-seven up near Lumpkin. The state patrol said he had to have been going at least seventy when he left the road. Car went through an abutment and slammed into a steep ditch filled with dried kudzu. Terri was in the front seat with him and Drew was in the back. His car door flew open and he was ejected and apparently knocked out. When he came to, the car was smoking. Terri and Jack were still inside the wreckage.

"The car had landed in the ditch at an angle with the right tires about four feet up from the dirt. Drew managed to get Terri's door open but he had to cut her seat belt loose in order to get her out of there. She had a broken arm and fractured pelvis. He dragged her a safe distance away then went back for Jack but..."

"He was too late," Clay said.

Bobby nodded and plowed a hand through his hair. "Jack was pinned behind the wheel. His legs had been crushed. As Drew headed back to the car, it caught fire and Jack started screaming, pleading with Drew to help him." Bobby's voice caught. "He was burning, man. The car was totally engulfed in flames. There was nothing anyone could have done."

"Sweet Jesus," Clay whispered. "What a fucking way to go."

"Terri went berserk. She tried to drag herself over to the car and Drew had to physically restrain her. When the cops got there, she told them Drew hadn't even tried to help Jack."

"Did they believe her?"

"There were those in Miller County who did, but I think most people knew it wasn't true. They knew how close those two boys were. No way would Drew have just stood there and watched his friend burn to death without trying to save him. Drew's a coward but he ain't that big a coward."

"I'm guessing he found out he was the baby daddy and did what they call the right thing," Clay said.

"Something like that. Drew called Big Jake from the hospital in Columbus where they'd taken the two of them. She was in there for a week or more with that broken pelvis. When Jake got to the hospital, Drew told him Terri was pregnant and the baby was his. I don't know if Terri told him or he just guessed but I'll give him props for manning up.

"Jake didn't want his baby girl's reputation sullied so he had a long talk with Drew. Drew and Terri were married while she was in the hospital recovering. As for Drew wanting to marry her?" Bobby shook his head. "He didn't."

"Why didn't he just tell her father to go to hell?"

Bobby shook his head. "You met Big Jake, son. You don't tell that man *nothing*. If Drew had dared open his mouth to Jake Thompson, Jake would have knocked his teeth down his throat. Wade Dunne is a mean son of a bitch and he used to beat the shit out of Drew every time the boy turned around, but Wade ain't nearly as mean as Big Jake. Drew took his medicine so to speak and never once said anything about it to anyone—except maybe his cousin Early. My thought is he felt a tremendous amount of guilt about Jack and not protesting the marriage was his way to atone."

"A hell of an atonement," Clay declared.

"I wouldn't have done it. If you ask me, though, things worked out pretty fucking good for Drew Dunne. He had his life handed to him on a silver platter."

"How so?"

"Drew had to quit college then and there that night at the hospital. God knows he didn't want to do that anymore than he wanted to marry Terri. He just wasn't given a choice in the matter. He wanted to be the first in his family to get a degree. He was shit out of luck in that department."

"What happened to the baby?"

Bobby shrugged, crushed his beer can in his hand. "Word was she lost it, but dollars to doughnuts, she had an abortion while she was in the hospital. Terri ain't cut out to be a mommy."

"Then what?"

"Big Jake created a job for him. He built the car dealership, paid for the inventory, the mechanics, the office help and the utility bills. He even picked the name of the business—Five County Motors. Made Drew the manager, allowed him to hire his cousin, Early, as head mechanic. Made his own son, Whip—you'll like him when you meet him, Clay—as sales manager. I hate to admit it but the dealership is one of the best in southwest Georgia and that's thanks to Drew."

"Got a head for business, does he?"

"Took classes online and at night school, got that degree he wanted so bad," Bobby said, then snorted. "Even if it was from one of them online colleges."

"Everyone's good for something, I guess," Clay said with a grunt.

"True that."

* * * * *

Allison went back to the kitchen to get something to drink for it was sweltering outside. The midafternoon sun was brutal. When she heard Bobby telling her husband what happened the night Drew's friend died, she stayed to listen and what she heard made her soul ache for the man she couldn't seem to get out of her mind.

"My thought is he felt a tremendous amount of guilt about Jack and not protesting the marriage was his way to atone."

Feeling as though someone had ripped the heart from her chest and not knowing why she was experiencing such an emotion, she quietly left the kitchen—easing the door open and shut behind her. Coarse male laughter from the living room covered her exit nicely and she returned to the swing without the drink she had gone to the kitchen to get.

She sat down and stared at the grass beneath the gently moving swing. No wonder his eyes had looked so sad, she thought. The man had gone to hell the night he witnessed his friend's death and she was fairly sure a part of him had been left behind there.

"Oh, Drew," she said. "I am so sorry."

She knew all too well what it felt like to exist in a portion of hell. Her soul resided there every day of her life.

Chapter Five

Big Jake came through the showroom like the force of nature he considered himself to be. He nodded at his son who was sitting slumped at his desk behind the small glass cubicle that was his office. A humorless smile pulled at the old man's mouth as Whip Thompson straightened up and reached for a stack of papers as though he had actual work to do.

"Fuckhead," Big Jake was heard to mumble. Everyone knew he had just a tad more respect for his only son than he had for the man toward whose office the old man was headed.

Those who had reason to be in the showroom seemed to suddenly find a reason to go out to the garage or into the storeroom or outside for a smoke break. No one wanted to be in the dealership when the skirmish between their boss and the man who actually owned Five County Motors began. Even the staunchest gossipmongers made themselves scarce for they'd seen Drew Dunne come in with what was obviously a bad hangover, and they would have to be blind not to have noticed the anger stamped on Big Jake's beefy face.

The only men who did not turn tail and run were Whip—who was studiously looking over a blank contract—and an older man with slicked back hair and a poor excuse for a mustache. That man shambled into the showroom and stood there to watch what was about to happen. On his face was a look of eager anticipation that his services would be required.

Drew looked up from his laptop when the door to his office opened without warning. He tensed when he saw his father-in-law framed in the doorway. He'd been expecting the man but not quite this early in the day.

"Let's you and me have a little talk, Andrew," Big Jake said. Leaving the door open so anyone interested heard his booming voice, he came over to sit in the chair facing Drew's desk. He wedged his bulk into the span of the seat, then leveled his eyes on his son-in-law as he leaned forward. His words came out from behind tightly clenched false teeth. "Just who the *fuck* do you think you are?"

Closing the laptop with a calmness he didn't feel, Drew pushed it to the side. "With all due respect, Big Jake, I know who I am."

"I know *what* you are and I know what you ain't," Big Jake snapped. He leaned back in the chair and it groaned beneath his weight. "You're nobody with delusions that you're gonna *be* somebody one day. Well, you ain't so you might as well get that notion right out of that head of yours."

"All I want is to be left alone," Drew said, wrapping his hands around the arms of his chair.

Big Jake's bushy white eyebrows jumped upward. His dark eyes narrowed. "You wanna run that by me again, boy?"

"I'm not a boy," Drew stated and hated that his voice wasn't filled with the conviction it needed.

"Wade," Big Jake shouted and Drew winced. His fingers dug into the padded arms of the desk chair.

Wade Dunne came sauntering to the open doorway and slouched against the jamb. "Yes, sir?" he drawled, his hard, cold eyes leveled on his son.

"You need to teach this boy some manners," Big Jake told him.

Dunne shrugged. "Been trying to do that all his life and it ain't took."

"Then I suggest you try again," Big Jake snapped.

Drew stared into the snakelike eyes of the man who had abused him when he was a child. The memory of his father's fists pumping into his face made the breath catch in his throat. The gut-wrenching pain of a hard boot to his belly caused his knees to go weak. Thoughts of the two times his mother had taken him to the emergency room with broken bones turned his blood cold.

Wade pushed away from the doorjamb, threaded his beefy fingers together and turned his palms forward—the joints popping. "My pleasure, Mr. Jake," he said. He took a step into the office, then grinned as Drew scrambled from his chair and put out a restraining hand in supplication.

"Not here," Big Jake said. "Take his uppity ass out back."

Drew shook his head. "There's no reason to—"

"Stop that fucking sniveling you little pussy," Wade cut him off. "Take your medicine like a man and be done with it."

The blood rushed to Drew's head and he heard it pounding to the violent rhythm of his heart. His father was going to hurt him—as he had many times over the years—and there was nothing he could do to stop him. He wasn't a fighter. Had never been a fighter but his father reveled in being one. Wade was good at it—could have been a pro had he not become a drunk instead. He'd beaten many a man to a bloody pulp and laughed while he did it.

"You ever known him to be a man, Wade?" Big Jake scoffed. His wide smile was mean, promising.

"Tried to make him one but that didn't take, neither," Wade replied and came toward Drew like a big cat stalking its prey.

"Please," Drew said. "I don't know what you want me to say but—"

"I think you said it all when you insulted my little girl," Big Jake said.

Drew kept the desk between him and his father. "I didn't insult her," he defended.

Big Jake arched a brow. "You didn't compare her to the coach's wife by saying Terri Anne was frigid and the other gal was hot as sin?"

"No, sir, that's not what I said," Drew told him. He remembered his words exactly. *"The difference between an ice storm and a sizzling fire."*

The older man's lips twisted. "You calling my little girl a liar?" he snarled.

"No, sir. I'm telling you that is not what I said."

"Sounds to me like he's got the hots for the new coach's little filly," Wade said with a grunt. "That true, boy? You wanting to stick that sniveling piece of shit you call a cock in that pretty girl's twat?"

"That better not be his intention," Big Jake said.

Drew judged the distance between the side of the desk where he was standing—his father on the opposite side—and the door. Even if he made it to the opening, he knew Wade would be after him. He was still a fast runner but there was nowhere he could run to stay away from his old man. Sooner or later Wade would find him and if it was later, the punishing fists would rain down harder and for a longer length of time.

"I've never lied to you, Big Jake. I never said Terri was frigid." Far from it, he thought. The woman was one of the county's biggest sluts, but he wasn't about to tell her father that—even though he suspected the old man already knew.

"Get your ass on over here, boy," Wade said. "I ain't got all day to fool with you."

Like Wade Dunne had somewhere to go and something to do, Drew thought. Mostly the bastard hung around the garage shooting the breeze with the mechanics or had his red nose up Big Jake's wide-load ass. Doing Jake Thompson's dirty work for him was the way Wade made most of his drinking money. That and hustling pool.

Drew squared his shoulders. Better to take it now and get it over with. He came slowly past the chair in which Big Jake was perched and walked to the door. He felt his father's hot, foul breath on his neck even though the old man was a good five feet away. Already he felt the hard knuckles slamming into his belly. Wade never left tell-tale signs of his abuse now that Drew was grown.

No one was in the showroom as Drew walked through it. Big Jake's son Whip was standing in the doorway of his office with his arms folded across his chest and a wide, hateful grin on his face. Whip had always hated Drew as much as Terri, but the two of them got along well enough since Whip was the sales manager of the dealership. At the moment, though, Whip's grey eyes were filled with satisfaction.

"Go on through the garage," Wade said from behind him.

Drew closed his eyes briefly. Everyone would be in the garage to see his walk of shame. Even Lenore, the black woman who he'd hired as the office manager. Next to Early, she would be the only one who wouldn't take pleasure in what was about to happen.

Just as he knew they would be, those who worked at the dealership and a few customers were milling about in the garage. The stench of used motor oil hung like a pall over the large space. Every eye was on him as he walked toward the metal door that led outside to the back lot. No one spoke but a few elbows were used to emphasize his humiliation.

Slowing down the closer he got to the door, Drew kept flexing his fists, though he knew he wouldn't be given a chance to use them against his father.

"Keep walking," Wade said loud enough for everyone to hear and his words were punctuated by a couple of snide snickers.

Pushing open the door, he blinked against the bright sunlight. He had barely cleared the threshold before Wade rammed a meaty fist into his right kidney. Sucking in a breath, he stumbled forward. Before he had time to react, he was spun around and that same hard fist was driven brutally into his belly twice with a speed that was nothing more than a blur. Agony spread like wildfire through his gut and the breath was snatched from his lungs. He doubled over—trying to suck air into his body—and his father's knuckles slammed into his chin to fling his head back and straighten his body. What followed was a succession of two more vicious jabs to his belly before he crashed to the hard-packed dirt. The jolt jarred his already tortured insides and made his teeth click together. He tasted blood and knew he'd bitten his tongue.

Wade stood over him with his hands on his hips, then prodded him on the thigh with a dusty boot. His voice was filled with hatred as he spoke, his tone leaving nothing to the imagination. He had enjoyed himself.

"You keep that filthy mind of yours off the coach's wife. You hear? If someone tells me you've been sniffing 'round her skirts, I'll break both your arms. Is that clear?"

Drew knelt there on one knee with his hand pressed tightly to his abdomen. The pain was so sharp he wondered if Wade had ruptured something inside him.

Wade leaned over to grab a handful of Drew's hair to jerk his head up. "I asked if that was clear, Andrew," he bellowed.

"Y…yes sir," Drew managed to gasp out. Tears of pain were blurring his vision but out of the corner of his eye he saw Early watching him—his face filled with concern. When Early started toward them, Wade spun around and pointed a finger at him.

"You keep your white trash ass right where it is, Rawls," he snarled. "He gets up on his own steam or he don't get up at all!"

Early froze. Though he hated Wade Dunne, he—like the rest of those who knew the man—feared him.

Wade hunkered down until he was at eye level with Drew. He rested one wrist on his knee, clenching his fist over and over again as though he itched to hit Drew again. "I want you to listen very carefully to me, Andrew," he said, the stink of his whiskey breath and rotting teeth terrible. "You ever talk back to that little girl of Big Jake's again and you and me are gonna go another few rounds. Next time I won't be so gentle with you. You hear me?"

"Yes, sir," Drew whispered. He squeezed his eyes tightly closed for the pain rippling through his lower belly was agonizing.

"Now get your sorry ass up and get back to work." When Drew didn't immediately obey the order, Wade reached out to cup his chin in a savage grip. "Open your eyes."

Drew was trying not to pass out but he forced his eyes open and looked right into those of his hateful father. He couldn't stop the look of pleading he knew came over his face as he stared into Wade's merciless face.

"Ain't nobody gonna help you," Wade told him. "Get up or stay on your knees like the coward you are."

Struggling to keep unconsciousness from washing over him, he knew Wade would leave him lying in the dirt—daring anyone to come to his aid—Drew strove to push himself up from the ground. The pain was so intense he almost lost it, but he slowly got to his feet with his hand pressed to his belly. A wave of nausea and vertigo overtook him and he lurched backward—almost fell—but somehow managed to keep his footing.

Wade stood up as well. He was a good head taller than Drew and broader in the shoulder. Though a beer gut hung over the belt of his stained khaki pants like dough from a popped tube of biscuits, the man still had lumberjack-sized arms and the thick thighs of a boxer.

"Sawed-off piece of shit," Wade said, then turned his head and spat. He started around Drew but leaned in to bump his shoulder hard against Drew's.

Staggering back, Drew had to bite the inside of his mouth to keep from crying out for the blow sent waves of pain through his chest and abdomen. He stood there and watched his father go back into the garage. Saw a few men clap Wade on the back as though he had won a championship bout against a worthy opponent. Heard laughter and knew it was at his expense. Early took a step toward him but he shook his head.

"No. Don't," he told his cousin.

Early would pay a stiff price for helping him. Wade would see to it. There was no way Drew could let that happen. Sucking up the pain, struggling to put one foot ahead of the other, he headed toward the door. As he passed Early, his cousin growled like a caged animal.

"That bastard needs to get stomped into a greasy pile of shit," Early said—voice low and tense.

Yeah, Drew thought as he entered the building. He wished he could be the one to do it. Doing so would erase all the pain the man had dished out to him over the years.

People were watching him. Unlike before, they were no longer silent. They weren't speaking loud enough for him to make out what they were saying but he knew it wasn't complimentary.

By the time he got to his office it was all he could do not to pass out. Thankfully Big Jake was gone. He'd done what he had come to do and now he would be reporting back to his precious baby girl. Drew could almost hear the laughter that was being shared between father and daughter.

"You're a coward," Whip told him as he came to stand in the doorway of Drew's office. "A sorry excuse for a man."

"You want something, Whip?" Drew said as he eased himself down into his chair—trying not to groan.

"Only thing I want is you out of my sister's life," Whip said. "She doesn't deserve a bastard like you."

"Did you get the quarterly report done, yet?" Drew asked, refusing to take the bait. He was beginning to shake he was in so much pain.

"Fuck you," Whip said and left.

Laying his head on the back of the chair, Drew was becoming more concerned that his father had done some real damage to his abdomen. The pain was spreading but it was centered around his navel. Trying to remember the anatomy lessons he'd had in school, he wondered if there was something in that area that could rupture.

"Are you okay?"

He lowered his head to look at the speaker, forcing a smile to his lips. "I'm fine, Lenore," he told the black woman standing just inside his office.

"You sure?" she questioned. The worry on her face touched him.

"Yeah, I'm sure. Nothing I haven't experienced before," he told her.

"You'd tell me if you were hurt bad, wouldn't you, son?" she persisted.

He nodded. "I would."

She kept staring at him for a moment or two, then half-smiled. "Okay, I believe you." She turned and went back to her office, which was between his and Whip's.

He put his head back again and closed his eyes. The pain was lessening—thank God—but he knew he was going to be sore for a day or two. There would be bruises on his abdomen and over his kidney where Wade had started the assault. Nothing he could do about it.

It was what it was.

Chapter Six

"Don't wait up," Clay told her as he headed for the door. "I may not be back tonight."

He was lying to her about where he was going. It wasn't even a plausible lie.

"Bobby and me are going possum huntin'. He's got a cabin on Lake Seminole. We're taking along a keg."

On a Monday night? she thought but kept her mouth shut. She didn't care where he went or how long he stayed away. She knew he wouldn't be back tonight and for that she was grateful. Any night she had to herself was a blessing.

She knew where he was going. She'd heard the phone ring earlier. She'd heard the lowering of his voice, the silky seduction of it and understood it was a woman—she didn't care who—on the other end. Experience told her it was probably the one she'd met at church the day before, the one he'd known and dated at college, but really? What did it matter? The cheating was going to happen one way or another. It was as inevitable as the sunrise.

She sat where she was on the sofa darning a pair of his socks as he closed the door behind him. With the darning needle paused to pierce the material, she listened for the sound of the truck door closing, the motor starting up, releasing a long breath when it did. The whining sound of the engine engaging as he backed down the driveway was music to her ears. She laid aside the darning and took the first calming breath she'd drawn in that day.

Supper was sitting in her stomach like a heavy rock. She'd never liked chicken liver—and especially not smothered in gravy that made it slick and even more unpalatable—but that was what Clay had wanted. Whatever Clay wanted was what she fixed.

And ate even if the food was hard to swallow. Thankfully he never allowed her enough of anything that she might gorge herself on it.

Her eyes shifted to the cabinet where she kept her sewing. Sewing was woman's work and the sewing basket was like a land mine to Clay Bennett. He would never touch it. If he needed something out of it, he ordered her to fetch it. Luckily that wasn't often. She bit her lip as she stared at the basket with her ears tuned to the sound of him returning on an off chance.

The clock in the kitchen ticked. Ticked. Ticked as the seconds passed. When she was sure he would not come back, she got up slowly from her chair and walked over to the cabinet. Like a thief, she looked around her as though expecting someone to stop her in mid-movement.

That was what he'd done to her, she thought. It was only part of the damage he'd wrecked on her self-esteem over the years. Like a well-trained coonhound she did everything he ordered and hated herself for doing it.

Hands shaking, she reached for the sewing basket and eased it from the shelf. She clutched it to her chest, then returned to her chair. She sat down with the basket in her lap, staring at it for the longest time. Beside her on the end table was a glass of sweetened tea. Inside the basket were two Mounds bars and a bag of hot 'n spicy fried pork skins. Mouth salivating, she unhooked the latch on the basket and lifted the lid. She sighed. Her treats were still there waiting for her.

Once more she looked to the door, listened for his truck.

Tick. Tick. Tick.

She lowered her eyes to the candy bars. Took one out and began to peel the crinkly wrapper from the sweet chocolate and coconut confection. The scent of the dark chocolate hit her nose and her entire body clenched with need. She brought the candy to her mouth and scooted the first piece of the two residing on the cardboard sleeve into her mouth.

Delight. Pure and utter, unrelenting and exquisite delight danced along her taste buds. Closing her eyes to the wonderful taste, she chewed slowly to better enjoy the indulgence she was forced to sneak from time to time.

Better than sex, she thought, but most everything was better than sex with Clay. Thinking that made her smile around the gooey goodness inside her mouth. When the phone rang she guiltily shoved the rest of the candy bar into the sewing basket and slammed the lid down. Her heart racing, she jumped up from the chair and with the basket still in her hands ran to the phone. Placing the basket on the kitchen table, she reached for the wall phone.

"Hello?"

"Is this Allison?" a female voice inquired.

Puzzled to hear a voice she didn't recognize, she acknowledged that it was.

"Hi, sweetie. We haven't met but I'm Heddy Tabb, the mayor's wife? Dick and I attend First Methodist so we weren't there to greet you on Sunday. I wanted to welcome you to Colquitt."

Relieved it wasn't a telemarketer, Allison released her death grip on the receiver. "Thank you, Mrs. Tabb. We're happy to be here."

Well, one of them was, she thought.

"How do you like it so far, dear?"

The woman's voice was friendly but there was just a touch of condescension and aloofness on the other end of the line.

"I'm sure we're going to love it," she replied.

"That's good. So here is why I'm calling. I am the chairwoman of the hospital auxiliary and we would love to have you join us. It would give you something to do two days a week, get you out of the house and all, and among like-minded women who are dying to meet you."

And learn everything they can about the new coach and his wife, Allison thought.

"I appreciate your invitation but…"

"Coach Bennett assured my husband, the mayor, that you would be delighted to lend a hand," Mrs. Tabb interrupted. "There's really not much to volunteering. We assist with filing, making copies, correlating brochures etcetera. We also escort patients and visitors, deliver flowers and provide reading material. Certainly nothing taxing and nothing you can't do. Shall we begin your orientation tomorrow morning?"

Feeling trapped, annoyed with Clay for making plans for her without so much as discussing them, Allison had no choice but to graciously accept.

"Good. White blouse and black pants with low-heeled shoes are our uniform. We'll provide you with a badge. I'll see you at eight." That said, the woman hung up without saying good-bye.

"Dang it," Allison said as she hung up. It wasn't that she wanted to be a woman of leisure. She didn't. She wanted—*needed*— something to keep her occupied but she would like to have chosen what that was. But as usual, Clay had chosen for her.

She went to bed that night angry and nervous. Jumping in right off the bat when she'd only been in town three days was uncomfortable for her. She would have preferred to ease into things. Get to know a few ladies. Make friends with a couple before delving into the waters of a small town where she knew only one or two people.

"I don't know *any* people," she said as she fluffed the covers around her. "I've met a total of four people and three of them were about as hostile as a hive of angry wasps."

But one had been friendly.

"Drew," she said, remembering the loneliness in his blue eyes.

Eyes that had held her captive from the moment she had looked into them.

Was it possible to fall in love at first sight? She thought she'd fallen in love with Clay but that hadn't been the case. It had been more falling in lust with the big man on campus. Love had never been a part of their relationship—his or hers—and never would.

She'd heard about the beating Drew took earlier that day and had been angry on his behalf. Hearing Clay and his new BFF Bobby talking about it at lunch had made her hackles rise.

"Boy got his ass handed to him at the dealership today," Bobby reported with a laugh. "Whole shop saw him on his knees in the dirt."

"Wuss," Clay pronounced with a snort. "I got no respect for any man who can't take care of business."

Allison wondered what kind of business that was supposed to be.

"He don't deserve respect. He ain't good for nothin' 'cept being a punching bag for old man Dunne," Bobby said.

"They put useless animals out of their misery," Clay replied. "Maybe someone should put that boy down."

The men laughed and that made Allison even angrier. Leaving the house, she had gone out to the swing—her refuge, the only place on the property where she felt safe. Her mind was on Drew Dunne and she hoped he was all right. A part of her wanted to pick up the phone and call the place where he worked to make sure he was but that would only cause him trouble if Clay found out. After Bobby left, she went back inside to clean up the kitchen.

"Me and Bobby may go hunting," he told her.

"Okay," she replied.

He left the kitchen to go back to the high school where he would spend the rest of the afternoon getting ready for the start of the school year the following week.

As she washed the dishes, her mind had been on Drew. She couldn't seem to get him out of her thoughts. Not that she really wanted to. His was the only encouraging face she'd encountered so far.

Lying now in bed, staring at the ceiling, she wondered if he had even given her a second thought. He was married but she knew from the way his wife looked at him that there was no more love in their union than there was in hers and Clay's. She knew Drew's wife abused him—as Clay abused her—so the marriage was nothing more than show.

"Do you ever make love to her?" she whispered. "Will she allow that? Do you even want to?"

If they had sex, she was fairly sure it would be perfunctory. She doubted there was any fire in that glacial miss with the hard stare and the thin, disapproving lips.

"Unless she likes it rough," she said aloud. Since she'd slept with Clay maybe that was how Drew's wife preferred it. If so, she'd more than likely got just what she wanted from Clay, for the man liked rough, violent sex. That seemed to be the only way he could enjoy it.

She knew that would not be the case with Drew. His hands would not be hard, grasping, painfully gripping. His would be a gentle touch, a loving touch. He would glide gently over a woman's body. He would take his time and…

"You have to stop this," she said, heat pulsing between her legs.

She reached for the remote control and pointed it at the flat screen TV that was Clay's pride and joy. He'd bought two of them— a forty-inch for the bedroom and a seventy-inch for the living room—with the money he'd gotten from selling her parents' house in Milton. The sets had all the bells and whistles, 3-D and extra speakers in every corner of both rooms. She hated them but at least they provided a few hours of enjoyment when Clay didn't have them on one of the sports networks, which was most of the time.

The TV came on with a soft, haunting refrain of music. A beautiful, black haired woman was lying on a brass bed with her arms beside her head, her fingers threaded through those of the man reclining atop her. His thick dark hair gleamed in the light of a candle on the nightstand. The camera was positioned behind his naked shoulder—focused on the woman's face and desire-filled midnight colored eyes.

"Love me, Declan," the woman said. "Love me as though there will be no tomorrow."

The dark head came down as the man slanted his mouth over the woman's. The kiss seemed to go on forever and Allison was hypnotized by the way he writhed his lower body against the woman's. When he lifted his head, a lilting Irish accent brought forth his words.

"Aye, Bess. For us there may never be another tomorrow."

The camera angle shifted and the man's face appeared on the screen as he looked down into the face of his lover.

Allison sucked in a breath. Her lips parted. She shot up in the bed, quickly pressed the pause button and stared in shock at the screen. Her heart pounded hard.

He, she thought, was why Drew looked so familiar to her. She was staring at the Irish actor Colin Farrell, and the two bore a very strong likeness to one another. While Farrell's eyes were a dark brown, Drew's were a soft, pale blue. The Irish actor's hair was darker, a deeper brown, maybe black, while Drew's was a dark chestnut. They looked to be about the same age, body build and height. The similarities were eerie.

"Mother of God," she whispered as she ran her gaze over the actor's handsome face. She shook herself and pressed the Info button on the remote to see what the name of the film was. It was obviously a period piece from the looks of it. When the title and synopsis came up, she felt another jolt go through her.

Since high school she had been enamored of the Alfred Noyes poem "The Highwayman." She'd had no idea the melancholy ballad had been turned into a movie. A hauntingly beautiful song done by Loreena McKennitt, yes, but not a movie.

"Ooh," she said on a long breath. Checking the time the movie had been on, she was unhappy to see it had already been on for over an hour. Wanting to see it from the very beginning, she pressed the search button, typed in the title and was overjoyed to see it would play again on another premium movie channel in less than half an hour. Without missing a beat, she set the DVR to record it. For this, she thought, only the seventy-inch screen would do.

Flipping back the covers, she swung her legs from the bed and thrust her feet into her bedroom slippers. All but running into the living room, she didn't bother with the lights. She fumbled for the remote on the table beside Clay's recliner, sat down and brought the footrest up. The TV came on with a harsh bright light less than ten feet from where she sat but it almost felt as though she were in a movie theater. The sound followed close behind and once she thumbed in the channel that would be recording, she sat there anxiously waiting for the stupid promos for other movies, other series to be over. When they were, when the movie started—with a long, sweeping panorama of the Irish countryside—she sighed with contentment.

* * * * *

Two and half hours later, Allison was back in bed.

Wide awake.

The movie had been wonderful. Sad and poignant but beautifully done with lush scenery and compelling cinematography. The actors had given stellar performances and the musical score had made her spirit soar along with the crescendos and haunting movements. Farrell had brought the highwayman to life with a cocky attitude, soulful expressions and a sensual smile that had melted her heart. Even the captain of the British soldiers sent to capture him had turned out to be more sympathetic than villainous. That he was played by handsome Irishman Emmett Scanlan was a plus.

As lacy shadows from the branches of the live oak outside the bedroom window wove patterns of light and dark across the ceiling, she stared at the shifting shapes and began to fantasize herself in the role of Bess, the landlord's black eyed daughter.

With Drew as Declan O'Shay, the wise-cracking, lusty highwayman.

Her very vivid imagination took over and she began rewriting the movie as she would have liked to have seen it.

Chapter Seven

He was in agony. There was no way he could turn on the bed that eased the pain. The dull, persistent ache that had been with him all day had become a fiery, stabbing moving slowly toward his lower right abdomen and radiating around to the small of his back. He felt feverish and had already thrown up twice. His abdomen seemed swollen to him—filling with blood? he wondered—and he was getting worried that something was terribly, terribly wrong.

And he was all alone in the house.

Terri had gone out a couple of hours earlier and Anita had left as soon as she'd finished cleaning the kitchen.

He tried to get up but the pain doubled him over and took his breath. Sweat was pouring down his face, pressing against his underarms and the center of his chest. The nausea hit him again and he barely had time to roll over to the edge of the bed before the hot bile flew.

The pain intensified as he strained. It was so strong that he felt as though he was being torn in half. He knew he needed to get to the emergency room but he knew he would never make it to his door—much less down the stairs. Panting, feeling faint, he fumbled above him on the nightstand until he found the phone.

He dialed 9-1-1.

* * * * *

"We had to break the door down," EMT Bubba Henry complained to the night nurse. "Do you believe that shit?"

"Front door was bad enough," Viv Chandler, his female partner, said with disgust. "But then we had to break *his* door down, too."

"What grown man locks his goddamned bedroom door?" Bubba demanded.

"With a security lock, too," Viv added.

"If you're scared shitless of your wife, you keep your door locked," Nancy Davis, the head nurse quipped. "If I lived with her? I would, too."

"Where was Terri during all that?" Kip Overton, the orderly on duty asked.

"Wasn't there is all we know," Viv replied.

"I've been trying to reach her but there's no answer at the house," Nancy said.

"It was his appendix, wasn't it?" Bubba queried.

"It's rare but, yes."

"Appendicitis is rare?" Bubba scoffed. "That's news to me."

"It is when it's caused by direct blunt force trauma to the abdomen," Nancy explained. "As I said, it's rare but apparently that's what happened with him."

"Blunt force trauma," Bubba said, then grunted. "How'd that happen?"

"From the beating his old man gave him this morning," Kip reminded him. "He got the shit beat out of him, with interest."

"Oh, yeah, I heard about that." Bubba acknowledged. "Shitty way to start the day, huh?"

* * * * *

In his room two doors down from the nurses' station, Drew heard every word the nurses and EMTs were saying but he really wasn't paying attention to them. He was still groggy from the anesthesia and the wound on his side where his appendix had been removed was throbbing. When he heard Dr. Trent Mackie's voice join the conversation he pushed the mental fog aside to listen.

"Have you been able to reach Terri yet?" Dr. Mackie inquired.

"No, sir," Viv answered.

"Did you try Big Jake's?" he asked.

"Whip answered the phone and said he hadn't seen her. Big Jake was already in bed and Whip didn't want to disturb him."

"God forbid the little bastard should wake his father up for something that has to do with Drew. Did you tell him what had happened?" Dr. Mackie asked.

"I told him."

"And?"

"He just laughed."

"Arrogant little snot," Dr. Mackie snapped. "I'm going to check on Drew, then I'm going home."

"Yes, sir."

The door to Drew's room shushed open and Dr. Mackie entered. He was still in his green hospital scrubs with his white surgical mask hanging below his chin.

"How you feeling, son?" he asked as he came up to Drew's bed.

"I hurt," Drew said.

"That's what that little button is for," the surgeon said with a smile. "Works really well if you press it."

Drew inched his hand over to the button that was attached to the morphine pump and did just that.

"You got any questions for me about the surgery?" Dr. Mackie asked him.

"No, sir. I guess I should be glad it was my appendix and not something Wade did to me."

Dr. Mackie cocked a shoulder. "It was probably going to happen anyway. The hits just rushed things along."

"If I didn't have bad luck…" Drew said with a sigh.

The surgeon smiled slightly, nodded, then the smile slipped away. He cleared his throat. "Drew?"

"Yes, sir?"

"I'm sorry."

"For what?"

Dr. Mackie's forehead crinkled as though what he was about to say was painful for him to do so. "How they treat you."

Drew sighed. "I'm used to it, Doc."

"You shouldn't be. I've never blamed you for Jack's death and they shouldn't, either. My son loved you."

"I loved him."

The surgeon's voice turned husky. "I know you did, son." He cleared his throat again. "You get some rest, now. I'll try to get hold of Terri for you."

"Don't bother. She wouldn't come anyway."

That seemed to hurt the older man even more. "Is there anyone else you want me to call?"

Drew hesitated and he saw Doc's eyes narrow. "What time is it?" he asked.

Dr. Mackie looked at his watch. "A quarter to eleven."

"He's still up. If you don't let Early know he'll raise hell."

"I'll call him and I'll call Whip to make sure he tells Jake you won't be at work tomorrow."

"Jake isn't going to like that," Drew told him.

"Tough shit. If he gives you any guff, direct him to me," Dr. Mackie said.

"How long am I going to be here?"

"Well, if there's no complications, probably Thursday. I want the wound to be well on its way to healing before I release you back into the wild." He put his hand on Drew's knee. "I'll see you in the morning. You call the nurses if you need anything, okay?"

"Yes, sir."

"Promise?"

Drew put the hand in which the IV was running to his chest. "Scout's honor."

Dr. Mackie pursed his lips. "You were never a scout, son," he said drily.

The father of his childhood best friend winked at him, then left, easing the door closed behind him. Doc's oldest son wasn't the only one in that family Drew loved. Doc had always treated him kindly, had never blamed him for what happened to Jack.

Or to Jack's mother, Miss Elizabeta, who had taken an overdose of sleeping pills only an hour after Jack's funeral. The woman had hated him as much as Jack's brother, Boyd—the assistant coach at MCHS. Idly he wondered how Boyd was getting along with Clay Bennett.

As soon as that bastard's face shifted through his mind, the face of his lovely wife appeared.

"Is there anyone else you want me to call?" Doc had asked.

It had been on the tip of his tongue to say her name. That was who he wanted at his bedside. That was whose eyes he wanted to see looking down on him with compassion.

With love.

"You've lost it, Dunne," he mumbled and shifted in the bed. His wound reminded him it was there and still fresh and he winced. Deciding it was best if he didn't move around, he lay as still as he could. Soon, his eyes became so heavy he could no longer keep them open and he drifted away on a placid lake of morphine. The last thing his conscious mind absorbed was the smiling face of Allie Bennett standing in the shadows of his deepest desire.

* * * * *

The hustle and bustle outside his room woke him. He heard the squeaky wheel of the meal cart trundling down the hallway and realized he was hungry. Gingerly he tried repositioning his body—relieved that the pain in his side was only a dull ache.

His room door opened and a young woman he'd known all her life came in with his breakfast tray.

"'Morning, Mr. Drew," she said. "How you feeling?"

"Sore," he responded. "How are you doing, Mavis?"

"Could be better but could be worse I s'pose," she replied. She put his tray on the rolling bed table and pushed it up the side of the bed. "Want me to lift up your head?"

He nodded. "That would help," he said as she took the bed controls and pushed the button to elevate the top portion of the bed.

"Raining outside," she told him. She took the lid off his plate, set it aside, then picked up his milk carton to pour the liquid into a glass.

"I hope you didn't get wet," he said. "You usually walk to work, don't you?" He knew she lived only a block from the hospital.

"Yes, sir. Mama drove me in to work today though. If she'd knowed you was here, she'd have come to visit." She cocked her head to one side. "How long you gonna be in here?"

"I imagine they'll let me go tomorrow. It's up to Doc Mackie," he answered.

"I seen him. He's making his rounds," she said. "You need somethin' else?"

"About six pieces of the greasiest bacon you can find." He was staring at the unpalatable looking clear liquid diet—broth, juice, soda pop and gelatin. Also on the tray was a small glass of what looked like urine sitting beside his coffee but he knew it was apple juice.

At least he hoped that was what it was.

"I don't think they're gonna let you have no bacon, Mr. Drew," she said saucily and headed for the door. "I'll be back to give you your bath."

"I think I can—"

"Hospital policy," she said, then turned to give him an audacious wink to let him know she was kidding.

"Shame on you, Mavis Jean Kent," he called after her.

He laughed to himself. At least one family in Miller County other than Early's liked him, he thought. Travis Kent—Mavis' father—had been Carlton Dunne's best friend growing up. The two men had been as inseparable as Drew and Jack had been. Mavis's mother, May, was Bea Dunne's aunt on her mother's side.

The breakfast was definitely not anything to write home about. At least the apple juice—even if it did look like pee—was palatable. It didn't take him long to finish the meager meal.

Or to be hungry all over again.

The nurse came in and took all his vitals—she had woken him at six a.m. to do the same—gave him a shot of antibiotics in his IV and told him she'd be back to bathe him.

"Everybody wants to bathe me," he said jokingly but she didn't crack a smile. She just stared at him as though he had insulted her.

"I will be back," she sniffed, turned, then flounced out of the room with her shoes squeaking against the floor.

"I will be back," he repeated in his best Arnold Schwarzenegger voice when she closed the door behind her.

For the next half hour he sat flipping through the channels of the TV attached to the wall. After running through the offerings, he turned it off. He was about to drift into a nap when Dr. Mackie came bustling in.

"How are you feeling?" Doc asked.

"Sore," he replied.

"To be expected. Let's take a look."

When the poking and prodding and note taking was done, Doc sat on the foot of his bed.

"I called Jake and told him you would be here until tomorrow," he said. "Early will be by on his way to work. I didn't call Terri. I figured Jake would call her and tell her."

"Not that she'd give a damn," Drew told him.

"Everything's healing as it should and I'd like to get you up and moving about this morning. Take it slow. No bending over or lifting anything heavy for at least a week. No running or lifting weights."

Drew made a raspberry. "I don't do that now."

Doc gave him a steady look. "Maybe you should think about doing it. Wouldn't hurt for you to bulk up a bit."

"And do what with it?" Drew asked. "Stand up to my daddy?" He shook his head. "The old man would put me down like a rabid dog."

"He won't live forever, son," Doc said. "As much as he drinks, I'm betting he's got a liver as hard as marble. That is if some meaner bastard than him doesn't take him out in a brawl." He folded his arms over his chest. "I saw him a couple of days ago. He doesn't look good."

"He never has," Drew said. "He'll outlive all of us 'cause he's too mean to die."

Doc took a long breath, then let it out slowly. "Just think about it. You were in good shape in high school but you've let yourself go. You could afford to lose about twenty pounds."

"To get down to my fighting weight?" Drew joked.

"To up your self-esteem, son," Doc said and unfolded his arms. He got to his feet. "You can't keep punishing yourself, letting yourself *be* punished for Jack's death. I don't like seeing you buckle under to Jake and your father."

"You gotta have something to want to live for," Drew said, staring the older man in the eye. "What do I have to live for?"

A movement at the door made both men look that way.

And she was standing there.

Smiling.

Nervous.

Looking as pretty as a picture.

Fresh. Sweet. Her face as gentle and innocent as a newborn's.

Her smile wavering as she realized he was not alone. Color invaded her cheeks.

"I'm sorry," she said and turned to go.

"Wait," Drew all but yelled. "Don't go!"

Doc gave him a surprised look, then swung his attention back to his visitor. "I don't think we've met," he said, walking toward her. He held out his hand. "I'm Doc Mackie. Trent Mackie."

She cut her eyes to him, then back to Doc. Hesitated only a second before slipping her hand in his. "Allison," she said. "Allison Bennett."

"As in Coach Bennett's wife?" Doc inquired and at her nod, he covered her hand with his other one. "Well, welcome to Colquitt, Allison. Do folks call you Allie?"

"I'd rather they not but yes, sir, they do," she replied.

"Then Allison it is," Doc said. He glanced around at Drew. He must have seen something on Drew's face that concerned him for he frowned. "Well, I need to finish my rounds." He turned back to Allison. "Again, welcome to Colquitt. I hope you'll be happy here."

Drew saw her gaze shift to him before she answered.

"I hope so, too, sir."

"Doc," the older man said. "Everyone just calls me Doc."

"Doc," she repeated and stepped aside as he headed for the door.

Once he was gone, she took a hesitant step toward the bed. Her eyes were suddenly filled with concern.

"When I saw your name on the list of patients, I was worried. You had appendicitis."

"Yes," he replied, drawing out the word. "What are you doing here?" Before she could answer, he waved his hand—the one with the IV in it—and winced as the damned thing pinched his arm.

"Careful," she said, coming over to the bed. "You could pull out the cannula."

"The what?" he asked, looking down at his arm.

"It's the thing sticking in your arm," she explained. "A hollow tube thingy so the IV solution can…" She stopped, shaking her head. "TMI, huh? I'm just parroting what a nurse told me earlier."

"You were visiting someone else?" he asked and felt jealousy rip through him like a crowbar.

"No, I'm volunteering with the hospital auxiliary," she told him. "Today is my first day and you are my first patient."

"Lucky me," he said, grinning.

"So," she said. "Appendicitis."

He nodded. "Hurt like a son of a bitch."

"Oh, I know all too well," she said. "I had mine removed when I was seventeen."

"Really?"

"Really," she said.

They were quiet for a moment—just looking at one another—until she dropped her gaze from his. When he laughed, she snapped her head up.

"What?" she asked.

"One of the five male fantasies," he said. At her puzzled look his grin widened. "Candy stripers."

Her face turned red. "I'm not a candy striper but I do understand the reference."

"I thought you probably would."

A crease formed between her eyes. "What are the other four?"

He surprised himself by actually giggling. He couldn't remember the last time he had giggled but it had probably been with one of Early's towheaded bratlings.

"Well, let's see," he said, arching his head back on the pillow. "There's French maid."

"Of course," she said.

"Nurse."

"That's not surprising."

"Cheerleader."

"Again, not surprising."

"And the old standby—Catholic school girl."

She blinked. "Even for a Southern Baptist boy?" she questioned.

"Especially for a Southern Baptist boy," he replied. "We've heard *all* kinds of things about Catholic school girls."

"Most of which are not true," she said.

"I'm sure they aren't," he agreed, then tilted his head to one side. "What about you girls? What are your five male fantasies?"

She thought about it for a moment. "Not sure there are five," she said. "I can think of three though."

"Which are?" he prompted.

"Cowboy, pirate and policeman," she replied, then her eyebrows shot up. "And highwayman. Yes, definitely—highwayman."

"Why highwayman?"

"Sexy as hell," she said. "Dangerous. Unpredictable. Arrogant and sure of himself. There is this poem—"

"'The wind was a torrent of darkness among the gusty trees. The moon was a ghostly galleon tossed upon cloudy seas,'" he quoted softly.

Her mouth dropped open and she stared at him. "*How* did you know that was the poem I meant?"

"I done got me some schooling, ma'am," he said with a grin, then shrugged. "Besides, it has always been my favorite poem. So sue me."

"Not 'The Charge of the Light Brigade' or 'The Raven' or…"

"'The Highwayman,'" he stated emphatically. He put a hand to his chest. "I'm a romantic at heart. I freely admit it. So sue me again."

He didn't think she realized what she was doing when she sat down at the foot of his bed. He certainly wasn't about to draw her attention to what she was doing.

"Have you ever seen the movie *The Highwayman* starring Colin Farrell?" she asked, her eyes bright with excitement.

"Who's Colin Farrell?" he queried.

"God's greatest gift to women to hear Bea tell it."

Allison jumped and scrambled off the bed at the sound of Early's voice. Her face had turned as white as a sheet.

"You must be Mrs. Bennett," Early said but there was no welcoming smile on his face. His shrewd eyes scanned her face before sliding slowly to Drew.

"Yes," Allison said.

"This is my cousin," Drew told her. "Early Rawls."

"Oh," she said and ducked her head. "It's nice to meet you, Mr. Rawls."

"Call him Early," Drew said. "But he's always late."

"Yeah. Funny," Early said curtly. "Seems like I was right on time today though."

Drew opened his mouth but before he could speak, Allison rushed over to the door. She looked around—her face still pale—and tried to smile at him.

"Get well soon, Drew," she said, then she was gone.

Early was silent as he stared at Drew.

"You better leave that woman alone, Drew. If you need your knob polished, go over to East Albany and get her done."

"It's not like that and I damned well don't appreciate you suggesting that is my intention toward Allison," Drew snapped. He had stored her preference of name securely in his memory and would never call her Allie.

"No?" Early asked.

"No," Drew stated. "Hell, no."

"Didn't look like that to me," Early said. "I was standing there in that doorway for a good five minutes and neither one of you even noticed me."

Drew narrowed his eyes. "You eavesdropping on me, Early?"

"You having some kind of goddamned midlife crisis?" Early countered. "If that's it, take that red job out on the showroom floor and tool around in it instead of looking to put your tool in some other man's garage!"

"It's not like that."

"Then tell me what it is like," Early threw back at him.

"I think I'm in love with her," Drew admitted.

Early stared at him as though he'd grown a second head, then threw his hands up.

"Sweet Jesus Almighty, Drew. Coach is gonna kick the shit out of you. What the hell's wrong with you falling in love with another man's wife? What about your own wife?" He shook his head. "You are playing with fire, old son. If Big Jake finds out you're even thinkin' 'bout cheatin' on his little girl, man, he'll cut your balls off and feed 'em to you with a big bottle of Louisiana hot sauce and some soda crackers."

"I can't help it, Early. I can't stop thinking about her," Drew defended.

"You better help it and you damned well better knock it off. You hearing me? You're going to bring holy hell down on your head if you don't!"

Chapter Eight

Allison hurried back to the reception area with her cheeks burning. She'd seen the look of condemnation in Drew's cousin's face. The man had looked at her as though she were a common streetwalker. Tears stung her eyes and all she wanted to do was run out the front door. She didn't want to face the other women—and especially not the mayor's self-important wife.

"Allie, what's wrong?" the woman behind the desk asked.

She couldn't remember the lady's name.

"Cramps," she said. "Bad cramps."

"Oh my," the woman—who was well beyond the age to experience her menstrual cycle—gave her a sympathetic look. "Then go home, dear. Get you a hot water bottle and lay down. That's what I used to do."

"Yes, ma'am," Allison said. She kept on walking toward the door—hoping the mayor's wife wasn't close by. For the life of her, she couldn't remember *that* woman's name, either!

"See you on Thursday," the receptionist called after her.

Scurrying out to the parking lot like a scolded dog, Allison wiped at the tears streaking down her cheeks. Why she should feel so guilty—she'd done nothing wrong—she didn't know, but her Baptist guilt was running overtime as she got into her car. Wrapping her hands around the steering wheel, she stared out the dirty windshield. All she saw were the condemning eyes of Drew's cousin.

"Lord," she whispered and crossed her arms over the top of the steering wheel, laid her forehead on her intersected hands and groaned.

She hadn't wanted to go to the hospital at all. She had been forced into it. The first thing Clay had said to her—practically the only thing he had said to her before he left for the high school that morning—was to do him proud. Him, she thought. It was always him. Everything was always about and for him. She'd left the house reluctantly and dawdled on the way to the hospital. She'd been ten minutes late. She knew the moment she walked past the doors that the woman consulting her watch, giving her a stern look, had to be the mayor's overbearing wife.

"You are late," the woman pronounced as though it was a major crime.

"I'm sorry," she'd managed to mumble.

"I would think on your first day you would want to make a good impression," the odious woman lectured. "I'll let it pass this time. Just don't make a habit of it."

All through what the woman had termed orientation, Allison had slunk along behind her like a redheaded stepchild. She'd barely registered half of what the mayor's wife was telling her and didn't particularly care. It wasn't until they stopped at the desk to check on who was convalescing at the hospital that she'd perked up.

"Drew Dunne?" the mayor's wife exclaimed. "What is *he* doing here?"

"Appendicitis," the woman behind the desk said, then lowered her voice. "I heard it was caused by the beating Wade gave him yesterday."

"Don't be ridiculous," the mayor's wife scoffed. "You don't get appendicitis from a beating." She sniffed. "Probably just slacking off. You know how those Dunnes are and especially *that* one." Her mouth twisted into a mean smile. "Has Terri been here to see him?"

"You know she hasn't," the other woman replied and they both laughed. "And neither has Big Jake."

Allison had listened to them gossiping about other people on the patient roster but had tuned out. She glanced at the chart, saw which room Drew was in and made a mental note of it. She was anxious to see him so she asked where she should start.

"I'll introduce you to the patients," the mayor's wife stated. "We don't want to spring a stranger on them."

It had been a sheer hell of expectation for her as they tramped from room to room, chitchatted with the patients, and she had to answer much-too personal questions the patients had about her and Clay. It was soon evident to her when they passed Drew's room for the third time that the snotty woman wasn't anxious to go in there.

"We missed that room," she said and watched the mayor's wife stiffen. "If you have something you need to do, I think I have the hang of introducing myself. If you don't mind, I can slip in there and—"

"Be my guest," the woman snapped. "I've no desire to speak with that loathsome man."

Fine by me, Allison thought and was sure it would be fine by Drew.

She lifted her head from her hands and gazed unseeingly at the hospital, remembering the way his eyes had lit up when he saw her standing in the doorway. The presence of the man in the white lab coat had surprised her so she'd turned away.

"Wait. Don't go!"

He'd sounded almost frantic and one look at his face told her if he could have gotten out of the bed to come after her, he would have. She'd been relieved and the doctor who was with him had been nice—even though there had been a bit of censure in his eyes as there had been in Drew's cousin's.

Were they—she wondered—that protective of him or that distrustful of his intentions? Were they accustomed to him flirting with other women so they were leery of her reaction to him?

He had been flirting with her, she thought, with all the talk about men's fantasies. But then again, she'd been flirting with him as well. Had his cousin not come in…

She took a deep breath, then reached into her purse to take out her car keys. All she wanted was to go home and think.

Think about Drew Dunne and the light that had been glittering in his beautiful blue eyes.

* * * * *

She walked in the door as the phone was ringing, so she hurried into the kitchen to answer. The phone had been installed when Clay had purchased the house, and to her knowledge this was only the second time it had rung when he wasn't there. The first had been the evening before when the mayor's wife had called. She hoped it wasn't her calling to complain or to chastise her for leaving the hospital so soon after her arrival.

"Hello?" she said, a bit leery.

There was no preamble that came from the other end of the call.

"He didn't mean anything by it. I'm sorry he made you run off. You didn't have to go home because of him."

She recognized his voice. It was that low, gravelly tone that did such strange things to her insides. Obviously he knew she'd left the hospital, had cared enough to ask where she was.

"It's okay," she said. Her hand tightened on the receiver, pressed it closer to her ear.

"No, it's not. He's just always looked out for me so…" His voice trailed off. "He's not a bad guy."

"I'm sure he's not," she said and pulled a chair out to sit down. "How are you feeling?"

She heard him sigh. "If people don't stop asking me that I'm gonna spit."

She laughed. "They're just concerned about you, Drew."

"That would be novel if it were true," he told her. "But it's more like they hope I'll tell them I'm still in agony so they can gloat."

"Oh, I don't think so," she said.

"Trust me," he replied. "It's true."

Her protective instinct kicked in and she caught herself before she actually growled into the receiver. She wanted to make sure he knew she wasn't like the other people he knew.

"Not of me it's not," she countered. "I am genuinely concerned about how you feel."

He was silent for so long she thought he might have hung up, believing her to be lying.

"Drew?"

"I'm here," he said. He didn't say anything for another long moment but it felt to her as though he was striving to gather his thoughts so she kept quiet. His next words confirmed that notion. "Thank you for coming to see me today. I really appreciated it."

"Well, I'd say it was my job but that wouldn't be entirely true," she said and realized her hand was shaking. "I wanted to see you."

"Yeah?" He sounded so eager, so ready to believe her it made her heart ache.

"Yeah. I was enjoying our talk."

"Me, too," he said.

"I was going to tell you about the movie."

He missed a beat or two then she heard, *"Ah,"* before, "The one with Collins in it?"

It took her a moment to understand what he meant. "Colin," she corrected. "Colin Farrell."

"God's greatest gift as I recall," he said and she heard the amusement in his voice.

"Actually, you and he could pass for twins." The raspberry he blew across the phone line made her grin. "It's true. When I first met you I thought you looked familiar but I couldn't place you until I saw the movie last night."

"I feel for the poor bastard if he looks like me," he told her.

She drew in a breath, then said, "I think you are a very handsome man, Drew. Even better looking than him."

"Have you met Dr. Grimes yet?" he asked.

She frowned—caught off guard by the abrupt change in the conversation. "Who?"

"He's our local optometrist. I think you should make an appointment. Obviously you are having trouble seeing clearly."

"You goofball," she accused. She was unaccustomed to being teased and it felt good.

Too good. So good she couldn't bring out the words she wanted so desperately to say.

"Am I keeping you from something?" he asked.

"No," she was quick to tell him, not wanting him to hang up.

"Good because I'm bored to death lying here. They were supposed to come help me hobble around the hallway but I haven't seen anyone since Early left."

"Just take it easy. No sprinting through the corridors chasing nurses," she advised.

He snorted. "Have you *seen* these nurses?" he asked, then she heard the unmistakable sound of fingers snapping. "No, that's right. You need glasses so I don't guess you have."

"You are incorrigible," she said.

"I'm bored and I'm…" There was a long pause, then his voice went deeper, even huskier. "Lonely."

She shouldn't say it. She knew she shouldn't.

"Me, too." She took a deep breath thinking in for a penny, in for a pound. "Listen, would you like to have lunch with me next week?"

Silence was like a slap in the face coming from the other end of the line. She heard him breathing—heavily—and thought she'd overstepped the bounds. She was on the verge of apologizing to him for her presumptuousness when he spoke.

"Yes, but it can't be here in town," he said.

Her heart was racing like crazy. "What about Albany?" she suggested. "I need to get some stuff for the house—groceries and a few odds and ends—and I was told there is a Wal-Mart up there."

"Yeah, there is," he agreed.

"I was planning on going Wednesday, have lunch and take a look around the town to see what's there." She tucked her bottom lip between her teeth and felt like a brazen hussy. "Could you meet me at Wal-Mart around eleven?"

"Yes," he said quickly. "I can do that."

"Okay, so that's what we'll do," she said. She felt light-headed, almost giddy.

And bad.

But not in a physical way but a wicked one.

"What about your wife?" she asked. "Will she give you any trouble if she finds out?"

"Will your husband give you any if *he* finds out?" he countered.

"Clay pays no attention to me," she said. "He doesn't care where I go or what I do so long as the house is cleaned, his clothes are ironed and I have his meals on the table at a set time every day."

"He pays no attention to you," he repeated. She heard him swallow. "Then you need a man who will."

A tremor rippled down her body. That was an opening she would have been deaf not to hear.

And stupid not to realize what he was implying. She hit the ball back into his court.

"Just as I believe you need a woman who will give you some," she said boldly.

His next words were almost a whisper. "Are you that woman, Allison?"

"I could be," she replied, then was quick to add, "Just as friends though."

"Of course," he was just as quick to reply. "Just as friends."

"Friends comforting friends," she stressed. "Nothing more."

"Nothing more," he agreed.

"Nothing more," she repeated. Her face was flaming and the giddiness was in full force. She needed to end the call before she wound up saying something she shouldn't. "I've got to go, Drew."

"Yeah, that's probably a good thing," he said.

And she knew. She *knew*! He was just as uneasy and tense as she was about their clandestine meeting to come.

"Bye," she said. "Don't overdo."

"I won't."

She hung up before she could say the three words that came rushing to her mind. Three words that shook her to the core.

Chapter Nine

Doc allowed him to go back to work Friday morning so long as he promised not to bend over or to lift anything heavy. He reasoned sitting behind a desk doing paperwork certainly wouldn't hurt him. At least it would help alleviate the boredom.

"I intend to have a talk with both Jake and Wade," Doc said. "If Wade touches you I swear to God I'll have criminal charges brought against him."

It was on the tip of Drew's tongue to tell him he might want to have a talk with Terri, too. She had a habit of hitting him whenever she was pissed at him about something—which was ninety-nine percent of the time—or simply when the mood struck her. He wouldn't put it past her to punch him in the side just to see what would happen.

Fortunately for Drew his father-in-law had gone to Atlanta for some kind of meeting and had taken both his daughter and Wade along with him. Terri because she had whined her way into going so she could shop and Wade as Big Jake's gofer. They wouldn't be back until late Saturday evening.

Which suited Drew just fine even though neither Jake nor Terri had seen fit to tell him they were going. Not that he gave a damn. They could stay there for all he cared. He had the house to himself and could breathe a sigh of relief that he wouldn't be subjected to either his wife's or her father's complaining.

For the tenth time that morning, he looked at the phone. He wanted so badly to call Allison. To talk to her. To hear her voice. Her laughter.

He smiled. He liked making her laugh. She seemed to appreciate his weird sense of humor almost as much as Early and Bea did.

Heart hammering against his rib cage, he reached for the phone again but the door to his office opened without warning and he snatched his hand back. He looked up to see Early framed in the doorway.

"You look like I just caught you jacking off," Early said.

"You need something?" he asked.

"Yeah, a tie-rod of Miss Elsie's car and she ain't gonna like hearing what it's gonna cost." He turned to go.

"Then call her," Drew told him.

Early spun around as though he'd been caught in a whirligig. "Me? I don't make them calls."

"No reason you can't," Drew said and looked down at his phone. His palm was itching to pick it up, dial Allison's number.

Early grunted. "Who were you going to call before I walked in?"

"Ghostbusters."

"Funny," Early snapped. "You were going to call *her*, weren't you?"

"Don't *you* have a call to make?" Drew queried. He picked up his pen to sign some papers—hoping Early would get the hint.

"Bea and I were discus—"

"You talked to Bea about this?" Drew interrupted.

"I talk to Bea about everything," Early said, taking a seat in the chair across from Drew. "We're worried about you. You know this is wrong."

"We haven't done anything wrong, Early."

"Not yet."

"Go call Miss Elsie," Drew said, dismissing him.

"'Thy shalt not covet thy neighbor's wife,'" Early quoted. "Remember that from Sunday school?"

"He's not my neighbor."

"Semantics, Drew."

"Hey, another new word. You're on a roll, Rawls."

"Screw you," Early said. "You know what other commandment goes hand in hand with not coveting your neighbor's wife?"

Drew tossed the pen to his desktop. "Don't say it," he warned. "I mean it. Don't say it."

"You're feeling guilty or you wouldn't be so pissy about this."

"Don't tell me how I feel. You have no idea how I feel."

"I know what you're thinking of doing," Early told him.

"What I do is my business and certainly not yours. I'm a grown man, Early. I know what I want."

"Fine," Early said, getting to his feet. "Go to hell. See if I care."

"You'd care," Drew told him.

"No, I don't think I would," Early said. He snatched open the door and stormed out.

"Trouble in paradise?" Whip asked as he came to stand in the doorway.

"Call old lady Dawkins and tell her she's going to need a tie-rod for her car," Drew ordered.

"You can call her," Whip said and turned to leave.

"No, goddamn it," Drew shouted. "*You* are going to call her!"

Whip's jaw sagged, his eyes widened. "What did you say?" he asked.

"I didn't stutter," Drew said from between clenched teeth. "Get on the phone and call her. That's not a suggestion. That is an order."

"You can't order me…"

"Yes, hell, I can," Drew said. "I am your boss. I sign your goddamned paychecks. You want to take it up with your daddy when he comes back, you do that. Run and tattle to him like you did when you were a boy. Tell him Drew is picking on you. Hell, tell him I stole your lunch money, kicked dirt on you. I don't give a shit. I'm sure Daddy will make it all better for his little Whipikins."

Everybody within earshot had to have heard the loud words coming from Drew's office. Lenore, the office manager, stuck her head out of her office, her thin brows hiked. Early came back from the shop area wiping his hands on a rag. With him were two mechanics. A low whistle came from one of them.

Whip squared his shoulders. "This isn't over, Dunne," he said.

"Make the call," Drew commanded.

"Not over by a long shot," Whip said.

Drew leveled his gaze on Whip. "Make. The. Call," he repeated.

Whip pivoted on his heel and went back to his office, slamming the door behind him. Drew looked down and saw the light on the phone that told him Whip was calling someone. He knew it was either old lady Dawkins or his father.

"What's gotten into you?" Lenore asked when she appeared at Drew's door.

"A whole bunch of crap," Drew mumbled.

"They got pills for that," she said with a twerk of her lips. She laughed to herself, then turned away.

Leaning back in his chair, Drew felt good about himself for the first time in forever. It had been years since he had asserted himself in that way and it felt right.

And he knew who to thank.

* * * * *

Saturday came and went quietly for Drew. He popped a frozen pizza into the oven, took a six-pack of beer out to the patio as he waited for the pizza to cook. The day was a bit cooler than it had been the week before and he was enjoying the respite from the late summer heat. Kicking his bare feet up on the glass patio table as he popped the top on the first beer and took a long, satisfying sip, he watched the water rippling in the pool as the cleaner made its mechanical rounds beneath the surface.

He rarely swam in the pool and—because of the cottonmouths—never in the pond. Every time he dove into the pool, Terri would come looking for him to do something she wanted done. It never failed. To him, it felt as though she didn't want him contaminating the water. Maybe she was afraid he'd piss in it.

Which he did when he knew she wasn't watching. He took great pleasure in standing on the coping, whipping out his cock and letting it rip. Petty revenge by a petty mind, he thought, but hey. It worked for him.

The timer dinged in the kitchen so he got up to fetch his supper. He hoped he had a chance to eat it before Terri and her father returned. She'd give him hell for eating the thing simply because she could. The woman begrudged every morsel of food that passed his lips. If she could lock him in her father's smokehouse and not have to pay the price for his murder, no doubt she would. Over the years he had wondered why she just didn't ask the old man to make him simply disappear. There was no doubt in his mind that Wade would be happy to provide the means and the disposal. There were quicksand beds in Miller County.

With a thick pot holder, he took the pizza from the oven, ran the cutter across it three times, then plucked a wicker hot pad from its place by the stove. With the pot holder still in place he picked up the hot pizza pan and took it and the pad out to the patio. Tossing the pad on the glass-top table, he set the pizza down and pulled off a piece before sitting back down in the chair. Feet up again, he brought the greasy wedge to his mouth. Munching thoughtfully, he wondered if Allison liked pizza. She looked like a pizza and beer kind of girl.

"Terri sure as shit isn't," he said around a mouthful of the pizza. His wife was a dry martini and rare steak gal. "The bloodier the better."

He wondered if her penchant for almost-raw food was what made her such a mean as hell bitch. Hadn't he read somewhere about a correlation between red meat eaters and a tendency toward violence?

Shifting in the chair, he felt a twinge of pain and winced. The incision was beginning to itch so he assumed that meant it was healing nicely. He'd been told to watch out for nausea, dizziness, fever—the usual culprits that would warn he had developed an infection. He wasn't worried about it.

He finished off the pizza, inhaled a couple of more cans of beer then, moved over to one of the chaise lounges, taking the last two beers with him. He sat them on the patio floor and stretched out on the chaise, crossing his legs at the ankles. The beer had made him sleepy—or maybe it was consuming an entire sixteen-inch pepperoni, mushroom, black olive and green pepper pie with extra cheese to go with the cheese in the crust. The thought of all that cheese made his mouth dry so he picked up the fifth beer, drained it in two or three gulps, then crushed the can in his palm. Just for spite, he pitched the dead soldier into the pool where it bobbed amid the waves. Bracing his hands behind his head, he closed his eyes and almost immediately Allison's face appeared in the darkness there.

"Clay pays no attention to me".

"Then you need a man who will."

"Just as I believe you need a woman who will give you some."

"Are you that woman, Allison?"

"I could be."

He couldn't get the words out of his head. Truth told, he didn't really want to silence them. They kept repeating as though they were on a loop. Each time he heard them in his mind, his body reacted— just as it did now. The erection pressed at the front of his cutoff denim shorts and strained to break free.

She smiled at him in the darkness and his cock hardened even more. It ached with need and he lowered a hand to the bulge. Taking care of his own needs had become a way of life for him so he felt no shame in what he began to do. It was just a fact of his existence. His palm slid back and forth—pressing against the tumescence—as his mind took him into that dark place where Allison was waiting for him…

* * * * *

She was gliding gracefully, effortlessly through the sparkling blue water. Her slender arm arced from the surface, then dug into the ripples to propel her along. Her black hair floated behind her in silky tendrils—the tresses of a mermaid. From one end of the pool to the other, then back again she cut the water so cleanly, so elegantly. The last four feet before she reached the place where he sat with his feet in the water, she dove beneath the surface and he caught just the briefest glimpse of a very sweet little ass. When she surfaced, she came up right between his spread knees. Her hands as she took hold of the coping were mere inches from his cock.

"Come in," she beckoned. "The water is wonderful."

"I'm good watching you," he said.

"I'd rather you be bad," she told him.

"Behave," he said with a grunt.

"Please come in," she pleaded. She turned her head and placed a light kiss on his bare thigh, then planted her feet against the side of the pool and jettisoned herself backward in the water. Her smile was saucy, seductive. Filled with challenge. She stopped midway the pool to tread water, to lift her hand and crook her finger at him.

"Come be bad with me," she said.

He crossed his hands over his waist, gripped the edges of his t-shirt and pulled it over his head. Tossing it aside, he slid off the coping and into the water. With sure, strong, even strokes he was in front of her, fanning his hands over the water to float there with her.

"Have you ever made love in the pool?" she asked. When he shook his head, her eyes took on a wicked gleam. "Do you want to?"

Before he could answer, she was gliding toward the shallow end with a powerful backstroke, though all the while her eyes were locked on his. He kicked at the water and lunged after her—ducking beneath the water to glide along like a fabled silkie. He came up right in front of her and wrapped his arms around her, pulled her to him. She wrapped her legs around his waist, her arms around his neck and her lips met his.

One moment her lush breasts were pressed to his chest behind her bikini top and the next they were flesh to flesh. Gone was the top, her bikini bottom and his cutoff jeans. His cock was riding the cleft of her ass as she clung to him.

"Better," she mumbled against his mouth. "Much better."

His hands were supporting her under her rump though the buoyancy of the water would have done the same. He just liked caressing her sweet little ass and it fit perfectly in his palms. She ground her core against his belly and that was all it took to set a massive fire in his blood.

A fire that only her body could quench.

He moved one hand between them, took hold of his cock and...

* * * * *

"What the hell are you doing?"

The loud, strident voice brought him bolt upright on the lounge. His hand was in the opened V of his jeans with his fingers wrapped around his shaft.

Terri and her father—as well as Wade—were standing over him staring down with looks of disgust, amusement and downright hatred. He jerked his hand from his jeans and quickly zipped them.

"I think we know what he was doing," Big Jake said with a crooked grin made all the more merciless by the repugnant gleam in his eyes.

"He's an evil, sinful boy," Wade said. "I always said he was."

"Get up and go in the house, Andrew," Terri ordered. "You've embarrassed me quite enough for one day." She kicked the leg of the chaise. "And in front of our fathers, at that."

For a reason he could not explain, he didn't move. He finished zipping his jeans but remained where he was.

"Did you hear what I told you?" Terri snarled.

"Hard not to when you're shrieking like a fishwife," he said quietly.

Terri gasped, sputtered and turned to her father. "Did you hear what he said to me?" she shrieked. "Did you hear what he called me, Daddy?"

Her father winced at the loud tone but didn't answer her. He was staring hard at Drew but when Wade took a step toward the chaise, Big Jake put out a staying arm.

"Leave him be," Jake said. "You hit him or hurt him in any way and Trent will sic the cops on the both of us."

"Who cares?" Terri shouted. "I told him to get up and go…"

"I'm not getting up and I'm not going anywhere," Drew told her.

"Go on in the house, baby girl," her father said. "I'll handle this."

"Let Wade hit him, Daddy," she said through clenched teeth. "Let Wade beat the ever-loving hell out of him."

"Go in the house, Terri Anne," her father ordered. "Now!"

Terri hesitated for a moment or two but when her father turned a stern eye to her, she flipped her hair over her shoulder and trounced away—stomping her feet like the spoiled brat he'd made her.

"Wait in the car, Wade," Jake said.

"If'n you want me to jack his ass out of that chair—" Wade began but he, too, was rewarded with a steely glare from Jake. He nodded, then strolled off as though he didn't have a care in the world.

Jake put his hands on his hips and stared at Drew. "You finally grow a pair, boy?" he inquired.

"I've had enough of her talking to me like I'm a servant instead of her husband," Drew replied.

"I told you the other day. You're nothing," Jake said.

"Then let her file for divorce," Drew said, clutching the arms of the chaise.

"There's never been a divorce in the Thompson family and there's not going to be one now," Jake stated. "The sooner you accept that, the better off you'll be."

"Then I'll move out."

"No, hell you won't," Jake said softly. "I'll not have the town gossips talking about my baby girl."

"Like they don't already?" Drew challenged.

"They talk about you. Not her."

"Then blame me for the whole thing. I'll—"

"You'll stay right where the hell you are," his father-in-law interrupted. "There's not gonna be any stigma attached to the Thompson name as long as I'm alive. Unlike you, my family has a reputation to uphold in this county."

Drew wanted to argue the point but there was no need. Jake Thompson's mind was as set as week-old concrete. He was trapped in a sham of a marriage with a woman who hated him and whom he hated, with no foreseeable way out. Until a week ago, he had resigned himself to living that lie and taking it as best he could. Now...

Now things were different.

"Don't even think about it," Jake said. "I can see the wheels turning in that head of yours. You try leaving my little girl and I promise you, Andrew, you will regret it. You will *deeply* regret it. I'll hire private detectives to track your ass and they'll bring you back to her in chains."

As soon as her father left, Terri came out of the house. He could tell by the fury puckering her face she would be after him with her fists and nails. Before she reached him, he got up and put the chaise between them.

"Coward," she shouted. She rushed around the end of the chaise but he stood his ground. When she would have slapped him, he knocked her hand away and stepped back.

"So help me God, woman, if you hit me I will fucking hit you back this time," he warned.

She stopped with her hand up to try it again. Her eyes narrowed to thin slits. "I'm gonna tell Daddy you threatened to beat me."

"You do that, Terri Anne," he said. "That's all you and that sniveling brother of yours know how to do. Something doesn't go like you want it to so you two go running to Daddy. Neither one of you know how to handle things like adults."

Her eyebrows shot up. "You bastard," she said. "How dare you talk to me like that? I'll throw your ass out of my house!"

"Then fucking *do* it, bitch!" he shouted at her. "Call Bobby Daniels and have him come out here and arrest my ass." He took a step toward her but she stumbled back. "You want me to get in a good slap or two so you'll have reason to charge me with domestic abuse? If you do, I'll certainly oblige."

She stood there quivering. He knew she wasn't afraid of him. It wasn't that. She was so enraged the adrenaline was pumping like mad through her body—causing a reaction.

"You'll pay for that smart mouth of yours," she said. She lifted her chin. "I've got somebody who will be happy to take care of your worthless hide."

"Who?" he asked. "The shithead who was fucking you the other night?" He laughed. "Good, then go to him. You two deserve one another."

He turned and headed toward the house—half expecting her to run after him and jump on his back. She'd done it before and given the chance would do it again. But she stayed where she was.

* * * * *

They were late getting to church the next morning. Had missed Sunday school altogether. Terri was having a bad hair day and was furious about it. She'd smeared her fingernail polish and had to take it off, redo it. The heel on her favorite pair of heels broke. Naturally she blamed Drew for all of it. Secretly he was having a good laugh at her expense. He had to admit, she looked downright awful. That made his morning and he was pretty sure it would make his day when the church women got a look at the frizzy mess his wife couldn't seem to curse into shape.

"If one person says something mean to me, she will fucking regret it," she grumbled.

He made no comment to her remark. She didn't expect one anyway. It was best to keep his mouth shut and his eyes on the road. Let her carry on her own conversation to whatever demon it was to which she reported. He drove in silence—as he did every Sunday— but instead of wondering what evil she was thinking up to throw at him after the services, he was thinking of Allison as they pulled up in front of the church. Of how badly he wanted to see her.

Ask and ye shall be given.

There she was, he thought as he turned off the engine. She and her husband were standing with Boyd Mackie—Doc's son—and Jan, Boyd's wife. Boyd was the assistant coach at MCHS and had been Jack's younger brother. Jan was the daughter of the family lawyer, Brooks Darnell Daniels. Jan was also Sheriff Bobby Daniels's sister.

Hair in that same tight bun, dress hem longer that was fashionable, Allison was standing demurely at her husband's side with her head down. She looked as miserable as he felt at seeing her that way. Anger welled up inside him.

"Are you going to get out of the car or not?" Terri snapped, drawing his attention away from where it wanted to be. "The door isn't going to open itself, you know."

Sighing heavily, he snatched the keys out of the ignition and shoved his door open. He slammed it harder than he meant to and heads turned toward him. Ignoring those staring at him, he came around the front of the car and to his wife's door. He opened it with his gaze directed over the top of the car and not at her. She wouldn't appreciate him putting a hand out to help her from the car—she never had—so he didn't bother. She got out, stood and shook her skirt.

"This car needs to be detailed," she said with a sniff. "Take it with you to work tomorrow."

"Yes, Miss Daisy," he said drily.

"Asshole," she hissed at him.

He looked down at her and gave her a smile he hoped would chill her to the bone.

"I'm getting tired of you talking back to me," she said and started to walk away but he stepped in front of her. His doing so surprised her and she drew in a quick breath.

"You are not my mother," he said in a low, steady voice. "You are not my boss. I'll say whatever the hell I want to say to you."

Her mouth formed a perfect O and when he stepped back, turned and headed for the church he heard her growl of rage. People were staring. He wasn't walking meekly behind her as he normally did but headed for the door with her scurrying to catch up to him.

* * * * *

Clay glanced at him as Drew passed them. He saw the bastard cut his eyes to Allie's—and hers to him—before he went into the church. When Jan raised a brow and exchanged a look with Boyd, Clay bristled. He reached over to take Allie's arm in a tight grip. She looked up at him and he saw fear—and what he thought could be guilt—shifting through her green eyes. He increased his grip until she flinched. He leaned toward her.

"Look at him like that again and I'll beat the hell out of you, woman," he said in a low voice only she was meant to here.

"He don't look no worse for wear considering," Jan commented as she stared after Dunne.

"Wade never leaves telltale signs, Janny. You know that," Boyd said. "He was hitting Drew in the gut."

"You saw the whole thing go down didn't you, Mack?" Clay asked, his gaze steady on Allie.

Boyd nodded. "I was coming out of the bank and saw folks going around the side of the dealership. Knew something was up so I moseyed over."

"I heard Dunne was on his knees in the dirt begging his old man not to hit him again," Clay said.

"Well, I don't know about that," Boyd replied. "I wasn't close enough to hear what was said but Drew was on the ground."

"Old man Dunne put him in the hospital," Jan said to Allie. "Wasn't the first time."

"Won't be the last, either," Boyd said with a laugh.

"Some men need to have their ass kicked," Clay commented. He dug his thumb nail into Allie's arm—pressing the fabric of the long sleeve into her flesh.

"He's had his kicked many a time," Boyd told him. "Ain't nobody I know deserves it more than Drew Dunne."

Jan nodded. "He killed Boyd's brother so whatever happens to him is what he's got coming to our way of thinking."

"I heard it was an accident," Allie said and Clay pressed his nail deeper.

"You don't know nothing about it, Allie, so you ought to just keep your mouth shut," he told her.

"Dunne didn't try to save Jack," Boyd said. "Saved his own hide and Terri Anne's."

"He knew which side of the bread his butter was going to be on," Jan said with a nod. "He'd knocked her up. Did it on purpose, too, so he'd have to marry her."

"Live on easy street the rest of his life," Boyd mumbled.

"Seems to me there was a method to the bastard's madness," Clay said.

"You better believe there was," Boyd said.

"We'd best get on in, now, Shug," Jan said to her husband. "We're about the last ones out here."

Clay kept a brutal grip on Allie's arm as he escorted her into the church. He found a pew near the back—well away from the Thompson family pew—and pushed her none too gently into it, taking the aisle seat beside her. Boyd and Jan found a seat a little further up.

A few latecomers like themselves greeted Clay, patted him on the back as they went down the aisle. A man in the pew in front of them turned and shook hands with Clay, nodded politely at Allie. When the man turned to face the front again, Clay leaned over to put his lips to Allie's ear.

"Did you see him at the hospital when you were there?" he demanded. He still had hold of her arm and tightened the pressure until her heard her moan. "Did you?"

"Yes," she said.

"Did you talk to him?"

"Yes."

The organ began playing and everyone stood but he did not relinquish his hold. The hymnals remained in the shelf behind the pew in front of them. There was no singing, no reciting of scripture. He did not let go of her until Brother Gilbert began his sermon.

"We'll talk about it when we get home," he said and removed his hand.

Through the rows of people, Clay saw the back of Drew Dunne's head. All he could think about were Bobby's words to him.

"You better watch him, Clay. He's got the worst marriage in the world. Far as I know he's never cheated on Terri Anne but he's got the want in his eyes in the worst way. I recognize that look."

And Clay had seen that look, too, when Dunne had glanced at Allie. It had been fleeting but it was there. A hungry look. A deep-seated need that could not be disguised. The bastard was full of it and he wanted to spill into another man's woman.

Yeah, the look was there, all right.

The more he thought about it the angrier he got for he'd seen that look mirrored in his wife's eyes as they'd followed Dunne into the church. It was all he could do not to emit the growl that was lodged at the back of his throat.

He didn't love Allie. Had never loved her but her family had money. Truth be told, they had more money than his family did and that was saying something. There was substantial wealth on both sides of her family, and on top of that her father and his father were fraternity brothers. He set out to seduce her. It was an easy conquest. A piece of cake. He needed to marry a rich girl because he knew his father wasn't going to leave him any of the money that was in the old man's numerous bank accounts. Those millions would go to his older brother ,Tyler, because their father, Kip, thought being a high school football coach—which had been Clay's dream since he was a boy—was a waste of time.

Marrying Allie had been a waste of time, too, as far as he was concerned. There was nothing about her that was in the least bit enticing.

Turning to look at Allie, he had to clamp his jaw tightly shut to keep from snarling at her. She wasn't a pretty woman by any discriminating man's standards. The only thing she had going for her was a wealth of thick black hair he would not allow her to cut any higher than her hips. That hair made a good tether when she was trying to get away from him.

He chuckled and she turned that nondescript face toward him— her eyes showing just the right amount of fear. He gave her his own kind of look that promised she wasn't going to like what he had in mind.

She was nothing more to him than a servant and a lay. And not a good lay at that. Even the worst skank he'd ever fucked was better in the sack than she was. The woman didn't like sex so why had she cast Dunne a look that said she was itching to have him shove it up her cunt?

He switched his stare back to Dunne—hating the man as he'd never hated any other man. He knew they'd been at Georgia together but Dunne had been so unimportant he didn't remember him. He did remember, however, the night Dunne had been injured down at Florida. They'd lost the game because of his sorry ass. For that alone, Clay despised him.

The congregation was standing again and opening their hymnals. Services were winding down and that was good. He was anxious to get Allie home for the talking-to he'd promised her.

Chapter Ten

Allison could barely walk the next morning. She was sore from her shoulders to her knees and the area between her legs throbbed with pain. Clay had been especially brutal with her when he threw her to the bed. He tore into her like a crazed person. It was rare he sodomized her but he'd pulled out all the stops and hurt her so badly she stayed curled into a fetal position most of the afternoon. She would have been there still had he not demanded she get up and fix his supper. Thankfully, he'd gone off to the school early and not jerked her out of bed to make breakfast for him.

Now as she hobbled into the kitchen to fix a cup of coffee, she held a hand to her belly where he had punched her one last time before rolling over to go to sleep. She thought of Drew and the beating he had taken.

"Just one more thing we have in common," she said as she stared out into the god-awful backyard that needed mowing.

Once the coffee had brewed, she took her cup out to the back stoop and sat down gingerly. She groaned—clutching the cup carefully between her palms. She was about to take a sip of the hot brew when the phone rang. She didn't move. Didn't attempt to get up to answer it. If it was Clay, he'd call again. If it was the mayor's wife—what *was* her name again?—she didn't want to talk to her. She was scheduled to work at the hospital on Tuesdays and Thursdays and half days on Saturdays. If the woman wanted her to cover someone else's day, that was just too bad.

But what if it was Drew? she thought. She was about to get up when the ringing stopped. She tensed, waiting for the ringing to begin again. That would mean it was Clay fuming about why she hadn't answered the first time. The phone stayed silent and she relaxed, sipped her coffee and stared morosely at the yard that was in desperate need of mowing. If it was going to be done, she'd be the one to do it. And the edging. And the raking when the time came. Anything that needed doing around the house that she could do—and some she really shouldn't like cleaning the gutters—would be left to her to see to. What went on in and around the house was her domain. Everything else was Clay's. At least that was his ironclad policy. He made the money so he disbursed it. He paid the bills. He wrote all the checks—she wasn't on any of his bank accounts—and he doled out an allowance to her as if she were a teenage girl. Twenty dollars a week for what he called female incidentals. The only exception was for grocery and household needs. There was a special checking account only for that and both their names were on it. He watched over every purchase she made and even questioned her about those he didn't like. There was never more than a hundred dollars in the account at any given time—the money replaced as he saw fit.

Heaving a long, tired sigh she took another sip of coffee and realized she was crying. That was something she did a lot so she rarely noticed when it started but this time she knew why the tears were falling. Clay had informed her he wasn't going to allow her to go to Albany on Wednesday. If she wanted something from Wal-Mart, he'd get it when he went over there after football practice.

She had been looking forward to getting away from the despicable little house she hated so savagely. Had looked forward to having lunch at some new restaurant. Had looked forward to driving around Albany, getting to know the town. But more than any of those, she had been looking forward to being with Drew.

"Drew," she said.

She'd dreamed about him last night. And the night before. And the night before that. He haunted her dreams and walked through her mind all during the day. She couldn't—and didn't want to—get him out of her thoughts. His smiling face and sensual eyes were the only things that were keeping her from screaming at the top of her lungs. At least in her dreams he could comfort her. Wrap his arms securely around her and she could lay her cheek against his chest and hear the steady beat of his heart.

Would he be as disappointed that she wouldn't be going to Albany as she was? She was almost sure he would be. They hadn't spoken at church. They'd only looked at each other in passing but something had passed between them. A promise. A need. She had felt it and she knew he had as well.

She frowned. Clay must have felt it or sensed it, too, for he had ushered her out of the church as soon as the congregation began filing out. He'd all but dragged her to their car and even went as far as jerking her door open and practically shoving her inside. She'd seen Drew looking their way as Clay backed the truck into the street.

She'd made the mistake of turning her head to look at him. Clay had reached over and slapped his hand to her thigh and twisted viciously.

"Get your fucking eyes on the road, bitch, or I'll go back there and turn him into a greasy spot on the ground!"

Clay had never—*never*—shown any jealousy over her. She didn't think he cared enough about her to give a damn. Why now was he doing so?

"Because Drew is Terri's husband," she said aloud now.

That had to be it. Even though Terri didn't want Drew, Drew had what Clay obviously wanted. There was no doubt in her mind that on the night Clay was supposed to have been night hunting with Bobby he was with Terri. No one could reach the woman to let her know her husband had been rushed to the hospital. Wasn't that a dead giveaway?

Not that she cared. He could wedge himself up inside Terri, or any other whore he wanted, as tightly as a cork in a wine bottle for all she cared. She began to hate him on their wedding night and that hatred had grown over the years. It was only her fear of him that kept her married to him. It was the money her family had left her that kept him married to her.

Money over which she had no control. Her father had seen to that.

"Women don't have a mind for finance," he'd told her. *"Your husband will see to the handling of your inheritance from your mother and me when we're gone."*

He hadn't counted on the boating accident that claimed his and her mother's life three months later.

Nor had he—or Clay—known about the trust fund her maternal grandmother had left for her in a bank in Tampa. The money was gathering interest month after month. By now it was quite a tidy sum looked after scrupulously by her grandmother's trusted lawyer. He never sent statements to her but she called him from time to time—secretly and always collect—to let him know how and where she was. At last count, there was over a million dollars in the fund.

"I know your father," her grandmother had told her on Allison's wedding day. *"And I think I know the kind of man you're marrying. I'll be putting something aside for you, dear. Don't let either of them know you have it. Promise me, Allison. Promise me you will never tell your father or your husband about the trust fund."*

A wise woman, her grandmother. She'd watched her own daughter be subjugated by Thadeus Bailey and didn't want the same for her only grandchild. Thanks to her, Allison had a nest egg that was there if she ever needed it. Everything else she'd left Allison had been taken and sold by Clay and the proceeds jammed into his own pockets. Irreplaceable treasures like the old pie safe he'd sold for $2000 and the steamer trunk her great-grandmother had brought to Florida from Ireland.

And the jewelry and the antique watches her grandfather had collected.

All of it gone. Never to be seen again.

"Why don't you just leave him?" a woman from church in Milton had asked her.

To someone who had never been in an abusive relationship it must seem like an easy thing to just leave. You simply pack your bag, hit the road, get lost, never look back.

"And hope he never finds you," Allison said aloud. She had no delusions about what he would do to her if—and when—he caught up with her. That he most likely would scared her so badly it made her stomach hurt. His threats over the years had kept her feet planted firmly in his shadow.

Yes, she had money. She was smart. She might not have graduated from college but she was intelligent. She might not be street savvy, but she wasn't stupid. She could recognize danger when it confronted her. How she would fare dealing with that danger was a concern right up there at the top of her list for staying with him.

There were other things that kept her chained to him as well.

She had taken her marriage vows seriously. She had made her bed and she had to lie in it. No one had forced her into the marriage. No one had held a gun to her head. Her decision to marry Clay had been the single most asinine thing she'd ever done and, in a way, she knew she was paying for making that mistake by not leaving. She realized that. She accepted it.

Then there was the embarrassment of having failed. That she could live with, but it would always be there in the back of her mind to remind her she had screwed up big time. Failure had never been tolerated in her family. Her parents might have had a bad marriage, too, but they never gave up on one another.

"You stay the course," had been one of her father's favorite sayings.

Religion—to some extent—played a part in her staying, too. Divorce still carried with it a stigma that would follow her the rest of her life. She didn't know if she could handle that on her own.

"I'm not sure I could make it on my own, period," she said to the straggly yard. "I've never been alone. The thought of being out there without friends, without family…" She shuddered. It wasn't just fear of Clay but fear of the unknown, of being alone that scared her.

And there was Clay and who and what he was. He was a popular man—well liked, envied, sought after. Who would ever believe a man like him would abuse his wife? Her word against his and who was she? A nobody. No one paid any attention to her when he was around. All eyes were on Clay.

"Excuses," she said. "They are all excuses."

But they were excuses that made her think twice each time she had the urge to run. What she kept hoping for was that he would leave her. That one of his affairs, his one-night stands, or whatever you wanted to call the dalliances, would lead to him wanting out of their marriage. If he ran away with one of his whores, the onus would be on him, not her. That was a dream she kept pressed close to heart.

"Maybe one day," she stated.

Grinding her teeth, she pushed herself up from the stoop—yelping as every muscle in her body protested the movement. She glared at the offensive backyard. She sure as hell didn't feel like mowing the sparse grass or pulling the weeds that constituted most of the green on the ground but she needed something to keep her mind off how pitiful her life was. She didn't need to sit there feeling sorry for herself.

And she needed to call Drew. Desperately needed to hear his voice. Not just to hear his voice but to tell him she wouldn't be going to Albany on Wednesday. She went inside, set the cup in the sink, then marched over to the phone. There was a slender phone book on the counter and she snatched it up, turned to the yellow pages and found the number for Five County Motors.

* * * * *

Drew looked up as Lenore came into his office. "Whatcha need, Lennie?" he asked.

She laid a sheaf of papers on his desk but kept the ledger she carried in her hand. "These are the invoices from the last couple of months. I think you need to look them over, Drew. Very carefully, then compared them to this." She put the ledger down atop the papers. "Something is way off."

He frowned. "The figures don't jive?"

She shook her head. "Not by a guinea mile," she stated. "He's embezzling. As sure as I'm standing here, he is. I just can't figure out how he's doing it."

Drew didn't need to ask who she meant. There was only one other person in the dealership who could be juggling the books and that was Whip.

"I'll look into it," he said.

The phone rang and he let Lenore pick it up.

"Five County Motors. This is Lenore. How may I direct your call?"

He smiled, ducking his head so she wouldn't see. It was such an elegant, professional way to answer the phone and it never failed to tickle him. By the way Lenore spoke, you'd think there were dozens of people for whom the call might be meant.

"May I ask who's calling?"

His head came up. "Gimme," he said, holding out his hand. He knew. He *knew*.

"One moment, please." She held the receiver away from him and reached down to punch the button to put the caller on hold. She arched a thinly plucked brow. "Mrs. Farrell is on the line for you."

"Give. Me. The. Phone. And. Leave," he said sweetly.

"Uh huh," she replied and handed the receiver over to him.

"And close the door behind you."

She gave him a long look, then almost—not quite—smiled. "Yes, sir."

He waited until the door was closed before punching in the button. "Hello?"

"I was beginning to think you weren't there," she said.

"I'm always here for you," he told her. "Mrs. Farrell."

She laughed—softly and sweetly—and he closed his eyes to the sound.

"Are you where you can talk?" she asked.

He looked down at the base set of the phone. There were no other lights lit. "Yes."

"I can't meet you on Wednesday," she said.

His whole world collapsed. "Why not?"

"Clay is going over after football practice so he told me to make a list of what I needed and he'd get it."

He clenched his hand around the receiver. "Do you think he knows you were planning on meeting me?"

"No, I don't think so. It's a matter of not wasting gas," she said.

"What?" He didn't understand.

"Clay is a miser when it comes to money. Why should there be two trips to Albany when one will suffice? He's going anyway so there's no reason I should. Drew…" She paused, then he heard her take a deep breath. "Is your wife going to Albany on Wednesday?"

"Not to my knowledge. Why?"

"Do you know where she was the night the ambulance came for you?"

He didn't. "Does it matter?"

"Clay wasn't home all night," she told him. "I think they were together."

That didn't surprise him.

"Do you care?"

"No. Do you?"

"Not a snowball's chance in hell do I care," he stated. "If she's with him, she's not with me and he's not with you."

"That's how I see it," she admitted.

"What about next Wednesday? Can we meet then?" he asked.

"I'll have to let you know."

"I really want to be with you, Allison." He thought he'd been too presumptuous because she was quiet for longer than was comfortable but then her soft, gentle voice came over the line to set his world to rights again.

"I want to be with you," she told him. "More than anything in the world I *need* to be with you."

This time he was quiet—taking in her words, cherishing them, savoring them.

"Drew? Did I shock you? Am I being too bold?" she asked and he heard the worry in her voice.

"No, sweetie," he said. "I need to be with you, too."

"I know it's wrong—"

"It's *not* wrong," he said. "We haven't done *anything* wrong. A man and woman can be friends, can help one another without it being immoral."

There was a knock on his door and he caught himself before he cursed. "Just a minute," he said, sharper than he meant to.

"You have to go," she said.

"Yeah. Can I call you later?"

"Any time before five," she said and hung up without saying good-bye.

He put the receiver down. "Come in."

It was Early and with him was one of the mechanics. Both men looked pissed.

"What now?" he asked.

"Whip fired him," Early said.

Drew knew the mechanic to be good at his job, honest and dependable. "For what?"

"You tell him," Early said to the man.

"Mr. Whip had me do a tune up Miss Gayle's car and I did. I gave him the invoice and he tore it up. He said we don't charge friends of the family. I told him he'd have to take it up with you and that's when he fired me."

"Well, you aren't fired, Philip. For one thing he doesn't have the authority to fire you or anyone else, and for another you were right in telling him to take it up with me. Go back to work and if he asks you to tune up somebody else's car, you come to me before you do. I'll make damned sure he knows that person is going to have to pay for it or it won't be done."

"Yes, sir," the mechanic said. He tugged on his baseball cap and left.

"Whip has got a burr under his tail this morning," Early said. "Son of a bitch yelled at me about there not being any Cokes in the drink machine."

"Ignore him. I do."

"You better keep his sorry ass in line." He grinned. "That's why you get paid the big bucks."

Drew snorted. "You make more than me and you know it."

"Yeah, but you got all the perks. The fancy mansion with the double swimming pool. The fully stocked fish pond. The Lincoln. The…" He snapped his fingers, shook a finger at Drew. "Oh, right. You don't got them, do you?"

"Get the hell out of my office," Drew said good-naturedly.

"Fuck you, too," Early said with a smile.

"You don't have the right opening, old son," Drew replied.

"I can go 'cross to the Piggly Wiggly and buy a jar of mayonnaise," Early told him.

"Get the hell out of my office, you filthy-minded pervert. And don't say anything to Whip. I'll take care of him."

"Wouldn't dream of it, cuz."

After Early left, Drew leaned back in his chair with his gaze steady on the ledger. Not that he was worried. He knew there were discrepancies in the ledger but only a sharp mind like Lenore's would have found them. He thought he'd hidden them well but apparently he'd slipped up somewhere. He would have to find a way to fix it. He hadn't gotten a degree in finance for nothing. He wondered what Big Jake would do if he found out his son-in-law had been embezzling money from the dealership since the very day it opened its doors sixteen years earlier.

He thought about the money he had squirreled away. There were reasons he had stolen the money. Not just because he got paid a piss-poor wage and figured he was entitled to more. That was part of it ,but pure spite was the majority of it. That he could, that he was smart enough to do it and not get caught bolstered his ego—one of the few things he had of his own. He purely enjoyed putting one over on a man who thought he was the smartest cock in the hen house.

Still, he worried what might happen if the old bastard caught on to his scheme.

"He'd put my ass in prison, that's what," he said quietly.

So? he thought. He'd be swapping one prison for another. At least in prison he wouldn't have to contend with Terri. Trouble was, he knew there would be a different threat to his ass there than the one she posed in *her* fancy prison. He wasn't a vain man but he knew he wasn't bad looking. He was slightly built. Both things that would make him easy pickings for men intent on making him their bitch.

No, prison was not some place he ever wanted to go. Which meant he had to find a way to put the blame of the cooked books elsewhere.

Like on Whip.

* * * * *

The following Wednesday hadn't worked out for her. Nor had the next. School started and there were dozens of things her husband insisted she do at home. He made the trip to Albany every week ostensibly to consult with coaches at the three high schools there. Before he came home—usually four to five hours later—he would have what was on the list she gave him. And wasn't it rather interesting that Terri took those same Wednesdays to make a trip over to Dougherty County to have lunch with friends? Wouldn't she and Bennett be surprised to learn their assignations allowed their spouses to have assignations of their own?

Not in person—for that would have been reckless in a town the size of Colquitt—but over the phone. Hours spent telling life stories and giving viewpoints about everything from books to movies to music to world news. Hours spent getting to know someone whose needs were as great as your own. Whose loneliness was abated by the ringing of a telephone.

If Drew couldn't be in the same room with her, at least he could talk to her. Her soft voice soothed the terrible ache in his heart. Her laughter made his soul sing. What if the only time he got to see her was at church? Though they never looked directly at one another, they were both keenly aware of where the other was. It was as though their beings had fused in some magical way. Rows of people might separate them physically but there was nothing keeping them apart in spirit.

Now he sat listening to her telling him about finding a baby robin in the backyard that morning and how she'd climbed up on the ladder to put him back in his nest.

"I wore a pair of new work gloves so I wouldn't get my scent on him. The mother bird would have rejected him otherwise," she said.

"So did he stay in the nest?" he asked.

"I've been watching his parents flying to and from the nest so I'm guessing he has. The wind must have blown him out the first time. He's not nearly old enough to fly."

"You've got a tender heart, lady," he told her.

"That's me. Giving all my maternal love to an animal because I can't give it to a child of my own," she said.

"Why don't you have any children?" It was a question he'd been trying to find a way to ask her and now an opportunity to do so had arisen.

"Clay had a vasectomy when he was in high school," she said. "Do you believe that? He hates children. Absolutely despises them. His brother, Tyler, has four and when we go visit Clay's family, he is simply atrocious to the poor kids. He and Tyler have even come to blows over how Clay treats them."

"I'm surprised any reputable doctor would have snipped him at that age," he commented—hating her husband even more for making it impossible for Allison to have a child of her own.

"He was visiting a friend of his who had moved from Georgia to Texas. They got drunk and drove across the border, paid a Mexican doctor to do it. It's a wonder he didn't get blood poisoning."

"So I'm guessing since he hates kids, adoption was out of the question," he said.

"Yes, it was." She paused. "How about you? Why haven't you and Terri had kids?"

He had told her why he'd married Terri. He'd told her about the pregnancy. He had also told her about the abortion Terri had insisted on getting.

"The only time I brought up adoption," he said, knowing that was what she was asking about, "she shut me down by saying she didn't want some other man's slime slithering around her house shitting, puking and pissing all over everything."

"She has a way with words, doesn't she?" Allison asked.

"Oh, yeah."

"Are you going to the first football game of the season Friday night?" she asked and he heard the hope in her voice. He knew she'd be made to go with her husband. With him down on the field, maybe they could sit within eyesight of one another. It was better than nothing, but it was too great a risk.

"Probably not. Friday nights are usually bridge night at her parents' house," he said.

"You play bridge?"

"I know *how* to play bridge. I sit there and go through the motions. It's a stupid game, I hate it and if I could get out of it, I would."

"You poor man," she said but he heard the laughter in her voice. "Oh, I'm going to Bainbridge tomorrow morning around ten to pick up some stuff for Clay at that sporting goods store downtown. You wouldn't happen to be going down there, too, would you?"

"Not a good idea, sweetie," he said. "As much as I'd love to see you, all we need is someone seeing us together and report it back to him or her."

She sighed. "Yeah, I guess you're right. It was just a thought."

"I'll be thinking about you though," he said and meant it more than she would ever know.

"I'll be fantasizing about you," she teased.

"Me and the highwayman," he said with a chuckle.

"You *are* the highwayman," she said. "As a matter of fact, that's my new nickname for you. Highwayman."

"I like that," he told her. "The only nickname I've ever had Early gave to me."

"What is that?"

"Shithead," he said drily. Before she could chastise him for his vulgarity—as she always did—he told her he had to go. He saw Miss Elsie Dawkins waddling through the showroom and knew he was about to be read the riot act.

"I'll let you go, then. Maybe next week I can make it up to Albany," she said wistfully.

"From your mouth to God's ears."

The door to his office swung open and a ninety pound granny with an artificial hip and a militant gleam in her eyes came strolling in.

"Get off that phone," Miss Elsie said. "I've a bone to pick with you, Andrew Allan Dunne."

"Allan?" Allison questioned for he'd never told her his middle name.

"Have a nice day, Miss Bess," he said. "Bye now."

"Bess who?" Miss Elsie demanded.

He hung up the phone. "Lord," he supplied, trying to keep a straight face. "Bess Lord. She's Land Lord's daughter."

"Don't know him and never heard of him. Now about this goldarn thing Whippersnap says I need…"

* * * * *

Allison smiled as she hung up the phone. "Andrew Allan," she said. "Allan and Allison." She thought about it. "No, Andrew and Allison. Andrew and Allison Dunne announce the birth of their son Allan." She giggled at the absurdity her wicked mind had formed.

Knowing Clay would not be expecting her to cook supper for him—since he always ate in at the Rib Shack when he went to Albany—she decided all she wanted was a big salad for her supper.

"Chased down with two Mounds and a bag of dill chips," she said. It would be well after nine or ten before Clay would come rolling in smelling like sex and whatever the hell perfume it was that Terri Dunne wore. Idly, she wondered what Drew would be eating since he, too, could have whatever he wanted.

As she went about putting the salad together, she imagined him stopping at The Polar Girl Restaurant on the way home and getting the double cheeseburger with bacon that was his favorite. Greasy and laden with artery-clogging processed cheese, he would get it to go along with a double order of onion rings, a cherry Pepsi and a slice of Miss Vivian's famous orange cake.

"Bon appétit, Highwayman," she said as she began washing the lettuce. "Enjoy it while you can."

Into a large bowl she dropped sliced cherry tomatoes, green peppers and pepperoncini peppers, green onions, sliced mushrooms, black olives and green olives, celery, broccoli, cauliflower, carrots, cucumbers, radishes, bean sprouts, a quarter cup each of walnuts, bacon bits and golden raisins, parmesan and a handful of shredded mozzarella cheese and—last but not least—a homemade virgin olive oil, balsamic vinegar and oregano salad dressing to toss with the veggies.

"Big enough for three people," she said as she looked at the bowl. "But I'm going to eat every last bit of it!"

Carrying it with her into the den, she turned on the TV and punched the remote that controlled the DVR. As the movie she'd watched every day for over two weeks began to play yet again, she tucked her legs under her in Clay's big, overstuffed chair and took the first forkful of salad.

Chapter Eleven

Still full from the salad she'd inhaled the night before, Allison forewent breakfast and headed to Bainbridge—a town about thirteen miles to the south of Colquitt. She had brought along some Celtic music CDs for company. One of them was by Loreena McKennitt and it was her CD she pushed into the player first. The fifth track was "The Highwayman" and she hit the skip button until that song began.

She'd dreamed of Drew the night before. Just as she did most nights. In the dream he was the highwayman, Declan O'Shay. He swept her up on his midnight black steed and they galloped along the seacoast as a full moon sailed across the heavens. He took her to a thatched cottage and carried her inside to lay her down upon his bed. There he made love to her over and over again as a soft rain fell beyond the windows. Even now she felt the delicious weight of his body pressing her down into the mattress. The caress of his hands upon her breasts. The stroke of it between her legs. His kisses were wine sweet and as passionate as the man himself. He had taken her with command and possessiveness.

It was the light bump that shook her out of her revelry but it was the yelp of agony that put her foot hard on the brake. She brought the car to a stop and looked in the rearview mirror.

"No," she cried and fumbled with the gear shift to put it in park. Not even bothering to turn off the car, she shoved open the door and jumped out.

The dog lay panting in the middle of the highway. She hadn't seen it. Her mind had been on the dream.

"No, no, no, no, *no*," she whispered as she knelt down on the pavement beside the injured animal. "Oh, sweetie, no."

Her hand trembled as she stretched it toward the dog. Blood was seeping from its mouth and she knew it was badly hurt. Her heart broke as she put her hands under its body. It yelped again and she snatched her hands back, afraid of hurting it more.

The sound of an approaching vehicle barely registered as she tried once more to lift the little animal. The heartrending howl of pain just wouldn't allow her to pick it up.

"Go open the door. I'll bring the pup."

She looked up and sucked in a harsh breath.

"Come on, Allison. Open the door for me. We don't have much time!"

He was already lifting the dog, ignoring the pitiful whimper and yowl of agony, not even flinching when the animal, out of pain and fear, bit him on the arm. He started toward the passenger side of the car he was driving.

She scrambled to her feet, hurried after him, glancing back to her car that was parked on the side of the road. "My car?" she questioned for lack of anything else to say.

"It's fine where it is. Get your keys, lock it up, then open my door, Allison. Now!"

Once she had the door open, he got in with the dog clutched tightly to his chest.

"It's gonna be all right, fella," he said in a calm voice. "We're gonna take care of you."

The animal was making a sound that tore at Allison's very soul. She looked down at the man holding it as tears streamed down her cheeks.

"There's a vet on the north side of town. Let's go," he ordered. "Now."

She nodded and shut the door, ran to her car, turned it off, pulled out the keys and locked the door behind her. She ran around the front of his vehicle and slid behind the wheel.

"I didn't see it," she said. "It ran out in front of me and—"

"Just drive," he said. His voice was firm, emotionless—which was what was needed at that moment—and filled with support.

She put the car in gear and stepped down heavily on the accelerator. It was the longest ten minute drive she'd ever taken

The dog was in with the vet. She was sitting on the bench outside the room shaking from head to toe. The receptionist had tried to comfort her but she could not—would not—be comforted. Her guilt wouldn't allow it. She had hurt a defenseless animal. It might die because of her. She felt as low as the scum on the underside of a snail's belly and couldn't stop crying. When he came out, she knew from the sadness in his eyes what he was going to say.

"No," she said, shaking her head.

He sat down on the bench beside her and took her hand in his. She looked down at that strong male hand and wanted to nestle her cheek into its palm. "I told them to put it down," he said.

"No," she whined.

He slipped his free arm around her, pulled her to him. "The little thing is in pain, Allison. We can't allow it to suffer. You know that, baby."

She looked into his eyes. His beautiful, kind blue eyes. "I didn't see it, Drew. I wasn't paying attention."

"It was an accident," he said. He released her hand to thumb away the tears from her eye. His voice was so gentle, so supportive. "You didn't mean to do it."

"I didn't see it." She broke down again. This time great wracking sobs tore from her.

He cupped her head in his hand and crooned softly to her, let her cry against his chest. When she'd cried herself out, when all that was left was hiccupping and an occasional low whimper of grief, he eased her out of his arms. The vet's assistant was standing beside the reception desk with a cardboard box in his arms.

"Would you take it out to my truck?" Drew asked.

She stared at the box and felt her heart breaking all over again. "He won't let me bury it at home," she whispered.

"You don't worry about that. I'm gonna take it home with me," he said. "I'll see to burying it."

She nodded as she swiped at her face. "Drew, I need to get my car. He'll be mad if I don't get his supplies," she told him.

"Sweetie, you're in no condition to drive," the receptionist told her.

"No, she isn't. Would you call the high school in Colquitt? Ask for Coach Bennett. Tell him what happened and that he needs to come get his wife. He'll need to bring someone along with him to drive her car back to town."

"You have to leave," she said. "Please, just go. You can't—"

"I'm not leaving you here alone," he stated emphatically. "I will stay until he gets here."

It was the worst possible thing he could do but she was grateful for his company. Hopefully they would get a chance to explain to Clay what had happened before her husband blew up.

* * * * *

The sound of brakes squealing, then a door being slammed hard brought Drew to his feet. Clay Bennett came storming into the vet's office as though his ass was on fire. He swung his hateful gaze straight at Drew, then marched over to him with his fists clenched.

"What the hell are you doing here with my woman?" he demanded.

"I ran over—" Allison started to say but Clay swung his angry face toward her.

"Was I talking to you?" he snarled.

"That's uncalled for, Bennett," Drew told him. "She's upset enough as it is."

Clay spun back around. "You got a problem, Dunne? You want one? You had no business coming here with my woman."

"What was I supposed to do? Keep driving? She was on her knees in the middle of the highway."

"She should have called *me*. I would have come for her," Clay snarled. "I will *always* come for her," He came toe-to-toe with Drew and seemed surprised when Drew didn't back up. "She is my *wife*. I will always come for her."

"Then take her home," Drew told him. "That's where she needs to be."

"Get the fuck out of here before I beat the shit out of you," Clay yelled at him loud enough that the vet and his assistant came out of the back.

"What's going on here?" the vet asked. "I could hear you clean outside."

"Mind your own business," Clay snapped without looking around. He crowded Drew even more but when an older man and a strapping young black man stepped to either side of him, he took a reluctant step back.

Drew looked over at Allison. "Are you going to be okay?"

"Don't talk to my woman," Clay bellowed. *"Don't you even look at her."*

"Sir, you need to calm down before I have my receptionist call the police," the older man said sternly. "I will not have a brawl in my clinic."

"You wanna take this outside, Dunne?" Clay growled.

"Clay, please," Allison said, getting up and coming over to him. She put a trembling hand on his brawny arm. "He was only trying to help."

Clay shrugged off her hand. "Go get in the truck," he commanded. When she hesitated, he literally growled at her.

Allison hurried out of the building.

"Does it make you feel like a big man to scare a little woman like her?" Drew asked.

"What I do with my wife is none of your fucking business."

"Like what you do with mine is none of *my* fucking business?" Drew threw back at him.

The man standing in front of him turned a bit pale. "You goddamned little prick," he ground out. "I'll—"

"Gentlemen, please," the vet said. "There is a lady present."

Drew looked at the receptionist. "I apologize, Katey." He raked a hand through his hair. "If you'll tell me how much the bill is, I'll pay it and leave."

"We'll send it to the dealership," she said, looking apprehensively from him to Bennett.

"Thank you," Drew said. "And thanks, Doc." He turned toward the door, peripherally aware of Bennett coming after him but then Jonas—Doc's assistant—stepped in front of Clay.

"Beggin' your pardon but there ain't gonna be no fightin' in this buildin', sir," the young man stated.

Clay made to push him aside to go after Drew, but obviously thought better of it. Instead, he pointed a finger at Drew.

"You come anywhere near my woman again and I'll shatter your life like a wrecking ball. You even look at her and I swear to God you'll regret it," he bellowed but Drew ignored him.

Allison was sitting in the passenger side of Bennett's truck with her face in her hands. When the door opened and she saw Drew come out she gave him a beseeching look. He shook his head, got in his truck and started it up. After one last look at her, he backed out of the parking slot and was gone.

* * * * *

On his way back to Colquitt Drew was grinding his teeth so hard it was giving him a bitching headache. All his life he'd backed down to males like Clay Bennett because he simply didn't have the build or the training to take them on. When he was in high school he was in pretty good shape but back then no one—other than Wade— laid a hand on him. Whether that was out of sympathy for the abuse he suffered at his father's hands or the boys were afraid of Wade, he didn't know. It didn't matter. It wasn't until he got to college where no one knew him that he'd had a fight or two. None of which he won. He'd had his ass handed to him because he knew next to nothing about fighting.

Then had come that fateful day on the UF football field when Chip Brantley had shattered his thigh.

Maybe Doc was right. Maybe he needed to bulk up, start training. He was developing a bit of a gut, but he hadn't really cared until Allison came into his life. He hadn't cared about how he was treated. Humiliation could eat away at a man's soul until there was nothing left of his bravery and that had happened to him.

Today, that bravery had come creeping back. It had its tail between its legs still but it was beginning to show its teeth.

And Allison had been the catalyst.

He had held her. Sweet, merciful Jesus he had held her to him. He had inhaled the gardenia perfume in her hair and felt the slightness of her slender body encased in his arms. He thought— though he couldn't remember if he had or not or just wanted to—he kissed the top of her head at one point as he tried to console her. It hadn't been an embrace of passion but one of comfort. It had seemed natural, right to draw her into his arms. He hadn't been thinking of anything except calming her, supporting her, absorbing the grief that was flowing from her.

But now, he thought about her body so close to his. His arms around her. His hand cupping her head. The way she had clung to him. The trust in her eyes as she looked to him to make things right. His entire being ached with the memory of her pressed against him.

He shifted in the seat, his cock aching with the memory, too. He reached down to rub the bulge.

"What I do with my wife is none of your fucking business."

Those words were like a whiplash between his shoulders. They burned all the way through to his core. The mere thought of Bennett putting his hands on Allison, his cock inside her, sent red-hot waves of scalding fury through Drew. He pulled hard against the steering wheel, then unwrapped the fingers of his right hand, clenched them into a fist, then beat savagely at the wheel.

"Goddamn son of a bitch!" he shouted at the top of his lungs. It stung to know Bennett had the right to do whatever he pleased to Allison—well almost—and there was nothing she could do to stop him. He'd seen the fear in her eyes. He knew precisely what the flinch he'd witnessed meant. Bennett had gotten physical with her at some point. That immediate response had told a tale that disturbed him deeply.

He was nearing the turnoff to his house. He'd taken an early lunch to go down to Bainbridge to surprise Allison and he was due back right about now.

"Fuck it," he snarled.

He didn't slow down as he reached the turnoff. He jacked the wheel to the right and spat gravel as he took the driveway. Terri's Lincoln was parked in front of the garage and that just pissed him off. She was blocking his side. It angered him so much he was tempted to ram the damned thing and push it into the garage. As it was, he laid his hand on the horn and kept it there.

Petty retaliation from a petty mind, he thought, but what the hell difference did it make? She sure as hell wouldn't come out to move the car so he just pulled right up until his bumper touched her.

"Just try to get out now," he mumbled.

As though she'd heard him, Terri appeared in opening of the bay. Her hands were on her hips and when he got out of the truck, she tossed her head.

"What do you think you're doing?" she asked. She looked him up and down. "Whose blood is that on you?"

"Parking on my side of the driveway," he said without missing a step. "What are *you* doing, wife?"

He started past her but she blocked his path. "I asked you whose blood that is!"

"Sorry to disappoint you, but it isn't mine. Now if you'll excuse me I need something to drink before I bury the dog that's in the back of my truck."

"Not on my property you won't," she snapped. "I want you to move that truck," she ordered.

He smiled. "No."

"You'd better."

"Or what?" he challenged. "You'll tattle to your daddy?" His smiled widened. "Go ahead but when you do, you tell him I think he should know where you've been going the past two Wednesdays."

Her eyes widened. "I don't know what you're talking about."

"Sure you do, Terri," he said. "You've been off fucking the new coach. He's been inside your cunt as many times as your tampon I would imagine."

She stiffened, squared her shoulders. "I'm not going to dignify that asinine remark by addressing it."

"Baby, you wouldn't know dignity if it jumped up and bit you on your scrawny ass," he said and continued through the garage.

"Unlike that trollop you're salivating after?" she yelled at him.

He didn't take the bait. Shutting the door to the mudroom behind him he twisted the lock. The little demon that was riding him hard giggled in his ear. He was halfway across the kitchen when she began pounding on the door. After swiping a bottle of raspberry white tea from the fridge, he twisted the cap, downed half the bottle, then wiped his mouth with the back of his hand. He walked through the great room and out the double French doors and headed for the gardener's shed to fetch a shovel.

Chapter Twelve

The mayor's wife—her name was Heddy Tabb—had left four voicemails. Allison heard her strident voice coming over the line as Clay listened to the messages. He turned to glare at her.

"You were supposed to be at the hospital by noon," he accused. He glanced at his watch. "It's one now."

"I'll call her and explain what happened," she said as she ran the heel of her hand under her chin. "I'll go in tomorrow instead."

"Well, now you've made that an impossibility, haven't you, Allie?" he snapped.

As she cowered against the base cabinet, she watched him as he dialed Mrs. Tabb. His whole demeanor changed as he spoke to the old bat. His blue eyes gleamed with humor but deep within them was the fiery spark that had ignited the moment he closed the door behind them. She listened as he told one lie after another to the mayor's wife.

"She gets these things about twice a year and when she does, she just goes to bed and waits them out. They're usually stress related and what with her hitting that poor little dog. She has a very tender heart when it comes to animals." He was quiet, then nodded. "Yes, ma'am. They're what you call cluster migraines and they really take their toll on her, let me tell you." Another long silence, then a purr was added to his voice. "I sure will. I'm going to check on her before I go back up to the school. Best thing for her is just to sleep." He laughed. "Thank you, Heddy. I truly appreciate your concern. You have a good one, now."

When he hung up, he turned and looked down at her where she was curled on the floor. His face was no longer jovial as his hands went to the belt at his waist.

* * * * *

When he'd tamped down the last shovelful of dirt, Drew leaned his wrists on the top of the handle and lowered his forehead to them. He shouldn't have dug the hole. Now his side was throbbing mercilessly. He didn't think he'd done any harm but with his luck, it probably had. Closing his eyes to the pain he stood there for a moment or two until the worst of it passed, then straightened as best he could. Swinging the shovel over his left shoulder, he headed back to the house. In the distance lightning stitched across the sky and he turned to look at it. Dark clouds were building rapidly and the wind was picking up. By the time he reached the patio, the first few fat drops hit the fieldstone.

The first thing he noticed was the French doors were closed and the blinds lowered over them. He wasn't a betting man but if he was, he'd lay odds Terri had locked every outside door, engaged the security alarm and effectively blocked him from gaining entry. He saw a blind in the middle of one of the doors move and knew she was watching him. Instead of trying the door handle, he leaned the shovel against the wall, took off his work gloves and tossed them on the table by the door.

"If anyone needs me, I'll be down in Boykin with Corinne," he said and turned to go.

The French door opened so quickly he could have sworn he felt the lintel vibrate.

"No, hell, you *won't*," Terri yelled, rushing out of the house. Before she could hit him with the hand she raised over her shoulder, he ducked under it and sprinted into the house. He heard her curse, then yell, "Bastard."

Taking the stairs two at a time, he laughed all the way to his bedroom. It was a good thing the ruse worked because his truck keys and cell phone were on his dresser and it would have been a long walk to Early's house.

Stripping off his shirt, which had dried blood smeared across the front, he looked at it, then stuffed it into the garbage. No one was going to try to get the stain out anyway. He undressed and climbed into the shower hoping the hot water would help the pain that was reasserting itself in his side.

It didn't, so he was quick with his shower, turned off the water, climbed out and wrapped a towel around his hips. As he got near the full-length mirror on the door, he stopped and took a good look at his body. He didn't like what he saw. A man in his prime shouldn't look the way he did. Putting his hands to his midsection, he was annoyed that he could take hold of a roll of flab that hung there.

"Get in here, Andrew."

Her strident voice made him jump. How the hell had she gotten into his room? he wondered, then remembered the door hadn't been fixed since the EMTs kicked it in.

"Did you hear me?"

Clenching his jaw, he opened the bathroom door but she wasn't in the room. The door was standing wide open.

"Son of a bitch," he snarled. His keys were gone from the dresser.

Hurrying from the room, he got to the foot of the stairs at the exact moment he heard his truck start up, then winced as he heard the gears grinding. Terri didn't know how to drive a standard transmission and the truck was screaming in protest. He flung open the front door in time to see his pride and joy bucking backward down the driveway.

"Stop," he shouted as he ran. Loose rocks from the gravel drive had migrated to the pavement in front of the garage and the soles of his feet found every one of the sharp edges.

The truck lurched to a stop about twenty feet from the garage. Terri got out, drew back her arm and pitched the keys into the tall pampas grass that grew in a long thick cluster along the side of the house.

"That's what you get for blocking me in," she hissed at him as she marched past to her car. She opened the door, then turned to glare at him. "For the love of Jesus, put on some clothes. Just looking at you makes me sick."

He watched her back down the driveway like a crazy woman, then whip the car onto the highway. She left rubber behind as she floored the accelerator.

For a long moment he just stood there staring at the place where she'd thrown his keys. It wasn't just the truck key that was on the key ring. There were keys to the safe-deposit box, the post office box, house, office and a few others.

"Shit," he said tiredly. He had duplicates of everything except the safe-deposit box key but that would be easy enough to replace. Trouble was, the duplicates were in his desk drawer at work.

Turning around to look at his truck, he realized he should get a magnetic box for a spare key to hide somewhere on the undercarriage. Probably learn how to hotwire a car, too.

And call someone over to fix the goddamned door to his bedroom.

Putting a hand to his right side he hobbled back into the house. The bottoms of his feet were hurting from the gravel. He went directly to the wall phone in the kitchen and dialed his office.

"Five County Motors, this is Lenore. How may I direct your call?"

"It's me," he said. "Would you buzz the shop? I need to talk to Early and listen, I'll need you to let him in my office to get something for me."

"You sick?" she asked.

"Sorta," he replied. "My side is hurting. While I'm waiting on Early would you please call Doc Mackie's office and see if you can get me an appointment this afternoon. I'd really appreciate it. Call me at the house to let me know what time he can see me."

"Will do. I'm gonna put you on hold. Feel better, son."

The music that started playing made him wince. Another cheating wife and dog song. How many were there out there? He made a mental note to look into buying some easy listening music instead of country.

"Hey, whatcha need?"

"I need you to look in the bottom right drawer of my desk. There's a gunmetal colored box and in it are a set of keys. Bring them out here to the house, willya?"

"Sure thing. Lenore said you were hurting. Need me to take you to the vet? Is it time for your distemper shot again?"

Though his cousin's words were meant to get a rise out of him, they hit too close to home and they made him angry.

"Just get out here," he said and hung up. He slumped against the counter for a moment, then pulled out one of the bar stools. He was about to sit down when the phone rang. He picked it up. "Yeah?"

"Doc said to come on up now," Lenore said. "I told him Early was on his way out there."

"Thanks, Lenore," he said.

While he waited for Early, he sat gingerly on the stool and laid his head on his crossed arms on the counter. The pain in his side wasn't worse but it was persistent with every breath he took. When he heard gravel crunching outside, he realized he couldn't very well go to Doc's office clad only in a towel.

Although there were probably some folks who wouldn't bat an eyelash at anything odd he did.

Trudging up the stairs wasn't an option so he sat where he was until Early came in through the mudroom. Idly he thought if Terri knew his cousin had a key to the house, she'd pitch one holy hell of a fit.

"You going like that?" Early asked as he walked over to him. "Flapping in the breeze like that is sure gonna turn the womenfolk on."

"Go up and get me some clothes, willya?" he asked. "There's no way I can make it up the stairs."

Early frowned. "That bad?" He put the keys he'd brought on the counter.

"Bad enough."

"I'm guessing something happened to your other keys," he said as he started toward the great room door.

"She threw them somewhere out in the pampas," he replied.

"Figures," Early pronounced. "I'll come back with my metal detector and find 'em for you."

Putting his head back down on his arms, he tried not to breath very deep because when he did, a lancing pain went through his side. He prayed he hadn't done any damage to his abdomen because he really didn't want to go back into the hospital.

"Here you go," Early said when he returned. He had a pair of jeans and a shirt draped over his arm and a pair of boat shoes in his hand.

"No skivvies?" Drew asked.

"One less thing to try to get on you," Early said. He dropped the shoes on the floor, then hunkered down with the jeans in his hands. "Put your foot in."

Drew thrust his foot into one of the pant legs, then did the same with the other before he stood up. He dropped the towel and grinned as Early looked away.

"Don't be dangling that puny thang in my face," his cousin grumbled. With his face turned to the side, he tugged the jeans up Drew's hips. "You can tuck it in your own self."

"Plan to," Drew said as he adjusted himself in the jeans, then zipped them. He tried to button the fly but the pressure on his side was too much and he left it alone.

Early got to his feet and held the shirt out for Drew to put his arms through. "Did she hit you or something?"

He snaked his feet into the deck shoes as he stuck the keys Early had brought him into his pocket. "No."

"You didn't do something to yourself," Early accused. "What happened?"

"I'll tell you on the way."

* * * * *

Doc shook his head. "A hole, Andrew? You dug a hole?"

"Somebody had to," Drew defended his actions. "I wasn't gonna leave the poor thing in my truck bed."

"I could have done it if you'd asked," Early said. He was leaning against the wall with his arms crossed over his chest.

"Well, the good news is it's not a hernia. You better be glad the abdominal wall is pretty tough," Doc said. "I think what you did was pull a muscle. I'll have Becky give you a shot of tramadol."

"What's that?" Early queried.

"A muscle relaxer," Doc answered. He looked at him. "You're driving, right?"

"Yes, sir."

"Good because he has a low threshold for strong meds—always has—and it's gonna knock him for a loop. You'll have just enough time to get him home and to bed before it really kicks in. I want him to sleep. I'll give you a prescription to have filled. When you do, you put it in his hand and not hers," Doc stressed.

"Gotcha." Early grinned. "Can I draw a funny mustache on him while he's out?"

"You better not," Drew mumbled.

"Not to say *she* won't," Early said with a wink. "Hell, she might even whack something off."

"You get someone to fix my damned door," Drew said. "That fat-ass Bubba Henry broke it."

"Only way he had to get you to the hospital, son," Doc reminded him. "Stay here and I'll send Becky in with the shot. She'll give you a list of things to watch out for while you're on the med. I'll call Jake and run interference for you."

"Again," Drew said.

"Any time it's needed, son," Doc said with a pat to Drew's back.

"He's a good man," Early said when Doc had gone.

"Always has been," Drew replied.

The shot hurt like hell but as soon as he pulled his jeans up, it began to take effect.

"He's gotta wait ten minutes before you take him home," the nurse said. "You can pull around to the side entrance. No reason for the people in the waiting room to see him staggering out."

"You're pretty, Becky," Drew said, grinning at her. "I ever tell you that?"

"Not that I recall," Becky said with a snort.

"Well, you are. Don't know why I never asked you out in high school."

Becky and Early exchanged a look.

"Might have been because she's twenty years older than you," Early said wryly.

"Shot's working," Becky said. "Go get your car, Early."

* * * * *

Early was having to hold his own stomach as he rolled Drew onto his back. His cousin had sang—at the top of his voice and in a key that probably only bats should have been able to hear—about some cheating dog messing with another dog's bitch and her not knowing who her puppy daddy was. The words had made no sense whatsoever and he'd nearly driven off the road twice he was laughing so hard.

"Easy does it," he said as Drew tried to get up. "Come on, now. Lay back down and let me get your shoes off."

"He sniffed her butt and she whomped him with her tail, told him to go on out and piss on the rail…"

"Good Lord almighty, Drew," Early said, shaking his head. "Just shut the hell up, willya. I'm dying here."

Getting Drew's pants and shirt off and him into a pair of boxer briefs was the hardest thing Early had ever had to do. If Doc hadn't advised undressing him so he'd be comfortable, he'd have left his cousin in his jeans and shirt.

"Take this dog and shove him. He ain't humping here no more. He done went and got her…"

"Shut up!" Early said. He couldn't take anymore.

Drew clamped his mouth shut. "Don't be mean to my dog, Rawls."

"You don't have a dog, Dunne," Early told him. "Not shut up and get to sleep."

Drew mumbled something Early didn't think was complimentary to him or his mother but let it pass. His cousin would be mortified the next morning and that would be time enough to let him hear the recording he'd been making with his cell phone as soon as Drew started singing.

Another mumble and then Drew rolled over to his stomach—which was how he normally slept—and began snoring.

Early chuckled, then went over to look at the door. He could fix it himself but it would take some doing and would be noisy in the process. He just had to hope Terri would leave Drew alone while he slept off the drug. Going to the closet, he found a lightweight blanket, took it down, then came back to the bed to throw it over Drew's legs.

"Dream of loose women with big boobs and little snatches," he told his cousin, then left.

Chapter Thirteen

He pushed up from the bottom of the bed, flowed over her, then turned to his side, drawing her with him to press her tightly to his side. One hand went to the back of her head to cup her face against his shoulder. Placing a gentle kiss on her brow, he put his leg over hers to meld her to him.

They lay like that for a moment or two without speaking, then she craned her head to look up at him. There was wonderment in her beautiful gaze.

"I had no idea," she whispered. Her fingers plucked nervously at the hair between his pectorals.

"That is only the tip of the iceberg," he said and kissed her again.

He was still as hard as stone—aching with need—but he just lay there holding her, not moving for fear he'd shame himself upon her.

"I want you inside me," she said. Her face turned red the moment the words left her mouth and she tucked her bottom lip between her teeth.

"And I want to be inside you," he said. He stroked her hair. "Are you ready for that, milady?"

She nodded.

One final kiss on her brow and he eased her from his arms. She turned to her back and opened her legs to him. He rose up, moved his body over hers. His cock pulsed as he wrapped his fist around it to guide it between her legs. He placed the tip to her damp folds and...

* * * * *

"Wake the hell up, Drew."

Drew shot up in the bed with a gasp. His head spun unmercifully and the inside of his mouth tasted like iron filings had been dumped in it. He had to grab hold of the edge of the mattress to steady the room.

"What are you doing in bed in the middle of the damned day?"

The strident, angry shriek coming from his wife's twisted mouth drove a sharp pain through his head.

"Answer me," she shouted as she stomped over to the bed.

"Shit," he mumbled. He glanced at her and saw the lady's maid from his dream and groaned. "Go away, you horse-faced shrew."

It was the wrong thing to say for she lashed out—hitting him on the side of the head with enough force to knock him sideways.

"Get the hell out of that bed. *Now*," she screamed so loud he had to put his hands over his ears to shut out the sound.

"Leave him alone."

It was Early's voice that interrupted whatever else Terri had been about to say. She spun around and opened her mouth to yell at his cousin but there were two men with him and she no doubt thought better of it.

"What are you doing here, and who are those men?" she asked.

"They are here to fix the door," Early said. He looked past her. "You all right, cuz?"

Drew nodded. "Groggy but the pain is gone."

Terri snapped her head toward him. "What pain?"

"I took him to Doc Mackie," Early replied for him. "Doc gave him a shot and that's why he's in bed."

"*What* pain?" Terri demanded as though she hadn't heard Early.

"I pulled a muscle in my side," he said. "Nothing for you to worry about."

"I'm *not* worried," she replied with a snort, then lowered her voice so only he heard her last words. "You can die for all I care."

That said, she spun on her heel and went to the door, all but shoving one of the men out of her way as she left the room.

"Bitch," Early pronounced. He came over to the bed. "You sure you're okay?"

"Yeah," Drew said. "Gimme my pants, will you?" He gingerly sat up and cautiously swiveled his legs over the side of the bed.

Early looked around at the men as he retrieved Drew's pants from the chair by the bathroom door. "Go on ahead and fix the door." He brought the pants to Drew.

"We're gonna need to put a whole new jamb on here," the taller of the two men said. "This one is too busted up to hold."

"Do whatever you need to," Early said. "Just send the bill to the shop."

"Will do."

Drew leaned back, thrust his legs into the pants, and then sat there with them unzipped as a wave of dizziness took over.

"Wanna come stay with me tonight?" Early asked. "Ain't no telling what she might do once we're gone."

Both men looked around with curious glances and Drew knew there would be another groundswell of gossip making the rounds before nightfall. He hadn't missed the look that passed between the two men when they saw the heavy-duty lock on the inside of the door.

"It'll be fine," he told his cousin though he should take Early up on the offer.

"You sure?" Early pressed.

"Yeah, I'm sure," Drew said on a long sigh. "You should get back to the shop before Whip has a fit." He got up and made his way into the bathroom.

"You call me if you need me," he heard Early say as he closed the bathroom door.

He went to the sink, took hold of the edge of the vanity and let his chin sag to his chest. His head was spinning violently and there was a mild twitch of pain in his side so he knew he needed to lie back down until it passed but he didn't want to take to his bed while the workers were fixing the door. Instead, he straightened, turned on the water, cupped his hands under the strong flow, then splashed his face until the cold water partially revived him. Running his wet hands down his cheeks, he peered into his own reflection in the mirror. He hated what he saw staring back at him.

Chapter Fourteen

The first really cold day of October came like a thief slinking out of the night. A hard freeze took all the dying blooms from the bushes and crinkled the leaves and dehydrated the last of the tomatoes clinging to the withered vines. A crisp wind skirled around the eave and blasted him in the face as he started down the driveway to the mailbox. Though all the important mail he and Terri received was delivered to their box at the post office, the *Albany Herald* newspaper arrived like clockwork every day—along with advertisements and the occasional piece of junk mail.

It was early—not yet six o'clock—and he had put on a pot of coffee to drink while he read the Sunday paper. His wife generally got up late every day and the Lord's Day was no exception. She'd stay wrapped in her covers until it was absolutely necessary to get up to get ready for church. Almost always, they got there late because tardiness was a way of life with Terri.

A car went by on the highway just as Drew got to the mailbox and the driver honked her horn. He lifted his hand to wave at the woman who had been the recipient of many of his wet dreams as he was growing up. He watched her tail lights come on and she stopped, backed up, then the passenger side window went down.

"Hey good-lookin'," she said, leaning down so she could peer at him through the window. "Whatcha got cookin'?" She winked. "Wanna cook somethin' up with me?"

"Hey yourself, beautiful," he replied. He went over to her car and leaned his elbows on the opening. "Where you going so early, Corinne?"

"I'm heading to Memaw's," she answered. "Today's her ninetieth birthday."

"No kidding? How is Miss June?" he inquired of the woman who had been a holy terror in Miller County back in the day. She was now a resident in an assisted living facility in Macon.

"Spryer than me and you," she told him. "Not a tooth in her head but that don't stop her from gumming up any steak you put in front of her."

He laughed. "You tell her I said hey."

"How you been?" Corinne asked. "I heard you had your appendix taken out."

"I'm right as rain now," he said with a cock of his right shoulder. "What about you? You doing okay?"

"Can't complain," she answered, then looked past him. "We're being spied on."

He turned his head and looked back up the driveway. His wife was standing on the concrete pad in front of the double garage with her hands on her hips. Even from a distance he saw the fury on her face. He sighed, hung his head, patted the car door opening twice, then pushed away from the car. He straightened on a long sigh, jammed his hands into his pockets. "Whoopee," he grumbled.

"She's going to give you holy hell for talking to the town slut," Corinne said.

"She doesn't need a reason to give me holy hell, baby," he mumbled.

"Better get your scrawny white ass back to her," Corinne told him.

"Yeah." He smiled, digging his hands into his pockets. "You drive careful, you hear?"

"As careful as Jeff Gordon," she said. "Tell your wife I said fuck you."

Drew laughed. "I don't think so."

"Hey baby, I *would* fuck you," she said. "Anywhere, anytime." She winked. "And in any way you wanted me to. That bitch is just plain crazy for not loving you." She put the car in gear and peeled rubber.

Squaring his shoulders, he pulled his hands from his pockets and turned to the mailbox to get the paper. When he glanced toward the house, he was relieved to see Terri no longer watching him.

He knew the reprieve would last only as long as it took him to walk from the road to the kitchen door.

* * * * *

He'd been right. As he drove them to town she kept up the same barrage of hateful, offensive comments she'd begun hurling at him as soon as he'd walked into the house.

"You nasty bastard," she'd shouted. "How dare you stand out there talking to that filthy slut where anybody driving by could have seen you?"

"No one drove by, Terri," he said. "No one saw us."

"They could have."

"Well, they didn't."

She narrowed her eyes. "You want to fuck that skank, don't you?"

The words came out of his mouth before he could stop them.

"I've already fucked her," he said. When she gasped, more words he knew he would live to regret left his lips. "I've fucked her a helluva lot more than I've ever fucked you."

"You and every swinging dick in the five counties," she threw back at him.

"Yeah, well, at least I got pleasure out of fucking *her*," he said between clenched teeth.

And of course she hit him. Several times before kicking him. Par for the course.

He eased up on the accelerator as they came into town. She was still mouthing off but he had tuned her out as soon as he'd pulled onto the highway and wasn't listening. When they arrived at the church, he took the last available parking space, put the car in park, turned off the engine and was out the door while she was in mid-sentence. He was halfway to the church door before she caught up to him—grabbing his arm and digging her long nails into his sport coat.

"You are a son of a bitch," she hissed. A sideways glance at her saw her lips stretched into a forced smile.

He made no comment, ushering her inside the church doors as a dutiful husband would. Eyes were on them as they made their way down the aisle to the family pew where her father was already seated.

It wasn't in Big Jake's wheelhouse to move over. Drew had to step over him and down two spots so Terri could sit between them. He didn't greet his father-in-law and had received no greeting to return. Sitting down, he saw Terri reach for her father's hand. He knew what that meant even before he heard Jake ask what was wrong.

"I'll tell you after church," Terri said and rested her head on her father's shoulder for a moment. As she did, Big Jake turned his hostile stare on Drew.

Throughout the church service Drew sat staring at the choir. Thad and Boyd Dykes—the local moonshine distributors—both had black eyes and cut lips. He wondered if they'd gone after one another or someone else had accommodated their habit of wanting to fight. Twice he caught Bobby Daniels glaring at him but that wasn't anything new. The sheriff hated him with more fervor than made sense. To his knowledge he'd never done anything to Bobby or the man's family.

Somewhere behind him he knew Allison would be sitting with Bobby's new best friend, Coach Clay. He didn't have to wonder why Bennett preferred to sit in the back behind the Thompson pew. He knew.

"You even look at her and I swear to God you'll regret it."

He wished he could see her face. He dreamed of her verdant gaze and longed to have it bestowed upon him. The gentle green eyes never failed to give him peace.

And hope.

He drew in a long breath, then exhaled slowly, looking down at the worn bible he'd taken from the rack on the pew in front of him as the preacher labored on with what Drew thought had to be the most boring sermon he'd ever had the misfortune of sitting through. Idly flipping through the book, his attention was caught by one of the verses in Proverbs—"Do not lust in your heart after her beauty or let her captivate you with her eyes."

That made him uneasy so he moved on. The next verse his eyes fell upon made the hair on his arms stir.

"But I say unto you, that whosoever looketh on a woman to lust after her hath committed adultery with her already in his heart."

He started to close the book but before he could the pages seemed to come alive and fanned forward until they landed on the first book of the bible. He felt a cold chill undulate through him as he read the words from Exodus 20:17—"You shall not covet your neighbor's house. You shall not covet your neighbor's wife, or his male or female servant, his ox or donkey, or anything that belongs to your neighbor."

He closed the bible so forcefully those around him turned to stare—including Terri who gave him a withering look that would have stopped a thundering elephant in its tracks.

"Sorry," he muttered, replacing the bible in the rack. He clasped his hands together and clenched them between his knees for he was keenly aware they were shaking. He turned his full attention to the preacher—half expecting the ceiling to fall down on him for not having been listening to the sermon.

"And lastly let us consider the words found in First James, verses twelve through sixteen," Brother Gilbert said, then cleared his throat before continuing. "'Blessed is the man who remains steadfast under trial, for when he has stood the test he will receive the crown of life, which God has promised to those who love him. Let no one say when he is tempted, *I am being tempted by God,* for God cannot be tempted with evil, and he himself tempts no one. But each person is tempted when he is lured and enticed by his own desire. Then desire when it has conceived gives birth to sin, and sin when it is fully grown brings forth death. Do not be deceived, my beloved brothers.'"

A chorus of amens followed and then Brother Gilbert smiled. "Before we have our closing hymn I would like to once again remind those who will be helping with the Fall Festival supper and bonfire this year to please remain behind after the services for their assignments. Now bow your head and ask for God's love and mercy and understanding."

Drew lowered his head, closed his eyes and listened to every word of the benediction. When Brother Gilbert was finished, he gave the hymn number for the postlude.

"Please turn to number three hundred and ninety-three, 'Blessed Be The Ties That Bind.'"

The congregation got to its feet and Drew along with them. He didn't reach for the hymnal. The old standard had been one of his uncle's favorites and he knew the words of all four stanzas by heart. As he began singing, it dawned on him that Clay Bennett had told Jake that his wife was going to join the choir. He frowned, wondering why she never had.

* * * * *

Allison sat quietly beside Clay as the pastor's wife handed out sign-up sheets for the upcoming Fall Festival that was celebrated in lieu of allowing the church's children to go trick or treating. God forbid, she thought, you allow them to dress up in scary costumes and have a little fun.

"What a crock of shit," Clay said under his breath. He thought Halloween was one of the great joys of childhood. She suspected he and his friends had done more tricking than treating. "Do you believe this is a city-wide thing?"

"It used to not be that way," Bobby said. He was sitting next to Clay. "When I was a boy, we went trick or treating and no one thought the first damned thing about it. Certainly didn't equate it to devil worship."

"Out in the Midwest, they don't even call it Halloween," Whip put in. "They call it Beggar's Night." He shook his head. "What's this world coming to?"

"I miss sticking dog turds in a bag and setting it on fire on some old fart's front steps," Bobby said with a chuckle.

"I can think of a few things I'd like to do on Halloween night," Clay said. He was staring across the room and when Allison turned to look at what had garnered his attention, she realized it was Drew Dunne at whom her husband was staring so hard.

Bobby looked that way, too, and grunted. "I can think of some things myself," he stated.

"I heard him and his wife don't sleep together and he keeps his bedroom door locked every night," Clay said. "Why you think that is?"

"To keep her from manhandling him," Whip replied.

"Or from beating the hell out of him," Bobby chimed in.

"You reckon?" Clay asked.

"She's as mean as a rattlesnake and as crazy as bat shit," Whip said of his sister. "If I was married to her, I'd keep my door locked, too."

"She can be a handful," Clay stated with a nod.

"I'm sure you'd know," Allison mumbled and when he looked at her with an arched brow, she lowered her gaze.

"What did you say?" he demanded.

"Nothing," she whispered.

"I didn't think so," Clay snapped. "Why don't you go get me some coffee?"

She was happy to leave the men even if it was to cater to Clay's warped sense of proprietorship. She heard them laughing as she walked away and knew her husband had said something crude and uncomplimentary about her. As she walked, she kept sneaking glances at Drew. He was sitting beside his cousin but she knew he was tracking her movement across the room. She could almost feel his eyes on her and that sent a tingle down her spine.

And that brought a memory of his hands and how they had gently, tenderly held the injured dog. How they had gently and tenderly held her, wiped away her tears, gave her comfort.

She turned toward him to find him staring right at her. His lips moved into a soft smile and she gave him one in return.

"Where's that coffee, bug?" Clay called from across the room.

Heat flamed in her face. Digging her nails into her palms, she turned away from Drew and continued to the folding table upon which the coffee urn sat. A part of her wanted to march right past that table and outside. That same part knew that Drew would follow her and if he did, there would be trouble. She didn't care about herself but she didn't want that for him.

Never for him.

With her lips pressed together and her entire being filled with hopelessness, she reached for a Styrofoam cup and placed it under the urn's spigot.

* * * * *

"She can't keep her eyes off him," Clay grumbled.

Bobby nodded. "I can see that."

"Seems to be mutual," Whip added. "He better not let my own man see him looking at your wife thataway."

"Don't seem to mind Clay seeing him looking at her like he wants to pounce on her right here in public," Bobby replied.

"Maybe he ain't afraid of Clay," Whip suggested.

"Well, he outta be," Clay said in an ominous tone.

Bobby leveled his gaze on Drew. "You know I just thought of something I could do to make matters a bit more—shall we say—informative for Mr. Dunne?"

"Informative?" Clay repeated as he turned back to Bobby.

"Yeah," Bobby replied, nodding. "That is if you don't care."

Clay swept his attention back to Drew. "Whatcha got in mind?"

"Something that will take the vinegar right out of that limp pickle," Bobby said with a chuckle.

"You do whatever the hell you want to him," Clay said. "'Cause if I have to go after him, things are gonna get real ugly, real fast."

"Don't worry. Gimme a few days and I'll get her done for you. What I have planned for Drew Dunne is gonna ensure he stays the hell away from your woman and he keeps his eyes to himself. I'm gonna put the fear of God in that boy."

* * * * *

The men were putting up the tables. The women were spreading tablecloths and arranging dishes on the long picnic tables that would soon be groaning with potluck treats prepared by the ladies—and the occasional gentleman—of the First Baptist Church. In half an hour, the congregants would be arriving for the Fall Festival supper.

Drew was slumped on a hard folding metal chair with his legs thrust out in front of him, crossed at the ankles, clasped hands bracing his head as he semidozed. He'd been at the church all day. The heat in the building was on too high and he was hot. He was also bone-tired, had the headache from hell pressing at the back of his skull and felt as though his mouth had been stuffed with cotton.

"Are you asleep?"

Her voice brought his eyes open with a snap. He dropped his hands down.

"Ah, no," he replied, uncrossing his ankles and sitting up. "Just resting my eyes."

"Thirsty?" Allison asked, holding up a glass pitcher containing a pale pink liquid. "It's lemonade."

He wanted to tell her he was dying of thirst, that he wanted nothing more than to drink from her lips. It was a stupid, poetic and lame thing to say so he kept his mouth shut and simply nodded. He sat up, armed the sweat away.

"I'd like some but don't get too close," he warned. "I stink."

She smiled. "You look tired," she said.

"I am."

"How've you been?" she asked as she poured him a cup.

"Fine and you?"

"I can't complain." She handed him the lemonade and watched him take a sip. He felt her eyes staring hungrily at his throat as he swallowed and knowing she was doing that made his cock throb.

He lowered the cup, licked his lips and his cock stirred again as her eyes dropped to his mouth. He had to say something. Anything. To break the awkwardness of the moment.

"It's delicious. What's in it other than the lemonade?"

For a moment she didn't speak, then seemed to mentally shake herself before answering.

"Ah, I…I toss in a jar of maraschino cherries when I'm blending the lemon juice and sugar."

"Well, it is really good," he said. "Special treat from a special woman."

She blushed. "I'm glad you like it."

"What is it he's liking?"

Drew turned to find Terri standing a few feet away. He clenched his teeth, hoping she wouldn't cause a scene.

"The lemonade," Allison told her. "Would you like some, Mrs. Dunne?"

"No, thank you, Mrs. Bennett," Terri replied, putting emphasis on the Mrs. "I'll just have some of my husband's. After all, what's his is mine."

Allison's gentle smile faltered. She swept her eyes to Drew, then away.

"Thank you, Allison," he said softly but she only nodded her acceptance of his thanks as she walked away.

Terri stepped over to her to block her path, then lowered her voice.

"You stay away from Drew, you conniving cunt," she warned. "I may not want his lying, cheating ass but I'm not going to let you have it! If you go near him again, I'll jerk a knot on your head."

Allison hurried away from her.

"I heard what you said," he told Terri. "That was uncalled for."

Terri snorted. "You just can't keep away from her, can you?"

"I've been sitting here for twenty minutes, Terri. I didn't seek her out."

"You didn't need to. The little slut came to you. Like a filthy fly to honey."

He stared at her. "Why do you have to be like that? *Why* in the name of God do you have to be like that?"

"You go after her and Clay will come down on your ass like white on rice."

"Like he goes down on your ass?" he countered. He got to his feet.

She smiled meanly. "Why, Drew, are you jealous?"

He smiled back at her—even more hatefully. Leaning down, he spoke just loud enough for her to hear. "Not one bit."

"You fucked her yet?" Terri asked. "If you haven't you will. Until then why don't you get you that nigger girl in your office and fuck the shit out of her?"

He straightened up. The fumes from the scotch she'd been guzzling had blasted him in the face. "Why don't you go crawl back into your bottle?"

She slapped him. Hard as she could. Loud enough to draw everyone's attention. Nothing new. People gaped, smirked, laughed. Out of the corner of his eye he saw Allison turning away.

But not before he's seen the anger shifting across her lovely face.

* * * * *

"Shit," Drew snarled as he saw the blue light pulsing behind him. His headache had gotten much worst after his wife slapped him so he'd left the church to go home to try and sleep it off. He automatically glanced down at his accelerator but he was going the speed limit. Slowing down, he tried to remember if he'd looked at his taillights lately. Did one have a burned-out bulb? Had it gotten broken without him knowing it? He pulled onto the side of the road, turned off the engine. It was after eight, dark as pitch, cold as a witch's teat outside as he rolled down his window. He heard the door on what he thought was a state trooper's car open and frowned when he heard the sound of a second door opening, then the crunch of footsteps on the asphalt. He looked up as a shadowy form came up to his side of the truck and was blinded by the glare of a flashlight aimed into his face, put up an arm to shield his eyes.

"Insurance and registration."

"Bobby?" he questioned, feeling a heavy sensation in the pit of his belly.

The command was repeated. "Insurance and registration."

"Can you get that light outta my eyes?" he asked and before he could shift in the seat to take out his wallet, the door of his truck was snatched open.

"Out of the car," came the order.

He blinked. "What?"

A heavy hand grabbed him by the upper arm and tightened painfully.

"I said get out of the car."

Daniels would have pulled him from the seat had it not been for the seat belt that was holding him in place.

"All right," Drew said. "Let me unbuckle..." He stopped as the passenger door was pulled open and he saw Nick Hatcher, one of Bobby's deputies, leaning into the cab. The heaviness in his gut became a lead weight.

"Get out of the goddamned car, Dunne," Bobby shouted.

Realizing he was in deep shit, Drew hurriedly unbuckled the belt and twisted around to get out of the truck. His feet had barely touched the ground before Bobby spun him around and shoved him against the truck bed.

"Hands on your head," Bobby ordered.

"What's this about?" Drew asked. "I know I wasn't speeding." He grunted as Bobby kicked his legs apart and began to frisk him.

"Lookie what I found, Sheriff," Hatcher said.

Bobby aimed the flashlight at the deputy and through the rear window of the truck Drew saw Hatcher holding up a small clear bag. The deputy shook it and grinned—his face looking evil in the beam of Bobby's flashlight.

"That's not mine," Drew said.

"Drew Dunne, you are under arrest for possession of cocaine," Bobby said. He grabbed Drew's right wrist and jerked his hand down to the small of his back. "You have the right to remain silent." The tight band of a handcuff was snapped onto his wrist.

"That's not mine," Drew repeated. "You know goddamned well it isn't!" He was being set up. Hatcher had planted the drugs or else had it cupped in his hand before he ever opened the truck door.

"Anything you say or do can be held against you in a court of law," Bobby continued, dragging Drew's other arm down to cuff it.

"Did Bennett put you up to this?" Drew asked as Bobby brutally pulled him away from the truck.

"You have the right to an attorney. If you cannot afford an attorney, one will be appointed to you," Bobby said. His hand was like a steel vise around Drew's upper arm as he pulled him toward the cruiser.

"You're not going to get away with this, Bobby," Drew told him.

"Do you understand these rights as they have been read to you?" Bobby snatched open the back door of the cruiser. "Do you understand these rights as they have been read to you?" he asked again.

"Yes," Drew said, gritting his teeth.

"Yes what?" Bobby

Drew spoke through his clenched teeth. "Yes, I understand."

"Well, fucking good for you, you sawed-off piece of dog shit," Bobby said. He put one hand on the top of Drew's head and pushed Drew's head under the top frame of the door, then shoved him into the backseat.

"Those drugs aren't mine," Drew shouted but he knew it wasn't any use. They were framing him and doing a damned good job of it.

They took him to the jail, shoved him down in a chair.

"I want my lawyer," he told Bobby.

"Ain't gonna be my daddy," Bobby said with a grin.

"Then call Ray Reynolds. He's…"

"Outta town," Nick Hatcher said. He was standing across the room with his arms crossed, leaning one shoulder against the wall, loudly popping the gum in his mouth. He grinned. "Won't be back until next week sometime."

"That leaves old man Jenkins and he's probably already to bed at this time of night," Bobby said. "I'll contact him first thing in the morning."

Drew just stared at him, knowing full well what Daniels was doing. "I'm entitled to a phone call."

"Well, ordinarily I would be happy to oblige you on that one," Bobby said. He shrugged. "But we're having trouble with the phone lines."

"Trouble with them all day," Hatcher put in.

Clenching his bound hands tightly, Drew struggled not to lose his temper. He knew that was what they wanted. In as calm a voice as he could muster he asked if he could have his cell phone that had been confiscated as soon as he'd been brought into the jail.

"You got any bars in here, Hatch?" Bobby inquired.

"Not a single one," Hatcher replied. "Must be the old wiring in the walls, I'm guessing."

Drew slumped in the chair. There was no doubt what the two men were doing and that he had no options. "So what now?" he asked.

"We get you processed," Bobby said with a grin.

They took him to a room where he was uncuffed and told to strip. That had been embarrassing enough but after they made him shower in front of them Bobby had stepped in front of him and the embarrassment became humiliation.

"Lift your ball sack," he ordered.

Then the humiliation became deep, abiding shame when they'd ordered him to bend over. Hatcher did the honors and was rough in doing it. He shoved his finger hard inside Drew's rectum and twisted viciously. It was all he could do not to straighten up, turn around and hit the bastard.

The faded jeans and blue chambray shirt Bobby had tossed to him smelled of cigarette smoke and piss but he donned the foul-smelling clothes as well as the canvas shoes and followed Hatcher to the cell where he knew he was going to be spending the night. He only hoped it would be the one night but a niggling fear pressing against his throat warned that it might not. When the cell door clanged shut, he had to steel himself not to shudder.

"You sleep tight, now," Hatcher said. "Don't let the bedbugs bite."

The moment the lights were turned out, he fumbled his way to the cot along one wall and sat down. Drawing his legs up on the bare mattress he knew it was going to be a long, cold, sleepless night.

* * * * *

Facing the wall, curled into a fetal position with his knees drawn up to his chest and his arms wedged between the smelly mattress and the wall, he came instantly awake as soon as he heard the clank of metal to metal. The room was still dark but his eyes quickly adjusted to the gloom. He didn't need to wonder who had entered the cell.

Before he could turn over they were on him. They flipped him to his belly, one held his arms and another his legs pinned to the mattress while a third reached under him and unbuttoned, unzipped his jeans.

He called them every filthy name he'd ever heard but they didn't say a word to him as the third man pulled the jeans down to his ankles. They were going to gang rape him. He knew it as surely as he knew his name.

It was Bobby's hand that grabbed his hair, pulled his head back. Bobby's foul breath in his face as he spoke.

"You like staring at Clay's woman, Dunne? You wanna fuck her? Is that what you think you're gonna do?" He pulled brutally on Drew's hair. "Huh? Is that what you got planned?"

"No," Drew denied, tears forming in his eyes from the pain and from what he feared was about to happen.

"She's a good, decent woman," Bobby said. "Not a whore like good ole Corinne Wexler. You don't fuck a woman like Allie Bennett 'lest you're her husband and if you're her husband, you can fuck her 'til she screams. Is that what you want to do, Dunne? Fuck her 'til she screams."

"No," Drew said, tasting blood in his mouth where he had bitten his tongue.

Bobby reached down and grabbed Drew's right buttock. "Want me to fuck you 'til you scream?" He pinched hard enough to make Drew groan.

"I think he does," Hatcher said.

"I'm not gonna put my dick is this bastard's asshole," Bobby said and slapped Drew as hard as he could on the ass.

"Then use something else," the third man said and Drew's blood ran cold when he recognized his father's gravelly voice.

"You want that, Dunne?" Bobby purred in his ear. "You want me to shove something hard and thick up there? Maybe poke you hard a few times, make you bleed?"

Fear became stark terror. If they raped him with God only knew what, they could hurt him badly enough that he'd be shitting in a bag the rest of his life.

"Please," he heard himself say and bit down on his tongue.

"Little peckerwood is scared," Wade said with a laugh. "Go on, Bobby. Do it. Fuck him with your nightstick. Shove it way up there and tickle his tonsils with it!"

Bobby let go of his hair and moved down toward the foot of the cot. Something cold touched Drew's rectum and he cried out.

"Bobby, don't!" he pleaded. "Please don't!"

"You gonna leave her alone?" Bobby asked and pressed whatever it was he was holding harder against Drew's flesh.

"I haven't touched her," Drew said. "I swear to God I haven't."

"And you won't," Bobby said. "You know why?"

The pain was bad as the nightstick came down hard across the top of his thigh with a meaty whack. The hit was hard enough to make him yelp.

"Next time we pick you up, it's not gonna be powdered sugar in that little bag. It's gonna be the real thing and you're gonna go to jail for real. You understand me?"

"Yes," Drew said. His voice was shaking—not so much from the terror that had seized him but from the pain lancing down his leg.

"And it won't be me and Hatch and Wade visiting you in your cell. It's gonna be three big dick neo-Nazi bikers who are gonna make you their bitch after they beat the living shit outta you. You hear me?"

They left him drawn in upon himself with tears streaking his cheeks, teeth chattering and heart pounding like a trip hammer.

Chapter Fifteen

He couldn't look at anyone as he left the jail the next morning. Hatch and Chip Collins—one of the other deputies—were snickering at him as they led him from the cell. Though he didn't think anyone saw him leaving the building, he still felt as though every eye in town was zeroed in on him. Head down, shoulders hunched against the cold wind, hands deep in his pockets, he turned the corner and walked up the street toward the dealership. He had no idea where his truck was or if it was in one piece. As much as he loved the truck he didn't care all that much about it right then. He was disgusted with himself, ashamed of not being able to fight back, pissed that he'd been subjected to such humiliation.

And he hated Clay Bennett and Bobby Daniels more than he had ever hated anyone in his life. He'd never wished anyone dead.

Until now.

Looking up as he reached the bank on the corner, he saw Early going into the shop. True to his name, his cousin was the first one to arrive every morning. When Early saw him, he stopped, put his hands on his hips and waited for Drew to cross the street.

"What the heck are you doing here at this time of morning?" Early asked.

"Walk with me to the cemetery," Drew said, cocking his head to the west.

"The cemetery?" Early repeated. "What for?"

"Walk with me, Early," Drew snapped and turned down the street.

"Where the hell is your coat?" Early asked.

"In my truck."

"Which is where?"

"I don't know."

"You're gonna catch cold tramping around out here with no coat. You need—"

"Forget about the goddamned coat, Rawls," Drew hissed at him. "I'm not cold. I'm too mad to be cold."

"Who yanked on your tallywhacker this morning?" Early grumbled as he fell into step beside him.

"Just shut the hell up," Drew ordered.

Early stared at him but wisely kept his mouth shut as they headed for the cemetery that was across the highway. Once they were there, Drew went to his mother's grave. Inside the ten by ten foot square of marble coping, a single black gravestone sat above the black marble slab that had her name, dates and Beloved Mother carved into the stone. The gravestone read Rawls and not Dunne and the slab was centered in the middle of the marker. There would be no room for Wade Dunne to be buried beside Drew's mother—not that she would have welcomed him when he died. At the foot of the slab was a black marble bench and Drew sat down on one end of it, Early at the other end. Drew's entire attention was riveted on his mother's grave and he was quiet for so long it must've concerned Early.

"You wanna tell me what's going on?" Early asked.

The bob whites called to one another in the trees surrounding the cemetery. The occasional snick of tires passing on the highway broke the silence. Somewhere a dog barked. Otherwise the morning was still.

"You're starting to scare me, cuz," Early said, putting out a hand to touch Drew's shoulder. When Drew flinched away from him, Early's face creased with concern. "Tell me," he insisted.

Drew bent forward with his clasped hands dangling between his spread knees. He closed his eyes and told Early what had transpired the evening before. When he was finished, his cousin shot up from the bench, plowed a hand through his hair and cursed as he paced.

"Son of a fucking bitch," Early said. He spun around. "Why the hell would he do that?"

"Because Clay Bennett told him to," Drew said. "They're as fucking tight as a virgin's cunt these days."

Early's mouth dropped open. It was rare that Drew used such vulgar words. Hell and damn and the occasional shit but fucking and cunt? He shook his head as though to clear the words away.

"But why?"

Drew looked up at him. "Because Bennett thinks I'm screwing his wife."

That snapped Early's mouth shut with an audible clicking of his teeth. He seemed to need to gather himself before he asked, "Are you?"

Instead of answering, Drew unclasped his hands and reached down to pluck a dried leaf from the ground at his feet. "Remember when I tried walking across the top of that old swing set at the house?"

"Yeah, you fell and damned near broke your neck," Early replied. "What does that have to do with—?"

"What happened to that kid, Early?" Drew asked. "What happened to the kid who wasn't afraid to do something stupid like that?"

"He grew up," Early said with a shrug.

Drew shook his head. "No, man. No. Growing up isn't why I'm scared of my own shadow. They've put me down and kept me down ever since Uncle Carlton died." He began to tear off pieces of the leaf. "I think my courage died with him."

"Courage to do what exactly?"

"To stand up to men like Bennett and Daniels. To take what I want and damn the consequences."

"You mean Allison Bennett?" Early questioned.

"Yes."

Early's eyebrows drew into a V. "What'd I tell you about her, Drew? Just 'cause you've got an itch…"

"It's more than wanting to sleep with her, Early. I want *her*. I want the woman behind that gentle smile," Drew said softly. "I love her. I want her and I'm going to take her from him."

There was a loud explosion of breath as Early gaped at him. "Sweet Jesus, Drew. Coach is gonna kick the shit out of you. What the hell's wrong with you falling in love with another man's wife? What about your own wife?" He shook his head violently. "What about Big Jake?"

"I'm going to take her and leave," Drew said.

"You do know you're talking about committing adultery," Early reminded him. "I know damned well you were sitting in church a couple of Sundays ago and heard Brother Gilbert talking about sin. Outside murder, screwing your neighbor's wife is the number two no-no in the commandments."

"I think the number two no-no is thou shall not have any false idols if I remember my Sunday school lessons," Drew said dryly. "Murder and adultery are numbers six and seven."

"Fuck you, Dunne," Early snapped. "You know what I mean. Adultery is a sin. You'd be committing one of the worst kinds of sin and what's worse, you'd be leading her into committing it with you, damning her to hell alongside you. You were brought up better than that. You *know* better than that!"

"I'm not asking you to condone what I'm going to do," Drew said, tossing away the leaf and dusting his hands together. "All I'm asking is that you not try to stop me."

"From what?" Early demanded. "Getting your goddamned self killed?"

"I'm going to marry her, Early. I want to spend the rest of my life with her. I want to go to sleep with her in my arms every night. It's not just my wanting her, aching for her. I want to *be* with her. Can't you understand that? Don't you think I deserve some happiness? Don't you think she does?"

"I'm not saying you shouldn't be happy, Drew. God knows if anyone deserves it you do. You know damned well I've told you time and again that you should have left that crazy-assed bitch you're married to many years ago. Hell, you shouldn't have married the woman in the first place."

"I don't think you were there when Jake made me marry her," Drew grumbled.

"Well, I was there when you got home and I told you then it was a goddamned mistake. You remember that?" Early nudged him with his knee. "You remember?"

"I am going to rectify the situation," Drew snapped. "I just told you that. I'm going to leave Terri and marry the woman I love. I'm going to find that happiness."

"So what do you want me to do while you're out there courting, getting your ass kicked or worse?"

Drew got up from the bench, thrust his hands into his pockets once more. "Just stay out of my way," he told his cousin.

"And if I can't?" Early challenged, his jaw thrust forward.

Drew stared into Early's worried eyes for a second or two. "Just do it," was all he said before he turned and walked away.

* * * * *

Allison heard the knock on the front door and reached for the kitchen towel hanging on the oven door. Wiping her greasy hands on the blue and white check cloth she walked through the living, opened the door and froze.

He was standing on her porch and his eyes were leveled on her. All that stood between them was the latched screen door. Fear shot up her throat and she put a hand there to still the suddenly wild beat of her heart.

"Let me in," he said quietly.

"What are you doing here?" she asked.

"Let me in, Allison. No one needs to see me standing out here," he told her and she saw his lips tremble. He wasn't wearing a coat and she knew he had to be cold.

Blood pounding in her ears, she fumbled with the latch, held open the door to let him enter. She looked past his broad shoulder at the houses across the way. Just because she didn't see anyone watching them didn't mean they weren't. She stepped back quickly, closed both doors, then turned to face him.

"You shouldn't be here," she said.

He was standing about six feet from her. His dark hair was tousled and his cheeks were red from the cold.

"Do you love him?" he asked.

She didn't hesitate. "No."

"Have you ever loved him?"

She knew he deserved honesty. "No."

He nodded several times, took a step toward her and stopped. "Do you love me?"

Her answer was barely above a whisper. "Yes."

"Does *he* love *you*?"

"No more than you love your wife," she replied boldly.

He took another step, paused, then withdrew his hands from his pockets. He spread his arms and she went into them, laid her head against his chest. One arm went around her and his right hand to the back of her head to hold her to him.

"I love you," he said. "More than I have ever loved anyone in my life."

"He'll kill you if he finds you here," she told him.

"He's not going to." He moved his hand from her head to her chin and lifted her face to him. "I want you to leave him."

"How?" she asked, searching his eyes. "I don't have any money here but I do have a trust—"

"I have all the money we will need," he said. He caressed her chin. "More importantly, you'd have me."

"Where would we go? He might not love me, Drew, but he doesn't like to lose at anything. He'd come after us. He'd track us down. There's no place—"

"We'll leave Georgia. Go out of the country," he stated.

"You need a passport to leave the country and I don't have one. Do you?"

"Yes and I can get you a passport. That's not a problem. Do you have your birth certificate where you can get to it easily?"

She nodded. "It's in my keepsake box."

He released her and stepped back. "Go get it for me."

"Drew—"

"Go," he said firmly. "I don't need to be here any longer than necessary."

When she returned and handed it to him, he read it, then looked up at her.

"You were born in Florida."

"Yes, is that a problem?" she asked, frowning.

"Shouldn't be," he replied.

"How long will it take?"

"I had to wait about three weeks to get mine," he told her. "It would have taken longer if I hadn't paid the expedited fee."

"Three weeks?" she questioned. "Where will we—?"

"I have a house in East Albany," he said, folding the birth certificate and stuffing it into the back pocket of his pants. "Out near Radium Springs. Nobody knows about it. Not even Early. We can stay there."

She put her thumb to her mouth and began chewing on a cuticle. "I don't know." She wasn't worried about herself. She was terrified for him.

"Here's what you need to do," he said in a quiet tone. "If you have things—small things—that mean a lot to you, things like pictures or jewelry, mementoes, put them in a cardboard box and set them out on the side of the garage tonight and I'll get them. Nothing heavy. Something I can easily carry a block or so. I don't want you to lose anything that you care about."

"What about you?" she asked. "I care about you."

He reached out to cup her cheek, smiling as she tilted her head into his palm. "You're not going to lose me, baby. I promise."

They were standing very close. His gaze dropped to her mouth, she parted her lips. He returned his eyes to hers. He held that look for a long time, then leaned in and as hesitant as any green youth lowered his head to hers. Gently, tenderly he pressed his lips to hers as they stared into one another's eyes. The touch of his lips was brief but it made her womb clench. It was not so much a kiss as a promise. Soft, sweet, infinitely tender. Asking her permission for more.

They pulled back, both stunned by their reactions. She knew there was no turning back now, and clearly so did he. They'd crossed a line over which neither would be able to step back again.

"I love you," he said, laying his forehead to hers. "Nothing is going to go wrong."

"Drew—"

"Nothing is going to go wrong," he repeated, then straightened.

"When are we going to leave?" she asked.

"Tomorrow," he answered. "Why wait?" He dug into his front pants pocket and pulled out a sheet of paper and handed it to her. "The directions to my house are on there. I've also drawn a couple of maps. As soon as he leaves for work, get in your car and drive south to Bainbridge. One of the maps tells you how to get from Bainbridge back to the road that leads over to Albany. Drive the speed limit and keep a close watch on your rearview mirrors. If anyone is following you, call the number that's also on the paper. That's my cell. We'll try again in a day or two."

"If they're following me, what do I do?"

"Go to the Wal-Mart in Bainbridge and do some shopping," he said. "Act normally. Don't make them suspicious." He glanced down at his watch. "I've got to go. Get your things together and put them where he won't see them. Okay?"

She nodded, looking down at her feet.

"We're going to have a good life together, Allison," he told her. "Once we are settled and in a country where we can safely do it, we'll get divorces and be free of all the crap we've had to put up with over the years."

"Yes," she said and lifted her head to look at him. "Free to love one another as we were meant to be loved."

He turned away as though he didn't want her to see his face and walked quickly to the door. She followed behind him, reaching out to take the side of the inside door as he pushed the screen door open.

"Oh, no," she whispered.

Drew looked back at her, then turned his head to see what had captured her attention. Staring at them from across the street was Lillian Hatcher, Deputy Nick's grandmother and Drew's piano teacher from childhood.

"Well, that's not good," he said. He looked back around at her. "What would your husband do if she told him about me being here?"

"Yell at me," she lied. She knew Clay would beat the hell out of her when he found out Drew had been in his house but Drew didn't need to know that.

"I'll go talk to her," he promised as she pulled the screen door shut behind him.

"You think that's wise?" she asked.

"Nothing ventured, nothing gained," he said, stepping off the porch. She watched him walk across the street to the old woman's house. She couldn't hear what he was saying so she closed the door to keep out the cold wind sifting through the screen, then leaned her back against it.

* * * * *

Drew forced his face into a smile he didn't feel as he crossed the old woman's yard. "Good morning, Miss Lillian," he greeted her.

"Not wise to visit that gal in broad daylight, Andrew," Miss Lillian said.

"Can I talk to you?" he asked as he reached her walkway.

"I don't know," she replied. "Can you?"

He ducked his head—feeling like a child again. "May I?"

"That's better," she said, then turned her back on him. "Come on in. Where's your coat, young man?"

"In my truck," he replied sheepishly as he climbed her porch steps.

"Keeping it warm, no doubt," she said with a sniff. She waited until he opened the door for her. Once inside, she walked through the very tidy living room into her kitchen. "You want a cup of coffee?"

"Ah, yes, ma'am," he said. Not really wanting it but since she'd offered...

"You and that young woman make a cute couple," she said to the accompaniment of rattling china.

He followed her into the kitchen. "Excuse me?"

"You heard me," she said as she poured a cup of coffee and turned to give it to him. "You may be tone-deaf, son, but you're not stupid."

Taking the cup from her, he sat at her table when she pointed to a chair and ordered him to park it. His adult years were rapidly dwindling away as he looked up at her. Once more he was the nervous little boy whose fingers she would slap with her ruler when he hit a sour note on the keyboard.

"How long's this been going on?" she asked, taking a seat across from him.

"There's nothing going on, Miss Lillian," he told her.

"Then it's fixin' to," she pronounced. "I see the way the two of you look at each other at church. I believe they wrote a song about such looks." She arched a brow. "Believe it's called 'Hungry Eyes.'"

He felt the heat rush to his cheeks and took a quick sip of coffee to hide it from her.

"Don't like that man of hers," Miss Lillian said. "Mean looking if you ask me." She stared him in the eye. "And he beats her."

Drew stiffened. He slowly lowered the cup to the table top. "Are you sure about that?"

"As sure as I am that you never did learn how to play that Chopin piece I assigned you for recital," she stated.

Absolute fury dredged a canal through Drew's very soul.

"Have you ever seen him hit her?" he asked.

"No, he's a pretty shrewd little bastard but when you hear him yelling at her and then you don't see her come out that door for a day or two, you know she didn't decide to take a minivacation. He's abusive to her, Andrew. I'd bet my last bingo dollar on it." She tilted her head to one. "Thing is, what are you going to do about it?"

He hesitated to answer. Not because he didn't trust her but because he was so angry he was afraid of what he might say or do to Clay Bennett. She took the matter out of his hands when she reached across the table and laid her wrinkled, liver-spotted and arthritic hand on his arm.

"You've had fifty miles of bad road with that woman Jake made you marry, son. Time you put your wheels on some good asphalt for a change. You don't have to worry about me spilling the beans on you. I won't. I don't owe Jake Thompson, his twit of a daughter or that man across the street a damned dime and wouldn't give any of them the time of day." She squeezed his arm. "Now, I'll ask you again. What are you going to do about it?"

"Take her and leave," he said.

"Good. Just be careful. Man like that is dangerous, Andrew, and given to exacting revenge on those who cross him. I'd hate it if anything happened to you. There's no telling what he will do."

"He's sleeping with my wife," Drew told her.

She didn't bat an eye. "Better him than you, wouldn't you say?" she asked with a twinkle in her rheumy eyes.

* * * * *

Walking back to town, Drew was surprised to see his pickup parked in front of the dealership. Bobby Daniels was leaning against the driver side quarter panel.

"Where you been?" Bobby asked as Drew came up to him.

"None of your business," Drew said, clenching his jaw.

"Maybe not mine but I imagine it's someone else's," Bobby said with a grin. "Think I should tell him?"

Drew started to walk past him, then saw Whip looking out the showroom window at them.

"Don't you forget what I told you about that little plastic envelope," Bobby said and his smile faded as Drew whipped around to point a finger at him.

"Get away from my truck," Drew ordered.

Bobby's eyebrows shot up. "Why, Drew Dunne, have you gone and grown a pair between last night and this morning?" he asked.

"Get *away* from my truck," Drew repeated. He clenched his hands into fists.

"Really? *Really?*" Bobby questioned, chuckling. "You really wanna do this, boy?"

"What's going on here?"

Drew caught sight of his father-in-law coming out of the dealership.

"Morning, Big Jake," Bobby said. He tipped the brim of his uniform hat.

"Sheriff," Jake replied. "You boys having words?" He looked from Drew to Bobby, then back to Drew.

"No, sir," Bobby answered. "Just two old friends shootin' the breeze."

"I'm not your friend," Drew said through his teeth.

"Don't you have rounds or something to do, Sheriff?" Jake inquired.

Bobby reached up to adjust the fit of his hat and nodded. "Yes, sir, I do." He flicked his gaze to Drew. "How's that pretty daughter of yours, Mr. Jake? Is Drew taking good care of her?"

"He'd better be," Jake said in an ominous voice.

"Yes, indeedy," Bobby agreed. "He sure should." He tugged down on his hat brim and strolled back across the street.

Jake was silent for a moment, just watching Drew as his son-in-law opened the door of his truck and reached for his coat.

"You got problems with Daniels?" Jake asked.

"None that I can't handle," Drew heard himself say and was astonished at the heat in his voice.

"You best leave the man alone," Jake advised. "He ain't the kind to step aside."

Drew slammed the door. "Neither am I," he said and walked past his father-in-law. He felt the older man staring at his back but he no longer cared what Jake Thompson—or anybody else for that matter—thought about him.

He hadn't been at his desk ten minutes before the door opened. He looked up to find Clay Bennett standing in the doorway.

"Don't think I don't know what you want, Dunne. Bobby warned you and now I'm gonna warn you. You leave my woman alone. Do you hear me? Because if you don't, I'll wipe the floor up with you, you little pipsqueak," Clay said. "You hear me?"

"Are you here to look at cars, Coach Bennett?" Drew asked. "If so, Whip will be more than happy to help you."

Clay lifted his left hand and shot Drew the finger. Without another word, he turned and stormed off.

Drew chuckled and went back to what he was about to do. His gaze fell on his wedding ring and he was staring at it when there was a knock on the door. "Yeah?"

Whip came in with a handful of papers. "These need to be signed," Whip told him.

Not bothering to look at his brother-in-law, Drew told him to put them on the desk.

"No, go on ahead and sign them—" Whip began but Drew looked up at him with narrowed eyes.

"I said to put them on my desk," Drew said. "I'll sign them when I get around to it."

Whip opened his mouth to say something but obviously thought better of it. He slapped the papers on the desk and pivoted away.

"And shut the door behind you," Drew ordered.

Whip slammed the door as hard as he could.

Drew stared down at his wedding ring for a long time—twirled it around his finger, then tugged it from his hand. He leaned over and dropped it into the trashcan where it made a hollow *tink*.

* * * * *

"Did you get it done?" Clay asked. He had his cell phone pressed tightly to his ear as he sat down heavily in his chair.

"Yep. No problem at all," Bobby replied. "You're good to go. Should be ready to go right now. Try it out and if you have any trouble with it, let me know."

"Will do. I owe you one," Clay said and hung up. He turned to look at the black base unit sitting on a shelf beside his desk. He stared at the twin blinking yellow lights and smiled.

Chapter Sixteen

He had no trouble finding the box she'd left beside the garage. He stood beside the house and listened to the drone of a sports program blaring from Bennett's TV. The man was no doubt sitting in the big easy chair he'd seen positioned in front of the big flat screen job and swilling down a can of beer. He wondered where Allison was, what she was doing. The thought of her in there with Bennett made his blood boil. When he heard Bennett yell for her to bring him another beer, he had to dig his nails into his palms to keep from ringing the doorbell and busting the bastard in the mouth.

"Soon, baby," he whispered. "Soon you'll be free of him."

He picked up the box and left.

* * * * *

It was raining the next morning—dark and dreary and bitterly cold for that time of year in Georgia—and the slap of the windshield wipers wore on Allison's nerves. She felt as if she were sitting on a red ant bed and kept shifting in her seat, constantly looking into the rearview and side mirrors for headlights. So far, so good she thought. There wasn't a car in sight behind her and she passed few on her twenty-one mile drive to Bainbridge. She had studied the map Drew had drawn and knew precisely where she needed to turn north to connect to the road to Albany. The paper he'd given her was tucked safely in her bra just in case.

Her mind had been on him all night long. She stood at the kitchen sink and pictured him stealthily executing his way to where she had left her box of treasures. The box contained a couple of photo albums, four framed pictures of her parents and one of her grandmother, a few knickknacks that meant the world to her. Finding the box gone this morning, she knew they were now in his care. The mere thought of him caring enough to give her a chance to collect things that reminded her of good childhood and young woman memories made him all the more dear to her. He was a good, decent man. A loving and kind man. A compassionate and thoughtful man. She knew her life with him would be wonderful.

If not free from looking over their shoulders.

"Once we are settled and in a country where we can safely do it, we'll get divorces."

She pictured them standing before a preacher or a justice of the peace. She could almost feel the cool circle of his love as he slipped it on her finger. She would place the ring on his finger with pride.

"With this ring I give you my heart," she would say to him. "I pledge you my troth and I thee wed."

Her gaze went to the ring on her left hand. It was an abomination, a brand, a sign of ownership and she would not live another minute with it on her hand. Braking the car, she pulled to the side of the road, put the car in park and brought her hand up. She stared at the cheap ring she had never liked, then tugged it from her finger. It took some doing. In all the years of their marriage, she'd never taken it off. She didn't dare. Once she was free of it, it almost felt as if a heavy rock had been lifted from her shoulders and she could breathe again. The bright white gold seemed to mock her as she looked down at the plain band. With her teeth clamped together, she put her hand on the button that would lower the passenger side window. Her intention was to toss the ring through the window and into the ditch where it would never be found then thought better of it. Instead, she unhooked her seat belt, leaned over, opened the glove compartment and threw the ring inside. Let Clay find it when she was gone. Let him know she had abandoned it as she had abandoned him. His brand removed. The tie that bound her to him severed.

She slammed the glove compartment door, then leaned back in the seat—closing her eyes as she took long, cleansing breaths. Removing the ring was her first step into the new life that waited for her in Drew's arms.

A vehicle passed and she snapped her eyes open—half expecting to see either Clay's truck or Bobby Daniel's. The car that was speeding away was a dark green sedan but she watched it until the taillights disappeared beneath the lowered sky. Taking a deep breath, she rebuckled her seat belt, glanced in the rearview mirror, then put the car in drive and pulled slowly out onto U.S. 27.

* * * * *

Everything had to be perfect, he thought as he looked about the living room. He'd come straight to Albany as soon as he left the house that morning, making sure he wasn't being followed. He kept looking at his watch, worried that she should have been there by now. Feeling sick to his stomach, he went into the kitchen, took a glass out of the cupboard and filled it with water from the sink. But after two gulps, he poured it out. The water did more harm than good on his queasy stomach.

"Calm down," he said aloud. "She'll be here. She *will* be here."

Unless, he thought, her husband had somehow gotten wind of their plan and stopped her.

"And he beats her."

Pure rage shifted through him for the thousandth time since Miss Lillian had uttered those words to him. Just thinking about them he curled his fingers into fists.

It never occurred to him that Allison would decide against coming to him. He knew she would join him if it was humanly possible. As the time dragged on and after the thirtieth or fortieth trip to the front window to peel the curtain back and look out, he was beginning to feel fear pushing aside the anger.

"Get yourself under control, Dunne," he said. When he did he thought of something Early had once told him.

"Talking to yourself is a sure sign of a deeply troubled mind."

He forced himself down onto the sofa. In front of him on the coffee table was Allison's box. It had been in the floorboard of his truck all night and he hadn't been tempted to take a peek at the contents, but as he sat there looking at it, his curiosity got the better of him. He sat forward to take out one of the photo albums. Opening it, the very first picture made his heart ache.

Allison as an infant. Lying on a fluffy white rug with a pale pink blanket covering her little bald head. Her smiling, toothless little face was so comical he laughed. Turning the page brought another laugh for there she was a year older with a mischievous glint in her pretty green eyes. Age two with chubby cheeks and a ridiculous topknot on her little head. Age three swaddled in a pink coat and with a barrette holding her shoulder length hair to one side.

Four.

Sweet Lord, at age four she captured his soul.

"Hello, little one," he said to the photo of the prettiest little girl he'd ever seen. She was wearing a pale green dress with very broad collars and her hair was well past her shoulders—one long curl dangling over her left shoulder—and tied back from her face with a matching green bow. Her little hands were clasped in front of her. It was obvious the photo had been taken in the summer. She had a golden tan on her slender arms. The sweetest, most endearing smile stretched across her mouth. That missing-front-teeth smile said she was a very happy little girl, loved by everyone and eager to have her photo taken.

Five. Six. Seven.

All the way through to high school. It was like watching a motion picture as he viewed the changes in her face. Her senior class picture was of a very self-posed young girl on the verge of becoming a woman. The smile in that picture was demure—almost shy—but it hinted at the sensual beauty that was to come.

Tracing the lips in the photo with the pad of his thumb, he felt the pull of his love for her tugging at his heartstrings.

He'd never known love before. Not as a man for a woman. Not as a lover for his true mate. It was something new and exciting to him but it was also a bit scary.

"I'll do right by you, milady," he said, thinking of the highwayman and his lady. "By all that's holy I will."

The crunch of gravel brought his head up and he snapped the album shut and returned it to its box before getting to his feet. His heart seemed to have jumped up his esophagus into his throat and he heard the blood rushing through his ears. The door seemed a long way away and his feet mired in quicksand—sucking at every step—but he managed to make his way there and reached out with a shaking hand to open it. He breathed a sigh of relief when he saw her in the car. She lifted a hand in greeting and cracked open her car door.

At that moment a loud crack echoed and lightening stitched across the heavens and lit the sky in an ugly shade of puce. A thunderous boom shook the house and the skies seemed to open like a burst dam as rain pelted the roof. His yard was already a quagmire—screaming at him that he needed to have the ground sodded. Georgia red clay puddles were scattered like miniature lakes across the entire front of his property. The deluge fell so heavily the concrete walkway was completely covered.

Caught in the downpour, he saw Allison's face only when an intermittent flash of lightning forked overhead. She had shut the door and was sitting there cringing with each new burst of sound.

"You don't like bad weather, do you, baby?" he asked.

He thought about grabbing an umbrella and going out to get her but the rain was now falling sideways and that wasn't a good sign. He knew with the torrential downpour and ferocious wind that was driving the rain sideways they'd both be soaked in a matter of seconds. He could only hope the storm was short-lived for Allison needed to stay right where she was.

Half an hour later, the rain had slacked enough that he could fetch the umbrella and go out to her. He went to the closet, got one and started back to the door just as the screen door opened and she came in.

"I think that was God's way of telling me I could use a shower," she said.

"You need a towel?" he asked as he hooked the umbrella on the closet rod and shut the door.

"Nah, I'm drip dry," she replied with a laugh. "I'm freezing though."

"Come here," he said, going to her with his arms out. "I'll warm you up."

She went into his arms as naturally as if they had been holding one another in that way for decades. She nestled her head against his shoulder and he wrapped his arms around her.

"I wasn't followed," she said.

"Good but I think we should go up to the post office right now and start the paperwork for the passport. I don't want to wait even a day," he told her.

She pushed away from him. "Drew, look at me! I look like a drowned rat."

"You look beautiful," he said, reaching out to hook a stray strand of her hair behind her ear.

She tucked that adorable lip between her teeth. "You sure?" she asked around the obstacle.

"Positive," he said. "Let me get my coat. We'll take my truck."

"I looked up what I would need online," she said as he went into the kitchen and took his coat from the back of one of the dinette table chairs. "I have my driver's license, library card and—"

"That'll be fine," he said. He came back to her, leaned in and kissed her nose. "We'll stop on the way back and pick up some hamburgers for lunch if that's okay."

"Works for me," she said, her smile bright as she gazed up at him.

"I've stocked the kitchen with…" He fanned the air. "Stuff but if there's other stuff you want, we can stop at Harvey's or Piggly Wiggly."

"Maybe I should look at your stuff before we go," she said. When he grinned and wagged his brows, she rolled her eyes. "You know what I meant."

He laughed. "Yes I do but trust me. I'll give you a good look at my stuff when we get back." Her blush was all the encouragement he needed to hook his arm around her shoulders. "Let's go, woman. Time's a-wastin'."

She hated the picture they took for the passport. Thought it made her look ten years older. Her hair was a mess and her face washed out. It depressed her and as they drove to Burger King she pouted.

"No one's passport photo looks good, sweetheart," he commiserated.

"Tom Keen's do," she said. "Every one of them."

He frowned. "Who's Tom Keen?"

She turned her head toward him. "Tom Keen? Hello! *The Blacklist*?" When he cast her a perplexed look she threw her hands up. "The asset or whatever he is from the TV show? Lizzie's husband? We think he works for Red or used to work for Red."

"I don't watch TV," he said. "I read."

"If you're gonna live with me, we're gonna watch TV and discuss the story lines," she said.

"Why does he have so many passport photos?" he asked. He didn't care one way or another but if it was important to her, he'd make it important to him.

"Because he has passports from Russia and Germany and all over the place. I think he's a super spy and he's sexy as hell," she replied.

"Well, then we *will* be watching that show together and discussing how much sexier I am than he is," he told her.

"Only if I can compare his stuff to yours," she said with a giggle.

It had stopped raining while they were in the post office filling out the paperwork but it started up again when they got onto Oglethorpe and crossed the Flint River.

"If this keeps up, Radium is going to flood again," he observed, leaning forward to peer up through the windshield.

"Is your property in the flood plain?" she asked, a touch of nervousness in her voice.

"I honestly don't know. I do know my yard is beginning to look like the Great Lakes," he replied.

By the time they got back to his house, the rain had stopped again but lightning was still fingering its way across the sky.

"I just noticed you have a metal roof," she said as he pulled in next to her car.

"I just put that in this past summer," he stated.

"How long have you had the place?"

"Two years now," he answered. "I wanted a place I could go where no one could find me." He turned off the truck, glanced at her. "My safe haven, if you will."

"It's a nice house," she said. "Small but from what I saw of the living room and into the kitchen, perfect for two people."

"We could live here pretty comfortably if we were allowed to," he said. "I'm going to miss it."

"What will you do with the house when we leave?"

"Give it to Early," he responded. "He can use it for rental property to have a little extra income. Chances are Jake won't fire him when I'm gone. My cousin is a master mechanic and one of the best I've ever known." He opened his door and started to get out but her words stopped him.

"I like Early," she said. "But he looks at me like I'm a scarlet woman."

He turned around in his seat to look at her. "He doesn't think that."

"No?" she questioned, running her gaze over his face—looking for the telltale sign he was lying.

Which he was.

"Of course not."

"If you say so," she said, opened her door and got out.

She'd caught him in his first lie to her, he thought and felt bad about it. He watched her as she skirted the front of his truck and hurried onto the deep veranda that ran the entire perimeter of the house.

He got out, was hit in the eye by a stray drop of rain. As though that were an omen, the rain started in again and he had to sprint to the porch where she was standing with her arms crossed.

"Don't do that again, Drew," she said softly.

"What?" he asked, searching for his house key.

"Lie to me."

He stopped with his hand on the handle of the screen door.

"Clay lies to me all the time," she said. "Our whole marriage has been nothing but a lie. Please don't start whatever this is with a lie."

"He likes you, Allison," he said. That much was true. "As to the other?" He shrugged. "Does it matter what he thinks?"

"It matters," she said. "I'm not a whore."

"Allison, I—"

She held up her hand to forestall what he was about to say. "I know you don't consider me in that way and yes, I am going to sleep with you tonight and every night from here on out. If that makes me a scarlet woman, so be it, but I'm not a whore. I am going to lie in your arms and take you into my body and give you as much pleasure as I know you will give me. I have been aching to do that since the day I met you, but despite all that I am *not* a whore."

Her words did things to his body he hoped she couldn't see. "I know exactly what you are," he said.

"Which is?"

"The woman I love and intend to marry as soon as we're both free," he said. He pulled open the screen door and thrust the key into the lock. "And I don't give a rat's ass what anyone thinks of either of us." He glanced at her. "I've been called a helluva lot worse things than a whore, believe me." The lock clicked and he opened the door for her to precede him into the house.

She went straight through the living room and into the kitchen where she began opening cabinets. He came to the doorway, leaned against it with his arms crossed over his chest and watched her inspecting everything.

"My stuff's over here, baby," he said in a growl-worthy tone. "Wanna inspect it?"

She ignored him but he saw her smile. "What would you like for supper?" she asked.

They'd eaten their hamburgers and French fries, drank their chocolate shakes in the parking lot of Burger King and food was the last thing on his mind at that moment.

"Whatever you want to fix," he answered and when she looked around at him with a deep frown creasing her forehead, he raised his eyebrows. "Did I say the wrong thing?"

"Clay always picked—"

"I'm not Clay," he interrupted in a firm voice. "You're the woman in this mix. You pick the food, you cook it however you like and I'll eat it. If you want my help in the kitchen, just ask. I can make a mean gravy and I'm not bad with spaghetti sauce and pasta. I can bake a ham with the best of them."

"I see cans of salmon," she said, accepting his statement. "How about croquettes, peas and carrots and stewed tomatoes?"

"Sounds like a plan," he said. "What can I do?"

"Peel and cut me up an onion," she said.

"Yes, ma'am," he agreed, pushed away from the doorframe and joined her in the kitchen.

He didn't have a TV but he had a CD player and a large assortment of music that—God be blessed—she liked as much as he. She found a deck of cards in a kitchen drawer and asked if he'd teach her how to play something.

"What?"

"Anything," she said. "I've never played cards."

"Not even in college?" he asked.

"I wasn't there long enough to do much except study," she told him. "My girlfriends were more interested in dating than playing games, although we did play Trivial Pursuit."

"Which we'll buy next time we go to town," he said. "Along with Yahtzee and a cribbage board and a backgammon set." He held his hand out for the cards, then patted the sofa beside him.

"I've never played cribbage but I do know how to play backgammon," she said. "I used to play with my grandmother. I'm pretty good at it."

"We'll see," he replied as he began shuffling the cards. "What we're going to play is a simple game of rummy. Easy and it goes pretty fast."

"Are we in a hurry?" she questioned.

Rain was still falling on the roof and he wanted nothing more than to be in bed with her wrapped in his arms listening to it.

"I'm kinda anxious for you to see my stuff," he said without looking at her.

"Then why are we wasting time with the cards?" she asked.

He lifted his eyes from the deck and locked them on hers. "Is that what you want?" he asked—holding his breath for her answer.

"Yes," she said.

He put the cards on the coffee table, stood and extended his hand to her. When she slipped her fingers into his palm, he drew her to her feet, then swept her up into his arms, lifting her as though she weighed no more than a toddler.

"Are you sure about this?" he asked, looking down into her face. Her arms were wrapped around his neck and he'd never felt more like a man than he did at that moment.

"Yes, Highwayman," she said. "I'm sure."

"So be it, Lady Bess," he said and heard the building desire turn his voice husky.

For once in his life he knew someone loved him—really loved him.

* * * * *

Rain falling upon the metal roof. Lightning flaring beyond the windows.

Locked in a cocoon of sensuality.

Locked in the arms of the one you love.

An unhurried drag of nails across taut, quivering flesh.

Deep kisses.

Deeper gazes.

The low rumble of thunder that rattled the windowpane. Another flare of light.

She lay on her belly beside him. Naked. Vulnerable. Beautiful to his eyes.

He lay on his side facing her. Naked. Invincible. Mirrored in her eyes.

Her smile. Sensual enough to make his cock stir yet sweet enough to bring out the protector within his chest.

Idly fanning his fingertips across the smooth perfection of her back. Down the deep cleft of her sweetly turned rump and along the silky expanse of her upper thigh. He was playing with her and she was going along without complaint. Without comment. Her eyes were dreamy as she looked over at him with her long hair spread out on the pillow beneath her head. All he'd done so far was undress her. Undress for *her*. Ran his hands over her satiny flesh. He hadn't touched her breasts or the beckoning softness between her thighs. She was a present on Christmas morning and he was taking his time unwrapping it as Declan had unwrapped his Lady Colette.

"What are you thinking?" she asked.

He wanted to ask her about the faint white lines that marred the smooth surface of her butt but he had a feeling he didn't want to know. He had a few lines like them on his own body—compliments of Wade's belt. That hers had come from a similar source made his heart ache.

"How soft you are," he said instead. He smoothed his palm over her taut buttock, trailed his fingertips along the crease that begged for further exploration.

"Are you deliberately trying to drive me crazy or is this your idea of seduction?" she inquired.

"I, milady," he said, "am taking my time. I've waited too long for this moment to rush it."

"Even if I would like you to speed things along?"

"Even if," he replied. "Humor me."

"You realize I am not a novice at this," she reminded him.

"Nor am I, but I will not have it said I'm one of those wham-bam-thank you-ma'am kind of guys. As the song says, I'm a man with slow hands."

"Infuriatingly slow," she said, then sighed loudly.

"Am I boring you?"

"I would *like* you to bore me but you seem content to simply torment me."

He gave her a slow smile he intended to be wickedness personified and that got her full attention. One fine midnight-hued brow arched with a taunting dare and her green eyes sparkled.

He accepted the challenge and raised up to hover above her. "Turn over," he commanded.

She obeyed without a word.

His gaze went to the darkly lush nipples that called out to be touched. Licked. Tasted. He put out his hand to rest his palm on her flat belly and he could have sworn he heard her purr.

"You're a beautiful woman, Allison. Do you realize men stare at you when you're walking out of the church?"

"If they do I've never seen them at it," she replied. "Why would they?"

He rubbed her taut stomach.

"The same reason all men look at a woman they know they can't have. They're fantasizing. Wondering what if."

"Women look at you," she said and when he blew a raspberry at the notion, she reached down to still his hand. "They do. I overheard two nurses say you're some mighty fine eye candy."

"Nice to look at but you wouldn't want to own him," he said.

"No one owns you, Drew," she told him.

"My wife and her father do," he replied.

"Why do you say that?" she asked.

"Because the house is in her name and the dealership is in Big Jake's name. He insists I put most of what he pays me into my retirement fund. Money for groceries, insurance, utilities and all that comes out of my salary. I never see the checks. He hands them over to Terri. I get what she calls an allowance but it's barely enough to keep me in socks."

"And to insure you won't leave her?" she questioned.

"I sure as hell can't afford to on what I take home. The only things I own outright are this house and my truck but I do have money. I have an ace in the hole they don't know about and I've been waiting for just the right time to play it."

"What do you mean?"

He grinned. "I've been embezzling money from the dealership for sixteen years."

She gaped at him. "What? *How?*"

"Jake made me take night classes in business and accounting. I got my degree online eventually. I didn't want to do it but after a few classes I saw that learning the ins and outs of accounting could be a big help. What it taught me was how to embezzle money without being caught. How to fudge on reports, cook the books, juggle fuel usage reports, and overcharge on maintenance to people who can damned well afford it."

"Wow," she said on a long breath. "And Big Jake doesn't know about it?"

"No and if he does find out, it'll look like Whip is the one doing the embezzling. He'd never prosecute his only son. Me? Well, he'd put my ass under the jail if he could but there's no way he can track where all the money went. It's in an off-shore account in the Cayman Islands," he told her. "Close to four million at last count."

She whistled. "You weren't joking when you said you had money. I'm in love with a crook."

"I'm not crooked. I'm broken, baby. So broken I don't know if I can ever be fixed. Between Jake and Terri and Whip, they've crippled me my whole life. Every time I think I can finally get on my feet, they knock me back down. Now I've got your husband and Bobby Daniels trying their hands at breaking me even more."

"It scares me what Clay might do if he finds us," she admitted.

"Does he whip you?" he asked.

She tensed. "Why would you ask that?"

"Does he?" He needed to know, fearing the answer. "I've seen the marks on your butt, Allison. Someone put them there. Was it him?"

"My parents and grandparents never whipped me," she said. It wasn't a firm yes to his question but it didn't need to be. He had his answer.

"He won't do it again," he said.

"I believe you," she said, putting her hand on his arm. "I love you so much for saying it."

"I've never known love, Allison. I've never been *in* love. I didn't know it could be like this," he said. "I love you more than life, itself. I would do anything for you."

"Then show me," she said softly. "Show me how much you love me."

The time for talking was over. He knew it. She knew it. He moved over her, settled his body between her legs.

"I want to take it slow," he said. "To savor every moment of this."

She smiled, put her hand on his cheek. "That's what I want, too."

"I've dreamed of being with you like this," he admitted. "Help me not to rush. Help me to give you as much pleasure as having you here is giving me."

It wasn't a mechanical kiss. It wasn't an unthinking touch of her mouth melding along his. She didn't just kiss him. She took possession of his mouth. *Mine*, the kiss said—loud and clear. He understood that as he never had anything else. With the press of her lips to his, she was claiming him. Branding him. Telling him he belonged to her and no other. He wanted his body to be the one she needed. The haven she came to when things became too rough around the edges.

He was hard and thick at the junction of her thighs. His cock ached. It throbbed. There was a coil of tension deep in his belly, a need that was growing stronger and more insistent with every passing second. His entire body was primed and ready.

She ended her kiss and he took up where she left off. He slipped his tongue between her lips to taste the rich honey of her mouth. Slowly he stroked her in the age-old imitation of the sex act. The tips of her breasts were pressed to his bare chest like burning brands. He writhed against her.

"Please," she whispered. "I need you."

Her words were the sweetest he'd ever heard. No woman had ever said those three words to him. Not even Corinne when they had been lovers. Hearing Allison say them brought tears to his eyes.

Gently, tenderly he wedged his hand between them to take hold of his shaft. With infinite care, he placed it to her soft, warm lips and pushed just enough to sheath its head within her sweet folds. Almost instantly her body clenched around him.

"God," he breathed. It was like paradise. So warm and so slick. Her silken channel drew him in deeper and deeper until he was lost there in her body.

She clung to his shoulders as he slowly rocked his body over hers. One moment her legs were bracketing his. The next they were clamped tightly around his waist as she lifted up to meet him stroke for stroke. Her inner muscle pulsed around him and he could no more have stopped his reaction than pull the sun down from the sky. He jerked and then began to pump into her with such force and abandon it shocked him. There was no way to curb the reaction. It was an itch that was boring into him with barbs that would not let go until release came.

And that release was fast approaching. He knew when it came, it would be the supreme moment of his life. With it would be cast away years of longing and loneliness and unfulfilled need. Perfect pleasure would fill every hollow place within him. Her body would take his where it had never been before.

Her body stiffened. She cried out as her vaginal muscles locked onto his cock. Ripple after ripple of her climax milked him until his cum shot hot and thick in her waiting body.

Yes, he thought as he thrust hard and deep into her to spurt the last lingering jet. She had filled in all the missing pieces of his heart, put back together the broken ones and arranged them in just the right places.

* * * * *

Slow. Soft. Infinitely gentle touches.
Long. Slower. Wet sweeps.
Lengthy strokes that filled. Fulfilled. Fully engaged the senses.
Low words. Lower touches. Fingers flexing around hardness.
Turning it soft.
Awakening it once more.
Hardness like velvet-covered steel.
Softness like the inner petals of a rose kissed with dew.
"I want to stay inside you all night."
"That might be very uncomfortable," she replied.
"Maybe, but we would be connected," he said with a smirk.
"I think we're already connected," she said.
"We'll get married and have 2.3 children," he said.
"Oh, *no*," she exclaimed. "We can't have a .3 child!"
"Why not?" he asked.
"Because it wouldn't be all there," she replied. "Trying to find clothes that would fit...Having to buy only one shoe." She shuddered. "No. No .3 child."

He gaped at her horrified expression. She was teasing him. Her lips were twitching, her eyes gleaming. He threw his head back and laughed.

"Woman you are—"

It was the sound of a car door slamming that cut him off. He rolled out of the bed and padded naked into the living room, pulled aside the curtain.

"Shit," he said.

"Who is it?" she asked.

"Get dressed. It's your husband."

Chapter Seventeen

"How did he find us?" she asked. She was standing in the bedroom doorway with a sheet wrapped around her.

"Get dressed," he repeated, easing past her to grab his pants.

"You're not going out there!" Her eyes were wide as saucers. "Drew—"

"He's alone and I have a baseball bat." He rammed his feet into the jeans.

"Drew, please," she pleaded with him. "Stay here. Call the police. You don't know him like I do. He's dangerous."

He wasn't listening to her. His heart was pounding fiercely. The taste of iron flooded his mouth as he plucked the bat from the place where it was leaning against the wall. Not bothering with shoes, he left the bedroom and her tearful voice behind.

When he opened the door and walked out on the porch, Bennett was standing beside Allison's car.

"What do you want, Bennett?" he asked, flexing his fingers around the bat handle.

"You know," Clay said, pointing at her car, "this looks just like my wife's car." He peered inside the vehicle, then looked back at Drew with a shit-eating grin. "Well, I'll be a monkey's uncle. It *is* my wife's car. Now what are the odds of that?"

Drew came off the porch. "I asked you what you wanted."

"What belongs to me," Clay said, his smile vanishing.

"Leave."

"Ain't gonna happen. I'm here to get what's mine."

"She's not going anywhere with you. Leave now and stay off my property," Drew ordered.

"I could tell you the same thing," Clay snapped and nodded.

Wade and Boyd came running around the side of the house. Drew spun around to meet the threat but it was too late. They rushed him but not before Drew got in one swing of the bat before the two men grabbed hold of him. It clipped Clay a glancing blow on the cheek and Bennett let out a bellow of rage, stumbling back with his hand to his face. Wade pulled the bat from Drew's hand and slung it away.

Clay came forward, grabbed Drew by the hair and jerked his head back.

"You trying to take my wife away from me you little dipshit? Huh? *Huh*? You think you're man enough to do that? Fuck, no you ain't. You think you can break up my marriage?" Vicious tugs. "Why don't I just break you up instead? How 'bout that? You hear me, you little prick?"

"Hard to get him to listen to anythin' I've ever said even when I beat it into him," Wade said with a laugh.

"Let's see how well he listens to *me*," Clay snarled.

With his free hand Clay hit Drew in the stomach twice very fast, then in the face, rocking him. He got a better grip on Drew's hair, anchored Drew's head, then hit him squarely in the nose. The sound of his nose breaking accentuated the pain. Blood gushed down the back of his throat making Drew cough. He spewed blood in Bennett's face.

"You goddamned little fucker," Bennett bellowed.

The blows came heavy and fast. His jaw. His temple. Both eyes. His nose again. Bennett had a wicked left hand and the firm grip he had on Drew's hair and the equally tight grip Wade and Boyd had on his arms didn't give Drew any option but to take the hits.

Allison came running barefoot out of the house. "Let him go, Clay," she yelled. She ran toward them.

"Catch her, Boyd. I got this one," Wade snarled and hip-bumped Boyd out of the way—looping his arms under Drew's.

Boyd nodded and snagged Allison as she tried to run to Drew. He locked his arms around her and jerked her to his chest, lifting her from the ground. Though she struggled and screamed at him to let her go, he kept tight hold of her.

"Clay, stop," she pleaded.

Drew's knees gave out under the vicious punches and he sagged in his father's grip as Bennett's fists changed direction and began pounding him brutally in the gut.

"Stop it," Allison yelled. "Clay, please. You're going to kill him."

"That's the idea," Drew heard Bennett say.

"I can't hold the little peckerwood much longer," Wade said with a grunt. "Fucking bastard is heavy."

"Then drop him," Bennett ordered.

Wade let go and Drew fell to his knees. The force of the collapse jarred him all the way from his knees to the top of his head. He could barely see for one eye was swollen shut and the other had a gash over it that was bleeding profusely. That didn't stop him from seeing Bennett bend over, pick up the baseball bat and come toward him.

"No," Allison screamed.

Trying to push himself up, unable to, pitching forward onto his right arm, fingers digging into mud and refusing to give him purchase, he saw Bennett bring the bat over his shoulder as though he was about to hit a line drive. He threw his other arm up to keep from being hit in the head. The bat landed on his forearm and the sound of a crack made him howl in agony. He fell sideways into the oozing mud and drew his knees up even as the bat came down once again, this time on his hip. The yelp that came from his throat when the ungodly pain hit unmanned him. He reached above him with his good hand—fingers clawing at the mud as he tried to crawl away. His hip felt as though it was dislocated.

"Oh, no you don't," Bennett hissed and bent over to hook his hand in Drew's belt to drag him back. "Come here you fucking bastard."

Mud packing under his fingernails, Drew slid backward over the ground. His chin scraped across a rock and pain flashed up his jaw.

"Clay, no." Allison was shrieking now, her voice tight with terror. "Please, no."

Twisting his head around at her horrified shout, looking up at the man standing spread legged above him, Drew watched Bennett lift the bat but before he could swing it again, Wade stepped between him and Drew. He grabbed hold of the bat to keep Clay from using it.

"Best not kill him, son," Wade advises. "He ain't worth spending your life in prison for."

"He fucked my woman," Bennett snarled.

"Yeah and you fucked him up good. Look at him. He's done for," Wade said. "Let it go at that. You done broke his nose and his arm—might even have broke his jaw. Ain't that enough?"

"No. Not anywhere *near* enough," Clay said but he released his hold on the bat. He hunkered down beside Drew, put his heavy boot on Drew's right wrist to pin his arm down. He pressed until Drew screamed with pain as his wrist snapped.

"You touch my wife again and I *will* fucking kill you." He pushed Drew over and shoved his face into a mud puddle, held his head down while Allison screeched in the background, pleading with Wade to stop him.

Worried, Boyd yelled, too, afraid they'd all be arrested for murder if the coach drowned him. "Damn, Coach, let him up! You're gonna drown him!"

Bennett ground his face into the thick, cloying mud, filthy water went up his nose and down his throat before Bennett released him. Sputtering and coughing, bleeding and puking muddy water, gasping for breath, it barely registered when Bennett shoved him to his back, then fished the keys out of his pocket. Bennett stood up and threw them into the bushes. As Drew struggled to breathe, Bennett unbuttoned his pants and pulled out his cock.

"Sweet Jesus," Wade said, laughing as Bennett's piss hit Drew in the face.

"Shit," Boyd exclaimed.

"If I could, I would," Bennett said, then drew back his foot and kicked Drew in the back and the explosion of pain turned the lights off in his brain.

* * * * *

Allison called out to Drew—terrified that he was dead. She sagged against Boyd, begging him to make sure Drew was still breathing.

"He is," Boyd said. "I can see his chest moving."

She could tell the man holding her was as worried as she was. It was in his voice. In the way he wasn't restraining her so much as holding her up now.

"Drew," she sobbed. "I'm sorry. I'm so sorry."

Clay—infuriated by her tears and apology—stalked over to her, grabbed her arm and jerked her over to his truck, behind the cargo bed and to the passenger door. He pulled it open. "Shut the fuck up, woman," he yelled at her. He shook her violently. *"Where's your pocketbook?"* When she didn't answer, he shook her again, twisting her arm until she yelped. "I asked you where your pocketbook is. You'd better answer me."

"In the house," she said. "It's in the house."

"Boyd, get her stuff," Clay ordered. "You and Wade drive her car back to the house."

"Yes, sir," Boyd agreed.

"Wade, you know what to do," Clay told the older man.

"You can't leave him like that," she cried, sobbing wildly, afraid what Wade might do.

"Watch me," Clay snarled.

"Please don't leave him, Clay. Please don't. He's hurt."

He drew his hand back and she cowered against the door. "One more word out of you and I'll knock your teeth down your fucking throat you cheating bitch." His own words brought pure evil to his eyes. "Did you suck his cock?" he demanded, eyes narrowed. "*Did you?*"

She shook her head. "No."

He shoved her into his truck, slammed the door hard enough to rock the pickup, then came around to the driver's side. He turned the key, put the truck in reverse and swung it around—the tires skidding in the mud.

Allison swiveled in her seat in an effort to see Drew.

"Turn around," Clay shouted at her. "Turn around or so help me, I'll go back and run him over with the goddamned truck."

Shaking violently, Allison turned back around. She looked in the side mirror instead.

Clay slammed on the brakes—throwing her forward against the dashboard. He reached over to take her arm in a punishing grip. "Do you want me to turn this truck around? Do you? I'll kill him, Allison. Swear to God I will. I'll squish him like roadkill."

She tore her eyes from the mirror. There was no doubt in her mind her crazed husband would do exactly as he threatened.

* * * * *

It was the smell long before the sound that brought him around. Rain was falling into his face and he could barely breathe. It hurt to breathe. It hurt to lick his lips. Lying in the mud with cold water filling his ears, he managed to open one eye to look up at the dark clouds boiling above him. His one good eye twitched against the invasion of the icy rain.

The sound was getting closer. It was reverberating through his skull. His mind registered what the sound was but he couldn't put a name to it. He just knew he should be worried. Slowly, he swiveled his head toward the harsh smell that was making it hard for him to breathe. He stared without really comprehending what it was he was seeing. It took him a few heartbeats to fixate on the sight, to assimilate the leaping colors, to identify the smell and when their meaning finally registered, he turned his face away.

Bright red engine. Piercing siren. Men in heavy clothing and helmets clamoring from trucks. Blue-clad men rushing to him, kneeling, looking down at him for a moment before exchanging horrified gazes. One of them put a hand to him and tipped him back into darkness.

* * * * *

He dragged her into the house and told her to strip, standing in the bathroom as she sobbed and shook. When she'd scrubbed herself to his satisfaction—right there in front of him—he went to the linen closet, took out a box of Massengill and lobbed it at her. She stared at the box and wondered where it had come from. She hadn't douched in years and the box certainly wasn't hers.

"Where did—?"

"Use it," he ordered.

"But—"

"*Use it*. I want you to wipe every trace of him from your cunt," he shouted.

His bellow set her to opening the box and removing the bottle and tube from it. Tears streaming down her cheeks, she screwed the tube onto the bottle.

He sat down on the edge of the tub to make sure she did as he instructed. As she struggled to insert the tube into her vagina, he pulled off his boots and socks and tossed them aside. Keeping his eyes on her, watching her every movement, he took off his shirt, then pitched it across the room. He stood, unbuckled his belt, unzipped his pants, then pushed them down his long legs. Naked, for he never deigned to wear underwear, he put his hand on his cock and rubbed.

She knew what was going to happen as soon as she was finished. He'd punished her too many times in the way he had planned for her not to know. The douching was different but that was because of Drew. The rape on the bathroom floor would be brutal, painful and humiliating. Then he would pick her up, carry her to the bed and do it again.

And again.

Then he would take his belt to her and apply it with heavy-handed strokes again and again and yet again until he was satisfied he'd punished her enough.

When he was finished, he would cradle her in his arms, gently push the hair back from her face, caress her cheek and ask her the same question he always did after he'd raped and hurt and shamed her. This time was no different.

"Do you love me?"

She provided the answer she had wanted to give for years instead of the one he expected. "You're my husband."

He stiffened, took her chin roughly in his hand and lifted her face so he could look down at her.

"I didn't ask you who I am, Allison. I know who the hell I am. I asked you if you love me."

She knew what would happen if she didn't give him the answer he wanted. "Yes, Clay."

"Do you love *him*?"

That was new. A deviation from the norm.

"Do. You. Love. Him?" he repeated. He tightened his hold on her chin.

She couldn't answer because she was afraid to. Afraid, not for herself but for Drew.

"Well, he loves you. You know how I know he loves you? He was more concerned with your safety than he was the beating I was giving him. He kept trying to look over at you. That tells me he's willing to lay his life down for you. Well, baby doll, he just might get the chance."

Searching his eyes, worried, she asked what she had to ask. "What does that mean?"

"It means if you go near him again, I'll kill him, Allison. I'll put a bullet between his fucking eyes."

When he was asleep with her locked so tightly in his arms she could barely breathe, she lay awake and silently cried. She was so worried about the man she loved. There was no way to know if he had survived the vicious beating the man she hated with all her heart had given him or how much damage had been done to him.

* * * * *

"His nose is broken. He has a concussion, a dislocated elbow, broken forearm and wrist, four broken ribs—one of which punctured a lung— bruised kidneys, split lip and numerous lacerations. He may have a detached retina. We're not sure on that."

"He going to be all right?" the deputy asked.

"Hopefully, though someone did their level best to beat him to death," the doctor answered.

"Robbery get out of hand?" the doctor's assistant asked.

"We don't think so. Paramedics said they found his wallet in the back pocket of his jeans. There was six hundred dollars and four credit cards in it. Muggers would have taken the cash, if not the cards, plus he had a cell phone in his other pocket," came the reply. "And then there was his house. Someone torched it and his truck. The truck is a classic and worth some money. Nah, we're leaning toward whoever did this had one helluva beef with him."

The doctor shook his head. "Well, they did a number on him, that's for sure. They tell you we called the emergency notification number in his wallet and the woman who answered asked why they were calling her?"

"Girlfriend?"

The doctor shook his head. "Would you believe wife? When we told her he'd been beaten up, she said he ought not to have been where he was and that he had it coming. She told us not to call her again."

"Messing with something he shouldn't have?" the assistant queried.

"Or with some*one*," the deputy replied. "I may need to talk to the wife and see if she hired some guys to teach him a lesson."

* * * * *

"Where the hell is Drew?" Jake asked Whip.

"Hasn't come in yet," Whip told his father. "Want me to call the house?"

"Get me some coffee. I'll call the goddamned house," Jake grumbled. He went into Drew's office and picked up the phone. When his daughter answered the phone, the gruffness left his voice. "Mornin' sweetheart. Where's that bastard you married?"

There was a slight pause, then Terri laughed. "I knew there was something I should have done last night," she said. "He's in the hospital over at Phoebe."

"For what?" Jake asked.

"Don't know; don't care," Terri said. "Listen, Daddy, I've got to go. I'm meeting someone for breakfast." She hung up before he could stop her.

Jake slammed the receiver down. "Son of a bitch," he snapped.

"He sick or somethin'?" Whip asked as he entered the office.

"Go get me some cigars and the *Albany Herald*," Jake ordered.

"Why me?" Whip pouted.

"'Cause I told you to," Jake shouted. "And send Rawls in here before you go."

*   *   *   *   *

Early rapped lightly on the door—wondering why Big Jake was at Drew's desk.

"Shut the goddamned door," Jake ordered.

Closing the door behind him, Early knew the old man wasn't going to invite him to sit down so he stood where he was, wiping his hands on the rag from his pocket.

"What the hell's happened to your cousin now?" Jake demanded.

Unease rippled through Early. "I don't know what you mean, sir," he replied.

"He's over in Phoebe Putney," Jake said. "I figured if anyone would know why it would be you."

"I haven't heard from him since yesterday morning," Early said. "I had to take Mrs. Harrelson's car over to—"

"Yeah, yeah, yeah," Jake said, waving away the explanation. "You can go."

"Do you want me to go over to Albany to check on—?"

"I want you to get your white trash ass back to work is what I want," Jake snapped. He narrowed his eyes. "That is if you want to keep your job."

"Yes, sir," Early said.

Despite the hatred he had for the man, Early was afraid of Jake Thompson. Any man in his right mind would be. It was a deep dark secret, but Drew told him Terri admitted her father had killed two men back in the day. He left Drew's office and went returned to the shop—concern for his cousin like a burning taper in his gut.

"What have you done, Drew?"

* * * * *

Hatch stuck his head in Bobby's office. "Sheriff Jackson from over in Dougherty County calling on line one, Bobby," he said.

Bobby nodded and picked up the receiver, punched the blinking button. "Hey, Bubba, how's it hanging?"

"Ten inches and growing," came the answer. "Say look, Bobby. I got me a man over here what got the tar beat out of him last night. You know anything 'bout that?"

"Prick's name wouldn't be Andrew Dunne by any chance would it?"

"That's the one. You know about it?"

"A little bit."

"His wife involved."

"Nah, though I can tell you she's gloating about it this morning."

"You wanna tell me what's going on with him?"

"Nothing other than to say he's an adulterous little bastard who got what was coming to him and leave it at that."

Sheriff Jackson snorted. "It's like that is it? Dipping the wick in some other man's honey pot?"

"Happens," Bobby acknowledged.

"Well, now, look here. I ain't gonna have this shit in my county, Bobby. They damned near killed that boy. Burned down his house and torched his truck. I can't have that going on here. What with the nigger gangs and the Dixie Mafia and the meth problem we're having to deal with? I don't need no Miller County boy coming up here and getting his ass beat on my turf. You get me?"

"I do, Bubba. I'll keep his ass out of Dougherty County. That good enough?"

Sheriff Jackson sniffed. "Guess it'll have to be." He paused, then asked, "Jus' 'tween you and me, who'd he screw that he shouldn't have?"

"Let's just say the wrong man's woman," Bobby said with a laugh.

* * * * *

Whip called his father as soon as he got out of the convenience store.

"What?" Jake snapped.

"Just thought you might like to know what I saw over here at the Jot 'Em Down," Whip said.

"Why the fuck do I care what you saw, boy?" Jake demanded.

"I was up at the counter getting your cigars when Coach Bennett walked in," Whip said.

"So?"

"So," Whip said, then lowered his voice although he was the only one in his car. "Coach came up to the counter to pay for his gas. When he handed Merle his money, I got a look at his knuckles. They were all chewed up like he'd been in a fight with somebody. You don't reckon it was Drew, do you? That they got into it? If that's what happened, you can bet Coach came out on the winning side."

"You think he caught Drew over in Albany with his wife and beat him up?" Jake asked. "Put the little turd in the hospital?"

"Wouldn't surprise me if that's what's happened," Whip said. "Coach was in here a day or so ago and I heard him tell Drew he'd better leave his woman alone—meaning Mrs. Bennett—and that if he didn't, he'd mop up the floor with him."

There was silence on the other end for a long moment.

"Daddy?" Whip questioned.

"Anything else?" his father asked.

"Coach had a nasty bruise on his face like maybe Dunne got at least one lick in before he went down."

"A lick," Jake scoffed. "That's about all the manhood he's got in him."

"That's about the size of it," Whip agreed.

* * * * *

"Morning, Big Jake," Bobby said when Hatch let him know who was calling. "How are things with you?"

"Whatcha know about a whuppin' Drew might've got up in Albany?"

"First I heard of it. Want me to check it out?" Bobby asked.

"Yeah, do that and do it now."

"Yes, sir. I sure will." Bobby hung up and leaned back in his chair to look at his visitor. "Seems Drew Dunne got the mother of a beat down up in Albany. Big Jake wants me to look into it. Whatcha want me to tell him?"

Clay grinned. "Give him half an hour, then call him back and tell him the cops said he got caught fooling around with another man's wife and had the shit beat outta him. No need to mention me. Whip saw my knuckles at the Jot 'Em Down. He'll know it was me."

* * * * *

As soon as Bobby relayed the message to Big Jake, the old man was out of Drew's chair and striding like a bull through the showroom. Though several people spoke to him, he ignored them, went outside and got into his car.

* * * * *

Drew shifted his right arm as best he could. The IV was stinging again. Glancing down at it, he was only marginally relieved to see there was no blood in the tube as there had been the day before when they'd had to restick him. He hurt enough in every muscle, bone and sinew in his body and his head was throbbing unmercifully. He couldn't move his left arm at all for it was in a cast from near his shoulder to his wrist and was lying on a pillow. The catheter rammed up his cock didn't feel all that good, either, and the bandage across his nose itched. All in all, he was one miserable son of a bitch. When the door opened, he let out a sigh of relief for the nurse had gone to get something for the pain. Seeing who had entered the room, he had to clamp down on his tongue to keep from groaning.

Big Jake stopped just inside the room and whistled. "Woo wee, Coach made mincemeat out of your face, didn't he?" He laughed,

210

sauntering a bit closer to the bed. "You ain't such a pretty boy now. That'll teach you to try running with the big dogs." He grunted. "Little mutt like you."

"May I help you, sir?"

Jake looked around at the nurse who had just entered Drew's room. He smiled his most engaging smile. "I'm his father-in-law," he told her. "Came to check up on him. How's he doing?"

"I've got a shot for him," she said, not returning the smile.

"Okay," Jake replied. He went over to the window to look out as the nurse administered the injection. After she left, he turned from the window to look at Drew.

"What the fuck did you do, boy?" Jake asked.

Drew was beginning to feel the pain shot and it loosened his tongue. "I'm not a boy."

"Well, you sure as fuck ain't much of a man or you wouldn't have let that peckerwood beat the shit out of you," Jake growled. "You ask me, you got just what you deserved. Too bad that beat down Coach gave you didn't finish the job and put your ass in the ground."

"You and Terri Anne would like that, wouldn't you?" Drew asked.

"It would have made my day and thrilled her no end. Don't nobody hate you as much as me and Terri Anne do."

"You two don't have a monopoly on hate, old man," Drew said defiantly.

Jake came over to the bed and braced his hands to either side of Drew, leaned in and with his lips peeled back said, "You done had one beating, you little prick. You wanna go for two? Want me to finish what Coach started? I'll make it so you can't open that smart mouth of yours for a month or two. That what you want, boy?"

Drew held the old man's silent glare and didn't reply.

"No?" Jake asked. "All right, then let's you and me be clear about somethin', okay?" He grabbed a handful of Drew's hair and pulled viciously. "You better listen to what I'm gonna say and you'd better heed my words, boy. If you *ever* cheat on my little girl again, there ain't nowhere you can hide, no hole you can crawl into that I won't find you, drag your sorry ass out and make you sorry you were ever born. And this here hospital bill? It ain't going on our group policy. You're gonna pay it outta your own pocket. You understand? I ain't paying the freight for your fuckup."

"Yes," Drew replied through clenched teeth.

"Yes, what?" He tugged on Drew's hair.

"Yes, sir."

"I didn't hear you, boy."

"I understand."

"You better. Now if…"

Drew tuned out the old man's words. He stared into the hateful eyes that were glaring back at him and wished Jake Thompson in his grave. Something had snapped inside him as Bennett beat him. The bastard thought he'd beat the hell out of him but Drew looked at it differently. Bennett had beaten the hell *into* him.

"You stay your ass over here in Albany until you don't look like you got put through a meat grinder. I don't want to see you back in Miller County until you are presentable."

Long after Jake had gone, Drew lay perfectly still staring at the ceiling. His head was no longer hurting but his anger was like a sandspur jammed under his thumbnail.

And he made a vow to himself. The next man who pulled his hair was going to die.

* * * * *

Early came to spend the day with him every Saturday and brought Bea with him on each of the three Sundays Drew was hospitalized. During the week his cousin called every day to check on him.

After the first week when he was no longer bedbound, Early helped him slowly transverse the halls with the IV bag in tow. They'd sit and talk until visiting hours were over. Not once had Early chastised him. Not once had they spoken of what had happened to put Drew in the hospital or who had done it. There was no need. The whole town knew.

They were going to let him go home the next day but he had nowhere to go. He couldn't go home to Colquitt just yet. Not until the casts were off his arms and he could halfway protect himself.

He'd purposefully avoided looking at himself in the mirror until that morning. With his arm and his wrist in casts, he'd had to rely on the nurses or Early to shave him, but a few days earlier he'd said fuck it and decided to let his beard grow. Curiosity about how the beard looked—since he'd never grown one—got the best of him so he steeled himself and looked into the mirror.

"Shit," he said.

It wasn't just the beating he'd endured that had altered how he saw himself in the mirror. Not the dark circles under his eyes or the crooked bump in his nose. It was far more than that. While he'd been recuperating life had etched a road map into his flesh. Dead end roads spread out from the corners of his eyes. Deepening ruts had been plowed at the bridge of his nose. East/West thoroughfares meandered lazily across his forehead, cutting ditches there. Southbound lanes bracketed the corners of his mouth like off-ramps. Highways and byways and pathways were beginning to crisscross his face. Now there were scars forming from the vicious beating— over his eyes, on his cheeks, his chin—to add to the construction.

Scars that were red now would fade into white lines eventually.

"More scars to add to my growing collection," he said to the mirror.

The scar on his side from the appendectomy. The scar on his thigh where the bone was held together with titanium rods and pins and plates. Terri could never bear to look at it, had never touched it yet Allison had kissed it tenderly and ran her tongue the length it. Would she kiss these new scars? he wondered.

The thought of her made him turn away from his reflection.

He was worried about her. Neither Early nor Bea could tell him much about her. They saw her at church on Sundays but at no other time. She no longer volunteered at the hospital and Bennett had sold her car. For all intents and purposes she was apparently a prisoner in her own home. He couldn't help but wonder what the bastard had done to her that day. Bea had assured him there were no visible marks on her but Drew remembered the fine white lines left by the bastard's belt that he'd seen on Allison's ass.

* * * * *

He started into the barbershop, thought better of it and decided he didn't need a shave and that he rather liked the way his hair curled around his ears. Fuck the shave and a haircut. He'd keep his two bits.

Walking on, he noticed a sign for a tattoo parlor and stopped to look in the window. There were sketches and actual photos of freshly inked tats in frames positioned in the showcase part of the window. A couple caught his eye and he decided to go in.

"Just to look around," he said.

And came out three hours later with a tattoo he had designed himself burning and itching on his right bicep. He'd cobbled the design together from several he'd found in the books on the counter and each portion of the seven-inch-long, four-inch-wide tat had a special meaning for him.

"Tell me about this design," he'd asked after studying the books for a while.

"That's a Celtic tree of life," the tattoo artist told him. "It signifies endurance and reminds us we should stand firm during times of great challenge."

"And this?" he asked, showing the woman an intricate knot design.

"That's the Dara knot," she replied. "The knot is like the roots of a tree. It signifies steadfast knowledge of who you are, the strength of spirit and the ability to see and know the truth."

"And if I combine them? What would it mean then?"

"That you have inner resources that strengthen you regardless of the circumstances you see around you."

"All right. See where these three knots are on the roots of the oak? Instead of plain loops, make them hearts like…" He opened another book of tats and pointed to an intricate Celtic heart. "And make the one at the bottom larger and put the initial A within it. In the other two E and C. And on each of the leaves spreading across the top of the tree put the date 11-02-2014. Make the leaves green and the tree brown but the hearts red."

"Just curious," she said. "What do the A, E and C stand for?"

"Allison, Early and Corinne," he told her. "The only three people in this world who accept me as I am."

* * * * *

He passed the pawnshop, took five steps, stopped, then pivoted around. Pushing open the door, a bell jingled overhead and he looked up.

"Annoys the shit out of me, too," the man behind the glass counter said. "Been meaning to take it down."

Drew leveled his gaze on the man. "Let's you know someone's come in though."

The man shrugged. "There is that." He leaned his forearms on the glass countertop. "What can I do you for?" He acted like he didn't notice the scars on Drew's face.

"I'm looking for a gun."

A nod affirmed Drew's words. "Pistol? Rifle? Shotgun?"

"Handgun."

"For?"

"Protection."

The pawnshop owner straightened up and waved his hand to indicate Drew should follow him. "Got just the thing."

Drew walked along the counter to the back of the store where a second counter ran perpendicular to the first. There were guns inside the glass case and the man took a key from his pocket to open it.

"You here by yourself?"

"Nope," the man replied. He glanced up at Drew. "If you're thinking of robbing me you better think twice." He jacked his thumb toward a mirror behind him.

"All I'm thinking about is getting even with the men who did this," Drew said, circling his palm in front of his face.

"Yeah, I would be, too, dude." He slid the glass door back and reached inside for a weapon. He laid it on the counter. "Springfield XDM 9mm 4.5. It weighs thirty-two ounces. Has a match grade barrel. Comes with two 19 round mags. Trigger pull is between 5.5–7.7 pounds and it has the shortest travel than any currently available polymer pistol. Along with a short reset, which keeps you on target with greater ease for faster, more accurate follow-up shots, this baby is a sweet piece of work."

"Accurate I'm not worried about. If I hit the target anywhere it will make my day," Drew told him. He picked up the gun and turned it back and forth in his hand. "Preferably in the crotch."

"Somebody really pissed you off, huh?" the man asked with a chuckle. "Tired of having sand kicked on you at the beach?"

"I'm getting goddamned *tired* of everybody telling me they're going to fuck my shit up." He pulled back the slide, sighted down the barrel. "They want to fuck with my shit, then they're gonna get that shit all over them."

"I heard that," the man said. "You'll want to use 124gr or 147gr Jacketed Hollow Point for the best protection. Hit your target anywhere and that target is gonna know some pain."

"That's my intention."

"You got a Georgia Weapons License?"

Drew nodded.

"I'll need to see it."

Reaching into the back pocket of his jeans, Drew pulled out his wallet, opened it and thumbed through the cards inside until he found the license. He handed it over.

"This will be in lieu of a background check if it's in order," the man said.

"It is," Drew said. "I haven't been hunting in a while but I keep the license up-to-date. How much?"

"Four hundred and fifty dollar, plus tax."

That was more money than he had in his wallet but he could always find an ATM to get more from one of the accounts he had there in Albany.

"Okay. Bullets?"

"Thirty-five fifty for a hundred. Extra nineteen-round clips are thirty-four dollars each."

"I'll take the gun, bullets, and an extra two clips." He looked along the counter. "What about a Taser? You have one of those?"

"You're going hunting for bear, ain't you, dude?" the man asked with a chuckle. He put out his hand. "Name's Gage, by the way. Gage Abbott."

"Drew Dunne," Drew said, taking the man's hand.

He went to the nearest ATM and came back with the money to buy both the 9mm and the Taser as well as the bullets and extra clips. After completing the purchase, Gage invited him to come hear him play at his sister's country-western bar.

"You'll have a great time. Trust me," Gage said. "I play a mean fiddle."

With no place to go and no time to be there, Drew agreed. He wasn't much for drinking anything other than beer but he had the sudden urge to tie one on. Brand new tat stinging, new beard itching, all he needed was some new duds to make him feel like a new man. He agreed to meet Gage back at the pawnshop after closing at five p.m.

Strolling along the street, he passed a truck with a For Sale sign on the side window. He went over to it, looked in the cab, which had a torn headliner and raggedy seat. In the bed that was rusted out. At the tires that had $500 rims but were nearly bald and shook his head. The paint job was good and the windows shone with a fresh cleaning but the rest of the truck was a disaster.

"Like me," he said.

Returning to the sidewalk he moved on down the street but his mind was on the truck. He needed transportation as much as he needed a place to stay. Motels, hotels were the easy part. He could do either but having wheels, mobility was more important. Mind on that, right hand on his cast to wiggle it as best he could to soothe the maddening itch, he reversed directions and went looking for a cab.

By the time he returned to Gage's shop, he had a brand new set of wheels and clothes he would never—could never—have worn before he took the beating.

"Shit, dude, you look like an outlaw," Gage greeted him.

And he knew he did. Looking into the mirror at himself from the chin down, he didn't look half-bad. Black shirt—on which he left the first three buttons undone. Black jeans so tight they gave him a hard on. Black leather boots to match the black leather belt with the broad silver buckle. Clothing made the man, he'd thought as he studied his reflection. It had taken some doing to pull the shirt sleeve over the damnable cast but he'd managed.

Lifting his gaze to look into his own eyes, he realized they had changed. They looked hard. Angry. Determined. With the five-day growth of beard, the scars over his eyes and his battered nose, he looked downright mean.

He felt mean.

"That's my truck," he told Gage and pointed to the black Chevy Silverado 1500 sitting at the curb.

"Nice ride," Gage said.

"You should have seen the one he torched," he said as he went around to the driver's side.

"Who torched it?" Gage asked. He looked at Drew across the hood.

"My old man," Drew told him. "Remember the house and truck at Radium that burned a few weeks ago?"

"Fuck," Gage said, sliding onto the seat. "That was you?"

"That was me."

"No wonder you're pissed, dude," Gage said with a grunt.

"Yeah," Drew said as he turned the key. "Had the fucking shit beat out of me, my house and my truck burned to cinders, my woman taken from me. Good times had by all except me and her."

"I read about it in the *Herald* but I don't remember there being a lady involved. Was she hurt?"

"God I hope not," Drew said. He put his arm on the back of the passenger seat and looked behind him to back out of the parking spot. It was a bit difficult to drive with the cast—harder yet to turn the damned engine on—but he was determined.

"But you don't know for sure," Gage stated.

"If the bastard did hurt her, I promise you he won't do it again."

"Nothing jacks my jaws worse than a woman beater. Guy like that needs his ass kicked. I can help with that," Gage said. He gave Drew a steady look. "I mean it, dude. I can *help* with that. You need some help?"

Drew shook his head. "Let's don't talk about it tonight. Tonight I want to get rip-roaring drunk and puke my guts up."

Chapter Eighteen

Having a hangover was worse than he remembered. He hadn't had one since college and the one rocking his brain at that moment was brutal. His eyeballs hurt and his hair felt as though it was crawling around on top of his head—a head that he was fairly sure was melting.

"Okay, so here's what you need to do."

He tried to focus on Gage's face but it kept slithering away— jerking like a marionette on a string—into the ether.

Or whatever the hell that wavy, undulating mist was that was surrounding the pawnshop owner and making his voice sound as though it was coming out of a deep well.

"You need to let me contact this guy I know."

"Who?" Drew managed to ask. He was trying to lie as still as possible but his body kept levitating off the mattress, then spinning around like a top.

"Don't know his name, dude. Nobody knows his name. You don't *want* to know his name. They just call him the Solution."

"Is that like the Situation?"

"The what?"

"Never mind. So if you don't know his name, how do you know how to get in touch with him?" He scrubbed his hand over his face, then looked at it. When had he grown a sixth finger?

"I know a guy who knows a guy who knows a guy who knows how to contact him. I can contact *that* guy. They call him the Negotiator."

"Makes perfect sense to me," Drew replied.

"You shouldn't go after your old man or this Clay prick. You go to jail and you don't get the girl. You dig?"

"Clay prick," Drew said, chuckled at the image the words conjured in his mind, then nodded and wished he hadn't for the room spun like a tilt-a-whirl and he leaned over the side of the bed and added another layer of puke to what was already there. The acrid smell hit his nostrils and he let loose another stream.

"Shit, man," Gage said. "You missed the trash can again."

"Sorry," Drew mumbled and eased his body back to the mattress—wishing it would stop rotating.

"Just say the word and I'll give the Negotiator a call."

"I'll get back to you on that," Drew told him. He drifted off as Gage started to explain the services provided by the man he called the Solution. The last thing he remembered hearing was Gage telling him he shouldn't drink so much.

* * * * *

Gage had left him at the Super 8, taken one of Drew's credit cards to give to the front desk to pay for the room and left him a note telling him where the card was and why he had taken it from his wallet. A quick inspection of his wallet told him Gage was a man to be trusted. There were nine one hundred dollar bills in the wallet left over from when he'd bought the truck and every one of them was still there.

That had been a week before and he hadn't seen his new friend since, though Gage had called a couple of times to make sure he was okay.

"You let me know when you need me to put you in touch with the Solution," he'd reminded Drew.

"Will do."

Now sitting in the motel room in the middle of the afternoon, staring at the phone, the remnants of the fast food meal he'd choked down for lunch smelling up the place, Drew knew he needed to go home.

"Home," he said.

Not that he had one. He was fairly sure Terri wasn't going to allow him to come back there. Her house had never been his home— anyone's *home*—for that matter. Early didn't have room for him, although his cousin would offer their sofa for his use. That wouldn't be fair to Early or Bea or the kids, and the thought of being around their happy little family unit was frankly more than he could bear. He was steeped in misery and knew he'd be in that frame of mind for some time to come. There was only one scenario that would or could make him better.

He reached for the phone, but stopped with his palm just above the receiver. For two days he'd been doing the same thing—reaching for the phone to call Allison, then chickening out.

"I saw her at the Piggly Wiggly and she smiled at me," Early told him. "She looked about as unhappy as a woman can look but she didn't look like he'd been abusing her."

"Does she know I'm okay?" he'd asked.

"Everyone in town knows you're all right so I'm sure she does."

That relieved his mind a bit but did not to alleviate the terrible loneliness that was eating at him like a hungry shark.

He needed to talk to her. He desperately needed to hear her voice. He ached to hear it. Longed to hear it. Longed to see her beautiful face. To hold her. To make love to her.

"Quit it," he hissed and jerked his hand away from the phone. Calling her would only cause trouble if her bastard of a sicko husband found out about it. He thought of a better idea instead. Picking up the receiver, he dialed 411 and asked for the number of a certain wise lady.

"Hello?"

"Miss Lillian? This is—"

"I know who it is, son," she said. "And I know why you're calling. I've been waiting for you to call. Would you like to talk to her?"

His heart leapt up into his throat and his fingers constricted tightly around the receiver. "Is she there?"

"Hold on," Miss Lillian said and the clink of the phone being put down went through him like a bolt of lightning. There were low voices in the background that he could make out, then heaven came on line.

"Drew? Are you all right?" she asked. He heard the concern in her voice along with the excitement.

"I'm fine, baby," he said, feeling tears welling up in his eyes. "How 'bout you?"

"Better now that I can talk to you," she said. "Where are you?"

"Still in Albany. I'm at—"

"Don't tell me," she said. "I shouldn't know."

That was probably just as well.

He had to ask. He had to know. "How is he treating you?"

"Like I'm an imbecile, but that's nothing new."

"He hasn't…hurt you…has he?"

"No."

He knew she was lying. He heard that in her voice as well, but he let it pass. There was nothing he could do about it at the moment. But he would.

"I'm coming home tomorrow," he told her.

"Drew, your wife has told everyone in town that she's not going to let you come back," she warned him.

"I figured as much. I'll find someplace else to stay. Don't worry about that."

"With Early?"

"No, there's just not any room there. Like I said, I'll find a place." He paused. "How come you're over at Miss Lillian's?"

"She's the only neighbor I'm allowed to visit," she replied. "Clay doesn't like her but I think he's a bit intimidated by her. She's the only friend I have in town right now."

"He's intimidated by her," he repeated. "That's good to know. I've wanted to call you but I was afraid he would answer."

"You wouldn't have reached me. He changed our phone number," she told him. "It's unlisted now."

"I half-expected that," he said.

"Allison, your husband's home," he heard Miss Lillian say in the background.

"I've got to go," she told him. "Please, *please* be careful. He hates you, Drew."

"No more than I hate him," Drew responded. "I know you can't say it where she'll hear you but I can say it. I love you, baby."

She surprised him. "I love you, too."

"He's on his way across the road, Allison. Hang up," Miss Lillian commanded.

"I've gotta go," she whispered.

"Wait. Put her on the line. I need to talk to her," he said more loudly than he intended but he didn't want her to hang up just yet.

"He wants to talk to you," Allison said and then she was gone, the receiver clunking on the desk again. He heard the doorbell ring and wished he could be standing behind it with his gun, then heard the bastard's hateful voice.

"Let's go. I've only got a half hour for lunch."

"And you couldn't get something in town?" Miss Lillian asked.

"Not when I have a woman to fix it for me," Bennett snapped. "Come on, bug."

There was the sound of a door closing and Miss Lillian calling Bennett an asswipe, then she picked up the phone.

"I detest that odious man," she said.

"Bug?" he questioned.

"That's what the little shithead calls her." She snorted. "That's about how she looks to him, I guess, and how he treats her."

"Is he hurting her?"

"Not that I can tell," Miss Lillian replied. "When are you coming home?"

"Tomorrow."

"I don't suppose you have somewhere to stay," she said. "I'd offer my spare bedroom but having you right across the street from her—"

"I appreciate that, Miss Lillian, but that would be like pouring gasoline on a smoldering fire."

"Sorry to hear about your house over in Albany, son," she told him. "That was just a rattlesnake-mean thing they did to you."

"Do people know who did it?"

"They have their suspicions," she replied. "Clay hasn't denied that he beat you up but he swears he didn't set fire to your house and that old truck of yours."

"He didn't," Drew said. "Wade did."

"Figures. So…" She sniffed. "What do you need me to do, Andrew?"

"Just keep on being her friend until I find a way to get her away from him."

"You be careful, son. No man takes kindly to his woman being taken out from under his nose even if he doesn't love her. To him, she's property."

"Yes, ma'am, I realize that but I wouldn't be much of a man if I didn't try to make things right for the woman I love. It may be a sin—"

"May be?" she countered. "No, son, it is, but sometimes sinning is the only way."

"Then let me run my plan past you," he said.

Part Two

Chapter Nineteen

The man who pulled up in front of the Five County Motors the next morning was not the same man who had walked out of it six weeks earlier. That man had cut his own casts off before it was time and set about regaining his strength and mobility for what he knew was coming. Mouths dropped open when that man got out of the black Silverado no one in town recognized, shifted his broad shoulders beneath the black leather jacket covering them, took off his shades and tossed them onto the dashboard. When he shut the truck door and turned around, there were more than a few collective gasps.

"Sweet Jesus Almighty God, is that Drew Dunne?" one of the mechanics asked.

He walked to the door of the dealership, pushed it open and strode—no, Lenore thought as she stared at him, *strutted*—to his office where Whip had taken up residence in his absence.

"You want some coffee?" she asked as he passed her.

"Please," he said. He gave her what she thought had to be one helluva killer smile with his white teeth made even whiter by the scruff that covered his upper lip, chin and cheeks. She lowered her gaze down past the black pants to the dusty black boots and whistled.

"I like your new look," she said.

"Me, too," he replied.

"He won't," she warned.

"Fuck him," he said, then glanced around at her. "Pardon my French."

She laughed and shook her head. In all the years she'd known him, Andrew Allan Dunne had never said an off-color word in her presence. Somehow that one vulgarity made him even sexier.

"Um hum," she said, fanning her face. The boy had finally become a man.

And that was exactly what he was, she thought. The beard, the clothes and the hair that was longer than she'd ever seen him wear it all combined to make him movie star handsome. The look in his blue eyes—a look she had never expected to see there—made him seem dangerous.

"Way to go, Drew Dunne," she said, turning away to fetch his coffee.

* * * * *

Whip looked up, down, then up again. His eyes widened and his lips parted.

"Get the hell out of my chair and my office," Drew ordered. When Whip only sat there staring at him, Drew went to the desk, put his doubled fists on the top and leaned across it. He put pure menace in his tone. "I said get the *fuck* outta my chair."

The blood left Whip's face. "Daddy's gonna—"

"Your daddy can fire my ass if he's so inclined, but I seriously doubt it," Drew said. "And if you aren't out of that chair in two seconds, I'm going to come around there and pull your lazy goddamned ass out of it."

There must have been something more than menace in his words that scared Whip shitless. He sprang out of the chair as though a gator had bit him on his fat ass. He skirted the desk with his face pale.

"I'm gonna call Daddy," he threatened.

"Oh, please do," Drew said. "I want to talk to him."

Whip scuttled out of the office like a singed dog and Drew heard his brother-in-law's office door slam shut. One glance at the phone and he chuckled as the light came on.

"You took him down a peg or two," Lenore said as she came in with his coffee.

Drew shrugged out of the leather jacket and tossed it on one of the chairs. "Give me a few minutes, then come back in and bring me up to speed," he told her. He thanked her when she put the coffee on his desk.

"Things have been real quiet since you've been gone," she said, running her gaze over his face. He saw her frown and knew she was looking at the scars.

"They're gonna get a whole lot louder now that I'm back," he told her. He went behind the desk and sat down. "Is Early here?"

"He went over to Dothan to pick up some parts but he should be back by noontime," she replied.

He nodded and realized she was staring at his chest. As he'd been doing since he bought a whole new wardrobe, he'd left the top three buttons undone.

"Like the shirt, too, boss man," she said, then turned around—her face a bit darker than normal.

It didn't take Jake Thompson long before he came bustling through the showroom and into Drew's office without breaking his momentum. The old man stopped in the doorway as though he'd hit an invisible barrier.

"What the hell are you wearing?"

"Shirt and pants, boots," Drew told him. "Forgot my underwear though."

Jake's jaw dropped. "How dare you come into my place of business dressed like a pool shark."

"The son of one anyway," Drew stated. He brought his left hand up to scratch at his chin and just as he had intended, Jake noticed what he wanted him to see.

"Where the hell is your wedding ring?" the old man demanded.

Drew leaned back in his chair. "I lost it."

"How the hell you lose your goddamned wedding ring?"

"If you didn't notice that one time you came to see me in the hospital, my arm was in a cast." He gave a nonchalant shrug. "My right wrist, too."

"What has that got to do with you not wearing my daughter's wedding ring?"

"You mean her brand?" Drew asked. "I have no idea where that thing is and I don't care."

"Then you'd better go buy you another one."

Drew just stared at him.

"Don't give me that sullen look. I'll wipe that look off your face, boy."

"Why don't you try, Jake?" Drew asked. "Matter of fact, I *want* you to try."

Jake blinked. "Excuse me?"

"You heard me." He said it with just a touch of disrespect and it went through Jake Thompson like a dagger.

"You get the hell out of that chair, boy," Jake ordered.

Drew smiled. "Do you *really* want me to?"

Just as Drew had done with Whip, Jake put his fists on the desk and leaned in. "You get up, go to wherever the hell it is you're staying and shave that shit off'n your face. Cut that ragged mop of hair and put on some decent business clothes. When you come back here—"

"No."

Jake's face turned red. "What the fuck do you mean, *no?*"

"Exactly what I said. I mean, no, I'm not gonna shave. No, I'm not going to cut my hair. No, I'm not going to change my clothes, buy a wedding ring or kiss your fat ass ever again."

"You are fired," Jake screamed at him.

"I don't think you wanna do that," Drew said quietly. "Not unless you want everybody in town to know that Whip has been embezzling from the company since you put him here."

The red leached out of Jake's puffy face. "That's a goddamned lie."

Drew reached over and pushed the intercom button. "Lenore, would you bring me in that ledger we were working on before I left and ask Whip to join us?"

"With pleasure," Lenore replied.

Jake parked his wide load in one of the chairs in front of Drew's desk, raked his angry gaze over the leather jacket laying across the other one, then turned his glare on Drew. "If you can't prove what you just said…"

"I can prove it," Drew replied, knowing full well he had cooked the books in such a way that Whip would look guilty.

"I heard you tell him he was fired," Whip said as soon as he came through the door. "Why's he still sitting there, Daddy?"

Lenore came in before Jake could answer. She extended the ledger toward Drew but the old man grabbed it out of her hand, told her to leave, shut the door and not disturb them. Drew looked up at her, smiled and nodded.

She knew, he thought. From the look on her face, she knew precisely what he'd done and—most likely—what he'd been doing for years. He knew because she winked at him before she turned to go.

Door closed, Jake began to thumb through the ledger.

"What's going on, Daddy?" Whip asked and Drew was pleased to hear the nervousness in his brother-in-law's voice.

Jake had heard it, too, and he looked up. "What the hell have you done, boy?" he asked.

"Done?" Whip repeated. "W…what do you m…mean, Daddy?" He ran his index finger under the collar of his crisp white cotton dress shirt, then tugged on his tie.

"You better tell me the truth," Jake said. "And you better tell me now." He leveled his narrowed eyes on his son. "Have you been taking money from the dealership?"

Whip took a step back and it was at that moment that Drew knew the bastard had and he hadn't caught it. Maybe Whip was a better businessman than Drew had given him credit for being. Well, now, he thought. Isn't *this* an interesting development?

"No, sir," Whip said, angrily shaking his head but he gave himself away with the way his bottom lip began to tremble. "I'd never do anything like that." He swung his attention to Drew and pointed a shaking finger at him. "If anyone's been juggling the books, it's him."

"Why would I do that, Whip?" Drew asked. He put his elbows on the chair arms, steepled his fingers and rested the tips under his chin as though he didn't have a care in the world. "I would have been too afraid of getting caught."

"Where'd you get the money to buy that truck out there?" Whip demanded and lifted his chin when his father switched a suspicious glower to Drew.

"I'm renting it," Drew said. "If you don't believe me, call Kingston Chevy and ask. When the insurance comes through on the house Wade burned down, I'll pay it off. Until then, I'll be making monthly installment payments."

Whip sputtered. He hadn't expected that answer.

"I know exactly how much money Drew has in his checking account," Jake said and at Drew's raised eyebrow, the old man snickered. "I even knew about that house you had in Albany. Don't think for a minute I didn't have people following and watching you."

That was a lie and Drew knew it but he simply shrugged. "I've got nothing to hide."

"You fucked Coach's wife," Whip accused.

Drew switched his gaze to Whip. "You may fuck your woman, Thompson. I make love to mine."

A deep stain invaded Whip's cheeks. "She's not your woman. She's Coach's woman. His wife."

"Not for much longer," Drew said. He unthreaded his fingers, leaned forward in the chair and looked Jake in the eye. "You can take the ledger with you to any accountant you like. You'll find out exactly what your son has been doing. How much money he's taken over the years. Now if you want that to become common knowledge in Miller County and the counties this dealership services, go on and fire me again. I'll walk right out that door and before sundown, everybody will be laughing about it over their supper tables."

Jake held Drew's gaze for a long time, then slowly closed the ledger. He laid it atop his son-in-law's desk, then settled back in his chair. "So you've grown a pair, have you?" he asked.

"Daddy, he's bluffing. He won't—"

"Go to your office, Whip," Jake said and Drew had to bite his tongue to keep from laughing.

"But Daddy—" Whip whined.

"Go to your office," Jake yelled. "I'll deal with your ass when I'm through with him."

Whip jumped and rushed to the door.

"And shut the door behind you."

Whip gone, Jake put his hands on his ponderous belly, spiked the fingers together and began rotating his thumbs around and around one another. It was a mannerism that had always annoyed Drew, but it told him the old man was cooking something up in his head—usually something that didn't bode well for Drew.

"Gonna have some scars on that pretty face of yours," Jake said.

"They'll add character," Drew responded.

Jake pursed his lips, studied Drew for a moment, then tilted his head to the side. "This isn't over, Drew."

"Didn't think for a minute it was," Drew acknowledged.

"You cheated on my little girl with the coach's wife."

"Who is cheating on me with the coach," Drew told him.

Jake's bushy eyebrows lowered. "You know that for a fact, do you?"

"Sure as it's raining out there again," Drew replied. He laced his fingers together and put them behind his head, leaned back more comfortably in the chair. "She admitted it, but I already knew. I've always known what your daughter was up to." He cocked a shoulder.

"I just didn't care. I can probably name you every man she's been with since our marriage. Bennett wasn't the first and I'll bet my pension he won't be the last."

"You calling my little girl a whore, Dunne?" Jake challenged.

"You know precisely the kind of woman she is, Jake," he said—deliberately leaving off any kind of respectful title. "You may not want to admit it, and I know damned well you don't like it, but you know. The whole town knows."

"You want a divorce?" Jake queried, eyes narrowed.

"Yes."

"Well, you aren't going to get one," Jake said. He heaved his bulk out of the chair, glanced down at the ledger. "This shit we've discussed stays right here."

"It does," Drew said, then smiled. "For now."

"Wade's out in the shop," Jake reminded him.

"Yeah?" Drew said. He shrugged. "People do love their gossip. Wade comes after me and the whole town is going to know about both your kids and all the really nasty little things the two of them have been doing over the years." He lifted his leg, rested it on the top of the desk and crossed his other leg over it. "Give me a fucking reason to tell them."

Jake left Drew sitting there grinning.

* * * * *

The motel owner didn't want to rent him a room.

"I don't want any trouble, Drew," he'd said nervously. "I just had the place renovated."

"I'm not going to cause any," Drew told him.

"It isn't you I'm worried about. If you bring that woman—"

Drew held up his hand. "I'd consider very carefully what it was you were about to say if I were you, Jimmy."

"I meant no disrespect to Coach's wife but everybody knows—"

"I doubt Allison and I are the first people to have an affair in Miller County, Jim. If memory serves you and Lola—"

"All right," Jimmy said. He turned and plucked a key from the board behind the desk. He gave it to Drew. "Just please don't do anything that I'll wind up having to pay for, Drew."

"All I want is a place to sleep," Drew told him. "I won't be bringing any man's wife here so you don't have to worry."

"Okay," Jimmy said but his tone left no doubt that he wasn't happy about the situation.

Drew had a few clothes in the front seat of his truck, some more in a couple of big plastic bins he'd bought at Wal-Mart. Under a light rain, he lugged everything into room nine and stacked them in the open closet beside the bathroom.

Inside one was his Dopp kit and he got it out, put his toothbrush, comb, aftershave and a few more items on the small vanity in the bathroom. He put a bottle of shampoo and a cake of glycerin soap in the shower. He pulled out the bin containing his brand-new laptop, iPod, earbuds, Kindle and a few John Sandford paperbacks he'd been reading while recuperating in the hospital. He placed the laptop on the table by the window and his iPod on the bedside table then looked around.

The room wasn't bad. It was clean and it smelled good. There was a combination air conditioner/heater under the window, which had a good blackout curtain hanging over it. It would never be home but it would do until everything was in place.

Until that time came, everything had to appear normal. He would go to work, go to church, be shunned.

Yeah, that's a given, he thought. After all, he'd seduced and corrupted their beloved coach's wife. He cuckolded the town's good man. For shame, Andrew Dunne. He was lower than the lowest scum in the filthiest fish pond in the five counties. He would be treated accordingly and he didn't have a problem with that. He no longer cared what the fine folk of Miller County thought of him. If he was being honest with himself, he thought, he never had.

Yes, he'd have to stay in Colquitt until his replacement passport was ready.

"Fucking idiot," he called himself for not having put it in a safe-deposit box instead of leaving it in a desk drawer at the house in Albany. It—like everything else—had gone up in flames. Thankfully, Allison's passport hadn't been issued yet and was now in one of the safe-deposit boxes of the Suntrust Bank.

There was one other thing he wanted to have—needed to have—in the room with him and he went out to the truck to get it. Leaving the Taser in the glove compartment, he took out the 9mm and took it into his room. It was loaded and that was the way it would stay.

Putting it under his pillow, he sat down on the bed and picked up the phone to call Early to let him know where he would be staying.

"Okay, Bea wants you over here for supper every night," Early told him when they connected. "Every night. Understand?"

"She afraid no one in town will serve me food, cuz?" Drew asked and when Early hesitated, he realized that was probably what both Early and Bea thought.

He looked around. "There is a little mini-fridge and a microwave and coffeepot in the room. I can get some sandwich meats, TV dinners—"

"You will eat with *us*," Early stated in a tone that said not to argue. "You know she always makes way too much food and most of it winds up getting tossed out to the coons. Damned coons make such a mess out there and—"

"All right," Drew said, laughing. "I'll come eat with you. Satisfied?"

"Somewhat," Early said with a sniff.

"But not tonight, okay? I've got some things I have to do."

"One of them things better not be Allison Bennett," Early warned.

A loud crack overhead followed by a loud rush hitting the roof grabbed Drew's attention. "Shit, it's raining again."

"Supposed to rain all day tomorrow," Early said. "Pretty soon we'll all be sporting gills."

"I'm gonna run. See you in the morning."

"Drew?"

"Yeah?"

"Be careful, please," Early said.

"Trust me, cuz. I will be."

As soon as he was off the phone with Early, Drew opened up the laptop. Pulling up an Excel spreadsheet Gage and he had put together, he started checking the list entered there. It was a list of things for a Go Bag.

"Hopefully you'll never need to use it," Gage told him. *"But if you do, it'll be there."*

First aid kit, maps and travel information, cash and change because ATMs might be inaccessible. Tool kit, Swiss Army knife, fixed blade and folding knives, flashlights, jumper cables, tire patch, assorted batteries and battery powered radio, lighters and matches. Passports, IDs, duplicate birth certificates, medical records if available and medicines if needed.

Other things like a tent, sleeping bags and blankets, pillows, air mattresses and portable compressor, weather appropriate clothing and binding material—duct tape, paracord, rope, electrical tape, zip ties and all-purpose wire.

He'd already begun assembling some of the items and he would be going down to Wal-Mart in Bainbridge to pick up most of the others. On Saturday he planned to purchase a camper top for the truck along with a propane powered camp oven, extra bottles of propane and outdoor cookware.

"You need to be prepared in case you have to camp out," Gage said. *"Might not be possible for you to check into a Hilton if you get my drift. These are things you need to know when you're running, dude. They can mean the difference between spending a night in a sleeping bag or a jail cell."*

Drew had been amazed at the advice Gage handed out like candy at Halloween.

"You need several passports. You go out of the country on a fake passport and come back in on the real thing," he said. *"What you need to do is map out a plan. Down to the last detail. Where you're gonna go. How long you're gonna stay. Where you'll go next and how you're gonna get there. I know a guy who can get you auto tags for any state in the union and any province to the north. You need a Go Bag and you need it stocked with stuff you might need.*

"Disguises and such for you and the little lady like wigs, fake mustaches and beards, colored contact lens, sunglasses and regular glasses. Hell, I can even get you some fake scars for your face from this chick I know who handles the makeup for the local community theater."

He wouldn't need the fake scars, he thought. He needed to cover up the ones he already had.

He scanned the list and checked off a few things he'd gotten since coming back to Colquitt. A pellet gun and slingshot were on the list as well as a rifle. He had all three but they were in his room at Terri's house and he didn't think she'd let him stroll in and pick them up but it was worth a try.

Shutting down the laptop, he went over and stuffed it under the bed, just in case. He picked up his leather jacket and put it on, then headed for the door. He stopped, went back and got his gun, stuffed it in his waistband at the small of his back. He just had to caution himself not to shoot Terri when she started in on him.

As soon as he pulled up at the garage he saw the pile of things mounded near the garbage cans and knew the sodden stuff was his. All his clothes, books, magazines—everything he owned that had been in the house—were in the pile. He wasn't surprised and he wasn't further surprised when the garage door went up and he saw Terri standing behind her car smirking at him. She raised her middle finger in salute.

"Fine," he said. "There's nothing there I really want anyway."

The pellet gun and slingshot were easily replaced. The rifle his uncle had given him for his twelfth birthday, however, could not. It was pouring rain but he got out of the truck and went over to the pile. He knew he'd find the rifle and started digging through the foul-smelling waterlogged mess.

"You are a fucking piece of garbage," she yelled at him.

He didn't have to worry about her coming out in the rain to attack him. She'd ruin her fancy hairdo and that would be one of life's greatest tragedies. He ignored her and tossed aside shirts, books and shoes to get to the stock of the rifle he saw wedged under one of his high school yearbooks. Seeing all four of the books laying there made his heart ache but it didn't matter all that much in the grand scheme of things. Allison had lost her beloved treasures in the house fire.

"Trash digging through the trash," he heard her say. "The worthless looking for the even more worthless."

"Fuck you," he said under his breath. He was soaking wet with his hair plastered to his head and rain cascading down his face. The rain was icy cold and he was beginning to shiver by the time he dragged the rifle from the pile.

"If you don't get off my property I'm going to call Bobby to come arrest you," she yelled, growing enraged because he wasn't responding to her jibes.

"Do it," he said but he knew she couldn't hear him in the downpour. He straightened and headed back to the truck.

"I hate your guts you miserable coward," she screeched at him. "I wish Clay had beaten you to death."

"Wasn't from lack of trying," he said softly as he opened the truck door.

"And she's a piece of fucking shit."

He paused and looked at her. He knew she was baiting him and he also knew if he took one step toward her she would run, call her father first, then Bobby, then Clay and the trouble would start. Instead, he just stared at her.

"Did you hear me? She's a whoring slut. A skank ten times worse than Corinne Wexler. A diseased twat who'll fuck any man with a dick."

"You really shouldn't talk about yourself like that, Terri Anne," he yelled at her, then got in the truck, grateful he'd left the motor running and the heater on. He shivered hard, chilled to the bone. He put the truck in gear, did a three-point turn and peeled out of her driveway. He swore it would be the last time his tires rolled down that particular patch of gravel.

Chapter Twenty

Fury had bought him lock, stock and barrel. It owned his ass like a pimp did his whores.

He stood there staring at his truck with his hands curling into fists and wanted to kill something.

All four tires had been slashed and there were two long wavering grooves all the way from the fender to the tailgate where someone had gouged it. The word PRICK had been spray-painted in silver metallic paint on the driver side door.

He should have known, he thought as he flipped his collar up, hunched into what little protection his leather jacket afforded him. Wade or Clay—hell, it could even have been Terri—had been busy overnight. While he'd slept somewhat soundly, someone had been fucking up his life yet again.

Hands thrust into his pockets, he walked past the truck and started walking through the rain. He could have called Early or Corinne. Either of them would have picked him up but he needed the walk. He needed the cold rain drenching him because his fury was so raging it was a wonder he hadn't erupted into spontaneous combustion.

It was only a few blocks—by city standards—to the dealership. Cars passed him and heads swiveled around to see who was trudging around in the torrential downpour. He could almost imagine their thoughts when they recognized him. Before too many hours had passed, there wouldn't be a living soul in Colquitt who didn't know what had happened to his truck.

When he got to the dealership, he went straight to the open garage door bay, his bedraggled appearance halting all movement and sound in the shop.

"Addison, get me four new tires for my truck and go out to the motel and put 'em on."

He looked around at the men gathered in the shop, saw Wade sneering at him and knew he was the culprit. Every man there must have guessed what had happened for they looked around at Wade. Every one of them put distance between themselves and Wade. If any of them thought Drew was going to let it drop there, they were mightily surprised when he unzipped his jacket as though ready to do battle with his old man.

"You got something you wanna say to me, *boy*?" Wade asked, then hawked up a wad of phlegm and spat it on the floor.

"Yeah, Wade, I do," Drew said. He lifted his shirt to show them the gun stuck in his belt and saw his father's smirk disappear. "The next son of a bitch who thinks to slash my tires or key my truck better be wearing a fucking bulletproof vest. You poke the devil often enough, he's gonna poke you back."

Wade's lips peeled back from his stained, rotten teeth. "You think I'm afraid of you, you sniveling little turd?"

"You better be," Drew said. "The boy you used to beat is now the man who will kill you the next time you lay your hands on him."

"You threatening me?" Wade demanded but his eyes were leery.

"No," Drew said. "I'm making you a promise, old man."

He pulled his shirt down, turned his back on his father and started through the garage into the showroom. He was almost to the door when Wade gave a thunderous roar and ran after him. Wade slammed into his son and tackled him to the floor.

"Call Bobby," Early shouted. He and another mechanic sprinted toward the two men who were now rolling around on the floor. Wade was punching Drew anywhere he could gain purchase but Drew had brought his legs up to lock them around his father and was dodging more blows than he was taking.

Early and the other guy got to them and both grabbed Wade's arms to pull him off Drew. Bellowing like a bull, Wade tried to shake them off but Early and Mack Carter weren't small men. They were physically strong from lugging around auto parts, tires and rims and neither one was a slouch in the brawling department. They dragged Wade backward even as he tried to kick Drew in the head. Drew scuttled backward, got his back to the wall and pushed himself up. His face was a mask of fury as he lunged at his father— connecting chest to chest with the older man and knocking him out of Early and Mack's grip.

The sound of running feet pounding on the pavement brought Early's head around even as he reached out to take hold of Wade once more. Mack grabbed Drew and swung him around.

"Stop," Bobby yelled. He pushed past the onlookers and bulldozed Early to grab a handful of Wade's shirt. "Knock it off, Dunne."

Mack had pinned Drew's arms to his chest but Drew was trying to buck free. He felt the murderous intent in his eyes and every man there knew if he could get his hands around his father's throat, he'd kill him. No one even noticed the gun that had been in Drew's belt lying on the floor.

"Goddamn it, I said *stop*," Bobby shouted. He shook Wade like a terrier with a rat, but staggered back when Drew's enraged father twisted violently out of his hold.

Wade was breathing heavy as he stumbled against the tool cabinet. The clank of something weighty hitting the concrete floor was loud in the suddenly silent room.

"What the hell's going on here?" Bobby snarled. He was looking at Drew—just as everyone was. "Let him go, Mack." He put his hand on the butt of his pistol. "Somebody better start talkin' to me. Who started this shit?"

Drew ran the back of his hand under his nose. It was bleeding again and his lip was split but he'd never felt more alive in his life. He'd never taken a shot at his father before that day and he'd gotten in several good blows with his left hand before his arm starting hurting like hell. He was afraid he'd rebroken his forearm but at that moment he didn't care. Wade was going to have a hell of a shiner and when he leaned forward to spit out two of his front teeth that was just icing on the cake.

"Answer me, Dunne," Bobby yelled at Drew. "Who started this?"

"He did," Drew said. "He tried to jump me from behind."

"Bobby," someone shouted and the sheriff turned in time to see Wade running at Drew with a dead blow hammer—a specialized mallet used to dislodge stuck auto parts. The head of the hammer was hollow and filled with lead shot. Wade had it raised above his head.

"Dunne, stop," Bobby ordered and drew his service revolver but Wade kept running toward Drew.

Drew slapped his hand to his waistband and when he realized he'd lost the gun, his eyes flared. He threw up his right arm as

Wade—screaming at the top of his lungs—came barreling toward him.

The older man never reached Drew. Bobby aimed and fired, hitting Wade in the shoulder and spinning him sideways. Wade tripped over his own feet and went down heavy.

"Get Dr. Mackie," Bobby ordered Hatch, who took off running. The physician's office was diagonally across the street and he could get there before the paramedics could.

Blood was pouring from Wade's shoulder but he managed to push himself to a sitting position. He turned deadly eyes on his son.

"I'm gonna kill you yet, boy," he said.

"Not if I kill you first," Drew said. He swept his gaze around the floor looking for his gun but Mack had already picked it up and shook his head when Drew held his hand out for it.

"Whose fucking gun is that, Carter?" Bobby asked.

"It's mine," Drew said. "And I want it back."

"Give it here," Bobby told Mack.

"I've got a permit—" Drew stated.

"You'll get it back after I sort all this shit out," Bobby told him. He looked down at the gun Mack handed him and then over at Drew. "This is some serious firepower. Did you come in here today to kill your old man?"

"Fucking little prick ain't got the balls to kill me," Wade snarled.

"He slashed my tires and keyed my truck, spray-painted my door," Drew said. "All I did was warn him and the son of a bitch tried to jump me."

"That's what happened, Sheriff," Mack said. "We all saw it. Drew was just protecting himself."

"Fucking backstabber," Wade called Mack. He locked glares with his son. "Every morning you wake up, you'd better thank your God Clay didn't kill you that day in Albany, boy. If'n it had been my woman you fucked, I would have put you in the ground."

"Shut up, Dunne," Bobby warned. "Anything you say can—"

"And what woman would that have been, Daddy?" Drew yelled. "It sure as hell wasn't my mother because you didn't give a damn about her any more than you cared about me."

"Do you know why that was, boy?" Wade sneered. "You really wanna know why?"

"Yeah, why don't you tell me, old man," Drew shouted back at him.

"It was because your mama was a whore just like the coach's wife. That's why."

Drew started forward but both Mack and Early stepped in front of him. "Don't you talk about my mother—"

"She cheated on me like that little slut cheated on the coach. You ain't nothing to me. You've never been nothing to me 'cause I ain't your daddy! Doc Mackie is your daddy."

Stunned silence settled over the garage.

"You're lying," Drew growled.

"Why would I? Huh? 'Bout goddamned time I told the truth of it. 'Bout goddamned time the town found out what kind of whore your mama was." Wade swiveled his head as Dr. Mackie came hurrying in with Hatch. "Tell 'im, Mackie. Tell him about you and that goddamn whore that was his mama."

* * * * *

Doc knelt down beside Wade, reached for the wounded man's arm but Wade knocked his hand away. "Stop acting like a fool, Dunne and let me see to your wound," he ordered.

"Not until you tell him about how you used to fuck his mama every chance you got. He's your bastard, you know. You knocked her up. I know she told you."

Doc sat back on his heels. "You're lying."

"That's what I told him," Drew said.

"Look at him," Wade demanded. "*Look* at him! I got brown eyes. Mary Nell had brown eyes. Why you think that little bastard's eyes are blue like yours, Mackie? Her hair was yellow. Mine used to be black as pitch. What color is *his* hair, Mackie? Huh? Huh? What color is his hair? It's the same color as Boyd's is and Jack's was. Got them red streaks running through it. Just like yours used to be."

Every eye went to Drew, then back to Doc.

"Don't you men see the resemblance? Don't you see the resemblance 'tween that little bastard and Boyd Mackie? 'Tween him and Jack? Hell, him and Jack could have passed for twins."

Bobby exhaled loudly. "Son of a bitch," he said quietly, his gaze steady on Drew.

Drew met Doc's shocked expression. He shook his head, turned and pushed the door to the showroom open and went inside.

"He's a drip off *your* dick, not mine," Wade grumbled. "Like father, like son, fucking another man's woman. Another man's *wife*."

"Shut your mouth," Doc said. "You just shut your filthy mouth." He turned to spear Bobby with a hard glower. "Call the paramedics. I'm not working on this bastard."

"Now wait a minute," Bobby said. "You took an oath—"

"Get somebody else to see to him, I said." He started after Drew, stopped and turned to look at Wade. "You ever go near that boy again and I'll send the Klan after you, Dunne," he warned. "They should have come after you long before now. There's a fucking bullwhip out there with your goddamned name on it."

Doc went into the showroom and was walking toward Drew's office but Lenore stopped him.

"He left," she said. "Just walked out in the rain and kept walking."

"Which way did he go?" he asked.

"Around the courthouse. He's staying at the motel so he may be going there."

Doc thanked her and went to the door. He looked toward the courthouse but in the pouring rain he couldn't see anything.

"You need a car to get back to your office, Doc?" Early asked as he came up behind the physician. "It's coming down pretty hard."

"Yes, I need a car," Doc said. "Didn't I hear Drew got a new truck? Where is it?"

"Down at the motel with four slashed tires compliments of that mean old bastard in there. Drew walked up here today." He dug into his pocket and took out his key and handed it to Doc. "That's my truck there."

"Thanks, Early."

It had been years since Trent Mackie had driven a stick shift but he got the hang of it by the time he got around the courthouse and started looking for Drew. It took him a few minutes but he finally saw the young man walking on the side of the road. He pulled up beside him and lowered the passenger window.

"Get in," he told Drew.

"No thank you," Drew said without looking at him. "I'm wet."

"What you're going to be is in the ICU with pneumonia if you don't get in this truck, mister."

Drew stopped walking but he still didn't face the man talking to him. He lifted his head and looked down the street as the rain sluiced down his cheeks.

"Did you love her?" he asked.

Doc didn't hesitate. "More than anything in this world," Doc replied. "She was the sweetest, most tenderhearted, gentlest woman I've ever known. She was the very breath in my lungs, Andrew."

Drew swiveled his head toward the truck. "That's how I feel about Allison."

Doc nodded. "You know, I wondered who Allison Bennett reminded me of and now I know. It's Mary Nell. They say a man tends to fall for a woman who reminds him of his mother. I guess you did."

"Yeah," Drew said. "I guess I did."

"Get in, son. I think you and I need to talk, don't you?"

Drew frowned. "How come you have Early's truck?"

"Just get in, will you?" Doc asked with exasperation. "It's getting cold in here with the damned window open and the rain's coming in."

Knowing Early would have a fit if he knew rain was pouring into his truck, Drew got inside. He was about to push the button to raise the window but Doc beat him to it.

"You look like a drowned rat," Doc told him. He reached over to turn up the heater.

"I feel like one, too."

Instead of driving on to the motel, Doc turned at the next street and headed north.

"Where are we going?"

"My house," Doc said. "You need some dry clothes and I need a dry martini." He glanced over at Drew. "Or two or three or four. It isn't every day you learn you have a grown son you knew nothing about."

"Sorry about that," Drew said, turning to look out the window.

"I'm not. I always liked you, son. You were good for Jack and he loved you like a brother. I wish I'd known you were. Things would have been so different for you."

"Boyd isn't going to like it," Drew said.

"Was he up in Albany with Coach?" Doc queried. "When Clay beat you up? Was he there that day?" When Drew didn't answer Doc sighed. "He was. I thought as much."

"He didn't lay a hand on me," Drew said.

"Don't lie to me, Drew," Doc said.

"I wouldn't lie to you, Doc. He didn't hit me."

"But he didn't stop Clay from doing so though, did he?" He pulled to the side of the road and stopped. He turned to look at Drew. "What exactly did he do? Did he set fire to your house?"

"No, sir. That was Wade," Drew said. "He torched my truck, too."

"What was Boyd doing while Clay was beating the shit out of you?"

Drew winced, looked away.

"Drew?"

"He was holding Allison," Drew replied. "Keeping her from getting involved and maybe getting hurt."

"But he didn't help you."

"He kept Bennett from drowning me."

"Drowning—?" Doc turned off the truck and moved in the seat so he was facing Drew. "Where?"

"There were puddles in my yard. Bennett pushed my face down in one and held me there. I couldn't get up because my arm and wrist were broken, my elbow dislocated. I heard Allison screaming. Wade and Boyd were telling Bennett to let me up. I thought the bastard was going to kill me." He met Doc's eyes. "The man is dangerous. As crazy and mean as Wade is? Bennett is worse. Much worse."

"Lord God," Doc said, then scrubbed a hand over his face. "And this is the man to whom we entrust our young men?"

"He's going to kill somebody one day," Drew said. "Mark my words. He will. I'd just as soon it not be me or Allison."

"You need to leave Colquitt," Doc told him.

"I'm going to, but I can't just yet."

"If it's a matter of money, I'll give you whatever you need."

"I don't need your money, Doc, but thanks for the offer."

"Well, you sure as heck couldn't have made much money over the years working for Jake."

Drew smiled nastily. "You'd be surprised."

"Why are you waiting?" Doc asked. "What's keeping you here?"

"Allison," Drew said. "I'm not leaving without her. We're going out of the country and I can't leave until I get my new passport. My old one burned up in the fire. It's going to take a couple more weeks."

"Then at least let me hire a bodyguard to protect you."

Drew shook his head. "I have to do this on my own. I have to stand up and be a man, Doc."

"You're not safe at the motel," Doc said. "Come stay with me. No one is going to dare come after you there."

"I'm not going to put you or anyone else in Bennett's crosshairs. You have no idea just how insane this bastard is. He beats her, Doc. A little woman like that and he *beats* her."

"I'll take this up with the school board," Doc told him. "I'll make sure they let him go. I didn't like him the first time I met him. Thought he was too damned slick by far with that ingratiating grin of his. Now I know why. I'll get his ass canned."

"Big Jake might have something to say about that. As much as he hates me—always has—he'd move heaven and earth to keep any enemy of mine close by."

"You let me worry about Jake Thompson. I used to beat his ass when we were in school and I can still beat his ass."

"He can cause trouble in other ways for you, Doc," Drew warned him.

Doc turned to look out the windshield, hooked his wrist over the steering wheel as he stared out into the rain. "You don't reckon he knew about me and your mother, do you?"

"He's your best friend," Drew said. "You tell me."

"We were so careful," Doc said. "I didn't tell a soul, but she must have."

"Or Wade figured it out. He's not the brightest bulb in the pack but he isn't as dim as a lot of people think he is."

Doc snorted as though that was debatable.

"He could have followed you at some point."

"That's a possibility."

"If Jake knew, that would explain why he didn't have a problem with me marrying Terri Anne."

"Because you were my son and not the son of the town drunk," Doc said quietly. He clenched his fist. "He had to have known."

"Makes sense if you think about it," Drew agreed.

"I'll tell you this much. We're not going to get anything done sitting here with you in those wet clothes," Doc said. He straightened up and reached for the key. "Once thing is for sure."

"What's that?" Drew asked.

"Things are going to be a helluva lot different from here on out."

Chapter Twenty-One

Allison sat at the kitchen table staring out the window. The drizzling rain was so depressing and it was keeping Clay and Bobby glued to the big screen. Not that it took the rain to do that. On any given Saturday and every week after church the two were joined at the hip watching sports programs and swilling beer until both were fairly well in their cups. She learned a lot of things she wasn't meant to know listening to them as they got drunker and drunker.

"Boyd just about had a conniption fit when he heard about Dunne," she heard Clay say. "Don't blame him. If I was to find out that little jackoff was kin to me—and a brother at that—I wouldn't be a happy camper."

"I didn't like having to shoot Wade but I couldn't let him kill Drew," Bobby said.

"You should've," Clay told him. "Save me the trouble."

"Don't say things like that," Bobby warned him. "You could be sitting in a cell right now if he had pressed charges against you up in Albany."

Clay blew a raspberry. "Fucking twat doesn't have the balls to do that and besides, it would have been his word against mine. Boyd and Wade sure as shit wouldn't have said anything."

"Your missus might've," Bobby reminded him.

"Not and kept her teeth she wouldn't," Clay snapped.

Once upon a time hearing those words would have put the fear of God in Allison. Now all they did was make her angry. Nothing Clay had ever done to her had come close to what he'd done to the man she loved. Seeing him hitting Drew, kicking him, slamming the baseball bat against his arm, trying to drown him had broken something evil loose inside her.

She wanted Clay Bennett and Bobby Daniels and Wade Dunne punished for what they'd done to Drew. Boyd Mackie not as severely but she wanted him penalized for his part in what had happened in Albany.

"But I want Clay and Wade six feet under," she mumbled.

She shuddered and got up from the chair. That was an awful thing to say, a sinful thing to say, but she meant it. Her heart was stone-cold toward her husband and only marginally less so toward Bobby.

She wrapped her arms around her for she couldn't seem to get warm. As she paced the kitchen—wincing every time Clay or his revolting friend whooped over some ridiculous football play—she thought about changing from her skirt and pullover sweater to sweats but that would mean going back through the living room. That would mean Clay remembering she was there and demanding she do something for him. She had no desire to garner his attention.

"Don't you get tired of hearing that old bat playing that goddamned thing?" she heard Bobby ask.

"She don't do it often, but yeah. I hate piano music. Give me a good electric guitar any day."

"I'd like to shove my electric guitar up that old broad's ass," Bobby complained.

The sound of two palms meeting made Allison roll her eyes. Clay and Bobby might be in their mid-thirties but they were still dirty-minded teenaged boys.

She went to the door that led out to the carport and opened it. The cold air made her shiver but she leaned her temple against the edge of the door and listened. Miss Lillian's hands might be twisted and stiff but she played beautifully and the song she was playing was the sweet, beautiful strains of "The Highwayman."

Allison pushed away from the door, then went out onto the carport slab. Despite the rain she walked to the end of the carport and stood there listening. It took her a moment to realize Miss Lillian was standing at her front door staring back at her.

If she's in the doorway, who was playing the piano? And why was the elderly lady standing there with the door open on a cold day like—

"Drew," Allison whispered. Even as his name left her lips, Miss Lillian stepped back and closed the door. A moment later the phone rang and she hurried back into the kitchen.

She knew better than to answer it. Clay had taken her cell phone from her and each morning he unplugged the landline phones and took them with him to school.

"This way you can't call him," he'd told her.

When he came home each day he brought the phones in with him, and only on Saturday and Sunday—when he was there with her—were they plugged into the jacks.

On the fourth ring, Clay came stomping into the kitchen and snatched the phone from the wall. "Hello?" he snapped. There was a pause. "Where the hell else would she be?"

It was Miss Lillian. She knew it had to be. No one else ever called for her.

"You can't do it for yourself? You're over there beatin' the hell out of that piano and you can't do something like that for yourself?"

Allison watched the anger shifting over his face—a face she had once thought was so incredibly handsome. Now the sight of it made her sick to her stomach and she wanted to throw hot grease in it.

"Oh, all right. How long is it gonna take? She has supper to fix."

Heart pounding, mouth dry, Allison felt light-headed as she stood there. He was going to allow her to go over to Miss Lillian's. She was going to see Drew.

"One hour and that's it," Clay agreed. He slammed the receiver into the hook. "The old biddy needs you to help her get her fucking Christmas decorations down from the attic. Let's go." He snaked out his hand and grabbed her arm, pulled her with him to the carport door.

No, Allison thought. What if he saw Drew there?

"Get your ass in gear, woman. You two bitches make me miss a touchdown and I'm not gonna let you forget it."

He practically dragged her across the street in the misting rain. Clomping up Miss Lillian's steps, he was about to punch her doorbell when the door opened.

"You got anyone in there with you?" he snarled.

"Only Tom Selleck but he's naked as a jaybird and wouldn't appreciate you ogling him," Miss Lillian said without missing a beat.

Clay snorted, released Allison's arms, then left her standing there on the porch.

"Come on in," Miss Lillian said, stepping aside. "You have one hour before that Neanderthal comes back for you."

Trembling, barely breathing Allison walked past her into the house and froze.

There he was.

Standing at the piano.

Looking better than any man had a right to.

It was the first time she'd seen him since that fateful day in Albany. As soon as Clay saw the big black pickup truck parked in front of the church that morning, he'd cursed and kept on going. She didn't need to ask whose truck it was for the hateful set of her husband's mouth was all the evidence she needed. And for the first time since they'd been in Colquitt, Clay missed the Sunday church service.

Because of the man standing in Miss Lillian's living room.

"Hey," he said.

"Hey," she replied and her gaze moved all over him.

All in black with a tantalizing scruff of hair on his face and such hunger in his eyes she felt her knees go weak. When he smiled at her—that sweet, endearing smile—her womb clenched.

He came from behind the piano and held out his hand.

"Well, what are you waiting for?" Miss Lillian said. "Go get him, girl."

She moved as though in a daze for a few steps, then with a soft cry she ran to him, flung herself into his arms.

"Take it into the guest room, kids," Miss Lillian said. "I've got some cooking of my own to do."

His smile turning to a broad grin, he slipped his hands under her ass and lifted her. She locked her legs around his hips, her arms around his neck. He chuckled at the fierce way she held him as he carried her out of the living room, down the hall and to a small, neat little bedroom. Without breaking stride, he kicked the door shut behind them, turned and pushed her against it. His mouth came down over hers.

It was an aggressive kiss filled with all the pent-up emotions she knew were roiling around inside him. His tongue was like a rapier as it pressed between her lips. The hard bulge beneath her ass told her he was more than ready for her.

"I need you," he mumbled against her mouth.

"Yes," she agreed. "Yes."

He insinuated his hand between them, dragged her skirt aside to tug at his zipper. The sound of it lowering almost made her come. She felt her body vibrate as he snagged the crotch of her panties, ripped it apart and the heat of his straining cock touched her flesh.

"I love you," he said and with one savage snap of his hips, was inside her.

There was too much hunger, too much need to go slowly. Too much lust raging between them for there to be anything but mindless sex there against the door. That it was banging with each upward thrust and she knew Miss Lillian heard the racket, only served to heighten the intensity of the pleasure surging through her lower body.

It shouldn't have. It should have shamed her, embarrassed her but instead it acted like a powerful aphrodisiac and she rode him as hard as he pumped into her.

He was bold. Assertive. Forceful as he took her. His upper body was sliding against her, his hips jacking upward to plunge his shaft as deep and as hard into her body as he could. She clung to him with his head pressed to her shoulder. Over and over again like a mantra she heard him telling her he loved her. When he came, she wasn't far behind. His seed scalded her and she felt each and every pulse of that jet flooding her cunt. Her muscles grabbed hold of him, milked him of every last spurt, then seemed to lock around him as though to never release his cock from her body.

"Great God almighty," he muttered against the side of her neck.

"You okay?" she asked for he was breathing heavy, panting, and his heart was pounding against hers.

"If I died and went to hell right now I'd die a happy man," he said in between gasps.

She stroked his hair. It was longer and damp at the nape. She liked it. No, she thought. She *loved* it this way. The soft curls were sexy as all get out. "You're not going to hell," she told him.

"There are a lot of folks in Miller County who would disagree," he said.

He was still inside her but she felt him slipping. His legs were shaking as he pressed her to the door. She unhooked her legs and he slid out of her with a groan. His essence eased down her thigh but where that truly bothered her with Clay, she didn't mind where Drew was concerned. As though he had read her mind, he reached into his pocket and took out his handkerchief.

"You should wash off before you go back over there," he said quietly. He stuffed himself back into his jeans, then zipped them. "He might smell me on you."

That brought her back to earth quicker than a snap and she nodded, took the handkerchief and turned away from him so she could wipe herself. He didn't look at her but moved to the bed and sat down.

"How is he treating you?" he asked.

"He ignores me most of the time," she said. Her cheeks burning, she turned around. She stuffed the handkerchief into the pocket of her skirt.

"And the rest of the time?"

His eyes looked so haunted now, so pained. She went to the bed and sat down beside him. He reached for her hand, brought it to his lips and kissed her knuckles.

"I no longer have a car, but I do have a keeper," she told him.

His fingers tightened around hers. "What do you mean a keeper?"

"A maid," she said. "A middle-aged white lady whose son is on the football team. She arrives just before he leaves every morning and leaves when he comes home."

"A jailer, you mean," he said and a muscle bunched in his cheek.

"She's nice but she gives him a report of everything I do during the day." She shrugged. "Which isn't much considering I never go anywhere. I don't dare leave the house. The only times I do are when we go to church or he takes me grocery shopping. He won't let me come visit Miss Lillian unless he brings me over here, then comes back for me. I half-expected him to come in today and look around to see if she was the only one here. It wouldn't have surprised me if he had."

"I was hoping he would," he said.

"Don't say that," she pleaded. "And I don't want to talk about him anymore."

"Okay," he said. He kept her hand in his possession, resting it on his thigh. "If things go as planned, I'll come to Miss Lillian's Sunday after next. I should have my new passport then."

"What about mine?"

"I have it. Took some doing. They didn't want to give it to me. They said you had to be there to sign for it but I know someone who knows someone who—" He laughed. "Let's just say I have friends who want to help."

"What are you planning?" she asked.

"Miss Lillian is going to call you to come over. She'll make the reason convincing enough that Bennett will let you. As soon as you walk through that door, you'll walk right out the back one. I'll be waiting. My truck will be parked a couple of blocks away." He took a deep breath, squeezed her hands. "We'll leave Colquitt and never look back."

She nodded solemnly, then eased her hand from his. "We don't have much time left," she said and pushed him so he lay down on his back. She put her hands on his belt buckle. "We shouldn't waste a minute of it."

"I can do that," he said as she unbuckled the belt, then popped open the button of his fly.

"I want to," she told him. "You're my man. Let me pleasure you."

She slipped from the bed to the floor, then pressed his knees apart, wedging her body between them. She tugged the zipper down and eased her hand inside the opening. Watching the muscles in his thighs bunch she drew him out slowly—wrapping her fist around his rock-hard shaft.

"You don't have to do this," he said and she heard his audible swallow.

"Look at me," she said.

He lifted his head from the bed to look down at her.

"There is not a part of you I don't love, Drew Dunne," she stated. "There is nothing I see that I don't like and nothing I would not do to have it."

With him still looking at her, she bent her head, opened her lips and slipped him inside her mouth as she stared up through her lashes at him.

He quivered from thigh to shoulders, the breath catching in his throat. His beautiful, gentle and loving blue eyes turned dark with desire. His lips that smiled so easily parted. His hands that had been beside him went to her head to tenderly spike his fingers through her hair. A bright sheen entered his gaze.

She used everything Clay had demanded she learn to pleasure Drew. One hand between his legs to gently rub his balls. The other hand wrapped tightly around his cock at the base while her lips formed firm suction around the ridge. Slowly she lowered her mouth down his shaft and then just as slowly drew back—sweeping her tongue over the broad head with each move back. A gentle twist of her hand with her mouth going in the opposite direction had him moaning as she sucked with just the right amount of pressure to make his blood boil. Swirling her tongue around and around him, lowering and raising her head, she flicked the tip of her tongue under the ridge.

"Allison!" he hissed and his hands tightened in her hair as jet after jet of his cum shot down her throat.

She took it all. Every last salty drop until he was spent and his legs were shaking and his flat belly quivering. His breath came in ragged heaves from his open mouth. His hands fell to his sides. Depleted. Drained. Totally spent.

By the time she had finished with him, he was clean and put back into his jeans, his zipper pulled up, button done and buckle back in place. With her hands on his thighs she pushed herself up and leaned over him.

"I love you, Drew Dunne," she said. "I would move heaven and earth for you."

"I would die for you," he told her.

"You almost did," she reminded him.

There was a very discreet knock at the door and they turned their heads toward it.

"He's coming across the street, dear," Miss Lillian said.

Allison gasped. "Oh, dear Lord. The Christmas ornaments! If he doesn't see—"

"They are on her kitchen table," Drew interrupted. He reached up to cup her cheek. "Go."

She could not resist one last kiss and lay across him to deliver it. His arms held her for only a second or two, then he pushed her gently away.

"Go," he said just as the doorbell rang.

"I love you," she whispered.

"I love you more."

She grinned. "Not possible."

Then she was gone.

* * * * *

"So, I've been meaning to ask. What do you think of your new daddy?" Miss Lillian asked when he came out of the bedroom a little while later. She was sitting on the sofa with a glass of wine in her hand. She indicated another glass and the bottle sitting on the coffee table.

"He's not ashamed of me," he told her. He poured himself a glass of wine, took a seat across from her.

"Why the hell would he be?" she demanded.

He shrugged. "It is what it is, Miss Lillian."

"Trent is a good man," she said. "Always has been and always will be. If I'd been a bit shorter in the tooth back in the day, I'd have nailed that fine piece of ass. Like father, like son."

He nearly spit out the wine he'd just tipped into his mouth. As it was he choked on it and started coughing.

"I knew, of course," she said. "Well, maybe not knew, but I suspected."

Dragging his fingertips over his lips to wipe away the wine. "Knew?" he echoed.

"That Trent was your father. You look just like him at that age. More so than Jack or Boyd. You have his eyes and his coloring. His build." She kicked off her shoes and brought her legs up on the sofa. "I'm surprised more people didn't see it, too."

"Jake knows," he told her.

"Of course he does," she agreed. "Why else would he have allowed you to marry that precious piece of dog shit that is his daughter?"

He gaped at her, stunned as she wagged her eyebrows at him, then shook his head. "Miss Lillian, were you hitting the bottle while Allison and I were in your guest room?"

"Maybe," she said, then shrugged. "Maybe you're just seeing the real me, son. Maybe I've been pretending to be this sweet, kindly old piano teacher all these years. Maybe I was a wild woman in my prime."

"I think the real you scares me more than the pretend you did."

She grunted. "Son, you weren't afraid of me. You were afraid of my trusty ruler."

He lifted his hand and looked at it. "I still have the scars to prove it, too."

Miss Lillian chuckled, then took a hefty sip of her wine. When she lowered the glass, she tilted her head to one side. "Want to hear what I think is going to happen come Monday morning?"

"I'm all ears," he said, trying another sip of wine and hoping she wouldn't say something else outrageous.

"Trent is going to go see Brooks Daniels and have his will changed to include you," she said. "Next, he's going to go see Jake Thompson and demand that Jake insist his daughter gives you a very quiet, very civilized divorce. No need for alimony since Trent will provide quite nicely for you. Then—" She drained her glass, then extended it toward him to refill. "Then the school board is going to serve notice on Clay Bennett."

He obliged, adding a bit more to his glass, then leaned back in the chair. "You think that's really going to happen?"

"I know it will, Andrew. That's the way his daddy and mama raised him. He's a good man despite having fertilized the rotten egg that brought Boyd Mackie into this world." She sipped the wine, then asked if Doc knew his son had been present at Drew's beating.

"Yes, ma'am, he knows," he replied. "I shouldn't have told him but—"

"Why the hell not?" she demanded. "He needs to know what kind of imbecile it is he raised. Trust me, Boyd's mother is the main reason Boyd is such a screw up, and Trent lost any hope for that boy long ago. You know all that trouble he got into at Georgia."

Drew did. He'd witnessed some of it.

"I think you know now why Elizabeta Mackie hated you so deeply."

"You think she knew?"

She nodded. "I surely do. You were the son of her rival. To give Beta her due, she loved Trent. She loved both her sons. She's was a snooty, uppity rich girl from Decatur County but she was a loving— if not judicious—mother to her boys."

"I used to catch her looking at me like she could stick a knife through my heart. I guess that explains all the animosity."

"Then there was the other boy," Miss Lillian said. "The one who loved you more than he ever loved anyone else. Jack's death hit Beta hard. She and Boyd blamed you—"

"As everyone does," he said, looking down into the wine glass.

"Not everyone, son. I don't. Trent never did. We may be few but we've always been loyal to you, Andrew. If I wasn't, you wouldn't have been allowed to take another man's wife into my guest room to do what you two did."

He felt the heat rising in his cheeks and couldn't look up at her. He finished the glass of wine, then got to his feet. "I should go. My truck's safe in the shop—I hope—so I've got a cold walk ahead of me."

"I'd offer to drive you but you don't need anyone seeing you fraternizing with me," she reminded him.

"No, ma'am, I don't. I'll go out the back way." He carried his wine glass into the kitchen and set it in the sink. He didn't expect her to follow and when she did, he looked around at her.

"Be careful, Andrew," she said, reaching out to lay her wrinkled palm against his cheek. "Watch your back."

"I will," he said. He took her hand in his and kissed her palm, then turned to the door.

* * * * *

As he wove his way through the jungle of shrubs and bushes that made up her backyard, he never saw her next door neighbor Alice Smith watching him from her kitchen window.

"Coach? Hi, how are you? Oh, this is Alice. Alice Smith. You know, from across the street? My nephew is the star quarterback for your team. Yes, that's him. Well, the reason I'm calling is I thought you might like to know who I just saw slinking out of Lillian Hatcher's house."

Chapter Twenty-Two

"Shit," Early said as he plopped down in the chair in front of Drew's desk. "I hate Mondays."

Drew looked up from the newspaper he hadn't had a chance to read the day before. "Why?" he asked in a singsong voice.

"Shit always, *always*, happens on Mondays," Drew said. He folded his arms across his chest and tipped his head back. "Parts you ordered on Wednesday the week before and that were supposed to have been in on Monday never are. Today ain't no different. Typical shitty Monday and I don't have that damned belt I need for Mr. Tipton's SUV. Now I'm gonna have to go over to Dothan and pick one up else Mr. Tipton is going to give me holy what for."

Drew folded the paper and laid it aside. Tipton Ellis was the only gay man he knew in Colquitt, and Tippie—as the ladies called him—was a terror when he didn't get his way. If his vehicle wasn't ready today, he would be in stomping his foot with his pastel colored sweater tied around his neck.

"Then you'd better be on the road," he told Early.

"I called Del and he can get your truck in tomorrow to have those scratches fixed and the door repainted," Early told him. He lowered his head. "You gonna be here tomorrow?"

"Far as I know," Drew said. "Why wouldn't I be?"

Early pulled himself up in the chair. "You need to be seriously considering getting out of Dodge, cuz. Matters ain't got no better with Wade in jail for assault. Your tires may be safe but you ain't safe from Coach and Deputy Dawg." He dropped his voice. "And now you got Boyd all riled up after he found out you're his brother."

"Half brother," Drew corrected.

"Snicks and snails, cuz," Early said with a wave of his hand.

"I'll be going up to Albany to check on my passport first thing in the morning. I was going today but Doc asked if I'd have lunch with him. If I get the passport tomorrow, I'm gonna shoot for Thursday for Allison and me to leave. I'll pick up the rest of what I need in Albany."

"The sooner you leave the better," Early said. He stood. "And just so you know? I saw Coach Bennett at the Jot 'Em Down when I stopped in to get the twins some tater chips for their lunchboxes. He gave me a look that would have scalded the quills off a porcupine. That man was pissed about something."

"That man is always pissed about something," Drew replied.

"Watch out for him, Drew. The way he was looking at me gave me a real bad feeling."

* * * * *

Babs Chauncey rapped lightly on Allie's bedroom door and called her name softly. Coach had told her his wife had developed one of her bad migraines the night before and would be sleeping in most of the day.

"Just let her rest," he'd said. "Don't bother her. Only thing for her to do is sleep it off."

But it was almost four o'clock and Babs—mother of nine and grandmother of twelve—was getting worried. There hadn't been a sound out of the bedroom all day.

"Allie?" she queried softly. "Sweetie, do you need anything?"

No answer.

Chewing on her lip, Babs—who was a devoted fan of all the CSI, NCIS and Law & Order TV shows—just couldn't shake the nagging worry that was growing with every passing hour.

"Allie?"

Still no answer.

She stood there a minute longer, then made up her mind.

As quietly as possible, she turned the door handle and eased the door open. The room was dark, draperies pulled together, and all she saw was the lump under the covers.

"Allie?" she whispered.

No answer. No movement under the covers.

Wringing her hands now in accompaniment to chewing her lip, she tiptoed to the bed. It was hard to make out anything in the dark but she managed to reach the bed without sprawling over something.

"Allie, honey, are you all right?" she whispered a bit louder.

There came a slight groan from the bed.

"Oh, thank heavens!" Babs said, putting a hand to her chest. "I was beginning to worry. Do you need anything?"

Another groan and a slight movement beneath the heavy quilt.

"Okay, I'll leave you alone. If you need something you just call out, okay?"

When she got no further sound or rustling, Babs backed quietly out of the room and closed the door behind her. Had she turned on the bathroom light, looked into the small room she would have seen the bloody towels and washcloths scattered on the floor and the blood-streaked belt that lay coiled in one corner.

* * * * *

The on again/off again rain that had plagued the county for four days had finally stopped by quitting time. Tipton Ellis had been the last customer to leave the shop. Drew set the alarm, locked up the building and headed out to the motel. As soon as he pulled in, he knew something was wrong. Jimmy Barstow was waiting for him outside the door to his room.

"I told you, Drew," Jimmy said as soon as Drew got out of the truck. "I told you I can't afford to have no trouble here."

"What happened?" Drew said. The door to his room was standing open.

"Somebody tore up my place, that's what!" Jimmy said, waving toward the door. "Thousands of dollars worth of damage! Thousands!"

Drew pushed past him and once inside the room realized Jimmy wasn't exaggerating. The room was a complete shambles. The bedcovers had been ripped to shreds. The mattress had been slashed. The lamps were broken and the shades crushed. The chairs had been smashed to pieces and the seats slashed. Something foul smelling had been poured all over the carpet. Across the wall over the bed someone had spray-painted the word ADULTERER in bold red paint that had ran down the wall in places. The drawers of the dresser and nightstand were in pieces and piled in a heap in the middle of the floor. Going over to the bathroom, he wasn't surprised to see the mirror smashed and cracks running through both the fiberglass tub and the sink inside the vanity—the doors to which had been broken off the hinges.

"Where were you when all this was happening?" Drew asked.

"I was in Cuthbert all day. Just look at this mess," Jimmy said. There were tears in his voice. "Just look at it!"

"I'll pay to have it repaired, Jim," Drew said as he stared at the open closet.

None of his things had been touched. The shirts and pants hung neatly on the wooden hangers. His second pair of boots and his dress loafers stood side by side on the floor beside his suit case. His socks and underwear had been removed from the drawers and were stacked neatly on the top of the dresser.

"Dear sweet Jesus," Jimmy said, sitting down hard on the destroyed mattress. He put his hands to his face. "Dear sweet merciful Jesus."

"I will pay for the mess, Jimmy," Drew told him again.

The distraught man looked up at Drew through his fingers. "I want you to leave," he said. "I can't have you staying here."

"I understand," Drew said.

Jimmy lowered his hands, looked around, let out a choked off sob and shot up from the bed.

"Just leave, Drew. Just get the hell out of my motel," he said as he all but ran from the room.

Standing there staring at the destruction around him, Drew felt really bad for Jimmy. Whoever had trashed the room—and he was fairly sure it had been Bennett and possibly Boyd helping him—had done so with vicious glee. He turned his attention to the red paint and sighed deeply.

"Must have been one helluva rockin' party."

He smiled and swung his gaze to the door. "Fun times, girl," he replied.

"Wouldn't have been any fun for you if you'd been here when they were tearing this place up," Corinne told him. "What the fuck is that smell?"

"Sewage, I think."

"Don't look like they messed with your clothes," she said, mincing her way across the sodden carpet, mouth twisted with disgust.

"Just wanted to eliminate me having anywhere to stay tonight," he said with a shrug. "Why they didn't touch the clothes just boggles the mind."

"I imagine Jimbo has politely asked you to vacate the premises?"

"In so many words, yes," he replied.

"Want me to help you pack all this up?"

"I can do it. You're gonna ruin your shoes."

"They're just shoes, stud," she said.

"Were you coming by for a visit or did you need something?" he asked, reaching for his suitcase.

"I'm the maid. Excuse me, housekeeping," she said. "Didn't you know that?"

"No," he said, surprised at the news.

"Yeah, well, it doesn't pay much but it keeps me in cigs and beer," she told him. "Only job I could get in Colquitt given my…ah…social standing."

"Ah," he commented. He guessed there weren't many career opportunities available to prostitutes in a small southern town.

"If you need a place to stay tonight, I've got room at my place," she said. "I also have a shotgun and a .357 Magnum there."

"Big bad mama," he quipped. "What you ain't strapped?"

"Who's gonna mess with the town twat?" she countered. "I'm a rather valuable commodity to the menfolk hereabouts."

"Don't talk about yourself like that," he said, stuffing the things from the dresser top into the suitcase.

"It's true," she replied. "You know it is."

He looked around at her. "Don't do it when you're with me," he stated.

There was a long moment of silence as he went over to pull shirts from the hangers.

"Didn't I hear you got yourself a gun?" She looked around. "Did they take it?"

"Rifle is in the truck. The nine mil is in the glove box."

"Maybe you ought to carry it on you, Drew," she said, worry turning her chocolate brown eyes soft.

"Maybe I should," he agreed.

"Look, I was serious. Come stay with me tonight. You can find someplace else tomorrow but I got the room and I promise I won't rape your tight little ass."

"Then why should I spend the night with you?" he countered.

"'Cause I'm your friend and I'd walk through fire for you," she said.

He paused in folding a shirt to look up at her. Once more there was silence, then she spun on her heel.

"I'm gonna go on home and wait for you there," she said. "I'll put some supper on. You know the way."

Before he could reply she was out the door. He stared at the empty doorway for a few moments, then exhaled tiredly.

Why not stay the night with her? She knew—just as he did— that there wouldn't be any hanky-panky going on. He was taken and she understood that. Hell, the whole town did.

He walked back to the closet to get the last pair of pants when he heard her return. "Forget something?" he asked.

"Yeah. You."

They were standing just inside the room.

Bobby, Boyd, Hatch and Wade. They moved aside to let Bennett past.

"Going somewhere cocksucker?" Bennett asked.

There was no place for him to go and five of them. The gun was in the truck. The only weapon at hand was a broken table leg lying on the other side of the bed. He dove across the bed to grab it but Bennett was faster. He slammed down atop Drew like a boulder and pinned him to the bed.

"Shut the door," Bennett ordered.

Someone grabbed Drew's legs as he tried to kick out from under the heavy weight pressing him into the mattress. Bennett had a hard elbow jammed into his spine and had his wrists locked in a brutal grip above his head.

He howled but with his face shoved into the ripped mattress his shouts were muffled. Struggling did no good when two men each had one of your legs and your arms were in the grips of two others. He felt the bed sag then something sharp pressed against his spine.

"Stop your bucking. I will fucking paralyze you if you don't!" He dug the tip of what Drew knew must be a knife into his flesh. "I said quit it."

He felt blood trickling down his side, felt the blade go deeper and stilled for fear Wade would make good on his threat. He knew the wound wasn't deep—just enough to bleed—but he didn't want to take any chances.

"Lift his head."

Bennett grabbed a handful of his hair and pulled Drew's head from the mattress. Another hand appeared in front of his face and he looked down to see two white pills pinched between Wade's dirty fingers.

"Open your mouth," Wade ordered.

He clamped his lips tightly together but once more the knife cut into him and this time must have hit a nerve for he yelped as stinging pain shot down his left leg. With his lips parted the pills were rammed into his mouth, then the filthy hand was clamped across his mouth.

"Swallow it." The pain rippled down his leg again. "I said swallow it."

"He'll swallow the fucking thing," Bennett said and let go of Drew's hair to pinch his nose closed.

Unable to breathe, lights beginning to dance behind his eyes he held out for as long as could but finally had no choice but to swallow the pills or suffocate.

"How long does it take for that shit to work?" Bennett asked.

"Ten to twenty minutes depending," Wade said.

"Fuck that. We don't have all night. Turn his ass over," Bennett snapped.

Wade's hand still clapped over his mouth, they flipped him to his back. He stared up into Bennett's savage face and knew hell was about to open up and suck him in. Sheathing the knife he'd used on Drew, Wade got off the mattress, but before Drew could shout for help, Bennett's hand was slapped across his mouth to silence him.

"Look at me. I said look at me, you sniveling little shit," Bennett shouted. "Did you enjoy your little fuckfest with my wife? I hope so because it's the last time you're ever going to enjoy using that dirty piece of flesh dangling between your legs!"

"We got a treat for you, boy," Wade said as he went to the foot of the bed. He bent forward and put his hands on the buckle of Drew's belt.

Screaming behind Bennett's hand, Drew barely heard the other men laughing as the man he had thought was his father started to unzip his pants. He knew what they were going to do to him and that was a fear like none he'd ever known.

It was the sound of the door crashing open—startling the men—that saved Drew from a fate any man would consider worse than death.

"Get your fucking hands off him."

Corinne's voice was like the voice of angels at the rapture.

"Fuck you, woman." Wade said spinning around.

"Fuck *you*, asshole," Corinne threw back at him. "This here is a Springfield XDM 9mm. There are eighteen rounds in the clip and one in the barrel. That's four bullets a piece for each of you and three for the prick on the bed with my man. Get your hands off him or so help me God I will splatter your fucking brains all over this room."

Wade looked to Bobby. "You letting a diseased piece of snatch keep you from doing your duty?"

"You better listen to her," Bobby says. "She's a crack shot." He clenched his teeth. "I should know. I taught her."

"You little pussy," Wade called the sheriff. "If you won't arrest her ass I'll—" He started toward Corinne.

She fired one round over his head and it hit the space in the middle of the scarlet A behind the headboard. Drew's eyes nearly bugged out of his head.

"Take another step and I'll put a 147gr JHP right through the center of your heart, Wade Dunne. I'd probably get the keys to the city for putting you down like the rabid dog you are."

"She can't get all of us before one of us gets to her," Bennett scoffed.

"Wanna bet?" Corinne asked. "Try me, you wife-beating son of a whoring bitch."

"She might could," Boyd put in, uneasily. "I ain't willing to test her."

"Let him up," she ordered. The gun in her hand never wavered. She held it in a two-handed grip and with a spread-legged, dipped-knee stance that said she meant business.

Bennett cursed but he released Drew.

"Can you walk, baby?" she asked Drew.

"I can try," he said. The pills were beginning to work. No doubt because of the adrenaline pumping through his system.

That and he'd never had a high tolerance for drugs.

He sat up shakily and swung his legs over the side of the slashed mattress. Boyd took a step closer to him—no doubt intending to use him as a shield so the others could rush Corinne—but she fired a shot into the wall right by his ear. The paneling splintered and pinged him on the ear. He yelled and jumped back.

"Next man tries that is going out of here in a body bag," she told them.

"You better listen to her," Bobby said.

"In the bathroom," she said and the barrel of the gun moved ever so slightly toward that room. "All of you."

Hatch hadn't said a word. He knew Corinne all too well and like Bobby he knew how good a shot she was. He wasn't taking any chances. He scurried for the bathroom with Boyd—still clutching his bleeding ear—right behind him.

"In. The. Bath. Room," she repeated, her eyes on Bennett.

"I say she's bluffing," Wade said.

"Why don't you take one more step and find out, cocksucker?" she replied.

"Get in the bathroom, Wade," Bobby said. "Just do it before she kills you."

"She wants to something fierce," Corinne stated.

"This isn't over," Bennett snarled as he left the bed and backed toward the bathroom.

"Oh, yes it is," she said.

Bobby and Boyd moved toward the bathroom but Wade stood his ground. His hand was inching toward the knife sheathed at his hip.

"Go ahead and try it," she warned. "I would like nothing better than to put you in the ground."

"You're in enough trouble as it is, Rini," Bobby told her. "Don't add murder to the mix."

"Bathroom," she said in reply.

"Come on, Wade," Bobby said. "Don't give her an excuse to shoot you."

Eyes narrowed into thin slits of fury, Wade backed toward the bathroom as Bennett had done.

"Where's your keys, baby?" she asked Drew.

"My pocket," Drew answered. His head was beginning to swim unmercifully.

"Can you make it out to your truck?" she asked Drew as Wade pushed into the bathroom with the other men.

"Yeah," Drew said and tried to get up. He sat right back down on the bed. It was obvious he couldn't.

266

* * * * *

"I'll help him."

Corinne jumped at the voice right behind her. Had she not recognized Jimmy's voice she would have spun around and shot him. As it was she kept the gun on the men crammed into the bathroom.

"You need to call the Georgia State Patrol and tell them what these men were going to do," she told Jimmy.

"I'm not calling anyone," Jimmy said, glancing at the men. "I'll help you get him in the truck so you can get him the hell out of here. That's as far as I'm gonna go."

"And you'll be sorry you did," Wade snarled at him.

"Shut that door," Corinne ordered Wade. "Shut it and I want to hear the lock click when you do."

"I ain't gonna—" Wade began but Bobby jerked him away from his position in front of the rest of them and slammed the door. The sound of the lock engaging came next.

"Get him out to the truck, then go get me that logging chain you have in the shed and a couple of those extra padlocks you have on hand," Corinne told Jimmy.

"For what?" he asked, eyes wide.

"Just do it!"

Jimmy started to leave.

"Take care of Drew first you fuckhead," she hissed.

"Oh, yeah, right," he said. He went over to the bed, slipped his arm behind Drew's back and levered him to his feet.

Which wasn't an easy task. Drew's legs were starting to turn rubbery and he had to cling to Jimmy to keep from falling.

"Get his keys and move his truck down a couple of spots. Here." She took one hand from her grip on the gun, although her eyes were locked on the bathroom door, and fished in her pocket for her own keys. "Bring my car over here and back it in where his truck is now."

Jimmy opened his mouth, thought better of whatever it was he was going to ask and started guiding Drew to the door. It took some doing for Jimmy to get him out to the truck, open the door and help him inside. He shut the door, then ran around the truck to get in the driver's side.

Drew sighed and the lights went out in his world.

"You boys all right in there?" Corinne called out to let them know she was still there.

"Fuck you," Wade shouted as Drew's truck started up.

When Jimmy returned with the logging chain and the padlocks he was panting.

"What do you need this for?" he asked.

"I want you to loop one end of the chain as close as you can around the bathroom doorknob and secure it with the padlock, then bring the rest of the chain outside and latch the other end to the ball hitch on my car. When you do that, I'll need you to pull the car forward a bit 'til the chain is taut. When I yell, you stop."

"Damn," Jimmy said. "Where'd you learn all this shit, Rini?"

"Doesn't matter," she said. "How is he?"

"Sound asleep," he said. "I propped him up and locked his door so he wouldn't fall out."

"Good man," she said.

The last thing Corinne did before she left the Colquitt Motor Inn was to shoot out the tires on the two vehicles that had brought Bennett and the others to the motel. Not satisfied, she opened the hoods and put two shots in each engine block.

And though she hated to do it, she put four more bullets in her own tires. Whoever came to rescue the five men in the bathroom was going to have one helluva time moving her car.

The last thing she saw as she drove away from the motel was Jimmy Barstow peeling rubber as he sped away in the opposite direction.

The last thing she heard was Drew snoring softly.

* * * * *

Justin Connor rolled over and reached for the phone on his nightstand. "Yeah?" he asked.

"It's Rini," a voice from his past said. "I need your help."

"Any time, any place, lady. What can I do for you?"

"I am at the Dreamland Motel out by the airport. Know the place?"

Justin chuckled. "You know damned well I'm familiar with it."

"Room one twenty."

"Half an hour," he said and hung up.

A man of his word, Justin was in his GTO and at the motel in the time he'd given her. There were no empty parking spots near the room she'd given him so he parked down the row and jogged back. He saw the driver's door of a shiny black Silverado open and Corinne Wexler in all her buxom beauty climbed out.

"Never would have pegged you for a pickup girl, Rini," he said as he came up to her. He swept out his arm, grabbed her around the waist and pulled her to him. His kiss was hard and deep—with a lot of tongue—before he released her.

"You haven't changed any," she said, stepping back.

"And I never will." He looked past her. "Who's in the truck?"

"A friend. That's why I called you. I can't lift him out and he's dead to the world."

"Dead?" he repeated.

"Out cold."

"Drunk?"

"Doped up," she said.

Justin looked down at her. "You resorting to using roofies on your johns now?" he joked.

"I don't know if that's what they gave him or not but he went down hard once it started taking effect."

"Could have been Special K," he said. "Ketamine."

"I know what Special K is," she said. "Can you get him out of the truck for me?"

"Sure thing," he agreed and went around to the passenger side. When he saw the twin gouges down the side he scowled. He despised anyone who keyed another man's wheels.

"It's locked," she said and eased him aside to insert the key in the lock.

"Who doped him?" he asked as she opened the door cautiously, for the man in the passenger seat was slumped against it.

"Some really mean assholes who were going to cut his balls off once he couldn't defend himself," she said. She reached into the truck to push against the unconscious man's shoulder to keep him from tumbling out.

"What the fuck did he do? Rape somebody? If he did, I'm not going to—"

"He fell in love with the wrong woman and that woman's husband is as crazy as they come," she replied. "If I hadn't have stopped them, they would have castrated him."

"Them?"

"Five men," she said. "Including Bobby Daniels and that dog shit Hatcher kid."

"Well, now. That's a whole 'nother can of different colored worms, ain't it?" Justin asked. He moved into position so he could slide his arms around the man's back and under his legs. At six foot five and 275 pounds, he had no problem lifting the deadweight that was Rini's friend.

She went ahead of him and unlocked the door to the motel room, then pushed it open to let him inside.

"Either bed," she said.

Justin nodded toward the one closest to the bathroom and waited until she'd pulled the covers back before gently laying the man down.

"Want me to you undress him for you?" he asked.

"I think I've had enough practice I can do that myself," she said with a laugh.

"What else can I do then?"

"You can take his truck and leave me your car," she replied. "You'll need to hide the truck. They might have an APB out on it."

"Why not just put another tag on it?" He really didn't want anyone else driving his Goat.

"You saw the scratches on the passenger side? That truck might as well have a sign with a blinking arrow pointing at it," she answered.

"Yeah, I guess it would. Not a problem but if you put even one little ding on my baby—"

"I won't," she said. She was tugging off her friend's boots, removing his socks.

"You know he looks familiar," Justin said. "Have I met him before?"

"He used to play ball for the Pirates," she said. "Drew Dunne."

"Crazy Wade's boy?" he asked.

"Actually," she said as she unhooked his belt buckle. "Turns out he's Doc Mackie's son."

"Fuck me," Justin said, snapping his fingers. "That's where I know this dude. He was Blackjack's friend."

"Yep," she said. She had Dunne's jeans undone and was tugging them down his legs. When he saw the scar on his thigh he nodded.

"And I remember how he got that." He shifted his gaze to Dunne's face. "I never met him but I saw him plenty of times when he played college ball before that Gator prick messed him up."

"A lot of things have messed him up," she said and began working on the buttons of Dunne's shirt.

"Here," Justin said. "Let me hold him up for you to do that." He put an arm behind Dunne's back and levered him gently to a slumped seated position.

"Damn, where did that come from?" she asked of the small cut she found on Drew's side.

"Doesn't look deep. A Band-Aid should fix it."

"I really appreciate your help, Justin," she said as he eased her friend down again.

"I'd do anything for you," he replied. "You know that."

"Just don't tell anyone he's here. I want to keep him here at least a few days until we can figure out what he's gonna do next," she said.

"Is his woman safe with her husband?"

"My guess is no, but I can't tell Drew that," she said. "Bennett has already beaten him near to death once before. Old man Dunne set fire to Drew's house and his truck." She glanced up at him. "Not this one but a sixty-six Chevy C10 that had been his graduation present from his uncle. You being a car man know how much he loved that truck."

"Yeah, I do," he replied.

"You need me to see about providing protection for the woman?"

"I'm going to call Early Rawls. Early is his cousin."

"How is old Early? I saw him a few months back over at the AutoZone and he was under the weather."

"He's fine as far as I know," she said. She started to pull the covers over her friend, then noticed his tat. "That's new," she commented and leaned down to look at it.

"Neat design," he said. "Looks like a tree."

She put a finger on one of the gnarled roots at the base of the tree and traced the letter C.

"That stand for you?" he asked.

She nodded. "I think it just might." She pointed to the E. "That would be Early and the A is for Allison, the woman he loves."

"Neat," he said. He looked at his watch. "I need to run, sweetie. I have to pick up the old lady in a few minutes. She's working the swing shift at Tiger World."

"Still stripping, huh?" she asked.

"Until her boobs drop and her belly sags," he replied.

"Tell her I said hi."

"Where's the keys to the truck?" he asked, digging in his pocket for the keys to the GTO. When they exchanged keys, he snaked his arm out once again and jerked her to him with the same force and enthusiasm as he had when he saw her out in the parking lot. This time the kiss was longer and he added a pelvic thrust to let her know he was still interested.

"Behave," she said against his lips and pushed him back.

"Can't blame a guy for trying," he said with a shrug.

"No but your old lady might," she replied.

* * * * *

After Justin left, Corinne kicked off her shoes, took off her jeans and blouse and sat down beside Drew on the bed. She got under the covers, then scooted up in the bed until her back was pressed against the faux headboard that was nailed to the wall. She reached out to smooth a lock of curly hair that had tumbled into his eye.

He looked so young and so defenseless lying there.

And too damned handsome for his own good.

He'd always been a good-looking boy but he had grown into a devastatingly handsome man. With his dark hair and vivid blue eyes—a killer combination—he could have been a movie star. Had things been different for him. He'd wanted to be a pro football player and didn't some of them go on to become actors?

"Rini?" he mumbled, startling her for she thought he was asleep.

"Yeah, baby. I'm here."

"I feel like I'm suffocating. Like there's this concrete block sitting on my chest, crushing me, pressing all the air out of my body."

She knew he didn't mean because of the drug they'd forced into him. He was talking about how he was feeling inside.

"There's a huge lump lodged in my throat and sometimes I think if I could just scream—scream at the top of my lungs—I'd feel better." He opened his eyes to look up at her. "I feel like I'm dying here."

His face was a mask of such heartbreaking pain it tore at her. It seemed to her he was coming undone, shattering, crumbling.

"I'm not going to let that happen," she swore.

"I'm on my knees, Rini. I'm so damned far down in this hellhole where they've thrown me I may never be able to get out. They've got their feet on my neck and I can't move in any direction."

"We'll figure it out, Drew. You didn't deserve this, baby," she said, stroking one of the fading red lines over his right eye with a fingertip. "You didn't deserve any of this."

She scooted down in the bed, turned toward him, then leaned in to place a kiss on his brow.

"I love you," she whispered.

"I love you, too," he said and fell asleep in her arms.

Chapter Twenty-Three

He came awake to the sound of a soft female voice. His stomach protested him moving so he lay still with his eyelids at half-mast and listened to what was being said. It took him a moment to realize it was Corinne's voice and that she was on the phone.

"Hey, Early," she said. "I didn't think you were ever going to answer the fucking call."

Pause.

"Yeah, well, he's here with me."

Another pause.

"You don't need to know where," she snapped. "Just know he's with me and that he's safe."

Longer pause.

"You don't know what happened last night at the motel?"

Small pause.

"Coach and some of his asshole buddies—including Crazy Wade—came after him and tried to cut his cock off, that's what."

A loud explosion of sound he couldn't make out and another pause before Corinne interrupted.

"I said he was all right, didn't I? You think I would have let them do something like that to my Drew?"

Short pause.

"All right then. Don't yell at me like that. I just thought you ought to know he's okay."

Another long pause, then words that hurt him all the way to his core.

"We've got to protect him, Early. He can't protect himself. Much as I love him, he just doesn't have it in him to be like he needs to be."

A pause followed by a hiss.

"No, I'm not saying he's weak. I'm just saying he isn't all that tough. Not like he should be. Like what he has to be in order to take her from that prick she's married to."

He slowly closed his eyes. The old adage that eavesdroppers never heard anything good about themselves was certainly true in his case.

"No, I've got a friend who loaned me his car and he took Drew's truck. We need to stay here a few days until things settle down, then you and me need to get him out of Georgia as quick as we can."

Then…

"How the hell should I know what to do about *her*? What do *you* think we should do?"

He clenched his teeth and turned over to his back—drawing her attention. He really didn't want to move but he had to piss and he didn't think he could get up on his own.

Just one more weakness he had to show Corinne.

Out of the corner of his eye, he saw her turn to look at him. "Hey, look," she said. "I gotta go, he's waking up. I'll call you back."

He fought to get up—that was the least he could do—but the nausea pushed at his throat and his head swam. He felt as though he had the worst hangover of any man in the world pounding at his body.

"How you feeling, baby?" she asked as she came over to him.

He held out his hand. "Help me up," he mumbled and hated himself for having to ask.

"Maybe you should just stay in bed," she told him but he took his head.

"And piss in it?" he asked. "I don't think so."

"Oh, okay," she said and moved back so she could lever him to his feet.

He stood, staggered and almost pitched back to the bed but she put an arm around him to steady him.

"Easy does it," she warned. "You're not going to a fire."

She helped him into the bathroom, kept an arm around him as he peed. Idly he thought it should embarrass him but it didn't. She'd seen his cock, touched it, sucked it and sheathed it inside her body enough when he was a teenager that she knew it almost as well as he did.

"Ketamine," she said.

"What?" he asked, turning his head toward her.

"We think it was ketamine they gave you."

He grunted. His head hurt too much to talk and his stomach was even queasier with him standing up. He really needed to lie back down.

"Never mind washing your hands," she said as he shook himself. She reached around him and pushed the handle down on the toilet. "Let's get you back in bed before your legs give out on us."

"I'm not helpless," he said.

"I know you're not," she replied as she walked with him back to the bed.

"No, you don't," he mumbled. "You don't think I'm man enough to protect myself or Allison."

"You were listening in on my convo, were you?" she accused.

"'He can't protect himself,'" he repeated as he crawled back into the bed. "Isn't that what you told Early?"

"In your condition right now?" She flung the covers over him. "You can't." She tucked the bedspread under his arms. "Shit, baby, you can't even stand up by yourself. If I hadn't have been there last night—"

"I'd have lost my potatoes," he said.

"No, you'd have lost your meat," she corrected. "All ten inches of it."

"Eleven when he's excited," he told her ,then tried not to smile at her pursed lips and rolling eyes.

"You wish," she replied. She straightened up and started to turn away but he took hold of her arm.

"Thank you," he said. "For saving whatever manly part or parts they were going to relieve me of."

"All in a day's work at the Colquitt Motor Inn," she stated. "We aim to tease."

He tugged on her hand. "And I do love you."

He watched her blush—which made her look twenty years younger.

"Yeah, well…" she said, then pulled her hand from his. She saw him rubbing his temple and asked if he needed some aspirin.

"I'd just puke it up the way my stomach feels."

"Try to go back to sleep, then," she said. "I'm gonna go get some coffee before I start having the screaming mimis."

"Yeah," he mumbled and snuggled down into the pillow. The pain in his head was starting to feel like a steel spike being driven into his right eye.

* * * * *

He woke to the sound of an airplane soaring overhead and wedged his eyes open. It took him a moment to realize where he was, then memory of the night before came back in a rush.

"Corinne?" he called but there was no answer.

For a second or two he felt so damned alone and vulnerable without her there.

He was ashamed of being so weak that a woman had to fight his battles for him. He sat up in the bed, woozy and sick to his stomach, and it took him a while to steady himself enough to get up and go into the bathroom. As soon as he lifted the toilet seat, he threw up until there was nothing left in his stomach and bitter bile stung his tongue. He sagged to the floor, then gasped as he saw another man sitting across from him until he realized it was his image staring back at him from a floor-length mirror.

"Coward," he told the doppelgänger. "You had to have a woman come to your rescue."

How lame was that? he thought. How utterly shameful.

The sound of the motel room door opening made him tense. He snapped his head around, felt his heart lodge in his throat, then settle down as Corinne came into the room.

"Hey, babe. You're up."

"I am."

"Need some help getting to your feet?"

"Nah," he said and pushed to a standing position. He still felt wobbly but found if he walked slowly with his hand dragging along the wall he could do well enough.

"I brought you some breakfast."

"I don't think I can eat it. Whatever the hell they gave me made me sick as a dog." He ran his hand over his mouth. "Have you had breakfast?"

"No."

"Then you eat it." He sat down at the little table by the window. "You sure?"

"Yeah, baby, I'm sure. I'd just puke it up."

"At least drink some coffee." She pulled a tall cup from the cardboard container she was carrying and extended it him.

He took the Styrofoam cup from her and peeled back the little white flap on the lid and took a sip. He lowered his head. "Thank you. I needed this."

"You're welcome."

Without looking up, he sighed heavily. "I don't mean for the coffee. I meant for last night. There's no doubt in mind what they would have done if you hadn't been there to stop them."

"I don't believe Wade would have gone through with it."

"I'm not so sure."

"I am. They were just trying to scare you."

"Well, they sure as shit did. Any time you threaten to cut a man's cock off, you're going to scare the shit out of him."

"I called Early while I was at the restaurant to see if he'd heard anything about what happened and he said it was the talk of the town," she told him.

"That's par for the course. Just another chapter in the wretched life of Drew Copperfield. Film to follow."

"He said Terri told everyone at the Piggly Wiggly that Clay wanted to give you an incentive to leave town and it worked."

"Considering I was unconscious when I left town I really didn't have a choice in the matter," he said drily.

"I'm sure she knew that but she made it sound like you tucked your tail between your legs and ran. Shit, Drew. You need to leave that crazy-ass woman before something bad happens to one or the both of you."

"I intend to," he said. "I'm going to leave Georgia altogether but I'm not going to go alone."

Corinne nodded. "You want to take the coach's wife with you."

"Yes." When she didn't respond, he looked up. "Early tell you something else you're trying to keep from me?"

"No, I was just wondering what Allison Bennett is thinking about all this," she said softly. "Is she wondering if you did turn tail and run?"

"She knows I wouldn't do that," he said. "She knows how I feel about her. What bothers me is why Bennett came after me last night. What changed?"

"Maybe he'd just been letting things simmer until they boiled over," she replied. "You've been keeping your distance from her, haven't you?"

He didn't answer. Instead he plucked at the little tab until he peeled it from the lid.

"Drew?" she asked. "You have been keeping your distance haven't you?"

He shook his head.

"You went over there?" she asked, her eyes wide.

"I went over to Miss Lillian's and met her there," he confessed.

"Did he know you were at Miss Lillian's?" she pressed.

"I didn't think so," he said.

"Would she have told him?"

"Miss Lillian?" he queried.

"No, baby! Allison Bennett. Would *she* have told him she met with you?"

"No," he said emphatically. "She's scared to death of him. She wouldn't tell him anything."

"But if he suspected you two had met, could he have *made* her tell him? Would he have done something to make her tell him?"

He thought about the belt marks on Allison's rump, then set the coffee aside. "Give me your phone," he told her.

"Who are you going to call?" she asked.

"Miss Lillian," he said. "Give me the damned phone, Rini."

"Why don't you let me call her," she said. "Just in case someone's there."

He frowned. "Yeah, you're right. I don't have her number though."

"I'll call directory assistance," she said and did just that, then agreed to have the call put through and charged to her cell.

He leaned his head back for it was spinning again.

"Miss Lillian? Hi, this is Corinne Wexler. Nella's daughter?"

He tilted his head on the back of the chair to look at her.

"I'm a friend of Drew Dunne's and the reason I'm calling is—"

Corinne cut her eyes to him.

"No, ma'am, he's fine. He's with me." She listened as the older lady on the other end said something that caused Rini to frown. "No, ma'am, that isn't what happened. I know if for a fact because I was there. If I hadn't have been there, they would have done something really awful to him."

Corinne's face turned scarlet red and she ducked her chin.

"What?" he whispered.

"Yes, ma'am, that's exactly what they were gonna do."

"Shit," he mumbled. "She knows, too."

"No, ma'am, I didn't see any emasculatome," Corinne said, then shrugged at him to let him know she had no idea what that was. He was fairly sure she thought it was some kind of musical apparatus. Trouble was, he knew exactly what it was and the mere thought of the instrument cattlemen used to castrate steers made him break into a cold sweat.

"Is she alone?" he asked.

"Yes, ma'am. I imagine that's true," she replied to whatever Miss Lillian asked.

He raised his head and snapped his fingers at Rini. "Is she alone?"

Rini pursed her lips. "Miss Lillian, he wants to know if you're alone. He wants to talk to you." She handed him the cell phone.

"Miss Lillian, have you talked to Allison today?"

"No, son, I haven't," she answered.

"Did you talk to her yesterday? Do you know if she's all right?"

"I haven't seen her but I could go over and check on her if you like. Babs Chauncey stays with her every day," Miss Lillian said with a snort. "I think you know why."

"Would you please go see how she is? Don't tell Babs you talked to me."

"Of course I won't, Andrew," Miss Lillian snapped. "What kind of fool do you take me for?"

"I don't take you for any kind of fool, Miss Lillian," he was quick to tell her. "I just don't want Bennett finding out I called."

"And he won't. What's that little gal's number? I'm assuming you aren't in town."

"No, ma'am, we're—"

"I don't want to know where you are," she interrupted. "Can't tell what I don't know. What's her number?"

"I—" He looked at Corinne. "What's your number?" She gave it to him and he relayed it to Miss Lillian.

"I'll call you back as soon as I can," the older woman told him and hung up before he could thank her.

An hour passed and there was no word from Miss Lillian. The coffee Drew had drunk was now coming back up in the toilet as he knelt on the floor beside it. When he heard the phone ring, he started to get up but a wave of dizziness hit and he slumped to the tile again.

"Hello?"

Pause.

"Yes, ma'am, it's me."

Longer—much longer pause—during which Rini said nothing. Concerned about her silence, he gritted his teeth and dragged himself up, holding onto the vanity to do so. By the time he staggered into the room, Rini was stuffing her cell phone into her pocket.

"What did she say?" he asked. "Did Miss Lillian go over there?"

"Yeah," Rini said, then looked away.

"And?"

"You're not going to like it."

"Tell me," he demanded.

"All right," she snapped back at him. "But lay back down before you fall your ass on the floor and I can't pick you up."

"What did she say?" he asked, ignoring her suggestion.

"She went over there and Babs answered the door. Miss Lillian asked to see the coach's wife but Babs told her she had a migraine and wasn't to be bothered."

"Migraine?" he repeated. "She doesn't have migraines."

"Are you going to let me tell this or keep on interrupting me?" she challenged.

He made his way to the bed because his knees were going all wonky again and plopped down at the foot.

"Okay, so Miss Lillian said she didn't like the way Babs wasn't looking her in the eye."

"Like you're not looking at me," he said. He felt his heart beginning to pound. Something was wrong. He could tell by the way she didn't deny his statement. He swallowed. "Go on."

"You know Miss Lillian," Rini said. "She doesn't take squat off'n nobody, so she demanded to know why Babs seemed all uptight and twitchy. After browbeating the poor woman—" When he would have interrupted her, Rini held her hand. "Miss Lillian's words, not mine. She said she pushed until Babs admitted she was worried about the coach's wife. That she'd been in bed two days and—"

"Two days?" he asked.

"Coach had told her she gets the headaches all the time and that when she does all she can do is go in a dark room and sleep it off."

"She doesn't have migraines," he repeated.

"Miss Lillian didn't think so either so she demanded to see the coach's wife for herself. She got Babs to admit she hadn't really seen her and hadn't spoken to her during the time she was sick."

"Some fucking caretaker she is," he snarled.

"Miss Lillian made Babs let her in and they went to the bedroom." She stopped. "You aren't going to like this."

"For the love of God will you just tell me?" he shouted at her.

In one long rush of words without taking a breath she said, "Miss Lillian went in and the room was dark so she had Babs turn the light on in the bathroom and when she did, Babs let out a loud cry and Miss Lillian rushed in there to find towels and washrags piled up in the bathroom all spotted with blood."

He felt the air leave his lungs and the blood drain from his face. He had to grab hold of the edge of the mattress to keep from pitching forward.

"Was she…? Is she…?" He couldn't say the words.

"Miss Lillian rushed over to the bed and pulled the covers back—expecting the worse—but the coach's wife just stared up at her. She was handcuffed to the bed and had duct tape plastered over her mouth. She had belt marks all over her from her shoulders to her feet but mostly on her back and ass."

Trying to hold back the nausea welling up in his throat, he stammered, "H…he whipped her?"

"Like she was a dog," Rini said. "Miss Lillian said they couldn't find the key to the handcuffs and knowing the coach's wife—"

"Stop fucking calling her that," he hissed. "Her name is Allison."

She ignored his outburst. "Knowing Allison needed medical care she called Doc Mackie. Told him not to tell anyway but to get over there right then, which he did. She told him to bring something to cut chain with. He didn't even question her, just got there in a shot and when he saw what Coach had done he cursed a blue streak. He was going to call Bobby but Allison told him Bobby already knew about it. He'd been there watching while her husband beat her."

"What?" he whispered.

"He watched," Corinne replied.

"Where is Allison now?"

"In the hospital."

"Is she all right?" he asked.

"She hadn't had anything to eat or drink since Sunday so Doc gave her an IV because she was dehydrated. Miss Lillian is with her. Allison knows what happened at the motel—some dumbass nurse told her—and she's worried sick about you. She told Miss Lillian to tell you not to come home."

"I'll kill that son of a bitch," he said, plowing a hand through his hair. "I swear to God I will see him dead and in the ground!"

"And go to prison for it?" she asked. "Be reasonable, Drew. Who would take care of her if you went to the electric chair for killing that worthless bastard?"

"I need to talk to Doc," he said. "He has to help her. He has to—"

"He's taking good care of her. He took pictures of her at the hospital and Miss Lillian said she took pictures of how she found Allison." She squatted down in front of him, put her hands on his knees. "That was Allison's idea so everything could be documented. Babs doesn't want to get involved 'cause she's afraid of what Coach might do to her son who's on the football team, but Miss Lillian said she'd testify to everything she saw and was told."

"Where is Bennett now?"

"At the school I guess."

"I need to talk to Doc," he told her again. "Let me have your phone." He tried to get up and slid right off the bed and onto the floor, knocking Rini down in the process.

"You need your ass in bed and I'm beginning to think you need a doctor," she said. "That shit they rammed down your throat should have been gone by now."

"Just help me the hell up," he grumbled. "Please?"

"Since you said please, I guess I'll have to," she mumbled.

Once she had him back in bed and covered to the waist, she handed him her phone. "His private number is programmed in now.

Miss Lillian told him you'd probably call so he said to give it to you."

"Thanks, Rini," he said, thumbing through the numbers.

"Um hum," she said, then went over to sit in the chair by the window.

"I've been waiting for your call," Doc said as soon as the call went through. "The patient is resting comfortably. She has eaten some Jell-O and broth and Lillian is making sure she drinks plenty of fluids. All the welts and abrasions have been seen to. There were seven or eight deeper cuts but they didn't require anything more than a butterfly bandage. The blood on the towels was menstrual blood so that's not a concern.

"Despite the obvious pain he caused her she's in relatively good spirits although she is worried sick about you. Don't—and I will repeat that—*don't* come back here until I let you know everything is safe for you. With our illustrious sheriff involved in this sordid mess, I've contacted an outside agency to look into the matter of the spousal abuse. I am going to see about getting a restraining order, too. I've got a call in to Judge Willingham but since he and Brooks Daniels are golfing brothers as well as frat brothers, the restraining order may take a while for me to get. Trust me, though, I am doing everything in my power to keep her safe. Every nurse and orderly at the hospital knows to call me the moment Clay Bennett or Bobby Daniels show their faces. Allison is not to be left alone with either of them for any reason." He paused. "Have I covered most of your concerns, son?"

"I want him kept away from her," Drew told him. "That's my main concern right now."

"It's being seen to. I'm not going to let anything happen to my son's girl."

"She's really all right?"

"Yes, son, she is. I wouldn't lie to you. Like I said, all that blood that scared Lillian and Babs was menstrual and not arterial and— truth be told—there wasn't that much of it. You know how women like to exaggerate."

"But she was handcuffed to the bed and her mouth taped shut?" Drew asked, opening and closing his left fist as he spoke to keep from hitting something.

"I didn't see the tape on Allison but Lillian removed it and had the foresight to have Babs get a baggie to put it in to preserve the DNA. It will have her fingerprints on it but maybe it can be used in a court of law if it comes to that. I took a few law courses back in the day and I'm thinking all of this can be used when Allison files for divorce. She has the grounds, that's for sure."

"What about the handcuffs?" Drew queried. "I'm assuming they belonged to Bobby."

"Can't prove it but I don't know why else Bennett would have any at his disposal otherwise. Pisses me off like a big dog to know Bobby stood there and watched that evil bastard beat that little girl. I told his daddy as much since Bobby wouldn't return my calls and when I went down to the jail he was conveniently on a call."

"Where's Bennett?"

"At school as though nothing untoward has happened. It's going to be all over town about Allison before nightfall. I can't keep the nurses from gossiping and this is big news. Frankly, I don't know how the bastard is going to spin it but you can bet your last wooden nickel he'll try. I'm meeting with the school board first thing in the morning."

"Just keep him away from her, Doc," Drew said. "That's all I ask."

"I swear to you I will. How are you doing, son?" Doc questioned. "Have you seen a doctor?"

"I'm all right. Just a bit queasy and light-headed. It'll pass. Rini thinks it was ketamine they gave me."

"Goddamned Wade," Doc snarled. "He has a drinking buddy who works for Ben Karnes, the vet over in Seminole County. I'll lay you dollars to doughnuts that's where that crap came from."

"Whatever it was it did a number on me," Drew admitted.

"Son, I hate to cut this short but my nurse just came in to tell me I've got a set of twins to deliver. If you need me, just call, but you stay where you are."

"Would you let Early know I'm okay?"

"I'll do that. Be careful, son."

After he hung up, Drew felt somewhat better although he was still worried about Allison and would be until he could rid her of the bastard who had hurt her.

And that was what he was going to do.

"Rini, look in my pants pocket and get my wallet, would you?"

"Whatcha need?" she asked.

"There's a card in there. Dark blue. Only one like it. Get it for me."

She dug into his pocket, took out his wallet and opened it. Her eyes bulged as she saw the cash inside.

"Fuck," she exclaimed. "What did you do? Rob a convenience store?"

"The Five County books," he said.

"Well, good for you, baby," she complimented. She found the card, handed it to him, then sat down beside him on the bed tailor fashion with an elbow braced on her knee and her chin propped on her fist.

He thumbed in the number, then handed the card back to her. His head was really hurting now and he was getting worried about the aftereffects of the drug he'd been given.

"Second Time 'Round Pawnshop, this is Gage," he heard on the other end of the line.

"Gage, it's Drew Dunne," he said as quietly as possible, for the back of his head was threatening to implode and he couldn't stop grinding his teeth, which made it worse.

"Drew. How's it hanging, dude?" Gage said and Drew could tell he was happy to hear from him.

"I'm just glad it *is* hanging," Drew said and glanced at Corinne when she giggled like a girl.

"Something happen?" Gage inquired.

"Yeah. I'll tell you about it sometime but right now I need to know if you still have that guy's name. The one with the solution."

"Ah," Gage said, drawing the word out. "Things got worse?"

"He put her in the hospital," Drew told him. "Chained her to the bed like an animal and beat her with his belt. Left her like that with her mouth taped up for two days."

There was a slight moment of then silence, then, "Gimme your number and I'll have him call you."

"I'm gonna give the phone to a friend of mine. Her name's Corinne. She's—"

"She's the gal who made you a man," Gage said with a laugh. "Put that little lady on the horn, dude."

Wondering what he had told Gage during one of their many drunken moments, Drew groaned inwardly and extended the phone to her. "He needs your number."

"Who is he?" she asked, taking the phone.

"A man I think you'd like," he said. "He did me a solid up in Albany."

"He the one what sold you the nine mil?" she asked with a frown. She put the cell phone to her ear. "I got a bone to pick with you about that gun he bought off you, my man, but here's my number." She rattled off her number.

As booming as Gage's voice was Drew heard him ask what her main malfunction was.

"That nine mil is a piece of shit. I don't know how much Drew paid for it but you robbed him."

"Then bring it in and I'll make it right," Gage said. "Did he have to use it?"

"No, but I did and it pulls to the left."

"Then aim further to the right," Gage joked.

"Fuck you," she said but smiled.

"If you insist. I may be cheap and I can be had."

"I'm *not* cheap but I can be had if you're as cute as you sound," she retorted.

"Please," Drew said. "I don't need to hear this."

Gage was laughing like a jackass, then he snorted so loud it made Drew flinch. "Look, mama. Tell him I'll have the Solution get in touch ASAP. You guys in Colquitt?"

Rini looked at Drew and he nodded. "No, we're over in Dothan."

"Home of the Peanut Festival. Go there every year. And the Vidalia Onion Festival and...ta dah...the Mayhaw Festival in your little neck of the woods. Loves me some festivals, mama."

"Tell me you're a biker and I'm yours," Corinne quipped.

"Harley boy all the way, baby, and I have an extra helmet," he replied.

"I don't need no stinking helmet," she told him then ended the call. She grinned at Drew. "I like him."

"I thought you would," he said, then slid down in the bed with his arm thrown over his face.

"Still hurting?"

"Like a big dog."

"Then get up," she said. "I'm gonna take you to the emergency room."

"No," he stated.

"Yes."

"No," he repeated. "They would have to report to the cops what they find in my system—if it's still there and it must be to be causing this much trouble—and the cops would call Bobby." He lifted his arm to look at her. "Do you want that?"

She twisted her lips. "No."

He lowered his arm again. "Then let it rest."

"No, 'fraid I can't do that," she said and started punching in a number on her cell phone.

"Who are you calling?"

"Remember Jason Connor from Bainbridge?"

He let his arm fall behind his head. He stared at her. "The pro wrestler? Three hundred pounds of muscle and meanness? The one they call the Velvet Hammer?"

"Yeah, that's him. It was his baby brother Justin who came to our rescue last night."

"Never met him."

"That's what he said about you but he knew who you were."

"He was a friend of Jack's," Drew said.

"A friend or a *friend*?" she inquired as she put the phone to her ear.

"I don't know," he mumbled. "How would *I* know?"

"Always wondered about Justin, although he and I were lov— Hey, stud, it's me. Do you have someone of the medical persuasion who could come take a look at my boy?" She shook her head as though the man on the other end of the call could see her. "He's really having a hard time kicking whatever shit they gave him. He's been vomiting, he can't walk straight and I can hear him grinding his teeth from where I'm sitting so I know he's in pain." She listened. "Yeah, that's what I said. He's grinding his teeth." She listened some more, then looked at Drew. "Are you seeing double?"

"Yeah."

"Yeah, he is. Uh huh. Uh huh, that, too. Okay, just tell him to knock five times, then two more so I don't shoot his ass." She ended the call. "He's sending over a vet."

"A vet?" he questioned.

"He says you have had an overdose of Special K—ketamine—and since the vet works with it all the time, he'll know how to treat the side effects. He said the guy can be trusted."

Forty minutes later there was the requested knock at the door and Rini went to open it. When she did, she looked up and up and up.

"Motherfucker," she exclaimed. "How tall *are* you?"

The vet chuckled. "Six eleven in my stocking feet," he said and wedged past her rolling an oxygen tank behind him.

She shut the door and leaned against it. "And are you in proportion to all that height, sweetie?"

He laughed again and came over to the bed with his black bag and the rolling tank. "I hear you're a bit under the weather," he said to Drew.

"I feel like shit," Drew replied.

"I bet you do. Well, first off, I'm going to give you some oxygen. That will help with the light-headedness. Then I'll give you an injection to combat the nausea and then you'll go nighty-night for a while. I'll stay until—" He looked around at Rini. "I'm sure everything's copacetic."

"Copacetic," Rini repeated. She was staring at him as though he was an ice cream sundae with a cherry on top. She even licked her lips in anticipation.

Hooking the elastic straps of an oxygen mask around Drew's head, then settling the mask over his patient's nose, the vet adjusted the flow of the oxygen, then reached into his black bag. He brought out a vial and needle.

"He hates shots," Rini said.

"Most men do," the vet quipped. He filled the syringe, set it aside, swabbed Drew's arm, then injected him.

"Shit, that burns," Drew complained.

"That's what they tell me," the vet replied.

"Such a baby," Rini told him.

"Let him give you—" Drew felt the rush sweep through him like wildfire. His mouth went dry and his body seemed to relax into the mattress. The last thing he heard was the vet telling him to have pleasant dreams.

Chapter Twenty-Four

Allison tried to get more comfortable but her body hurt all over. She eased to her side and lay staring at the blinds on the window. It was raining again and she felt so alone. Miss Lillian had gone to the cafeteria to get lunch and Doc had already been in to make his rounds earlier. The nurses were busy with a gentleman down the hall who was screaming bloody murder for whatever reason. She wished Drew was there but was glad he wasn't.

"I didn't tell him everything," Doc had told her. "If I had, he would have broken the land speed record getting back here. I tried to play down your injuries so he wouldn't worry."

For that she was grateful. Drew didn't need to know Clay had blackened her eye, split her lip and severely bruised her jaw with his fist. The strikes from his belt had been bad enough but the bruises on her arms and ankles hurt the most where he had twisted her flesh unmercifully as he restrained her. If Drew ever found out why he had held her down and for whom he would kill Clay and Bobby.

"You're a dirty whore and we're gonna treat you like one," Clay had yelled at her.

She shuddered. The memory of Bobby Daniels's hands on her, his body covering hers made her ill.

The sound of her door opening broke off that horrible thought of her husband's friend grunting his way to release. She twisted her head around to see who had come in, then stiffened.

"Clay," she whispered and opened her mouth to scream but he moved too fast. He was on her with his hand clamped across her mouth before she could release her breath. He bent over her and put his face close to hers. She smelled the liquor fumes coming from his mouth.

"You and me need to have a little talk, slut," he said.

* * * * *

Right after rounds, Doc had gone to the courthouse to talk to someone about getting a restraining order against Clay Bennett. He cooled his heels for nearly an hour before the bailiff told him the judge would see him.

"She has to be the one to request the order," Judge Garfield told him. "She's the victim, Trent. Not you."

"She's in the hospital," Doc reminded him. "Can you get someone over there to take her statement?"

"Probably tomorrow," Garfield said, leaning back in his over-padded chair. "We've got a lot on the docket today."

"Is that you talking or Brooks Daniels because Bobby is involved in this sordid mess?" Doc snapped.

Garfield frowned. "Are you accusing me of something, Trent?"

"If the robe fits," Doc stated.

The judge threaded his fingers together and put them behind his neck. "I'll get someone over there first thing in the morning."

"You do that," Doc said. He got up from his chair. "If you don't, I'll take this matter over your head."

Garfield just smiled.

* * * * *

"This is how it's gonna go," Clay told her, his hand pressed brutally to her mouth. "I'm gonna take my hand away but if you scream, I'll break your goddamned jaw. You understand?"

She nodded as much as his heavy hand would allow.

"You better understand," he said, then eased his hand back. His face was a harsh mask of pure hatred as he leaned over her. When he slowly straightened, he never took his eyes from her.

"Don't hurt me, Clay," she pleaded.

"Then you'd better do what I say, huh?" he sneered.

"Yes," she agreed and hating herself for the whine in her voice.

"So this is what you're going to say from here on out. Some bitch is going to come in here tomorrow to take a statement from you. That interfering old doctor has asked for a restraining order against me but he ain't gonna get one and here's why. You are going to tell that nosy bitch that you and me engage in a little *Fifty Shades* shit from time to time. You're going to tell her you like for me to tie you up and whip you with my belt. You're gonna tell her it turns you on. When she asks why you didn't say something right off the bat, you're gonna tell her it was because you were ashamed to admit you're into bondage and stuff like that." He reached out to cup her chin—gripping it in a savage grasp. "Are you hearing me, Allie?"

"Yes," she acknowledged. She felt a tear roll down her cheek. "You're gonna say you love me, but that every now and then you need a little extra cock on the side to keep things interesting. You know how it hurts me, but you don't care because you need the rush of dirty, hot sex to turn you on. You're gonna tell that woman that you're a whore, you know you are, but you just can't help it."

"Clay, please," she begged. "Don't make me—"

"And you know why you'll say all that and make that bitch believe you? Well, I'm gonna tell you." He pinched her chin even harder until she moaned. "I can't get to that cowardly asshole you've been fucking, but I *can* get to his cousin," he said. "And his cousin's family. That little wife of Rawls's is a mighty tasty dish. I know some men who would love to clean her plate." His face turned even more hateful. "Then there's that busybody old woman across the street. She could fall, break a hip, not be found for days. That Wexler girl could come up missing. Whores do all the time."

"Please—" she groaned.

"And I'll get 'round to him again, Allie. I promise you that," he said. "He won't stay away from you for long and when he comes back? I'm gonna do more than threaten to slice off his cock. I'm really gonna do it. The only way you're gonna prevent that is to tell him you never want to see him again because if you don't, that boy is gonna know a whole 'nother world of hurt."

* * * * *

Doc couldn't believe what he was hearing. He didn't say anything as Allison spoke to the woman Garfield had sent over to take her statement. He wanted to but the pleading look in the young woman's eyes kept him from doing so. After the older woman left, he reached for Allison's hand.

"What did he threaten, Allison?" he asked but she shook her head. "*Who* did he threaten? I know he was here. Miss Lillian saw him coming out of your room."

"Just let it go, Doc," she said and started crying all over again, something she'd done most of the afternoon and night the day before.

"I can't, Allison. Did he threaten Drew? Did he—?"

"Please let it go," she sobbed and started to shake so violently he took her in his arms to calm her down. "Please."

Miss Lillian had been sent from the room when the woman from the court had arrived but Allison had asked him to stay. As she'd told her nasty, unbelievable story to the woman whose eager eyes were filled with spite, he'd known she'd wanted him there so he would know the truth behind her lies. The whole scenario she'd spun for the woman had made him physically ill and knowing what he knew had happened to Allison, his fury rose up like a roaring inferno.

"He can't ever know," she said, clinging to him. "Promise me you won't tell him."

"Tell him what?" he asked. "That every word you told Lucinda Craig was a damned lie? Or that you are protecting him from your husband by having her spread that lie all over town? She will, you know."

"I know," she sobbed. She buried her face against his chest. "God help me, I do."

He stayed with her until she stopped weeping, then he kissed her on the forehead and went out into the hall. Miss Lillian was sitting on a metal chair across from the room. She got to her feet.

"I heard every last word of it," she said, her eyes militant. "We can't let that little peckerwood get away with this."

"And we won't," Doc said.

"What are we going to do about it?" she asked, hands on her ample hips.

"Who do you think Bennett threatened her with? You?"

"Me, Early, Bea," she said. "Anyone who is precious to Drew and that includes the gal he's with right now."

"Corinne," he stated.

"He's gonna go after her for a certainty," Miss Lillian said. "She shamed him and those other men. They won't let that stand, Trent."

"You may be right," he agreed.

"Damned straight I am," she stated. "You'd best call her and tell her to keep that boy as far away from here as she can get him."

"We need to find a way to get Allison to him," Doc told her. "Get her away from Bennett before he does something worse to her."

"Like holding her down for Bobby Daniels to rape?" Miss Lillian asked.

Doc stared at her. "What?"

Miss Lillian nodded. "She didn't have to tell me. I knew as soon as she said Bobby stood there watching. That little bastard did more than watch. You think about all that menstrual blood on those towels. Those men had a go at her. Both of them."

"Lord, I hope you're wrong," Doc said. "If that's true and my son ever finds out, he will kill both of them."

* * * * *

Drew looked over at Corinne. "Is that a radio?"

Corinne got up from the bed and looked out the window. There was no one there but the music was coming from just outside the door. She eased it opened and looked down.

"It's a cell phone."

The Disney song "Heigh-Ho" from *Snow White and the Seven Dwarfs* was merrily playing.

His heartbeat accelerated. "Bring it here."

Rini bent over, picked up the phone. She looked both ways down the walkway but no one was loitering about. She shut the door and brought the cell phone to Drew.

Drew took a deep breath and answered. "Hello?"

"Mr. Dunne?"

"Yes, is this—?"

The man's voice had a strong Irish accent and authority as he interrupted.

"If you will look in the glove compartment of your borrowed car, you will find I have provided you with two burner phones. They are untraceable. I have marked them one and two. There is a reason for that. For the first phase of our operation I will be calling you on phone one. This will take some time so please put phone two in a safe place. You will use it after the completion of phase one. Is that clear?"

"Yes, but—"

"Listen carefully to me and do not interrupt. When I phone you, the only four words I want to hear from your end of the conversation are 'I'm listening' when you answer the phone and 'yes' or 'no' when I ask you a question. I will ask if this is Mr. John Smith to which you will answer yes. I will then brief you on what has transpired. You are to say nothing else to me. Absolutely nothing. You are to ask no questions, make no comments. Is that clear?"

"Yes."

294

"Good. I will make two calls to you on phone one and one—perhaps two calls—to you on phone two. If there is to be a second call on phone two, I will so inform you at a later date. When I have briefed you, I will ask if you understand. You will answer either yes or no. If no, I will repeat myself only once more, ask again if you understand and then I will hang up whatever your answer is, yes or no. You are paying me to do a job for you and that is precisely what I will do. Once I start, I will finish. Is that understood?"

"Yes."

"Since I will use a burner phone each time I call you, there will be no way for you to contact me to call it off. Once begun, the solution will not be derailed. Cut and dried and to the point, Mr. Smith. Is that clear?"

"Yes."

"Are you sure you want me to solve your problems for you?"

Drew didn't hesitate. "Yes."

"Perfectly sure?"

He ground his teeth. "Yes."

"All right, then. Payment is ten thousand for each assignment I am undertaking. That is a steep discount on my regular price because you are a close, personal friend of my employer. What I need from you is thirty thousand in cash. Leave it in the glove compartment of your car. I will retrieve it at my discretion. Is that clear?"

"Yes."

"Do you want time to reconsider?"

"No."

"Excellent. Two bits of information for you. Solution two will be taken care of first because I have it in sight. Then I will see to solution three. I will save solution one for last. There may or may not be a bonus solution I will perform for you at no extra charge but that remains to be seen. That is at the discretion of my employer. Now when this call has ended, please remove the SIM card from the phone you are using, break it in half, flush it down the toilet, then take the phone and throw it into the nearest river or stream. Make sure no one sees you do this. Is that clear?"

"Yes."

"When I have completed solutions one and two you will then remove the SIM card from phone one, break it in half, then flush the pieces down the toilet. Dispose of the phone in the nearest river or stream. Again, make sure no one sees you do this. Is that clear?"

"Yes."

"When next I call, it will be to burner phone one. Is *that* clear?"

"It is."

"What did you say?" came a nasty snarl.

"Yes."

The man hung up.

"How did he know why I contacted him and where the hell we are?" he asked. He stared at the phone as though it could give him the answer. "And why four assignments instead of just the three? Who else is he including?"

Rini asked what had been said and when he told her, her eyebrows shot up. "What the *fuck* did you do?" When he didn't answer, she hurried over to him and grabbed his arm, shook him. "Did you just hire a contract killer, Drew?"

He felt a hard shiver go through him at her words, then slowly lifted his eyes from the phone to her face. "That wasn't the kind of solution I wanted."

"Apparently it's the one you're gonna get," she said. "He's going after Wade and Bennett and Terri?"

"I think so but I don't know who the fourth person is."

"You are a crazy motherfucker," she said.

"If you want out, leave now," he said. "It's probably best you do. I don't want you caught up in—"

"I'm with you for the long haul, babe," she said.

"You could be charged as an accessory to murder, Rini," he warned.

"If the man you just talked to is a pro—and I'm assuming he is—nothing is going to blow back on you. That means nothing is going to blow back on me, either."

"Nevertheless, I think—"

"Wade and the coach," she said as though he hadn't spoken. She tapped the nail of her index finger on her cheek. "They deserve it but—" She tightened her grip on his arm, then said, "Bobby or Big Jake or Boyd." She shrugged. "Could be any of those three. They all three deserve it."

"Boyd," he said. "He's just peripheral damage in this."

"Whip?" she suggested.

"Shit no. He's nothing more than a gnat."

"Then it's Bobby," she stated.

"Has to be Bobby," he said. "The others aren't that important."

"And Bobby was there when Allison was being beaten," she reminded him.

"It's Bobby."

"Gotta be," she granted. "No big loss."

"You got that right," he mumbled.

Then something the Irishman said finally registered with Drew. He sucked in a ragged breath. "Holy Mother of God. His *employer*," he said.

"What? Who's employer."

"He said he was giving me a discount on what he normally charges because I was a friend of his employer."

"Who is that?" she asked.

"Gage," he said quietly. "Gage is his boss."

* * * * *

The first call from the Irishman came at just past midnight. Rini had gone out to Justin's car to fetch the phones. One was on the nightstand and the other was in Drew's coat. His heart leapt to his throat as he answered.

"I'm listening."

"Mr. Smith?"

"Yes."

"Mr. Smith, there is a slight problem on this end. Nothing for you to be overly concerned about but the situation needs to be addressed. I believe you should be the one to handle it. Do you understand?"

"Yes."

"Here is the problem. I have ascertained that solution number one is going to be removing a certain object from the hospital tomorrow morning. He will then be taking that object to Marietta where he intends to keep said object for the unforeseeable future. There is in Marietta a private sanitarium where such objects are placed and often forgotten. Do you understand what I am saying?"

Drew closed his eyes. "Yes."

"I am about thirty feet from solution number two and will not be able to get back to the place where solution number one is in time. Can you intercept solution number one and retrieve said object?"

"Yes," Drew said through clenched teeth.

"Excellent. That is as I believe it should be. Please do not harm solution one. That is my job and you do not need to have something like that hanging over you. It could be a very electrical situation for you. Do you understand?"

"Yes."

"I would imagine solution one will take the normal route to Marietta, which is up U.S. nineteen. This is where I think you should be waiting in your borrowed car at the approximate time I believe solution number one will pass the interception point. Also, I believe this might be the correct way to handle the problem."

Drew listened to the instructions and nodded with each point the Irishman made. He laughed at one of the man's suggestions.

"Do you agree with my recommendations?"

"Yes."

"Excellent. You will find what you need in the glove compartment of your borrowed car."

The call was disconnected.

Chapter Twenty-Five

Drew wouldn't let Corinne go with him though she shouted and shrieked and threatened him with all manner of bodily harm. After an exhausting argument, she'd finally given in to him but not before she had hurled dire warnings at him. He'd left her at her house in Brinson with a look on her pretty face that should have dropped him where he stood.

As he sat in Justin's really rad GTO with his iPod jacked into his ears and the skirl of Bruce Springsteen's "Mrs. McGrath" pushing at his eardrums, he kept his eyes on the road ahead. Any minute now—if the Irishman was correct—Bennett would come tooling along with Allison. The mere thought of the bastard taking her to some sanitarium to incarcerate her made him furious. What he had planned for Clay Bennett would go a long way in tempering that fury, though he knew it wouldn't fully dissipate until Bennett was no more. He would not be happy until the bastard was pushing up daisies with his size thirteen feet. His only regret was that he would not be the one to put him in his grave. Maybe he could go to the bastard's funeral, then stay behind at the cemetery to spit on the mound of dirt covering him.

"Fuck, Dunne, that's cold," he said softly.

He wondered when he had gotten so goddamned mean. Could have been the brutal beating he'd taken at the hands of Clay Bennett that had finally knocked some sense into him but he figured it was more than that. It went deeper than what Bennett had done to him. That was just the latest beating he'd received from life.

The threat at the motel? Yeah, that had added to it but it had been what had happened to the woman he loved that had been the last straw. A man could take only so many kicks to the head before he broke. It was how—and when—he put the pieces back together again that was the telling point.

He glanced at the glove compartment where he'd stored the two items he'd retrieved from his truck. Meeting Justin Connor at his house had proved to be interesting. Especially when Justin went over to lovingly stroke the GTO and had spoken to it as if it were a woman.

"He likes his car," Rini whispered.

"Yeah, I can see that," Drew replied. "Just a wee bit too much for comfort, I think."

He liked his truck, too, but he hadn't named it. Justin had named the GTO Leslie.

"You really should give your truck a name," he'd insisted to Drew. "A male name for a truck, of course."

"Of course," Drew had agreed.

"Well?"

"Well, what?"

"What are you going to name it?" Justin asked.

At a loss to know what to say, Rini had solved the problem for him. "He's gonna call it Malachy."

"Stupid name," Justin pronounced.

Malachy it was, he thought then chuckled. It *was* a stupid name for a truck.

He tensed for just over the rise he saw a silver pickup coming toward him. There was no mistaking Bennett's road hog of truck. Leaning over, he opened the glove compartment and took out the Taser. He got out of the GTO, tucked the Taser in the waistband at his back and then stepped out to position himself just far enough behind the car to where he knew Bennett would see him as he passed. With his arms folded across his chest, he moved to the edge of the road and waited.

And sure as shit, Bennett looked right at him as he passed.

But not before Drew saw Allison's shocked face staring at him from the passenger seat.

Bennett slammed on the brakes. With a squeal of the tires the truck fishtailed, then came to rest at an angle halfway on the road and halfway on the grassy side. It said a lot for the bastard's frame of mind that he left the truck that way, opened the door to come storming toward Drew with his fists clenched.

"You fucking son of a bitch," Bennett shouted at him. "I'm going to beat the shit out of you,"

Drew waited until Bennett was ten feet or so away before he slowly reached behind him under his jacket and pulled out the gun. He brought it around in front of him and aimed it at Bennett.

"Whoa," Bennett said, eyes flaring. He put his hands up to his shoulders. "There's no cause for that."

"You don't think threatening to cut my dick off doesn't give me cause to shoot you?" Drew asked.

"It was a threat, nothing more. Put the Taser down and we'll discuss this like men," Bennett said.

"I don't think so. You've got four or five inches of height on me and probably fifty pounds. You're in shape and I'm not," Drew told him.

"That's not my fault, you fucking coward," Bennett replied. "If you ain't man enough to take me, that's your problem, not mine."

In his peripheral vision Drew saw Allison—her coat pulled around her—standing behind her husband's truck. He took his eyes off Bennett for just a second to look at her and when he did, Bennett charged him with an enraged roar shattering the morning air.

Drew didn't blink an eye. He fired the Taser and two small dart-like electrodes shot out the end, the barbs catching in Bennett's jacket. The charge sent Bennett to his knees, his muscles contracting, head bobbing and he pitched to his side shuddering violently, smacked his head on the asphalt and knocked himself out.

"Shit," Drew said with disgust. "I wanted to Taser him a couple more times."

"You don't want to kill him," Allison said in a casual tone.

"No?" Drew said, stuffing the Taser back into his waistband.

"He's not worth you going to prison for," she said and started toward him.

"That's what everyone keeps telling me. Can you drive his truck?" He took two zip ties from his pocket, knelt down beside Bennett, flipped him to his belly, then made quick work of binding his wrists and his ankles as tightly as he could pull the plastic ties.

"Yes."

"Then get in and pull in behind me," he told her. He looked to the north and south to make sure no vehicles were in sight. He knew their luck wouldn't hold too much longer.

"Aren't you afraid I'll run him over?" she inquired.

"I imagine you want to, baby, but let's not do it," he told her. He turned Bennett over again, then grabbed his arm to bring him to a slumped sitting position. Leaning over, he put his shoulder to the unconscious man's chest and hefted him up.

"What are you going to do with him?"

"You'll see," he said. He carried Bennett to the GTO. The lid to the trunk was open a crack and he pushed it up, then bent forward to dump Bennett into the trunk. Once more he dug into his pocket and pulled out a syringe.

"What's that?" she queried.

"Ketamine," he said with a grin. "Same stuff he gave me except a smaller dose." He pulled the plastic cap off the syringe with his teeth, then slammed the payload into Bennett's thigh. A slight groan made him chuckle.

"Nitey-night," she said as Drew closed the trunk lid.

"Turn the truck around and follow me," he told her. "We don't need anyone to see it parked like that."

She nodded, then released her tight hold on her coat, reached out and grabbed him by his. She pulled him to her, took possession of his mouth with a ferocity that made his cock leap. When she'd kissed him thoroughly, she pushed him away.

"How you like them apples, baby?" she asked, walking backward to Bennett's truck.

He chuckled. "There's a turnoff about a mile down the road," he told her. "Just follow me."

"Anywhere you go, Highwayman," she said.

He grinned as he got into the car. Pulling onto the road as she whipped the truck around. The heavy thump of music was so loud he could hear it as she pulled up behind him. He kept watching her in the rearview mirror as they drove down the road. She was smiling and rapping her palms on the steering wheel.

He'd never loved her more than at that moment.

* * * * *

He flipped on his right turn signal and slowed down. The path down which he drove was nothing more than twin ruts between two cotton fields. Once beyond the fields, it continued for about a mile through spreading live oak trees. He stopped near a thick cluster of them and got out.

Allison drove up beside him with the radio blaring. The silence was deafening when she turned off the engine. As she joined him at the back of the GTO, she was humming.

"Like that song, do you?" he asked as he opened the trunk.

"He hates that radio station," she said, then frowned when the lid popped up and she looked down at her husband. "Are you going to castrate him?"

"Would you like me to?"

"I'd like nothing better. So are you?"

"In a manner of speaking," he said. He reached into his back pocket and pulled out a switchblade. He flicked a button and the business end of the knife flipped up.

"Ah, Drew?" she questioned. "I wasn't being serious."

"I'm not going to harm a hair on his head," he told her. "Trust me. You're going to like what I have in mind."

Then he set to slicing the clothing from Bennett.

"Not much of a dick," he observed as the tighty-whities came away.

She reached over to cup him between the legs. "Not like this one, no."

He sidestepped her touch. "Behave, woman."

"Your loss," she said.

"As much as I'd like to do bad things with you right now, I don't want to do them on the cold, hard ground."

"There's the backseat of your car," she said, then glanced at Bennett's truck. "Or the front seat of his truck. That would be ironic, wouldn't it? Doing it in his precious truck? Your choice."

"A nice warm bed is my choice," he replied.

"You know what? He's turning bluish," she said.

"There's a blanket on the backseat," he replied. Although he would just have soon let the bastard freeze to death that would have been murder. He told her to get it.

"Can't we let him turn into a Popsicle?" she asked.

"Like minds, baby," he said. "But no."

"Too bad," she said with a shrug. She opened the rear door of the GTO, reached in to retrieve the blanket. She handed it to him.

After molding the blanket tightly around the naked man, Drew picked him up and carried him to the back of the truck.

"Lower the tail gate, sweetie," he ordered.

Allison shook her head. "I was joking, Drew. He'll freeze for sure back there."

"We don't have far to go. He'll be just fine."

After placing Bennett in the bed of the pickup and shutting the tailgate, he said, "Let's go."

"Where to this time?"

"Back to Colquitt," he answered.

"Drew, no," she said, shaking her head. "If Bobby sees you, he'll arrest you."

"For what?"

"For anything," she said. "For breathing."

"He's not going to see me," he said.

"Where are we going that he won't?"

"To the courthouse."

Her eyes widened. "Have you lost your *mind*? You don't think he or one of his men might not see you in the broad daylight?" she countered.

"They don't know this car and if they see anyone, it will be you. Let's go."

* * * * *

Allison chewed nervously on her thumb nail as she followed Drew into Colquitt. People might not recognize the muscle car he was driving but they would sure as hell recognize Clay's truck. With her behind the wheel, she was bound to garner attention. He never let her drive his precious truck but—then again—no one but Bobby knew that. She was terrified Bobby or Hatch or one of the other deputies would see her and when Drew pulled into one of the parking places in front of the courthouse, she drove in beside him, her heart pounding rapidly against her rib cage.

Drew got out of the GTO—leaving it running—but no one seemed to be looking his way. With the black knit watch cap pulled down over his ears to hide his thick curly hair, the sunglasses, black gloves and dark clothing, she would have bet money on people turning to stare but they didn't. Instead, they seemed to go out of their way not to. If finally dawned on her that he presented such a dangerous presence they weren't feeling obliged to acknowledge it. Even when he went behind the truck and pulled the blanket off Clay, no one was paying attention.

"Get in the car, babe," he told her as he passed her window, rolling up the blanket as he went. "We need to boogey." He got in the car, tossed the blanket into the backseat.

"Sweet Mother Mary," she said. She couldn't get out of the truck fast enough. Lowering her head, she opened the passenger door of the GTO and slid inside.

"Buckle up," he told her.

"He's going to get pneumonia," she said.

"He won't be there that long," he said. He put the car in gear and backed out of the parking place. "Open the glove box and give me the phone marked X."

She leaned over to do as he asked and saw there were four phones in the glove compartment. She rifled through them until she found the one he wanted. When she handed it to him, he thumbed in a number, put the phone to his ear as he rounded the square to head back the way they'd come.

"Yeah, who's this?" he said, listened, then grinned. "Well, Deputy Dawg Hatcher, this is the man you were going to help castrate the other night. Remember me? Just thought you might like to know Clay Bennett is sorely in need of your help. He's in the back of his pickup on the square." His grin widened. "You have a nice day, Deputy."

Allison watched him roll down his window. As they passed a couple of people walking in front of the drugstore, he yelled to them.

"There's a naked man in the back of that silver Dodge Ram." He pitched the phone out the window, then rolled up the glass. "Burner phone. No prints," he said in way of explanation. He settled back in his seat.

"People are going to tell them about this car," she warned him.

"Won't matter. By the time they find it, we'll be long gone."

Chapter Twenty-Six

"Who lives here?" Allison asked as they pulled up before a neatly kept double-wide mobile home with a broad wooden deck running the length of the front.

"A friend," he hedged.

"*The* friend?" she asked as the door opened and a woman appeared. "What's her name again? Loreen?"

"Corinne," he said and wondered when he'd told her about Rini. He glanced at her. "I told you about her?"

"No. Miss Lillian told me about her," she said.

A bit uneasy that the two women had been discussing Corinne in connection to him, he squirmed in the seat.

"She's the one who got you out of town after the incident at the motel."

He let out a long breath. Maybe that was all Miss Lillian had said about Rini.

"She works—well, *worked*—at the motel as a maid. She may no longer have a job there," he told her.

"Why is she waving us away from the trailer?" she asked.

Drew frowned. "I don't know."

"Maybe she has a client," she said.

The breath caught in his throat and he slowly turned his head toward her. "You know?"

"Of course, I know," she said. She leaned forward. "I think she's wanting you to pull the car around back."

"Oh, yeah. That makes sense. They'll be out here soon enough."

He pulled around behind the mobile home to find a large metal shed with a carport attached to it. Rini's car was parked beside the carport instead of under it so he drove the GTO under the corrugated metal roof of the carport.

"She has a nice place here," Allison said, looking around.

"It was her grandmother's," Drew told her.

"She inherited it?"

"No, her grandmother has Alzheimer's and is in an assisted living facility in Macon. Rini doesn't own the place outright. Her uncle does and she rents it from him." He turned off the engine.

"And just to be clear? She doesn't bring men here out of respect for her grandmother."

"I wasn't being judgmental, Drew," she told him. "I am grateful to her for helping you."

"I know you weren't," he said and realized he was more than a bit defensive about Corinne.

A screened porch had been built onto the back of the mobile home. The door to it opened and Corinne came down the three short steps with Early right behind her.

"You'd better get," Corinne said. "It won't take them long to come out here looking for you." She tossed him the keys to her car.

Early nodded at Allison but didn't greet her. He turned his full attention on Drew. "You know where to go?" When Drew nodded, Early told him to leave Rini's car there and they'd pick it up later.

"Justin will be waiting for you at the motel in Dothan," Corinne said. "He'll have your truck gassed up and ready to roll."

"Did he swap my tag out?" Drew asked.

"Yeah and he buffed out the scratches down the side, painted the door for you," Early replied. "By the way, I know how Bennett found you guys up in Albany."

"How?" Drew and Allison asked at the same time.

"He had a GPS tracker on her car. I found it when the man who bought it brought it in because the dash lights weren't working right. I found it plugged into the OBD."

"The what?" Allison questioned.

"The On Board Diagnostic port under the dash," Early supplied. "I'll be willing to bet your old truck had one, too, cuz."

"They put it on when they took it the night I was arrested," Drew said.

"Arrested?" Allison asked.

"I'll tell you about it later," he told her.

"Since your truck didn't have an OBD, they probably put it underneath with a magnetic mount kit," Early surmised. "I'll bet you my next paycheck Bennett has a tracking platform somewhere and knew just where your vehicles were at any given time. They show up at the same place at the same time and that's all she wrote." He shrugged, then glanced at his watch. "Now, get. And don't worry about this truck. We checked it over, it's good to go."

"And be careful," Corrine said. She ran over to him, threw her arms around his neck and gave him a hard hug. "Promise me you'll be careful."

"I promise," he said.

She released him, then looked Allison in the eye. "He's something in bed, ain't he? " she asked.

Allison didn't miss a beat. "I hear I have you to think for that."

"Allison—" Drew groaned.

"Damn right you do."

"Thank you."

"My pleasure."

"Mine, too," Allison said with a laugh.

"Shit," Early whispered. He cast Drew a shocked look.

"And thank you for protecting him the other night," Allison said. "I owe you a debt I'll never be able to repay."

"No need," Corinne said. "Just do right by him. That's all the payment I need."

"I swear to you I will," Allison agreed. She turned to Early. "Early?"

"Yeah?"

"I'll take good care of him."

Early nodded. "I know you will. Now go. Shoo!"

"I love you, cuz," Drew said.

"Back at'cha," Early said and looked away.

Drew smiled at Corinne. "I don't want to get you into trouble. I wish you'd go with us."

Rini waved away his concern. "Baby, I was conceived in trouble and been in it ever since the minute I was born," she told him. "Your daddy ain't gonna let nothing happen to me."

"Will you just *go*?" Early shouted. "Get. Scram. Skedaddle. Bye now."

Drew laughed, took Allison's hand and walked her to Corinne's Toyota. He opened the passenger door for her. He gave Rini and Early one last look, then got in the car.

"They love you," Allison said.

"Yeah, I know," he replied. "They're my family." He reached over and took her hand, brought it to his lips, then put it on his knee. "Now you're my family, too."

"Forever and a day," she said, squeezing his fingers.

* * * * *

They picked up his truck from Justin, then headed upstate to Montgomery. He wanted to make it to Nashville before nightfall. From there, he planned to head north up to Kentucky through Ohio, along Lake Erie, cut across the tip of Pennsylvania and head north by northeast to Watertown, NY. It was going to be a long drive but he figured that would be the last place anyone would be looking for them. If he took his time, stayed under the radar by keeping strictly to the speed limit and obeying all traffic laws, the chances of them being stopped were almost nil. With the new Florida tag and the camper top, good old Malachy, the truck, wouldn't be what the troopers would be looking for.

The first night on the road, when they had entered the little nondescript motel, he realized she was nervous. She stood just inside the room there twisting her fingers together, unable to meet his eyes as he plopped down on the double bed. An alarm went off in his head; fear that she regretted having run away with him. He sat up.

"Allison?" he questioned, his hand out to her. "Have I done something...?"

She shook her head. "Nothing is wrong," she said. "I want to be here and I'm going to sleep right there beside you but just give me a minute, okay?" She put her hand to her chest. "I feel like I can't quite catch my breath."

It hit him like a ton of bricks that her thoughts had gone back to Colquitt, to Clay and Bobby and the horror they'd put her through. He dropped his hand.

"I'm in no hurry, baby," he said softly. "Take your time." He smiled. "I love you."

She nodded. "I love you, too." Her chin quivered. "More than you will ever know."

He longed to get up from the bed, go to her, take her into his arms, soothe her but a little voice warned him to stay put. To let her come to him in her own sweet time. Even though his heart was aching for her, he forced his body down on the mattress and with a nonchalance he sure as hell didn't feel, locked his hands behind his head and looked up at the ceiling.

"Not a bad place as no-tell motels go," he commented.

"I've never been to a no-tell motel before," she said. She came over to the bed and sat down gingerly on the mattress, careful not to touch him. She kicked off her shoes.

"Well, you can check it off your bucket list, now," he told her.

She was quiet for a long time, then sighed deeply. "I really do love you," she said again.

"I love you more," he replied.

"Not possible," she said, then eased her body down beside his. For a moment she was tense, then he could feel the tension easing out of her. At last she turned to face him and when he swiveled his head toward her, she smiled.

"Hey there," he said.

"Hey yourself," she answered.

He smiled, then reached out to lace his fingers through hers.

"Love me," she whispered.

"I do," he said.

"No," she said. "*Love* me."

He searched her eyes. "Are you sure?"

"Yes," she said. "I want you to erase everything they did to me. I want you to make me forget it all."

He knew she would never forget but if it was the last he thing on God's green earth, he was going to do all he could to replace that horrible memory.

* * * * *

Two days later, they reached their destination, visited a small mom-and-pop grocery to stock up on essentials, got a pizza and a six-pack of beer, six Mounds bars, a big bag of jalapeño flavored Cheetos, and headed for a rustic redwood cabin that had been built out in the middle of nowhere. As he drove, Allison read the directions they had found in the glove box.

"You will find the electricity on, the furnace quietly humming in the background, logs stacked just outside the kitchen door and the cabinets fully stocked with all the comfort foods of home," a note attached to the MapQuest printout read. "Enjoy."

"He thought of everything," Drew said as they walked into the cozy interior of the cabin. The cabin was small—with only one bedroom—but it was perfect for what they needed. Built off the back

310

of the cabin was a nice-sized home gym equipped with a Bowflex, speed ball and a heavy bag.

"Smells like fresh-cut pine in here," she said.

"As long as the bed is firm and the covers warm, it could smell like a hog lot for all I care," he replied. He sat down to take off his boots, rubbing his right foot through the heavy woolen socks.

He was bone tired, nearing the end of his reserve. His shoulders were tense, he had a slight headache and he was hungry. It was all he could do to keep his eyes open while they ate the pizza. By the time he'd finished his third piece the beer did him in, the bed seductively whispered his name.

"Go on," she told him. "I'll clean up."

"Clean up what?" he asked. He held out his hand. "Your man wants his woman beside him in yon bed, wench."

"Does he now?" she asked.

"He needs to be"—he grinned—"handled before he goes to sleep."

"Is that right?" She slipped her hand into his. "Mayhap I can do something to ease him into slumber, milord."

He pulled her against him, wrapped his arms around her and kissed her slowly, gently yet with so much pent-up passion they both shivered.

He laid his forehead against hers. "I need you."

She eased out of his arms, took his hand to lead him from the great room down a short hallway to the bedroom.

"Let me," she said as they reached the bed. She put her fingers to the bottom of his thick sweatshirt and tugged it up and over his chest. She did the same with his long-sleeved t-shirt. His eyes were on hers as she unbuckled his belt, unbuttoned him and lowered his zipper. As he sprang free, she arched a brow. "Where is your underwear?"

He looked down and pretended to be shocked. "Somebody took my underwear?"

"Pervert," she said, then pulled his jeans down his hips. She had to bend over to do so and his cock was at eye level.

"You like what you see, milady?" he asked softly.

"Eh," she said with a shrug. "It'll do, I suppose."

His hand on her shoulder to steady himself, he stepped out of the jeans. Naked, he turned and dove for the bed. He flopped down on his belly and protested as she pulled off his socks.

"My feets is gonna be cold," he said.

She ignored him. "Roll over so I can pull the covers back," she ordered.

"My feets are cold," he told her.

"I'll warm your feets," she snapped. "Let me pull the covers back, Drew."

He flipped to his back, sat up and grabbed her, pulled her down atop him and encircled her in his arms.

"My feets isn't all I want you to warm," he said.

"I'm not doing anything until you let me pull the covers back," she said, then pursed her lips. "I mean it. We're not going to ruin this really beautiful comforter with your"—she arched a brow— "you-know-what."

"My you-know-what is going inside you," he said and arched his hips to press his erect cock against her lower belly.

"Your you-know-what has a tendency to slip out of *my* you-know-what," she reminded him. "Now let go."

He growled but released her. Instead of rolling over, though, he got out of the bed to give her a chance to play with the covers as she wanted. Once she had the comforter, blanket and sheet down, he flopped back on the bed. He held his arms out to her and arched his fingers several times as though he were a toddler asking for a treat.

"You are incorrigible," she said. "May I remove my clothes before I join you?"

He grinned, then wagged his brows. "If you do it slowly and with great feeling."

She snorted. "I'm too cold and too tired to strip for you, Dunne," she said.

As she took off her clothes he put his hands behind his head and watched her every movement. Each one was poetry in motion to his way of thinking. To him, she was the most beautiful woman in the world. He loved her so deeply he felt it in his soul. She was everything to him and he wanted to be everything to her. His heart was filled with such peace, his body with such longing, he could barely contain the feelings.

The last piece of clothing she removed was her panties and when she turned to the bed, he whistled in appreciation. As he had at the two motels they'd stayed at on the way to the cabin, he pretended not to notice the healing bruises covering her sweet body.

"Will you get under the covers?" she asked. She sat on the mattress, then stuck her legs under the sheet.

"Hey. You can leave your socks on but you took mine off?" he challenged. "You think that's fair?"

"I have poor circulation in my feet," she said. "Believe me. You don't want my cold toesies rubbing along your calf in the middle of the night."

"I believe you should pay a toll for being allowed to wear socks to bed when I can't," he told her as he joined her under the covers.

"What kind of toll?" she asked.

"The kind that is exacting," he said. He slid down in the bed—disappearing beneath the covers—and slid on top of her. He parted her legs and put his mouth to her cunt, tongue thrusting inside.

"Oh, *that* kind of toll," she giggled.

"The only kind that matters," he mumbled against her.

She raised her knees to give him better access, then tossed the covers back. They landed on his ass and he snagged them with one foot to push them farther down the bed. He slid his hands beneath her, lifted her to him to sink his tongue deeper inside her velvet warmth.

"I don't mind paying this toll at all, milord," she said, raking her hands through his hair. When his lips closed around her clit, she sucked in a harsh breath.

"I like exacting it," he said and knew the vibration of his voice on her sensitive nubbin would send a shiver down her.

He was right. Her hands clenched in his hair.

She tugged gently on his hair. "Come here, Highwayman," she said.

He grinned and slithered up her body. She wrapped her arms around his shoulders, locked her legs around his hips, then wedged one wool-covered heel securely at the cleft of his ass.

"Ride me," she ordered huskily.

"With the greatest pleasure."

He took his cock in hand, put it to her slick entrance, then arched his hips. He slid into her with one sure stroke.

As the snow ticked at the window, he took his time and claimed her slowly, deeply, unlike the two previous nights when their lovemaking had been fierce and rapid. He possessed her with every fiber of his being. She denied him nothing. Took all he had to offer and gave equally in return.

* * * * *

He woke to her hand between his legs. "You want some of that?" he mumbled.

She stroked him. "Um hum. Feel up to it, Highwayman?"

"I believe I could be accommodating, Lady Colette."

"I prefer Bess," she said, though she had certainly enjoyed him telling her about his dream of Lady Colette.

"Sweet Bess it is," he agreed.

She snuggled against him as she stroked his cock. "You need to keep me warm anyway."

"Why's that?"

"It's snowing out there."

"Better than in here," he quipped.

"You know I've never understood that about TV weathermen," she said.

"What?" he asked, confused by her abrupt shift in thought.

"Why do they say it's raining *out there* or it's snowing *out there* or it's windy *out there*? Where else would the weather be if it's not *out there*? It isn't *in here*." She tugged on his cock. "And why do they feel the need to keep saying *right now*? It's snowing *out there right now*. *Right now* its twenty-eight degrees in Des Moines with a twenty percent chance of—"

He smacked her on her pretty little ass. "Hush, woman," he said. "I'm trying to arouse you."

"Too late," she said. "I'm already—"

He rolled on top of her, pinned her down and slammed his hands under her buttocks to impale her.

Which very effectively put an end to the weather broadcast.

Right then.

In there.

* * * * *

She lay on her back, he on his side facing her with his arm flung over her breasts, his thigh covering her groin. It was a proprietary position of possession, ownership, control and it made her feel very protected and wanted. Treasured.

"What are you thinking about?" he asked.

"Did you ever love Terri?"

It surprised him that she was thinking of his wife because he'd been thinking about her bastard husband.

"Did you?" she pressed.

"No and neither did Jack. She was always following us around like a stray puppy and that annoyed the hell outta me. Jack ignored her but he knew he was going to have to marry her one day if he stayed in Colquitt. She hated me because I think deep down she knew he preferred me to her."

"When did you know?" she asked. "That he was gay?"

"Miss Lillian?" he asked, hoping it had been her who had told Allison.

"Yes."

He shrugged. "I think I always knew. When we were younger it just seemed right that boys stuck with boys. When we were about fifteen, we were wrestling and he pinned me to the mat. Hell, he always pinned me because he was bigger, taller, heavier and stronger than me. But that day he pinned me on the mat on my belly and I felt his erection rubbing against my ass. I went berserk. I bucked him off and we didn't talk for a week or two. He finally came over one night to apologize to me. He swore it would never happen again. That he was thinking about Terri when we were scuffling but I knew better. As we had gotten older—when most of us started getting girlfriends—Jack showed no interest whatsoever in being with Terri or any other girl. I might have been young but I wasn't stupid."

"What about you? Did you have a girlfriend in school?"

He shook his head. "Sweetie, my prospects were at the very bottom of the totem pole. Hell, not even at the bottom. They were in the concrete *beneath* the base. Even poor girls knew I couldn't give them anything and besides, they looked at me and saw my father. Who in their right mind would want that?"

"I wish I'd known you back then," she said. "Or at least in college."

"Why? I certainly wasn't anything to write home about, baby. I wasn't the boy you took home to meet your mama."

"You didn't know my mama," she said. "You wouldn't have liked her but then neither did I. My grandmother? That was a different story. I adored her and she loved me. I think she would have liked you."

"*I* didn't even like me back then," he said. "I doubt she would have."

"You know what I think?"

"That weathermen are absolute tools?"

She laughed. "Well that, too, but I think you're too hard on yourself. You're a kind, sweet and gentle man who has had a few too many kicks from life's boot but all that's going to change now."

"How?"

Before she could answer, the cell phone the Irishman had marked with the big bright number one rang.

"Now that's different," she said of the ringtone which was from the movie *Dirty Dancing*. The melodic tones of "I've Had the Time of My Life" were definitely different.

He reached for the phone where it lay on the nightstand and answered, "I'm listening."

"Mr. Smith?"

"Yes."

"Mr. Smith, I am sorry I did not get back to you a couple of days ago but I had a slight complication. The complication has been resolved and I regret to inform you solution two has met with a tragic end in a rather seedy pool hall in Jacksonville. Do you understand?"

"Yes."

"Do you wish the details?"

Drew thought about it for a moment, then replied, "Yes."

"Solution two engaged in fisticuffs with another bar patron—a gentleman who was not as inebriated as he pretended to be and whose pugilistic expertise was far superior to his opponent's. Solution two took quite a licking. He went down hard out behind the pool hall never to tick again. Do you understand?"

"Yes."

"My condolences, Mr. Smith."

The caller hung up.

Drew returned the phone to the nightstand.

"Who was that?"

"Someone I know," he replied.

"What did he want?"

"He called to tell me Wade is dead," he said.

Chapter Twenty-Seven

Drew sat watching the snow piling up beyond the cabin. They'd been there two days and the snow had been falling off and on the entire time. Behind him, Allison was still sleeping, snuggled down into the thick wool blanket so that only her tousled hair and the tip of her nose could be seen. Tomorrow they would cross into Canada using the counterfeit Canadian passports he had found in the glove compartment of his truck along with the real ones. Once across the border, they were to make their way to St. John's, Newfoundland, until the Solution had finished his mission.

"I don't want to know how your friend accomplished this," Allison said as she viewed the passports. In the photo on her fake one, she had short blonde hair and glasses. In his, he had red hair, an eye patch and a jagged scar beneath it that ran all the way to his chin. There was a note with the phony passports that read: you have a limp and she is nine months pregnant. Accessorize as needed.

"He seems to be a man of many talents," Drew said. He was more impressed with how the Irishman had gotten the real passports and put together all manner of forged documents from birth certificates to drivers' licenses to Social Security cards. How he had managed to find—or have someone else find—the Go Bag Drew had been preparing blew his mind. The duffle bag was safely ensconced in a toolbox beneath the camper top that had been added to his truck while it was under Justin's care. Gage—or the Irishman—had been a busy boy. He had a sneaky suspicion Justin knew Gage or knew *of* him.

"Are you worried about something?"

He looked around. Allison was sitting against the headboard watching him. "How long have you been awake?" he countered.

"Long enough to watch you staring out that window, looking uneasy."

Heaving a tired sigh for he had barely slept the night before, he pushed out of his chair and went over to the bed. He sat down, then stretched out so he could lay his head in her lap, slide his arm along her side to hold her to him.

"Were you thinking about Wade?"

"No," he replied. "I won't think about him ever again."

"Then what?"

"If they catch us with phony passports when we cross the border tomorrow, they'll deport us and we could be arrested. "

"Do you think Clay or your father-in-law are looking for us?" she asked.

"I think Bobby most likely has an arrest warrant out on me for some made-up shit. I don't know about you. Your bastard of a husband is mean enough to have named you as my accomplice and you know people saw you with me on the square. If we're caught, I know I'm going to jail. That's a given. Just the thought that you will be extradited to Georgia to face Bennett's wrath scares the shit out of me," he said as she stroked his hair. "The jail term for using a fake passport carries a minimum ten-year sentence in the U.S. I have no idea what it is in Canada but that won't matter. They'll ship us back over here in a heartbeat to get rid of the problem."

"Someone has been playing on the internet again," she said with a sigh.

"I'm thinking we should stay here in the States and not try using the passports."

"Or we could use our real ones," she reminded him.

"If there is a warrant out for me—or us—we'll be arrested when we turn them over."

"Well, there is that," she said.

"No, I think we should stay here. We can use the disguises in the Go Bag until all the threats have been eliminated."

He clamped down on his tongue. He hadn't intended to say that and tensed as he waited for her to ask him what he meant. Considering her hand had stilled in his hair, he knew it was coming.

"What have you done, Drew?" she asked in much the same tone of voice Corinne had used.

"You don't need to know," he said. He held his breath. "What you don't know won't get you sent to prison if it all comes unraveled."

She was sitting there perfectly still with her fingers threaded through his hair. When at last she spoke, there was resignation in her voice.

"No, I suppose I don't need to know."

He relaxed until her next words came.

"Are all the threats to us going to be eliminated?" she asked.

"Three—possibly four—will," he said and could hear her mentally naming the potential eliminations.

"The fourth?"

"I don't know who that is but I suspect it's either Jake or Terri," he answered honestly.

"No loss either way," she said and began stroking his hair again.

"That's it?" he asked. "That's all you're going to say?"

"What more do you want me to say, Drew?" she asked. "That I approve?"

"I know you don't approve," he replied.

"Then you don't know me as well as you think you do," she stated. "Get up."

He lifted his head and turned it to look at her. "Are you that angry?"

"Get up," she repeated. When he did and was standing beside the bed, she tossed the covers aside, sat up. "Come here."

He moved closer but not close enough for her for she reached out to snag her fingers in his belt to pull him to the very edge. Once there, she took hold of his belt buckle. The jingle of the belt coming undone—was there anything more erotic sounding? The tugging of the shirt from his pants, the slow unbuttoning and the even slower peel of the garment down his shoulders and from his body made him instantly harden. Not rushed. Not hurried. As though they had all the time in the world to enjoy one another. Keeping eye contact the entire time except when he lowered his gaze to her moistening her lips. The fusion of her eyes with his as she pulled down his zipper and reached inside the fly for his straining flesh was nearly his undoing.

"Remind me to lecture you on this propensity you have for not donning underwear," she said a moment before she leaned over to take him into her mouth.

* * * * *

Later that night he was naked in their bed. Lying on his side with her arm under his, her fingers twirling a lock of hair on his chest as she molded her front to his back.

"What is it with you women and chest hair?" he asked.

"We like a nice field of grass for our girls to play in," she replied.

At first that made no sense to him but when it did, he laughed. "I guess it's the same reason guys like a patch of grass at the beginning of the runway," he told her.

"You are a dirty old man," she accused.

"Does *he* have hair on his chest?" he asked and wanted to kick himself for doing so.

"He's as bare there as a baby's behind," she said. "Not manly at all." She ran her palm over his chest. "This is as manly as it gets.

"What about her?" she countered. "Does she have grass at the beginning of the runway?"

"No, she's as smooth as a baby's behind, too. Gets her thing waxed every six weeks."

"He gets his chest waxed. Maybe that's why they have such a thing for one another," she said.

"Maybe they are getting them waxed at the same time," he suggested.

She laughed at that. "I've always thought women who get themselves completely denuded are just a bit on the weird side. Did she ever do anything kinky?"

He grunted. "Yeah. Whenever I would need to go to auto shows up in Atlanta or wherever, she never went with me but as soon as I came home, she'd demand I strip, then turn around so she could see my back and ass," he told her.

"Why?"

"To make sure there were no scratches on me."

"Scratches?"

"She liked to rake her nails down my back on those rare occasions she insisted I screw her. Not deep enough to leave scars but deep enough to draw blood. She got off on it."

"She—"

The cell phone came to life with the *Dirty Dancing* ringtone and they both tensed. It continued to ring but Drew made no move to answer.

"Want me to get it?"

"No," he said finally. "I don't want this coming back on you." He picked up the phone. "I'm listening."

"Mr. Smith?"

"Yes."

"Mr. Smith, I regret to inform you a law enforcement officer has been killed in the line of duty. Do you wish the details?"

That stunned Drew for Bobby hadn't been among the three people he expected to be eliminated first.

"Mr. Smith?" the Irishman repeated in a stern tone. "Do you wish the details?"

"Yes."

"Excellent. It seems the officer died while attempting to serve a warrant. The suspect opened fire, hitting the officer twice. Once directly in the groin and once in the femoral artery. Unfortunately the officer bled out before help could arrive. Do you understand?"

"Yes."

"I am not entirely sure you do. Let me be more precise and let me assure you the person in question has always been solution number two and not the bonus solution. Do you understand?"

"Yes," he replied but he really didn't. The Irishman's next words made it all too clear.

"The officer was shot in a part of his anatomy he used to defile a lady who could not defend herself. *Now* do you fully understand?"

Drew closed his eyes. He knew exactly what the Irishman was telling him. "Yes," he said, his voice breaking.

"I knew you would. Please follow the instructions I gave you regarding this phone. My next call with you will be to phone two."

The call ended.

Allison reached over to put her hand on his arm to get his attention. "Who?" she asked.

He turned his head to face her, looked at her a long time, felt like hitting something—anything—then told her, "The man who raped you."

She searched his eyes. "I never wanted you to know."

"I realize that but you should have told me."

"And then what?" she questioned softly.

Fury was making him sweat as he rolled out of the bed. "I would have killed him."

"Yes and gone to the electric chair for it." She lifted her chin. "I wasn't about to let that happen."

"You should have told me," he repeated. He went to the window where the snow was almost halfway up the panes. He had the urge to put his fist through the glass. The sound of her leaving the bed and padding over to him was what kept him from doing just that. She slipped her arms around his waist, laid her head on his back.

"I love you," she said.

He reached down to cover her crossed hands on his bare belly. "I love you more."

"Not possible," she replied.

The feel of her naked breasts against his back went a long way in calming the rage that was boiling in his blood. Bobby Daniels's face rose up out of the rime on the windowpanes and once again he wanted to slam his fist into the glass.

"Why?" he asked and had to fight to keep the tears at bay. "Why did he do it?"

"Why did Bennett *let* him do it?" He had to know. He needed to know how any man could so such a thing.

"They'd been drinking," she said. "When Alice Smith called him—"

"The Alice Smith who lives next door to Miss Lillian?" he interrupted.

"She saw you leaving that day and she ran to the phone to tell him," she answered.

He turned in her arms to stare down at her. "Does she know what he did to you?"

"I think the whole town does," she said.

He shook his head. "No, I mean Bobby. Does she know what Bobby did?"

"No one knows except Doc and maybe Miss Lillian," she told him. "I doubt either one of them said anything to anyone else about it. I don't want anyone to know."

He ground his teeth. "If it's the last thing I do before they put me in my grave, I'm going to tell Alice Smith what I think of her."

"Drew—"

"I mean it, Allison. That interfering bitch is as much responsible for what Bobby did as Bennett was. If she'd kept her mouth shut, it wouldn't have happened."

He knew she understood that from the way she cast her eyes down. He pulled her into his arms, wrapped them tightly around her. "Baby, I'm sorry," he whispered.

"I don't want anyone else to know what he did to me," she told him.

"I'm not going to tell her. I wouldn't do that," he swore. "But I am going to make damned sure she knows how I feel about her."

For the longest time he held her with his chin resting on the top of her head, their naked bodies pressed closely together. It wasn't until he swept her up and carried her back to bed that he realized she was silently crying. When she'd cried herself to sleep, he eased out of the bed and went to the gym to take his frustration out on the heavy bag.

* * * * *

A week and a half later found him shoveling snow—yet again—from the front porch and back deck of the cabin. It was six degrees with a wind chill of negative thirty-two degrees when he came in to warm up before going out to make sure the truck was okay. It was parked inside a detached garage and he had plugged in a battery warmer in case they needed to leave suddenly. There was a snow blower in the garage as well but he had no idea how to use it. If push came to shove, he reasoned he could make it work.

He decided—and she agreed—they should stay where they were until the last phone call came. He had thought long and hard about it and not attempting to cross over into Canada, staying put, made more sense than risking being caught. Keeping a low profile would be easy enough. There was plenty of food in the cabin, enough wood for the fireplace, propane for the furnace and stove should the lights go out during what had become a full-blown blizzard.

Allison seemed happy. The bruises and cuts were healed and the shadows in her eyes were fading. When he came in to thaw out, she was humming as she went about making a pot of Brunswick stew for their supper. The smell of the barbequed pork, tomatoes, corn and onions made his mouth water. She was an excellent cook. What was more, she enjoyed cooking for him. He'd put on ten pounds since they'd been at the cabin.

He sat down by the fire to pull off his snow boots. "I can't wait to try that tonight," he told her.

"I thought I'd bake some cornbread," she told him as he peeled off the snowmobile suit he'd found among the things that had been provided for them. "I found a can of chopped chili peppers. Want me to add them to the mix?"

"Sounds good. Any coffee left? My insides are mostly slush at this point. Georgia boys got no business shoveling snow." He hung the snowmobile suit on a straight-backed wooden chair to dry in front of the fireplace. The roaring flames were like a siren calling to him so he went over to warm his hands, chaffing them together as he stared into the fireplace.

"I'll fix you a cup," she said. She poured him some of the streaming brew, then brought it over to him. She looked down. "Andrew Dunne. Are your socks wet?"

He wriggled his toes. "Yeah."

"Take them off right now before you catch cold," she ordered. "I'll get you another pair."

"Yes, ma'am," he agreed and sat down on the floor to do just that. He didn't think he should tell her his toes were frozen stiff.

She came back with a thick pair of beige wool socks. As she handed them to him they heard a strange noise outside. "What the heck is that?" she asked.

He got up, padded over to the front door and looked out. "Huh. It's a truck with a plow on the front," he said. "It's blading the driveway." He reached for the door handle.

"You keep your ass right where it is, boy," she snapped. "You're not going out there barefoot and with no coat."

"I want to thank the guy," he said.

"That's all well and good but you're not going to until you put on your socks and boots and coat," she stated.

"Yes, mom," he grumbled. He did as she ordered. Before he could open the door, she whistled. He turned as she lobbed his watch cap at him.

"Cover up," she said.

"Nag, nag, nag," he said but jammed the cap on his head.

The snowplow driver waved at him as he made a sweep of the heavy snow off to the side of the cabin. He stopped and lowered his window. "How's it goin'?" he asked.

"Better now that I don't have to plow that damned drive," Drew told him.

"Mr. O'Malley called me last night to ask me to see to it for you," the man said. "From that accent I'm guessing shoveling snow ain't been your thing."

Drew went over to the truck and stuck out his hand. "Bill Frazier," he said for that was the name on the fake passport.

"Van Brookes," the man introduced himself. "Mr. O'Malley told me to ask you if you needed anything from town." He jerked a thumb over his shoulder. "I live about a mile down the road and I could pick up whatever you might want."

"We're fine," Drew told him. "Thank Mr. O'Malley for me." He shoved his freezing hands into the pockets of his coat. He took a chance. "Love that accent of his, don't you?"

"Sometimes I can't understand it but my wife thinks it's sexy," Brookes laughed. "She thinks *he's* sexy."

"Does he get up here often?" Drew inquired.

"When he can," Brookes replied. "He comes up here to go fishing up on Lake Ontario. He's had me and the wife over for supper a time or two." He shivered as a blast of cold wind went past Drew and into the cab of his truck.

"I better let you go before we're both frozen stiff and my missus comes out here to drag me back inside by the ear," Drew said with a laugh. "Can I pay you for—?"

Brookes shook his head. "All taken care of. If you need me, I'm in the book." He waved, then rolled his window up.

Drew sprinted back into the house with his teeth chattering and his fingers feeling as though they would fall off. He hurried over to the fire.

"O'Malley," he said as he took off his coat.

"Pardon?"

"I believe the Irishman's name is O'Malley and this is his cabin."

"The man on the phone?" she wanted clarified.

He nodded as he held his aching hands to the heat. "Comes up here to go fishing." He glanced around at her. "The man in the truck said his wife thinks he's sexy."

"It's a well-known fact that all Irishmen are sexy," she said. She gave him a look that sent heat straight to his groin. "Especially mine."

"This is true," he said smugly. He slid his hand down his crotch. "Want me to prove it?"

She pretended a yawn. "Not at the moment but hold that thought." When he cupped himself she giggled and turned away—tossing "Pervert" over her shoulder.

"But I'm *your* pervert," he called after her.

Taking off his boots, he stretched out on the thick area rug in front of the fireplace with his toes to the heat. Bracing his head in his hands, he looked up at the exposed beams of the ceiling and felt a contentment he hadn't felt since—

"Since never," he said aloud.

He was happy, he thought. Happy and satisfied and at ease. He went to bed each night feeling secure and safe, holding the woman he loved in his arms, knowing she'd be there come morning. He slept soundly and woke refreshed, his woman's back against his front and his arm around her. He got up eagerly to start a new day knowing there would be no drama, no accusations, no nasty insults. The day never dragged on for there was never any situations to make it so.

"You want a sandwich?" she asked from the kitchen.

"Yeah, babe," he replied.

And for the first time in his life, someone thought of him and his needs and saw to those needs without pissing and moaning and making him feel as though he should get down on his belly and crawl in gratitude.

"Ham or chicken salad?"

"You choose," he replied. "I'm easy."

"Yes, you are," she said. "A man-whore of the first degree."

He chuckled. Even her insults made him happy for they were aimed at amusing him and not hurting him.

She came over to him and held out a jar. "I can't get it open."

He sat up, took the jar, then popped the lid with ease. He handed it back to her.

"My hero," she said.

"I aim to please," he responded.

"We'll see about that later," she said saucily and flipped her long braid as she pivoted on her heel.

He watched her walking away and thought how absolutely adorable she looked in a pair of light grey sweats and with her feet encased in only a thick pair of his wool socks.

"Clay never let me go barefoot," she'd told him. "I like going barefoot."

"Then you can go as barefoot as a yard dog in the summer," he'd assured her.

When lunch was ready, she brought two plates to the great room and placed them on the coffee table before going back for the iced tea that was their staple with every meal. He craned his head around to see what was on the plates. As usual, she'd piled his with three sandwiches—chicken salad—corn chips, a pickle and a large dollop of potato salad.

"I'm going to be as big as a barn if you don't stop forcing me to eat all this food," he complained as she came back with the glasses of iced tea.

"Nobody is forcing you, Highwayman," she said. She sat on the rug beside him, twisted around to get their plates, handed him his.

"Waste not, want not," he muttered.

"Drew?" she asked. "What are we going to do once everything has been taken care of?"

He took a bite of his sandwich. "What do you mean?"

"Where are we going to go?" she asked. "What are we going to do?"

"What would you *like* to do?" he asked.

"I'd like to open up a day care center that will offer after-school opportunities for latchkey kids," she said.

"Okay," he agreed.

"Just like that?" she countered.

"We've got the money," he replied. "Why not?"

"What will you do?"

He shrugged, thoughtfully chewing on his sandwich before answering. "Get a job doing anything but shoveling snow. Make myself useful. I don't want to be a burden on society."

She rolled her eyes, munched a corn chip. "Seriously, Drew. What do you want to do?"

"I haven't thought beyond getting out from under all the shit that has been thrown at us," he told her. "Once everything is settled, I'll sit down and take stock."

As though the gods had been listening in on their conversation, the second burner phone came to life. This time the ringtone was "I Can See Clearly Now."

"You can't say he doesn't have a wicked sense of humor," Allison remarked.

The cell phone was on their nightstand and he got up to get it. She followed him into the bedroom.

He took a deep breath before answering. "I'm listening."

"Mr. Smith, I regret to inform you there was a tragic accident in Decatur County, Georgia, early this morning. A man and his lady friend—a woman estranged from her husband—were killed when the car the gentleman was driving left the road at a high rate of speed and crashed into a concrete abutment. An autopsy has yet to be performed but it is believed both the male and his female companion were inebriated at the time of the accident and quite possibly cocaine might have been involved. Both passengers were trapped inside the car. Do you wish further details?"

"No," Drew was quick to say. He didn't want to know how Allison's husband and his wife had died.

"Very well. I should tell you there will be a refund for this particular solution. This was, indeed, an accident. Do you understand?"

"Yes." History repeating itself, Drew thought.

"Please retain this phone. The gentleman who employs me has asked me to handle the bonus I mentioned to you during our first conversation. I would ask that you give me a day or so to accomplish this last task."

The Irishman hung up.

"Clay?" she questioned.

"And Terri." He sat down on the bed with the phone still in his hand.

She blinked. "They were together?"

"Traffic accident that our man says he had nothing to do with," he said.

"Clay always did drive recklessly. Thought he owned the road."

"So did Terri," he said. "It's believed they were drunk."

"That isn't a surprise," she said. "He had a drinking problem."

"So did she," he told her.

"What now?"

"He's going after Jake next," he said softly.

"Did he say that's who it is?"

"He didn't have to."

She took a seat beside him. "No, I guess not."

He'd lost his appetite. He looked at her. "How do you feel about this?"

She rubbed her hand up and down her thigh. "I don't feel anything," she replied. "You?"

"Nothing," he said. "Absolutely nothing and I should."

"Yeah, me, too," she agreed.

"Does that make us bad people?" he asked.

She reached for his hand. "I think it makes us human."

Chapter Twenty-Eight

She was worried about him.

He hadn't said much the rest of the day. Not even the Brunswick stew made much of an impression on him. He'd complimented her on it but then lapsed into silence that lasted the remainder of the meal. He'd offered to help her with the dishes and she'd waved him away.

He had gone to the gym where he'd spent a lot of his time since their first morning at the cabin.

And he'd gone to bed without her. When she came in to join him, he was on his side with his eyes closed but she knew he wasn't sleeping. She gave him his space, refrained from touching him although every feminine instinct in her body screamed at her to take him in her arms. Morning light found his side of the bed empty.

He was standing with his hands in his pockets—shoulders hunched—at the sliding glass doors that overlooked the deck and the broad expanse of snow beyond. Part of her wanted to go to him, slip her arms around him, but another part warned that wasn't what he wanted or needed right then.

So she didn't say good morning but followed the delicious smell of French vanilla–flavored coffee into the kitchen.

"Bring me a cup, would you, babe?" she heard him ask.

"Sure thing," she said in a much chipper voice than she felt.

Taking the cup in to him, he took it with one hand, then slid his arm around her to bring her to his side.

"It's finally stopped snowing," he commented.

"Are those deer tracks?" she asked as she spied deep impressions in the snow that edged the deck.

"Stride looks about right."

"Did you ever go hunting for deer with Early?"

"No," he said. "I don't like venison." He took a sip of coffee. "Besides, it would be like shooting Bambi. I just couldn't do it."

They drank their coffee and stood there staring at the mostly untouched expanse of pristine white snow that undulated across the backyard. The bright sunlight made it look as if the gently rolling ground was bejeweled with diamonds.

"I thought about what you said," he told her.

"About what?"

"Wanting to open a day care center. I think that's a great idea."

"I have so many ideas," she said. She looked up at him. "Did I tell you I speak French and Spanish?"

His eyebrows shot up. "No, you did not."

"Well, I do and I could teach or tutor in those languages. I'm also a math whiz kid and could tutor in that subject as well as chemistry."

"I could teach them how to embezzle money from their employer," he said with a wink.

"I doubt we should add that to the curriculum," she replied.

"I guess not," he said. "But I *am* a helluva accountant. After all, that's what my degree is in."

"Then you could get a job as an accountant," she said.

"I'd rather be neutered with a dull rusty spoon," he grumbled.

She laid her head on his shoulder. "All I want is for you to be happy. To do whatever *you* want to do."

"Ironically enough, I enjoyed my job at Five County," he said.

"Then we could open up a dealership somewhere," she suggested. "Do we have the money to buy a franchise?"

"Oh, yeah," he said. "We do and then some."

"About my trust fund. We've never talked—"

"And we're not going to talk about it now," he interrupted her. "Your money is your money. I'm not going to touch it."

"It's *our* money," she corrected.

"Not going to touch it," he repeated. He finished off his coffee.

"You can be such a stubborn cuss," she said on a long breath.

"You wouldn't have me any other way."

"I don't know about that," she muttered.

"I really like the idea of having a dealership of my own," he said. "The question is where."

"Too bad I can't buy Jake's," he said quietly.

That surprised her and she eased out of his hold. "You would go back to Colquitt?" she queried.

He shrugged. "It's my home," he said. "I was born and raised there and despite all the crap I've had to deal with over the years, there are still people there I care a good deal about. Early, Bea and the kids, Rini and Miss Lillian. I can go back now that they're no longer in any danger."

"If going back there would make you happy, then that's what we'll do but—"

"But what?"

"I'm not sure the town will be all that happy to see me back," she said. "I'm a fallen woman."

"And I'm the man who made you that way."

"Joke 'em if they can't take a screw," she said.

He laughed, leaned down to kiss her on top of the head. "You know what the motto of Colquitt is?" he asked.

"They have a motto?"

"Most cities do," he replied. "Their motto is, Pull for Colquitt or pull out."

"That way you won't get her pregnant," she said with a giggle despite the frown he bestowed on her.

"For shame, woman," he chastised.

"Hey, like I said. If they can't take a joke, screw 'em."

"Would it be uncomfortable for you if we went back?"

"Not as long as I had you by my side but where would we live? Will she have left you the house?"

"Hell, no. I don't know what's in her will but I know damned well *I'm* not. She probably left it to Whip," he said. "Him? Would he have let you the house?"

"Possibly," she replied. "Probably but I wouldn't want to live there. I hate that house."

"What would you do with it?"

"Sell it or rent it out," she said. "Give the money from it to charity."

"We could build one for ourselves."

"We could design it just the way we want it," she said.

"We could."

"Do you think Whip might sell you the dealership?"

"Not a snowball's chance," he said. "He'd run it into the ground before he'd let me back in there considering the way he feels about me. Hell, he'd *burn* it to the ground before he'd sell it to me."

"And the town can't sustain two auto dealerships," she said.

"No, but it doesn't necessarily have to be a car dealership. I could get Early to go in with me and we could open a garage. I like tinkering on trucks and he's a helluva good mechanic. We could sell used cars and do classic car and truck restorations and rebuilds.

There's nothing like that in Colquitt and if we could pull in customers from the other four counties, get a rep for doing quality work, Early could make a damned good living."

She sensed the wheels turning in his mind. His eyes were gleaming as he looked out across the deck.

"I could hire Lenore to be our office manager," he said. "Mine and Early's. How does Rawls and Dunne Garage sound?"

Leave it to him, she thought, to put his beloved cousin first.

"Sounds good," she said. "Let's go sit at the table and start planning just what we want. I'll list all the things I want at my day care and you list what you want for the garage, then we'll start sketching out the plans for our house."

"You really don't mind going back?" he said. "You know there are going to be people who think I'm responsible for the deaths."

"I don't care what other people think," she said. "I never really have."

"What if the mothers won't bring their kids to you because of me?" he asked.

"Every woman in Colquitt knows by now how Clay used to beat me. The man tied me to his bed, left me without food or water, put me in the hospital. The woman you were married to abused you mentally and physically at every turn. My husband and your wife died in a car crash together because he was drunk. You didn't put a gun to their heads to make them do that. It was an accident. Your father used to beat you, tried to castrate you. Some man in a pool hall in Jacksonville beat him to death in a brawl. You weren't there and couldn't possibly be responsible for Wade's death. Bobby? He died in the line of duty. That is one of the hazards of the profession. Do you really think people are going to hold all that against *you*?"

"And Jake?" he asked.

"If it is him the Irishman is going after—"

"It is," he said. "I know it is."

"All right. If that's the case, Jake will meet his end in a way that won't come back on you. You can count on that," she said.

"You sound so coldhearted about it," he said.

"Maybe so, but in one way or another, all five of those people hurt you over and over again. They made your life miserable. Wanted you dead and tried. The world—and you—will be better off without them in it."

* * * * *

For the next several days they worked on designing the new life they would be sharing together. They scoured the internet for home plans and interior design, landscaping. Googled day care centers and learning centers and garages. While she looked for teaching supplies, books and toys, he looked for manuals, parts and equipment.

They debated on whether or not they should go back for the funerals of their spouses and reasoned that they shouldn't return just yet. No one knew where they were so how were Drew and Allison to know Bennett and Terri had been killed?

"I could call Early," Drew told her. "But Jake could very well have had someone tap the phone at work. I wouldn't put it past him. I'd just as soon no one be able to track us."

Both of them ignored the cell phone on the nightstand. They avoided looking at it altogether. It was like a scorpion sitting there with its stinger arched.

They were both free but felt they shouldn't do anything about it just yet. It was best to put a few months behind them before they married, another month or so before they went back to Georgia. By then, the matter would no doubt be settled and all possible danger eradicated. As each day passed, the tension caused by the waiting to hear from the Irishman grew steadily. It was nerve wracking and neither slept all that well with one ear cocked for the burner phone to ring for the last time.

Every day he disappeared into the gym. Worked out like a fiend for hours on end. He'd come out of the room sweating and tired, but happy. He now had chiseled pecs, washboard abs, a rock-hard belly, killer biceps and an ass off which a quarter could bounce. The extra weight her cooking had added to his body was all muscle.

And he had stamina.

As their last round of lovemaking had proven.

"Justice of the peace or minister?" he asked as they lay in bed with the Sunday paper spread out on the bed.

"Minister," she said. "I'd always thought marriage vows are sacred."

"They're supposed to be," he said. "Mine weren't."

"I guess mine weren't, either," she admitted.

"Don't worry about it. Those vows weren't sacred to our spouses, either. Both of them cheated on us long before you and I met."

"Other than him, you are the only man I've ever slept with," she said. She turned to him. "Other than Rini?"

"I haven't been innocent, babe. There were a couple of women," he said. "When I went out of town."

"I don't have a problem with that," she said and went back to reading the comics.

"Why not?" he asked.

"Men should be experienced. Few women want a man who knows no more about sex than she does."

"So me having cheated on Terri doesn't bother you?"

She shrugged. "She got what she deserved. She really wasn't a wife to you, was she?"

"No."

"And she didn't love you."

"That would be an understatement."

"Then, it's a moot point," she stated.

"You know we're justifying our actions," he said.

"Baptist guilt," she said. "Think we should stand up in front of the congregation and confess our sins?"

He looked at her.

She looked at him.

Together they said, "No."

* * * * *

They were sinning again.

Fifth time that day.

Third time that night.

His cock was buried deep inside her. She was wrapped around him like sticky on a lollipop. A fine sheen of sweat covered those parts of their bodies that were rubbing vigorously against one another. His growls and her purrs filled the bedroom and the headboard was banging the wall with as much force as he was banging her.

He'd learned she was not the fragile little Southern girl he thought her to be and liked it a bit rough at times.

She'd learned he had the staying power of a jet engine at full throttle and with just the right amount of tweaking would gear up even higher.

He stiffened, threw his head back and roared as he came.

She cried out as the most intense orgasm he'd ever given her took hold of her.

Arms trembling as he thrust one last time, he collapsed atop her, slammed his arms around her and rolled so she was lying stretched out atop him with her legs between his.

"Damn boy," she said. She dropped her cheek to his heaving chest.

"I think you broke me," he gasped. He was trembling from the force of his release.

"I'm going to be sore in the morning," she replied.

He grunted in acknowledgement of her words, then closed his eyes. He must have dozed off for a few seconds for the sound of the zydeco melody of "I Can See Clearly Now" startled him and he jumped. When he jumped, Allison yelped, for she too must have fallen asleep after such a rigorous bout of lovemaking.

"It's him," she whispered.

Mouth dry, he reached for the phone. He didn't think the tremor in his hand had anything to do with what he and Allison had been doing earlier. He pressed the talk button, then put the phone to his ear.

"I'm listening."

"Mr. Smith?"

"Yes."

"Mr. Smith, I regret to inform you of the untimely death of an elderly gentleman of your acquaintance. Do you wish the details?"

Drew clutched the phone tighter. "Yes."

"It seems the gentleman in question suffered a massive heart attack while visiting the grave of his only daughter. Do you understand?"

"Yes."

"The will of one of the parties killed in that accident in Decatur County stated the deceased's estate would go to her father and at his death to her brother. The brother is now the sole beneficiary of her estate. Do you understand?"

"Yes."

"In regard to the other will, the executrix is being sought by a private investigator at the bequest of the deceased's family. I am, however, a very close, personal friend of the investigator. You might even say I know him better than anyone else ever will." The Irishman chuckled. "Do you understand?"

Drew smiled. "Yes."

"Good. I will tell you that an advance look at that will states the executrix is the sole beneficiary of her husband's estate. Do you understand?"

"Yes."

"Excellent. This concludes our business, Mr. Smith. You will find the sum of ten thousand dollars in the glove compartment of your truck. The money is a refund for solution number one. Please handle this phone in the same manner as the first. It is my fervent wish—and the wish of my employer—that you will not need my services again but if you should, you know how to contact me. I sincerely wish you and your future wife every happiness. Good-bye."

"Thank you," Drew said.

"My pleasure, Mr. Smith."

And then the Irishman was gone.

Chapter Twenty-Nine

The couple who walked into Hardee's that morning drew the attention of everyone there. Conversations were halted in midspeech. Eyes widened. Mouths dropped open. Only one man showed no surprise at seeing them but he was grinning from ear to ear.

"You do know how to make an entrance, cuz," Early said.

"You know my wife, don't you, Early?" Drew said loud enough for everyone to hear.

Gasps filled the room.

"I believe I have had the pleasure," Early said. "Hello, darling."

"Hey," she said. Her cheeks were red but she held her head high as she slid into the booth opposite Early and her husband sat down beside her.

"Bea would have been here but the twins are home sick," Early said.

Drew extended his arm behind Allison, laid it on the back of the booth and settled into his seat. "We'll head out there after we take care of business here in town," he said.

"My wife might not be coming but my dates are here," Early said and smiled at the older woman who had just entered. Beside her was a younger woman with a saucy walk and a wicked glint in her eye.

"I hope they get an eyeful," Corinne said as leaned down to give Drew a peck on the cheek. "Lemme in, Rawls."

Early got up to allow the women into the booth, then sat back down. "They're married," he told them.

"Good," Miss Lillian proclaimed. "Mazel tov."

"Thank you," Drew replied.

"Where'd you get hitched?" Rini asked.

"Atlanta," Allison provided. "We had to wait three days to get the license."

"That's not the only news we have."

"Oh?" Miss Lillian asked.

"We're back to stay," he told her.

"Are you sure that's a smart thing to do?" Rini asked, exchanging looks with Miss Lillian.

"Probably not," he replied.

"But this is his home and we'll be damned if we're going to allow anyone to run him—or me—out of it," Allison said.

"You know the house went to Whip," Miss Lillian said, then looked at Allison. "And I hear you have your house up for rent."

"It was never my house, Miss Lillian," Allison said. "The only thing good about it was that it was across the street from you."

"Where will you two live?" Miss Lillian asked.

"We're going to build a house," Drew said, then leveled his gaze on Early. "That is if you can spare some of that unused pasture you keep saying you're going to put a fish pond on."

Early's eyebrows shot up. "Are you kidding me?"

"No," Drew said. "That's another reason I want to take Allison out there. I want her to see the land. If she doesn't like it, we'll find something else."

"It's family land," Early said. "It's *your* land, cuz. Of course you can build on it." He grinned. "Hell, I *want* you to build on it."

"Those brats of his will be over there all the time," Rini warned Allison. "You ready to put up with that?"

"I love children," Allison said. "I always wanted a houseful."

"She wants to open a day care and after-school learning center," Drew told her.

"Well, lordy mercy," Miss Lillian said. "Ain't that something?"

"Would you be willing to teach piano there, Miss Lillian?" Allison asked.

Tears glistened in the old woman's eyes. She reached across to place a wrinkled hand on Allison's arm. "I would be honored," she said, her voice cracking with emotion. "If I can teach your poggleheaded man how to play, I suppose I can teach anyone."

"I'm sitting right here, Miss Lillian," Drew said drily.

Miss Lillian just grinned at him.

"And would you be willing to help out as a teacher's aide?" Allison asked Rini.

"*What?*" Rini gasped. "Those women won't want me within a mile of their kids."

"Well, hell's bells, Corinne Wexler," Miss Lillian said. "They'd rather have you with their kids than with their menfolk. Take the offer, gal!"

Rini looked around at the shocked eyes of the people in the restaurant. A couple of the men were clients of hers.

"You aren't serious," she whispered to Allison.

"Yes, I am," Allison said. "Everybody deserves a second chance, Rini. You saved my husband's greatest asset and I'd do anything for you."

"His greatest—?" Early said, then whooped with laughter.

"She is very fond of that asset," Drew said with a wink.

"Overly fond," Allison mumbled. She looked Rini in the eye. "Will you do it?"

"You may not be able to get any children to come there if you hire me," Rini warned.

"I'll take my chances."

"I'll tell you this much," Miss Lillian said, raising her voice and casting her gaze around the room. "If Mary Magdalene could be at the right hand of Jesus, there isn't any reason whatsoever that Corinne Wexler can't be at the right hand of Allison Dunne."

"It *is* the Christian way," Drew agreed. "To forgive and welcome home the prodigal child."

"Which is his way of saying, you're gonna have to go to church from now on," Early told her.

Rini sighed heavily. "Okay, but I'm not wearing no stupid frilly hats or gloves."

"Oh," Allison whispered. She was staring at the door.

Drew turned his head to see Alice Smith walking in. Miss Lillian's neighbor saw him and stilled like a deer caught in headlights.

"Why don't you join us, Alice?" Drew said, sliding out of the booth.

"Drew, no," Allison hissed at him.

He walked right up to the woman who didn't seem to know whether she should bolt out the door or run for help to the other people gawking at her. She was literally rocking back and forth from one foot to the other.

"What's the matter, Alice?" Drew asked. "Cat got your tongue?"

"I...I..."Alice clutched her handbag like a shield in front of her.

"Nothing to say today?" Drew inquired. He stopped right in front of her and folded his arms. "You had plenty to say the day you called Clay Bennett to tell him you saw me sneaking out of Miss Lillian's house."

"I...I..." The middle-aged woman was shaking like a leaf.

"I think everyone here knows what happened after you made that phone call," Drew said. "I know I do.

"Allison knows because she was on the receiving end of Clay Bennett's belt. Miss Lillian and Babs Chauncey know. They were there. They saw the damage he did. They saw the bloody belt lying on the bathroom floor. Miss Lillian took pictures of Allison handcuffed to her own bed with welts and cuts all over her body. Corinne knows. Early knows. If Doc Mackie was here he would tell you he knows as well."

He turned to encompass the people staring at him. "All of you know what happened after Alice called. That was the day Clay Bennett beat the hell out of his wife, then chained her to their bed, taped her mouth up so she couldn't call for help. If I hadn't called Miss Lillian to ask her to check up on her, God only knows what else might have happened to Allison. I know someone from the hospital told you they had to put in an IV line because she hadn't had anything to eat or drink for two days."

Accusatory eyes went to Alice and held.

"Would you like to see the pictures Miss Lillian took or that they took at the hospital, Alice?" he questioned. "Like to see what your interfering, gossiping tongue caused?"

"No, I..." Alice spun around and would have fled had Drew not snaked out a hand to grab her arm. She yelped but he pulled her to him, bent his head and said something that completely leached her face of color.

"Do you understand?"

Alice nodded like a bobblehead doll. "Y...yes," she said.

"Excellent," he said. He let go of her arm, smiled, then turned his back on her to walk to the booth.

"What did you say to her?" Allison asked in a low voice. When he didn't answer, she asked again.

"You don't need to know," he said.

"Whatever it was he said made her pee her pants," Rini said.

People shifted their attention to where Alice had been standing, then laughter broke out in the restaurant.

"She'll never live that down," Miss Lillian said.

"Serves the bitch right," they heard someone say.

"Damn straight," someone else commented.

Then those in the restaurant went back to what they'd been doing before Drew and Allison walked in.

"Folks around here are like hummingbirds," Miss Lillian said.

Early frowned. "Meaning?"

"Short attention spans," she replied. "They flit from one thing to another almost quicker than the eye can see."

Early sat forward in his seat and lowered his voice. "Well, cuz, this is your lucky day. Here comes the brand new sheriff to welcome you home."

Drew looked around, not surprised to see Nick Hatcher pushing the door open.

"That's all we need," Miss Lillian said. "I hate that people know I'm kin to that boy."

Hatch came right up to the table with his hand braced on the grip of his service revolver. He tipped his hat to Miss Lillian.

"Morning, Mamar," he said.

"Were you raised in a barn? Take that damned hat off, Nicholas," she snapped.

Off came the hat and up came the blood into Hatch's slat-thin face.

"What do you want?" Miss Lillian demanded.

"I don't want no trouble with him, Mamar," Hatch told his grandmother. He wouldn't look at Drew.

"There won't be any trouble unless you cause it," she told him. "Are you going to cause this man trouble, Nicholas James?"

Hatch lowered his head, scuffed the toe of his boot on the floor as though he were ten years old again. "No, ma'am."

"Then what is your purpose in coming over here?" she asked.

"Just to tell him I don't want no trouble with him."

"Then look the man in the eye and say that," she ordered.

It seemed to take all the courage Hatch had to lift his head and switch his gaze to Drew.

"Congratulations on your new job, Hatch," Drew said. "I'm sure you'll make a fine sheriff."

Clearly that had not been what the young man was expecting. He opened his mouth to speak but what came out plainly wasn't what he meant to say for he winced.

"Bobby is dead."

"I heard," Drew said. "Please extend my condolences to his father and sisters."

"Shot by someone he was trying to arrest." Hatch swallowed loudly. "We ain't found him yet."

Drew nodded, put his arms on the tabletop and clasped his hands together. "I assume you know who the man is."

"Man named Vince Kent," Hatch said. "Ever heard of him?"

"No, can't say that I have."

"Why would he have?" Rini asked.

"Just askin'," Hatch said. "Askin' everybody."

"Excellent way to apprehend a criminal," Miss Lillian said. "By just askin'."

"Coach is dead, too," Hatch stated.

"As is the woman he was with when he plowed them into a slab of concrete," Early reminded him. "Drunk as a skunk and high on cocaine. Isn't that what the county coroner down in Bainbridge said, Hatch?"

"The car was in good condition?" Drew inquired.

Hatch blushed. "Ah, yeah."

"No brake or mechanical problems?"

"It was an accident," Hatch said. "That's been proven."

"Pure and simple," Rini said.

"Cut and dried," Miss Lillian added.

"Now Big Jake is gone, too," Hatch stated.

"Heart attack, wasn't it?" Drew inquired.

"Dropped dead right by his daughter's grave," Hatch added.

Drew cocked his head to one side. "Is there a reason you're telling us what we already know?" he inquired.

"Just seems a bit strange, is all," Hatch replied.

"Strange how?" Drew asked.

"People you didn't get along with all dying within a month of one another," Hatch told him.

"Are you accusing him of something, Nicholas James?" Miss Lillian snapped.

"No, ma'am," Hatch answered.

"Was an autopsy performed on my father-in-law?" Drew asked quietly.

"Yeah," Hatch said.

"And?"

"He died of a heart attack," Hatch said.

"Overweight, chain smoking, heavy drinking seventy year old whose idea of exercise was climbing into his car. Who would think a man like that would be a candidate for a heart attack?" Miss Lillian queried.

"M-mamar, p-please," Hatch whined. "I'm trying to talk to Drew."

"Then talk and don't stammer," Miss Lillian. "And for the love of the Lord, stand up straight, boy."

Hatch squared his shoulders, his face scarlet.

"Any suggestion of foul play where Big Jake is concerned, Hatch?" Drew asked.

"No."

"Well, there you go," Early said. "What is your point, Hatch?"

"Just saying."

"Then say it somewhere else, boy," Miss Lillian ordered. "You are annoying us. Go away."

"Bye, now," Rini said.

"Boyd's lookin' for you," Hatch said, hitching up his pants and in doing so almost dropping his hat. He had to scramble to keep it in his possession.

Drew smiled. "And I'm lookin' for him." He winked, clucked his tongue. "And Whip."

"Don't want no trouble, Drew," Hatch was quick to say.

"Ain't gonna give you none, Hatch," Drew replied.

Hatch pointed a shaking finger at him. "I'm gonna hold you to it."

"You do that, Hatch," Drew said. "And again, congratulations on your new job."

"About that night at the motel…," Hatch began, but Drew shook his head, a muscle grinding in his cheek.

"Now's not the time to discuss that. We'll get around to talking about it sometime." He smiled nastily. "Just me and you."

Once more Hatch opened his mouth to speak, obviously thought better of it—again—and nodded. He slapped his hat on his head, turned and slunk away.

"Out of all my grandchildren, Nicholas has been the biggest disappointment. Boy never has had a lick of common sense," Miss

Lillian pronounced. "Making him sheriff is like handing a loaded gun to a chimpanzee."

"He's gonna run right to Boyd," Early said. "By the way, he's the new coach."

"Figured that would happen," Drew said.

"You're gonna have trouble with Boyd," Rini said. "He's been bad-mouthing you ever since Bobby's funeral."

"Before that," Early corrected her.

"Now what?" Miss Lillian said with a grunt.

A man was approaching the table with his baseball hat clutched in his grease-stained hands. He was one of the mechanics from the shop and a distant cousin of Corinne's. He gave Drew a tremulous smile. "Sorry to interrupt, Mr. Dunne, but Mr. Thompson heard you was here and asked me to come ask you if you would come by the shop."

"Mr. Dunne?" Early asked, then laughed. "Hell, Boudreaux, since when have you ever called him Mr.?"

"Since people starting dropping like flies," Rini joked.

Boudreaux frowned at her, then returned his attention to Drew. "What should I tell him, sir?"

"Tell I'll be along later today," Drew said.

"But…" Boudreaux cleared his throat. "He's expecting you now, sir."

"Well, I'm busy at the moment, Philip," Drew said. "I'll get to him when I have the time."

Boudreaux nodded. "I'll tell him, sir."

"You do that," Early said.

After Boudreaux left, Drew took in a long breath, then let it out slowly. "Mr. Dunne," he repeated.

"You can expect that from now on. They're scared of you, son," Miss Lillian said.

"Why?" he asked.

"Why indeed?" she countered. "You ever see *The Man Who Shot Liberty Valance*?"

"When I was a boy," he replied. "I'm not making the connection."

"You're Jimmy Stewart and Clay was Liberty Valance," Allison said.

"Precisely," Miss Lillian agreed.

* * * * *

Allison loved the land where Drew wanted to build their dream home. They walked the area for a half hour or longer, then went up to the house to see Bea. His cousin's wife hugged him so tightly he could barely breathe, then threw her arms around Allison as well.

"I am so happy to have you in the family," Bea said.

"Us, too," the twins said in unison but their mother wouldn't let them any closer to Drew and Allison than the hallway. They stood there in their pajamas and stocking feet giggling.

Drew slipped his arm around Allison's waist. "I want you to stay here with Bea for a while."

"Why?" Allison asked, then looked at Bea. "Not that I'm not enjoying the company."

"I have some things to see to in town," he said.

"Then I want to come along," she insisted.

"No," he said in a stern voice.

"Drew—"

"I said no," he said again. He removed his arm.

"He's gonna be doing man stuff," Bea said. "Ain't no changing a man's mind when he's about doing man stuff."

Allison clearly didn't like it or approve but she knew him well enough to know there would be no changing his mind. "You'll be careful?" she asked.

"I'm always careful."

"That's the first lie I've ever heard you tell, Andrew Dunne," Bea said. "You're going straight to hell for sure." She wagged her finger at him. "You won't pass go and you won't collect two hundred dollars. You'll be burning in the fiery pit."

"That's a given, Beatrice," Drew stated. He looked at his wife's uneasy face. "I'll be careful, baby."

"I'm serious, Drew," Allison insisted. "I worry about you."

"Nothing is gonna happen to me," he said, kissed her on the forehead, then turned to the door. "Can't say the same for anyone who gets in my way though."

"He's changed," he heard Bea say as he left.

"That's what I'm afraid of," Allison replied.

* * * * *

Whip was standing at the filing cabinet when Drew knocked on the door. He looked around with his hands in the files, then paled. "Drew," he said.

"Whip," Drew said. He crossed his arms over his chest and leaned his shoulder against the doorjamb. "You wanted to see me?"

Shutting the file cabinet drawer, Whip nodded. "Would you take a seat, please?"

"I'm fine right where I am," Drew said.

"Yeah, but what I have to say is private," Whip said. "I'd like to keep it just between you and me."

Drew stared at him for a moment, then shrugged. He pushed away from the door. "You want me to close the door?" he asked.

"Please."

Drew closed the door, then took a seat in front of Whip's desk. He lifted his foot, braced his ankle on his knee and sat back comfortably in the chair.

"Daddy left me the business," Whip said as he sat down in the chair that had once been Drew's.

"I assumed as much."

"Terri left me that god-awful house of hers." He stared hard at Drew as though trying to assess how Drew felt about the news.

"Better you than me," Drew said. "What are you going to do with it?"

"You want it?"

The question surprised Drew and he had a hard time hiding his expression. "Ah, no," he said. "I've hated that house since the day they broke ground on it."

Whip sighed heavily. "I don't know what the hell I'm gonna do with it. I'm not gonna be able to sell it for anywhere near what it's worth," Whip said, plowing a hand through his hair. "There's not a soul in Miller County who can afford it."

Drew nodded. "That's true."

"Daddy left me his house and since I'm already living there and it's the family home, I'm gonna stay."

"Makes sense," Drew said.

"You sure you don't want Terri's house?"

"Positive," Drew replied. "Allison and I are going to build a house next to Early."

"I heard you two got married," Whip said. "Congratulations. I hope you'll be happy together."

That didn't just surprise Drew, it shocked him.

"I mean it," Whip said. "That wasn't being sarcastic."

"Okay," Drew said, drawing the word out as he sat there wondering what the hell had happened to Whip Thompson.

Whip sat forward with his hands clasped tightly on the desktop. "Here's the deal," he said. "I did all right handling the business when Daddy was alive to tell me what I should and shouldn't do. When you were over in Albany all those weeks, I thought I was doing a bang-up job. But with Daddy gone and with him his advice, I'm struggling here, Drew. I'm way outta my depth. We're losing money hand over fist." He wiggled in his chair. "Since it's obvious you're back home to stay, would you be interested in working for me? Doing the same job you did?"

Another shock went through Drew. He realized Whip must really be in over his head for him to admit such a thing and to ask for his help.

"Give it some thought," Whip said. "Talk it over with the missus. I don't expect a reply today. I—"

"I won't work *for* you," Drew interrupted. "But I will buy into the company if you want a sixty-forty partnership. I figure an infusion of say, five hundred grand, would put updated machinery and new tools in the shop, some more used cars on the lot, maybe contract a few more mechanics."

"Where the hell would you get that kind of—" Whip's eyes widened and he slumped back in his chair with a loud *whompf* of air leaving his lungs. "Son of a bitch," he whispered.

Drew smiled at him.

"I *knew* you took that money," Whip said.

"Prove it," Drew said.

"You know fucking well I can't," Whip said. "Do you have any idea how much trouble you got me into with Daddy?"

"Don't play the innocent here, Whip. You were skimming," Drew said.

"Not no five hundred grand worth, I wasn't," Whip snapped.

"You want to take my offer or not?" Drew asked.

Whip thought about it for a moment, looked past Drew's shoulder to the showroom floor, then pursed his lips. "Fifty-fifty," he said.

"Sixty-forty," Drew said. "Nonnegotiable."

"It's my family business," Whip insisted.

"But I'll be running it," Drew pointed out. "There's more to it than just sitting there behind the desk, Whip. I think you've found that out already."

"We are gonna keep the name."

"If we do, I want to open up a satellite garage to do rebuilds and restorations on classic cars and trucks," Drew said. "I'll give you five percent of our profits."

"Ten," Whip said.

"Five," Drew said. "Or the name gets changed to Thompson-Dunne Motors."

Whip flinched. "Five is highway robbery but okay." He stood, held out his hand.

Drew got to his feet. He hesitated, then grasped his ex-brother-in-law's hand.

"Don't take any more money from this business," Whip said.

"Ditto," Drew replied.

Chapter Thirty

There were three men standing at his truck when Drew came out of the dealership. He recognized two of them but the third he'd never seen before. One of the men was leaning against the front grill with a nasty look on his face.

"Boyd," Drew greeted him.

"You're not welcome in this town," Boyd said. "You need to take that woman of yours and leave. Now."

Drew saw people on the sidewalks watching them. A few had come out of the courthouse and were standing on the lawn. Shop windows had faces peering out of them and he couldn't help but think of blackbirds sitting on a telephone wire.

It wasn't *The Man Who Shot Liberty Valance*. It was *High Noon*.

"You always were a coward," Drew told Boyd. "Always did need to have others help you do your fighting. Just like Clay Bennett did."

The man Drew didn't know took a step forward but Boyd pushed away from Drew's truck and held out his arm to block him.

"You don't think I can take you man to man?" Boyd demanded.

"I know you can't," Drew said. He wanted to brag that he had spent the last few months working out every day at O'Malley's cabin but he didn't. "You need your two goons here to hold me for you like you and Wade held me for Bennett?"

"No, hell, I don't," Boyd said.

"All right," Drew said. "Then let's go out behind the shop and discuss this."

"Fine by me."

Drew's spine tingled as he turned his back on Boyd. He half-expected to be jumped, but to give the other man his due, Boyd fell into step beside him.

"I'm gonna whip your ass," Boyd stated.

"You can try," Drew replied.

As they passed the garage bays, three of the mechanics as well as Whip appeared in the opening.

"I've called Doc and Hatch," Whip said. "You're gonna keep this fight clean, Boyd." He pointed at the two men following Boyd. "My men are gonna make sure you do."

"I'd appreciate it if our men can keep Boyd's lackeys from interfering, Whip," Drew told him.

"This is just between you and me," Boyd snapped.

"Then why'd you bring your bully boys?" one of the mechanics asked.

Boyd didn't answer. He followed Drew around the corner of the building and to the grassy patch that edged the property.

As Drew headed for the winter-burned grass, he took off his leather jacket and tossed it to Boudreaux.

"Don't let that take up with you, Philip," he told the mechanic, then began rolling up his shirt sleeves.

"No, sir, Mr. Dunne," Boudreaux acknowledged. He folded the jacket against his chest.

The sound of running feet brought Hatch and two of his deputies to the fight. "What's goin' on here?" Hatch asked.

"Just a disagreement between brothers," Doc Mackie said as he came out of the back door of the garage. "Let them handle it, Hatch."

"Fighting is against the law," Hatch stated.

"Bullshit," Doc said. "Fisticuffs are a time-honored way men have of settling their differences."

"You're not gonna try and stop them?" Hatch asked.

"No," Doc said.

The people who had been watching from the courthouse, sidewalks and shops suddenly appeared at the periphery of the parking lot. Most were men, but there were a few women scattered among them. One sweep of his eyes across them let Drew know he knew each one. What his and Allison's life here in his hometown was going to be from that day forward depended largely on how the fight went. He intended to make sure—no matter how brutal it got—that he was the man left standing.

Boyd took off his heavy corduroy jacket and threw it to the ground. He rolled up the sleeve of his sweater, spit in his hands, then doubled his fists, took a fighting stance on the grassy patch.

"No unsportsmanlike conduct, boys," Doc said. He leveled his gaze on Boyd. "Your inheritances depend on how you handle yourselves here today."

"Why are you lookin' at *me*, Daddy?" Boyd asked.

"Because I know you, son," Doc replied. "Keep it clean or so help me God I'll cut you out of my will this very day."

Boyd cut his angry gaze to Drew. "You see what you've done?" he snarled.

"I haven't done anything," Drew said. He raised his clenched fists. "Yet."

Early and Rini pushed their way through the crowd that had gathered.

"Can he take him?" Drew heard Whip ask Early.

"I don't know," Early said.

"Sure he can," Rini stated. "Just watch him."

Drew and Boyd circled one another, took a few experimental jabs—looking for an opening. They bobbed and weaved around each other as the tension in those watching mounted. Drew didn't want to execute the first blow. He didn't want to be the one to draw first blood. He wanted to put Boyd down but he wanted it on record that Boyd threw the first punch.

And he did. It connected with Drew's jaw and staggered him. He stumbled back, dodged a second blow aimed at his face, then brought his fist up under Boyd's arm and slammed it into the other man's gut. A loud whoosh of air escaped Boyd's mouth and he doubled over. Drew's second punch clipped Boyd's chin and drove him backward.

"I'd say that boy's been practicing," Doc said to no one in particular.

All the years of backing down, taking Wade's abuse, accepting without defending himself against Terri's and Jake's insults, being handed his ass by more people than he cared to remember came bubbling up to the surface.

The explosion that came from Drew's fists, the steely determination the people were no doubt seeing on his face as he hammered away at Boyd's body went a long way in giving him back his manhood. He had no intention of crippling Boyd or doing a great deal of damage to the man, but he did intend to put him down and keep him there.

He didn't lose his temper or his objective. He simply carried out the punishment with controlled, measured and well-timed punches. Boyd kept moving back—stumbling, blindly lashing out but not connecting that often. There was fear in his eyes now and a growing worry.

A quick fist to the point of Boyd's chin flipped the man around and he fell to one knee in the graveled area beside the grass. He grunted but managed to push himself up quickly enough to take a roundhouse swing at Drew. Drew ducked under the blow and landed one of his own in Boyd's solar plexus, then another.

Boyd went to the ground again—this time crashing onto the parking lot, landing on his back.

"You had enough?" Drew asked.

"Fuck no," Boyd snarled and twisted over to shove himself to his feet. He spat out a mouthful of blood, then rounded on Drew and came at him with a roar—wrapping his arms around Drew in a tight bear hug, lifting him from the ground.

A fair fight meant a fair fight and as badly as Drew wanted to ram his knee into Boyd's groin, he pulled back his head and butted him instead. The hard hit dropped Boyd's arms from around him and staggered him. It also gave Drew a sudden, blinding headache as he danced away from his opponent.

Boyd shook his head, stumbled, then put his fists up again. He moved slower as they circled one another. He kept shaking his head, no doubt to clear it. He made a tentative jab at Drew, missed and Drew's punch hit him squarely on the nose, breaking it. The loud crunch made those gathered groan. Boyd went down to his knee again with blood streaming from his nose.

"Enough?" Drew repeated.

With his hand cupped under his nose, Boyd glanced at his father.

"I'd stay down if I were you, son," Doc advised. "Your brother's beat you fair and square."

"Not my brother," Boyd snapped. "Never *be* my brother!"

"I feel the same way," Drew told him and when Boyd shifted his glare to him, he shook his head. "It is what it is."

"But I am your father," Doc stated. "Whether you claim one another or not doesn't matter. I fathered you both. Everyone in town knows that. You can call each other whatever you will, that doesn't change the fact that you are brothers."

"Half brothers," Drew corrected.

"No kin at all," Boyd hissed. He stumbled to his feet and went over to retrieve his jacket. He nearly went down again when he bent over to pick it up. He staggered but managed to keep standing. He gave Drew a mean look. "This isn't over."

"Yes, it is," Doc said. "Do anything to your brother and I promise you, Boyd, I will change my will that very day."

"That's not fair, Daddy," Boyd said. "I am your son."

"He's my son, too," Doc stated.

"No, he's your *bastard*," Boyd shouted. He turned, staggered again, then pushed his way through the mechanics who were blocking his path.

"Go after him, Doc," Drew said. "I think I broke his nose."

Doc nodded. "You're a fair man, Drew," he said.

Drew didn't reply. He held his hand out for Boudreaux to give him his jacket.

"Good fight, Mr. Dunne," Boudreaux said.

"Drew," came the correction. "Don't call me Mr. Dunne again."

"Yes, sir," Boudreaux agreed.

Early shook his head. "Bad precedent there, cuz. You earned his respect."

Drew shrugged away the comment. He draped his arm around Early's shoulder. "Let's me and you go talk about the new garage we're gonna build," he said.

"We're gonna have a new garage?" Early asked, stunned.

"Yes, we are."

"What about us?" Boudreaux asked. "Can we come to work there?"

Drew smiled. "You're gonna be working here, Philip. How does head mechanic sound to you?"

"Working for Mr. Thompson, still?" Boudreaux queried with a frown.

"For Mr. Thompson *and* me," Drew said. "I'll be going into partnership with him."

"You're kidding," Early gasped.

"And in partnership with you in our new garage," Drew said. "How does that sound to *you*?"

"Like manna from heaven, cuz," Early replied. "Like manna from heaven."

* * * * *

The weather had turned unseasonably warm for February. Drew and Allison sat in the truck and looked at the foundation footings that had been poured for their new house. The redwood cabin would bear a strong resemblance to O'Malley's place in Upstate New York but on a larger scale. Four bedrooms, one just for Miss Lillian when she came to visit. Another variation of the design was the wraparound deck that had been Allison's idea, as had the skylight in the kitchen that was Drew's.

They were planning the landscaping as they surveyed the site in the lowering sun.

"I was looking in the gardening section on the Log Cabin webpage," she told Drew as she sat nestled against his shoulder, their fingers entwined on his thigh. "I want to put in a lot of pampas grass—both white and pale pink—and redtop. Lots and lots of redtop lining the gravel driveway. Along the walkway, I think blood grass instead of the traditional boxwood."

He nodded. "And magnolia and mimosa trees. Gardenia over there and plenty of honeysuckle to grow on the split-rail fence Early and I are gonna build."

"Smell good plants," she said. "Don't forget the banana and trumpet vines, too."

"I want a big double swing hanging from that live oak," he said, pointing to the big, sweeping tree that was laced with Spanish moss.

"I want double swings on the front part of the deck and one on the back part plus four of them in that big octagonal gazebo we saw at the Home and Garden show."

"A swing each for us, Early and Bea, Rini and Gage, and Lenore and Thomas. Don't forget the fire pit in the middle of the gazebo for when the weather turns cold."

"I hadn't thought of that," she said. "We'd have to vent the copper roof. What would we do when it rained?"

"I'm sure there's some kind of sliding thing or other that will cover the vent for those times," he suggested.

"That would work."

They watched the sun go down in the west, then looked toward the east where the moon was rising. In an hour or two it would be sailing like a ghostly ship across the sky.

"I think we should put in some big pots to grow herbs in," he told her.

"Oh," she exclaimed. "And a big raised vegetable garden inside railroad ties. A big garden."

"Raised?"

"To keep the snakes out," she stated. "I want purple hull peas and crowder peas, field peas and black-eyed peas. Butter beans and lima beans."

"Tomatoes and okra, bell peppers and cucumbers," he said. "Broccoli and cauliflower and radishes. All the stuff for a big salad."

"Don't forget the eggplant and summer squash and zucchini," she added.

"Carrots and several kinds of lettuce, celery and you know what?" He nodded. "I'm gonna have Early go with me out to the woods and see if we can't find some hog plum trees to transplant by the garage."

"And scuppernongs. We gotta have scuppernongs," she said. "To go with the fig trees I want to put in. I can't wait to cook some fig preserves."

"You know there are mayhaw trees down along the river," he told her. "You know how to make mayhaw jelly?"

"Do I know how to make mayhaw jelly?" she repeated, then blew a raspberry. "Boy, please. You and Early go shake those mayhaw trees and see what kind of jelly this girl can make."

He laughed. "Anything else you think we need?"

"Maybe a pond between the two properties for you and Early and the boys to fish in?"

"Sounds good."

"And a tire swing," she added.

He frowned. "A tire swing?" Then nodded. "Oh, for the Rawls' brood," he said.

"No," she replied. "For this one." She laid her hand on her tummy.

Drew stared at her. "W…what?"

"It seems there is nothing wrong with your little swimmers," she said. "Nothing wrong with my eggs, either. Doc says around October we're going to be needing a crib and a stroller and—"

He pulled her to him. His heart was pounding so hard in his chest he thought it might burst. "A baby?" he said. "You're having a baby?"

"Uh hum," she agreed.

"*My* baby?" he mumbled.

"It better be yours," she said.

Epilogue

As it turned out they needed two tire swings.
Two cribs.
Two strollers.
One of each for Avery and his twin sister Bailey.
Soon they would begin work on that .3 child.
Life was good, Drew thought.
Very, very good.

ABOUT THE AUTHOR

Charlee, as she is known to her readers, is the author of 100 novels, the first ten of which are the WindLegend Saga. She was married 43 years to her high school sweetheart, Tom, until his untimely death in April 2009. She is the mother of two grown sons, Pete and Mike, and the proud grandmother of Preston Alexander and Victoria Ashley and the giddy great-grandmother of Amber Dawn.

A native of Sarasota, Florida, Charlee was adopted at birth and grew up in Colquitt and Albany, Georgia. She says of her heritage: "I was born in Florida and raised in Georgia, so that makes me an official Sunshine Cracker!" She now lives in the Midwest where she enjoys the changing of the seasons.

Her hobbies are reading, writing, and quietly communing with her beloved husband, Buddha Belly, as he guides her gently from somewhere beyond the here and now. She is owned and operated by seven cats who only allow her to leave the house for catnip, kitty kibble, and clumping kitty litter.

She loves to watch *ANYTHING* in which **Allan Hawco**, Michael Trucco, Victor Webster, or Chris Vance have starred, and patterns her heroes after these fine actors as her tribute to the many hours of enjoyment they have given her.

She collects statues of the Grim Reaper, Anubis, gargoyles, and windchimes. One of her prized possessions is a Grim Reaper windchime sent to her by a fan from England.

Her signature Reaper novels have a huge loyal following and currently she is at work on a new dark fantasy set in Australia.

Did you enjoy this book? Drop us a line and say so! We love to hear from readers, and so do our authors. To connect, visit www.boroughspublishinggroup.com online, send comments directly to info@boroughspublishinggroup.com, or friend us on Facebook and Twitter. And be sure to check back regularly for contests and new releases in your favorite subgenres of romance!

Are you an aspiring writer? Check out www.boroughspublishinggroup.com/submit and see if we can help you make your dreams come true.

www.ingramcontent.com/pod-product-compliance
Lightning Source LLC
Chambersburg PA
CBHW061316170626
46817CB00001B/205